THE VINES

A NOVEL

SHELLEY NOLDEN

Map illustration by Travis Hasenour
First Hardcover Edition

Published by Freiling Publishing, a division of Freiling Agency, LLC.

P.O. Box 1264,
Warrenton, VA 20188

www.FreilingPublishing.com

Library of Congress Control Number: 2020920419

ISBN 978-1-950948-40-6

Printed in the United States of America

For my mother, with love,

and all the essential workers and health care heroes who've selflessly served throughout the COVID-19 pandemic

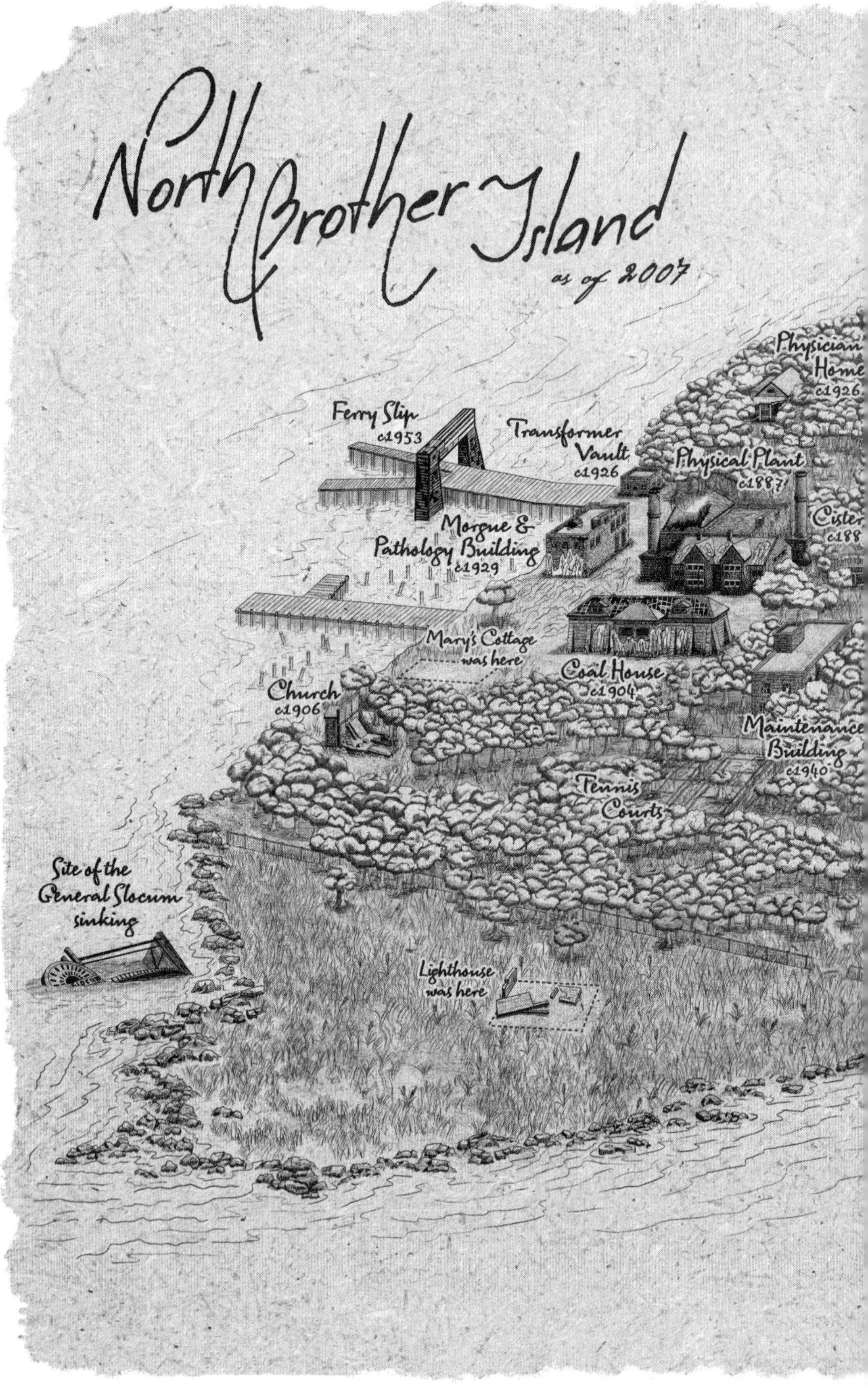

North Brother Island

as of 2007

Physician
Home
c1926

Ferry Slip
c1953

Transformer
Vault
c1926

Physical Plant
c1887

Morgue &
Pathology Building
c1929

Cister
c188

Mary's Cottage
was here

Coal House
c1904

Church
c1906

Maintenance
Building
c1940

Tennis
Courts

Site of the
General Slocum
sinking

Lighthouse
was here

Tuberculosis Pavilion
c1942
Store House
c1907
Male Dormitory
c1885
Staff House
c1885
Service Building/School
c1928
Nurses' Residence
c1905
Garage
c1892
Extinct Structures
Mary's Cottage
c1907
Lighthouse
c1869

2007

Forty-four years since the abandonment of Riverside Hospital on North Brother Island, north of Hell Gate in New York City's East River

July

A thick keloid encircled the young woman's throat like a noose, ready to seize her last breath. Though any one of the other faded wounds gripping her slender, muscular body should have already claimed it. Humming an achingly sad tune, she reached for an elixir bottle beside the cracked porcelain tub in which she stood. As she twisted, a tangled, worm-like network of whip marks on her back met the glow of dawn pervading the forest.

For the past four decades, indigenous and invasive plants had been hell-bent on destroying the remains of Riverside Hospital. Unchallenged by the collapsed outer wall of the first-floor bathroom, a shaft of sunlight irradiated her glistening skin.

Maybe she's a ghost, Finn Gettler thought from behind a cottonwood as the woman lathered her hair. Thousands had died here, many more had suffered. But not everyone who should have perished had. This, only his family knew. A chill passed across the back of his sweat-slick neck, and he shivered.

Finn didn't believe in the paranormal world. If ghosts were real, however, this shuttered contagion hospital would have spawned them.

A distant shriek pierced his eardrums. The sound must have come from one of the black-crowned night herons nesting at North Brother Island's southern end.

The woman tilted back her head and released water from a camp shower bag; it flowed down her long hair to the top of her calves, where the dirt-caked tub shielded the rest of her from view.

During his stint in the Peace Corps in Africa, not once had he seen a body so mutilated. Nor, in his twenty-eight years on this earth, one so graceful. An impossible combination, yet there she stood.

His heart pulsing, Finn pressed himself against a tree trunk strangled by a mulberry vine. There was something "off" about this place he'd been longing to visit his entire life. He could feel it; an aching brittleness, as if he'd already been reduced to the same decaying state as the bird carcass his boot had crunched in the darkness an hour earlier.

As she raised her arms to rinse the suds, he could see the contours of her biceps. More warrior than victim from the looks of it, she likely wouldn't appreciate his help. Or his gaze. Neither would his girlfriend, but if Lily were here, she'd be just as alarmed by this woman's appearance.

A mosquito buzzed near his neck, seemingly undeterred by his bug spray. The woman couldn't possibly hear a slap above the rising noise from the birds, but she might notice the motion, so Finn held still.

She twisted to scrub her back.

Her physique and tank-top tan lines reminded him of the rock climbers he'd encountered during his expeditions thus far in his quest to cross the world's twenty most dangerous bridges. Her body, however, looked more like it had gone through a blender than fallen from a cliff.

Is she using this island to hide from whoever's been hurting her? Finn wondered.

With a sudden premonition that they weren't alone, he eyed the forest.

No one materialized from the whispering green.

Slowing his breathing, he turned to study her for signs of recent abuse.

Her eyes now closed, she continued singing the same melancholy tune. Her voice had a raspy edge; only someone confident in her solitude would croon—and expose herself—like that.

The makeshift shower likely meant she hadn't kayaked through the predawn East River chop, as he'd done to avoid detection by the NYPD Harbor Unit. She must have camped here overnight.

To avoid an awkward confrontation, Finn thought it best to sneak back to his kayak, hidden in the brambles near the docks. Yet he couldn't compel himself to move.

The squawking of the herons intensified. Soon, he realized, the blur of early morning would sharpen into clean lines. He had to get going, but his trek through the island's interior with only a flashlight had disoriented him. And the deteriorating buildings that he'd passed in the dark now looked frustratingly unfamiliar.

He removed his sketchbook from his hiking pack and glanced at the map. A month ago, he'd drawn it after committing the original, annotated in German, to his nearly photographic memory. In the shed at his parents' Long Island home, he'd found the schematic along with a dozen of his father's old excursion logs.

During Finn's childhood, his family's clandestine research at the abandoned hospital, where his grandfather and great-grandfather had worked, had been a constant source of anxiety. Completely excluded, Finn hadn't even been allowed in their Upper East Side laboratory.

Frustratingly, mere months after he had completed an undergraduate degree in physics that should have earned him a role in the project, 9/11 happened. Almost instantly, the NYC waterways became flush with patrols. Her father, Rollie, had claimed it was too risky to continue collecting the environmental samples from which they hoped to pinpoint an elusive immune system boosting chemical reagent.

To both Finn and his brother, Kristian, Rollie's justification for shelving such vital research seemed flimsy and suspect.

So, when Finn came across the cache of records while looking for his camping gear, he'd decided it was time to do a little digging.

Even without the woman's grim presence now, the aura of misery surrounding the trees and dilapidated buildings would have remained. The stench of rot pervaded the campus. *Something* had made his father suddenly fear this place, where he'd spent most of his childhood and too much of his adulthood.

Listening to his gut had gotten Finn out of dicey situations before. Now it was telling him to slip away before that intense woman caught him gawking at her.

He studied the notes on his map. The project logs had been written in German. Preparing Finn for the eventual day he'd have access to them, Rollie had spoken the language to him throughout his childhood. Hopefully Finn hadn't mistranslated a critical detail.

Resisting the urge to pull off his sweaty T-shirt, Finn inventoried the three decrepit buildings within view, then spotted a rusted chain-link fence draped in porcelain berry, a vine that grew almost a foot a day. Beyond the barrier stretched a blanket of ivy, interspersed with Norway maples. It had to be the tennis court, which meant the woman was showering in the staff house.

According to the diagram, he'd need to cut across a meadow to reach his kayak, while watching out for *Giftefeu* (poison ivy). Rollie had noted its presence on his map.

A sharp gust zipped past Finn's ear.

Lodged in the trunk of the cottonwood, a surgical scalpel vibrated only inches from his head.

He raised his hands to protect his face.

The knife had come from behind; he spun to locate its owner.

Above, the leaves shook from seagulls and ospreys taking flight.

Despite their cawing, the forest seemed quiet. Oddly and creepily so.

Her singing had stopped, he realized.

The air whistled again, and a second scalpel hit the wood with a *thwack.* He ducked into the foliage and yanked his pack in front of his chest. Shielding his eyes, he studied the knife suspended in the tree. This one had been thrown from a different direction; there had to be at least two assailants.

If these same men had caused her scars, Finn had to get the hell out of there.

But how could he leave her, assuming she was still alive?

At the start of his second year in the Peace Corps, he'd requested reassignment to the civilian relief effort in war-torn Ivory Coast. The night the rebels took control of Danané, he'd seen what could happen to those left behind. It still caused nightmares and regret.

Cold sweat dripped from his brow.

The forest was too still; he was being watched.

He tasted blood and realized he'd bitten his tongue. Another scalpel could whiz through the air, this time landing in an eye or the back of his head. Unlike all those who'd been incinerated or transported to Potter's Field on Hart Island, his body would rot where it landed.

If Finn had respected his father's ruling that North Brother had become too risky, he wouldn't now be defenseless and alone, about to die on a deserted island surrounded by eight million people.

The faint hum of traffic underscored the proximity of help; so close, yet so far.

He knew his best option was to flee. Surveying the greenery, he spotted the tennis court fence that marked his escape route. Yet he didn't bolt.

Either his invisible enemies were defending the woman, or they wanted to kill her, too. Assuming they hadn't already sliced her throat, Finn and she, together, might be able to make it to his kayak. The currents would quickly carry them beyond the range of those blades.

With the daylight, a patrol might notice them leaving, but he'd gladly take an illegal trespassing charge over death.

A pokeberry plant blocked his view of the decaying bathroom. He eased aside a long, thin cluster of dark berries, revealing only more vegetation. He would have to get closer.

Shifting his pack onto his back, he realized that he'd dropped his sketchbook and turned to reach for it.

The air trilled.

A third scalpel—this one from above—stabbed the moleskin cover. Protecting his face with his hands, he looked up.

On a thick branch, almost directly overhead, perched the woman.

Her blue eyes were trained on the bridge of his nose as if she were a sharpshooter scoping her target.

So she is on their side, he thought, *but what are they doing here?*

Barely blinking, she continued to stare at him.

He diverted his attention.

Droplets landed on a bracket fungus, darkening its orange hue. Finn peered upward, realizing they'd fallen from her hair, now in a loose ponytail. She was wearing a faded tank top, khakis, and men's steel-toed boots. Even with the racket of the birds, he should have heard her climbing the tree.

If he grabbed the weapon wedged in his book, he knew she'd react swiftly. He dared not rifle through his pack for his utility knife.

"I'm unarmed," he said, showing his palms.

"I'm not."

Silver glinted near her ear, and Finn distinguished an olive-green work glove from the leaves partially shielding her head. She was holding a scalpel. With a flick of her wrist, she could lodge it in his skull.

Finn leaped backward. Despite the plants around him, there was no place to hide. "I didn't see anything." He raised his hands. "I swear."

"You saw plenty."

He winced. "I meant—I'm sorry. It was dark. I didn't even . . . whatever you guys are doing here; it's your business."

"Guys?"

He scrutinized the foliage again. "You mean you're all women?" Dread gushed into his stomach as he pictured other women with similar scars and equal anger.

"No," she said in a stiff tone. "I was refuting your use of the plural."

To have thrown all those scalpels, she would have needed to be in three places practically at once. Or impossibly quick. "That can't be."

"I wish it weren't the case," she said, her voice catching in her throat. Keeping the knife raised, she settled into the crook of the branch.

Finn sensed an opportunity to retreat. Using his bag as a shield, he unfolded his long body. "I'm going to back away slowly, get in my kayak, and forget this ever happened."

From this higher vantage point, he could better see her face. Even with her brow furrowed, her cerulean eyes and dark, long lashes overwhelmed the rest of her features. Spots of shade from the leaves above dappled her skin.

She swallowed hard, the noose-like scar around her neck tightening. "Do you really think you can forget me?"

Recalling her marred torso, he felt a tenderness toward her—irrational given the weapon in her grip. "How many of those have you got?"

"Enough to kill you."

"No wonder you're flying solo," he muttered.

She shifted, and a branch hid her face.

Apparently, she'd heard him. Finn groaned.

Her penetrating eyes reappeared, and he met her gaze.

"So, Peeping Tom," she said and coughed into her shoulder, "what's your actual name?"

Once she had his personal information, he'd have to worry about her showing up at his Brooklyn Heights apartment. But if he didn't answer, she might not let him leave.

"Cook," Finn said quickly, picturing the explorer who'd claimed to have reached the North Pole a year before Robert Peary. "Frederick Cook."

The woman huffed, and Finn wondered if she'd recognized the name.

She extended her free hand. "Toss up your papers."

"My what?"

"You must have a driver's license or draft card."

Surreal. He held back a quip about the draft ending around thirty-five years earlier, and that his wallet was buried at the bottom of his pack, where it would stay. He scanned the forest for signs of a second aggressor, though he sensed she'd been telling the truth.

A breeze, laced with traffic fumes, rustled the green-white flowers of the vines.

She tossed the scalpel toward the sky.

Finn jumped back, cowering as it plunged toward him.

It didn't puncture his skull, nor did it land nearby.

He looked up.

Metal winked in her hand.

Again, she flipped the steel upward and caught it by the handle—clearly a signal that she could wait all day for him to comply.

His best defense would be a version of the truth. "I was curious, okay? This place is wild, and I don't mean wild as in *wilderness*. What makes this island amazing is that nature fought back against greed and exploitation and actually won. Sure, the place has a dark past, but pretty soon these invasive species will have destroyed all evidence of that. To think, from the Bronx, basically, all you can see is a dome of green. People have no idea."

She leaned toward him. The set of her jaw had softened, and her eyes had widened.

He rubbed the beaded bracelet he always wore, a gift from a family in Séguéla. Her trust would be much harder to earn. "When you look at the island from the west, the morgue and physical plant behind it jut out like soldiers trying to keep their heads above quicksand. It's only a matter of time before nature claims them, too."

Sunlight, seeping through a break in the canopy, illuminated copper streaks in her brown hair. Her entire being seemed to glow. He reminded himself that it was only a trick of the light; she was no angel.

"This place seemed untouchable," he said, "yet at the same time inviting." He didn't regret his decision to come, but he certainly wished he could undo the way he'd come upon her. "I didn't mean to invade your privacy. I should have backtracked as soon as I saw you."

She withdrew into the canopy.

"Should have, would have, could have," she said, now unseen. "Here's another conditional verb to conjugate: *would have lived*. That's the future perfect, correct?"

He shrugged. It wasn't a verb he cared to analyze.

Her face reappeared. "I'll have to check." She glanced behind her and then back at him. "Later."

He raised his index finger. "*Will live* avoids the issue altogether."

Still no smile.

At the top of her reach, she jabbed the scalpel into the tree trunk.

Finn exhaled with relief. Maybe she *had* appreciated his wit.

She reached into a pouch at her hip and retrieved a handful of silver. Below the first, she wedged three more blades into the bark. "I doubt it's become socially acceptable to spy on a woman while she's indecent. Not that societal norms matter here. Only my rules."

The taste of blood in his mouth; he pictured quarts of it soaking into the dirt beneath him. "I'm sorry, I really am. It's just . . ." If he admitted that he'd been captivated by her beauty, she'd blind him with two of those blades.

"It's not worth the effort," she muttered as she ran her index finger downward, touching the handle of each scalpel, their *pinging* reverberating through the air. "You've been here for, what"—she glanced in the direction of the sun—"three hours? That long, you're as good as dead."

Finn squeezed his shoulder blades together. "What's that supposed to mean?"

She scowled. "Explaining anything to you would be a waste of . . ." Her eyes narrowed. "You're a Gettler, aren't you?"

His focus snapped to her face. "How'd you know?" She couldn't, unless Rollie was still coming here.

"The Aryan nose and exceptionally white teeth give you away."

Finn did have Rollie's straight nose and narrow chin, though his dad's sharp features had softened with age. But fifty years of four cups of coffee a day and the belief that the new whitening treatments were a vain waste of time had left Rollie's teeth far from pearly. The woman couldn't be thinking of the same man, Finn decided and squinted up at her.

"Cat got your tongue?"

He couldn't let her conclude that she'd rattled him. "I'm Finn. Nice to meet you."

"But that's Irish . . . and your eyes: they're green. Not that it matters; you're a Gettler." She climbed to the next branch, in line with the column of knives. "Get off my island."

Her island?

That claim would be better pondered from afar. "How do I know you won't plant one of those in my back as soon as I start running?"

"You don't."

Without deliberation, he slung his pack over his shoulder and sprinted toward the field, where he would be completely exposed.

Over his heavy breathing, he listened for the breaking of branches behind him and detected nothing.

Reaching the meadow, he sped up. Above his hiking boots, weeds and poison ivy raked his bare shins.

A whistle sounded, followed by a *fwunk.*

His joints locked.

If she'd hit him, he'd be feeling extreme pain. Finn exhaled with relief.

Her dusty voice came from behind, high up. He whipped around, and the sun momentarily blinded him.

"The orange," she said from the branches of a maple. "Leave it."

His mouth gaped. She must have traveled through the canopy.

He regularly scaled trees for his job as a landscape lighting designer, yet he couldn't move that fast. No one could.

She pointed at his bag.

As he'd left home that morning, Lily had tucked an orange beneath the cord crisscrossing the front pocket. He lowered his pack to retrieve it and nicked his hand on a scalpel embedded in its flesh. Beads of juice clung to the metal. Finn extracted the instrument.

She maneuvered to a far branch, putting the trunk between them.

The knife seemed heavy. An instrument like it—or this very scalpel—could have caused her scars. He inspected its ivory handle, tracing a small crucifix etched near the hilt.

Just holding the prize from the killing of an elephant made him feel vile.

He let it fall.

Although thin, she didn't appear to be starving. Throughout his travels, he'd encountered many fascinating people but none who'd exuded both her toughness and vulnerability. He felt a compulsion to learn what she'd been through, and if it were ongoing, though he sensed that the longer he remained in her presence, the more of an enigma she would become.

For not respecting her privacy earlier, he owed her far more than a bruised piece of fruit.

He removed the insulated bag that contained enough food to keep him going until nightfall, when he'd planned to glide past the patrols. Along with the orange, he tossed it near the tree where he'd last seen her.

He knew he should run. Instead, he waited for her to reappear.

Barely audible over the hoarse squawking of the herons, a morning announcement drifted from the PA system for the neighboring Rikers Island correctional complex.

It was as if their encounter had never happened. As if she didn't exist.

Yet he knew she was still watching him. Despite the burning rash that would result from reaching into the poison ivy, he picked up the scalpel—proof that she'd truly been of this world—and raced toward his kayak.

Two weeks later

July

Lily Skolnik clung to the shed along the property line of the Gettlers' Long Island shore home. Concealed by the encroaching sycamores, she listened to the beating of waves on the distant, rocky shore; the cawing of seagulls; the scratching of black elder branches against the weathered planks; and the heaving of her breath, louder and more primal than all else.

To calm her thudding heart, she fingered a sumac leaf and inhaled the plant's citrusy scent. Usually, she loved coming here to get away from the congestion and concrete of the city. But, today, she wished she were still at home, enjoying a cup of green tea and a Sudoku puzzle.

Instead, here she was, about to spy on her boyfriend.

Before she could lose her nerve, she pressed her ear to the lichen-encrusted wood. From the far side of the windowless wall came a *thunk*, followed by a metallic clanging.

Lily knew that Finn had sneaked away from his mother's birthday celebration on the back patio to have another look at his father's journals. But something else in there must have caught his attention.

She wished she were with him. Or that she could have been content to keep an eye on Rollie and Kristian, as Finn had asked her to do. Normally she would have eagerly helped, but Finn hadn't been the same since he'd returned from North Brother Island two weeks earlier, and she needed to know why.

What had he discovered among those ruins? Four years ago, during their third date—a tour of Alcatraz—Finn had casually mentioned his family's multigenerational involvement in another haunted past. Two years later, after swearing her to secrecy, he'd sheepishly explained that one of his great-grandfather's patients had recovered from typhus, then scarlet fever, with miraculous speed. Ever since, his family had been looking for the elusive, immune system boosting chemical reagent that they believed she'd ingested. "My dad's too serious a guy to chase a myth," Finn had countered when she'd questioned their theory.

It had taken him another year to reveal that his grandfather, who'd treated hundreds of patients at Riverside, had also been a doctor in Hitler's Schutzstaffel. She understood his hesitation: although her mother had never taken her to a synagogue, Lily was Jewish. Two of her great-uncles had died at Auschwitz.

If Finn had found proof that his grandfather had conducted involuntary medical experiments on those exiled on North Brother, it would explain his sullenness since showering off the stench of the East River.

Repeatedly she'd begged him to tell her what he'd seen. Each time, he'd told her he wasn't ready to talk about it, that he was still "processing."

Nervously picking at a hangnail, she pictured him now, paging through his father's handwritten observations of NYC's forbidden island—currently off-limits in their conversations.

It hadn't started that way, she thought bitterly, wiping perspiration from the back of her neck. Even in this shade, the air felt like the hot, steamy breath of a stranger too close on a packed subway car.

Three days before Finn had stolen onto North Brother, he'd asked her to go with him. She had, after all, accompanied him on all five of his dangerous bridge expeditions thus far, despite being too terrified to cross any of the canyons.

Though she had no desire to poke around ruins teeming with asbestos, she'd wanted to be there with him on North Brother Island. She had the means: a kayak stowed beside Finn's in their basement locker. Only her job as a horticulture coordinator for the Central Park Conservancy had held her back. If the Harbor Unit caught her trespassing in the federally protected heron preserve, she'd surely lose her job.

Maybe she should have risked it.

A gust, carrying a trace scent of kelp, buffeted her sundress and the sensitive ferns at her feet. She allowed the breeze to batter her cheeks and liberate sections of long, black hair from her ponytail.

This must be how Finn feels when he's halfway across an abyss.

When he'd first floated the idea of turning his fascination with bridge construction into an extreme hobby, she'd called him crazy. So had Rollie.

As far as Lily knew, it was the first time Finn had ever brushed away his father's heavy guiding hand.

After their first expedition, the Gettler family had gathered in their Upper East Side apartment for a digital slide show. As Finn narrated the images of lush forest, a bemused smile occupied Rollie's face. But when the first view of the precarious Ghasa suspension bridge appeared, he scowled. "How reckless. Hasn't our history taught you to value life above all else but God?"

Finn flinched and dropped his chin.

A charged silence filled the room.

Lily fumbled for the right words to defend him, but none came. She couldn't disagree with Rollie's concern for his son; her worry matched his.

"You have to stop this," Kristian said from a leather armchair in the corner, "It's just too dangerous. And stupid."

"Fuck off."

Immediately, Finn apologized to the group.

"It's not like I haven't heard that word before," eight-year-old Milo quipped, glancing at his father through the gap in his shaggy, dark blond hair. He turned to Finn: "Have you got a shot looking down from the bridge?"

"Milo," Kristian said, "don't encourage him."

Finn coolly shut his laptop and strode from the room.

Two bleak, cold blocks from the apartment building, Lily caught up with him. Without a word, she slipped her hand into his coat pocket and wrapped her already icy fingers around his warm skin. One of the things she loved most about Finn was how alive she felt in his presence, perhaps because he seemed so unconcerned with death.

Lily knew that if Rollie found Finn rifling through his old journals now, he'd be furious, despite the project's dormant status. In his soft yet commanding demeanor, Rollie routinely preached respect and family loyalty. Even she had been on the receiving end of that message.

While somewhat awkward and disturbing coming from her boyfriend's father, she would have welcomed that same expectation from Leonard, her father. A familiar aching sensation stretched across her chest.

Maybe she should have stayed with the others on the patio, where she'd been painting a watercolor of the craggy shoreline far below while Sylvia watched from her wheelchair, a rare smile on the side of her face not paralyzed. Lily loved making her happy; she should have prioritized that over her curiosity.

Soon everyone—including Finn's aunt and her twenty-three-year-old twin sons—would be wondering where the couple had gone.

But as long as she was already here, she might as well take a quick peek, she decided and peered around the corner. The pawpaw shrubs and blue joint grass rising from the bluff rippled in the wind. What she could see of the two-acre lawn that stretched between her and the house remained empty. Any moment, though, someone might decide to stake out the croquet set.

Not to mention, Finn could emerge.

Her temples pulsating, she pulled herself upward on the ledge to see through the high, narrow window, her toes leaving the ground.

Finn stood only a few feet away with his back to her, a sheet hanging limply from one hand.

Near him, atop an old wooden spool table, sat a wire animal cage.

Her stomach clenched as she dropped, and she suppressed a scream. She glanced toward the field; no one had seen her.

Leaning against the shed, she tried to re-create a visual of that crate. Something—or *things*—had been in there. *Moving.*

A tingling sensation overcame her eyes, and white flecks streaked her vision.

Why would the Gettlers have lab animals here? she asked herself, already fearing the answer.

Her panic attacks always began this way, but she couldn't give in to this one. Her right shoulder began to twitch.

"No," she said, too loudly.

Slowly, she counted to twenty.

The tingling faded. Lily smiled at this small victory.

She had to know what was in that cage.

At the edge of the thicket, she spotted a short log and set it beneath the window.

Although wobbly beneath her sandaled feet, it gave her the height she needed. She peered into the room and sucked in her breath.

Hanging from the top wire latticework were several bats, their wings wrapped tightly around their furry bodies as they slept. One of them had woken early and was crab-walking, using its sharp claws, along the front of the crate. Its mouth opened, revealing small, daggerlike teeth.

Finn must be watching it, Lily thought and smiled despite the circumstances. He loved anything nature-related, just like her. Each month, when the *National Geographic* arrived, they curled up on the couch with bagels and lox and read the issue straight through.

Given this critter's big ears, beady eyes, and horseshoe-shaped mouth, she might have considered it cute, if it weren't so creepy that these animals were here in the first place.

In search of an explanation, she shifted her gaze to the workbench just below the window. Spread across it were the journals, the knapsack from which they'd presumably come, and an open carton of individually wrapped syringes.

They had to be for the bats, she surmised. *But what are they injecting them with?*

Grunting, she pulled herself another inch higher.

Her hands lost their hold. The heel of her sandal snagged the log, causing it to roll, and she fell. Her knees hit the rocky dirt.

Based on his hunched shoulders, he appeared to be as disturbed as she was by the presence of laboratory animals on his parents' property. For all she knew, he might have seen more of them on North Brother. Acutely aware of how little she knew about his trip and thoughts since then, Lily breathed in the scent of the sandy loam.

Her nausea receding, she raised her head.

Halfway across the lawn, Kristian was charging toward her, unhindered by his loafers and chinos.

Adjusting the bodice of her sundress, she scrambled to her feet. To head him off, she rushed forward, then slowed to avoid arousing suspicion.

"Time to eat?" she asked as they neared each other.

"That was quite the tumble," he said, panting from the exertion. "You okay?"

"I'm fine," she said, conscious of Finn still within the shed only ten feet behind her.

He wrinkled his brow and scrutinized her. "What hurts?"

"Seriously, I'm good." She retied her hair and straightened her shell necklace. The slightest dishevelment might cause him to worry that her neurons had been misfiring.

"Your patellae took the brunt of it."

Lily lifted the hem of her dress, and the sight of dirt-streaked crimson triggered a stinging sensation. If Kristian discovered Finn now with that cage uncovered, the confrontation might provide some answers, but the fallout for Finn wouldn't be worth it. As head of pediatric neurology at Memorial Sloan Kettering, Kristian was closer to Rollie, an internist with his own practice. Surely Kristian would tell their father that Finn had been nosing around.

She had to draw Kristian away from the shed.

"Can you help me find a bandage?"

"Yes, but your heart rate may still be elevated." He took her wrist to gauge her pulse.

"I'm not *that* frail," she said but didn't pull away. Her petite stature, in comparison to the Gettler men—Finn and Rollie were more than six feet tall, and Kristian's heft made up for him slightly missing the mark—didn't help her case.

"Sorry," he said, dropping his hand. "You can take the doctor out of the hospital, but . . ."

She smiled gently. "God knows I've given you a few scares."

He raised his sunglasses and peered at her, his sky-blue eyes cluttered by long lashes. "Finn said your anxiety has been worse lately."

Avoiding his probing stare, she studied her hands, which made her feel more self-conscious. Her nails were whittled down to the flesh.

Kristian tapped his hawk-like nose. "You'll call me if you find yourself checking more than six squares on that chart?"

"I promised I would." Just this morning, while Finn had been in the shower, she'd taken out the laminated checklist of "Signs of Depression/ Anxiety" and had shaded eight of the ten boxes. Then she'd wiped the sheet clean.

His gaze shifted to a spider, spinning a web beneath the eaves of the flat roof. "Like cancer, mental illnesses are treatable. Neither should prevent you from joining our family."

Her smile fell. Fourteen years apart in age, the half brothers had grown up separately and now had little in common. Yet clearly Finn had shared with him her reservations about marriage.

The extent of his family's knowledge about her medical issues and their relationship had always been disconcerting. Considering how private they all were, it was pretty hypocritical.

"I shouldn't have said that." Kristian ducked his chin in apology. "It's just that I see how much he loves you." He shoved his hands into his pants pockets. "All we're guaranteed is the present. Yes, you almost died. Twice.

But you also received two second chances, thanks to science. Make the most of them."

She blinked to hold back the tears. Only Kristian, with his oddly calming black-and-white perceptions, could address her this way. Whenever Finn tried to tell her to stop worrying, the conversation quickly shifted to an argument that ended in deadlock.

"Enough about that." He let his arms swing to his sides. "Where's Finny? Mom won't start her birthday dinner without him, and her pain's an eight. We need to get her to bed soon."

Lily had always admired Kristian's devotion to his stepmother, despite his job and own family's demands. His birth mother had died from congenital heart failure when he was only seven. Two years into a Doctors Without Borders trip to Cambodia, Rollie met Sylvia, an International Red Cross volunteer from Romania. Rollie brought her to the United States to meet his son, and six months later, they married at City Hall.

According to Finn, from the start, Sylvia had viewed Kristian as her own, so it made sense that he adored her. Still, even biological sons often aren't that dedicated to their moms. Finn tried, but there was little he could do to alleviate her ever-worsening arthritis, nerve palsies, and polyneuropathy—all side effects of her chronic Lyme disease. Seven years ago, she'd been bitten by a tick carrying a rare, antibiotic-resistant strain of the virulent bacteria *Borrelia burgdorferi*.

"He can't have gone far." She sidled over to the fence and peered down at the beach. "Milo was bugging him earlier to go crabbing. Maybe they're at the tidal pools."

Kristian shook his head. "Milo's at the kitchen table, doing his pre-calc enrichment."

"Really? You should give Boy Genius a day off now and then."

"He can't. He's got big shoes to fill someday," he said, without any indication it was a joke, and glanced at the shed. "Maybe Finn's in there"—he arched his dark eyebrows, laced with unruly gray—"and you were about to meet him for a—"

The door swung open.

"Hey," Finn said, squinting.

She locked her gaze on his eyes, searching for evidence that the bats had shocked him as much as they had her.

He looked away and twisted the visor of his Mets cap back to the front, and she sensed he was hiding something.

"What were you doing?" Kristian asked.

"Looking for my belaying kit." Finn tucked his chin-length, sandy brown hair behind his ears. "You seen it?"

"Yeah, I used it last weekend at the Gunks, when I had nothing better to do with my day off."

Finn fake-laughed. "That sense of humor. I'm so jealous. Is dinner ready?"

"The steaks have probably cooled twenty degrees by now, and I still need to treat those scrapes on Lily's knees."

"I'll do it," Finn offered.

"That's outside your wheelhouse, Finny. Besides, you need to conserve energy for dish duty, while the rest of us are enjoying dessert."

"I'm not the one who needs to go light on the birthday cake."

"My body fat percentage is modestly above the norm only because I've got a real job," Kristian said over his shoulder as he began walking toward the patio. "The type that doesn't involve climbing trees and screwing in lightbulbs."

"Hmm." Finn cocked his head. "How many doctors does it take to screw in a lightbulb?"

"Zero," Kristian said without slowing. "I've got someone who does that for me."

"Because you don't know how!" Finn called out.

"Hey now, be nice," Lily said, though she knew neither had been offended. As an only child of divorced parents, she couldn't help but feel a little envious of their continual verbal sparring.

"What happened?" Finn asked, leaning forward to inspect her knees.

She didn't believe he hadn't heard her hit the ground. Though, sometimes, when concentrating intensely, he did tune out everything around him. "It's nothing." She stepped away. "I just tripped on a log. What about you? You okay?"

From the set of his jaw, she knew he wasn't. Clearly, he was bothered by that evidence of ongoing virology research.

But she couldn't be the one to mention it and give away the fact that she'd been snooping. She could only hope he would bring it up. "What did you find?"

He shook his head and glanced toward Kristian, now more than ten yards away.

She doubted he could hear them. Either Finn was being extra cautious, or it was an excuse.

"You'll tell me on the way home?" She wrinkled her nose at how desperate the question had sounded.

"It's complicated." He raised his hat to wipe his brow. "I know that's not what you want to hear, but I need some time to process it."

Her stomach ached; no way could she eat now.

Abruptly, Finn stopped.

As she strode past, he grabbed her upper arm, causing her to reel backward.

To steady herself, she clutched him, yet the relief that he wanted her beside him kept her dizzied.

Finn pressed his hand to hers. She felt something soft and looked down.

In her palm was a single bluebell blossom. She hadn't noticed this breed of wildflower growing on the Gettlers' property, nor had she seen him stoop to pick this one.

"It's beautiful," she whispered. "Thank you."

"I'm sorry. What I found . . . I don't know if my dad's the man I thought he was, and that's not exactly an easy thing to talk about. Okay?"

Sickened by the statement, she managed to nod. "I'm here when you're ready."

She tucked the stem under the strap of her dress, then brushed her lips across his cheek.

He entwined his fingers with hers, and they fell into step.

For the next two hours, she would have to interact with Rollie as if nothing were wrong, including smiling at all his cheesy puns, which she struggled to do under normal circumstances.

She didn't blame Finn for his reticence in sharing what he'd found. Firsthand she knew that reality can be far harder to face than uncertainty.

One week later

August

In the darkness, Finn crouched among the wild grasses encroaching on the seawall. Even without the light pollution, he would have felt exposed beneath the waning gibbous moon, unthreatened by a single cloud. A storm system was expected to hit New York City early the next morning. By midnight, twenty hours from now, the chop of the river would become unnavigable. Long before then, he planned to leave this rock. Hopefully *with* the woman.

He repositioned a folded, inflatable raft and rope within the hull of his concealed kayak and scrutinized the horizon, still untouched by natural light. Within the pitch-black forest, this place was even more so "her island." Until he convinced her that he was on her side.

Finn squirmed. Ever since he'd found that square of yellowed paper tucked in Rollie's final journal entry, dated August 28, 2001, queasiness had been his constant companion. "You're done with Riverside," his mom had written. "She's suffered too much already."

Moments later, he'd heard a rustle behind him and ripped away the sheet, revealing the cage of bats. A horrifying range of possible connections among Sylvia's declaration, the scarred woman who despised his family, and the evidence of ongoing research had snatched his breath.

Finally, he had insight into why Rollie had been so vocal and absolute in his decision. Yet the implications of his mother's written request had left Finn shaking. In all that he'd overheard as a child about catalysts, environmental studies, specimen samples, and antibodies, there'd been no mention of human test subjects.

Yet it hadn't been uncommon for his parents' conversations about Rollie's latest site visit to shift from the dinner table to their locked bedroom, leaving Finn unable to finish his meal alone because of the pit in his stomach.

Now he couldn't shake the dread that the woman he'd encountered was somehow involved against her will, and that his father's efforts were possibly ongoing. Considering Kristian's frequent rantings about government ineptitude in curbing outbreaks, as evidenced by the initial SARS-CoV response, he very well could still be involved, too.

His mother, a renowned feminist, had quit her paralegal job in the mid-1980s to attend women's rights and peace rallies in Washington, DC. Even though she now couldn't hold a pen, the fiery poems and essays she'd written for three decades had earned her a permanent place in women's studies curricula at colleges across the country. If she'd known that the Gettler men's "vital research" entailed involuntary human testing, she wouldn't have stayed with Rollie. The note, however, implied that's precisely what she'd done.

While retrieving the knapsack that housed the journals, wedged in the bow of his dad's kayak, Finn had found a MetroCard with an expiration of 04/27/09. Evidently Rollie had recently visited the island. The easiest way to get a kayak to either of their launch points was by carting it on the subway.

Finn guessed the scarred woman was at most twenty years old, which meant she'd been a young teen back when Sylvia had penned that edict.

If Rollie had been using this woman, or a string of vagrants, to test the effects of various locally sourced chemical compounds on the immune system—while a day nurse tended to his wheelchair-bound wife—he couldn't be doing so by force, given her strength and prowess. He must have an ongoing means of manipulating her into submission. Finn prayed to God that it didn't relate to the scars covering her body.

Rollie's desire to hide from Sylvia his continued activity here would certainly explain why he'd lied to Finn.

To stay alert, Finn tugged at the corners of his eyes. Over the past week, he'd barely slept. The father he'd always known—a man who'd been strict yet also kind, generous, and fascinated by Finn's comic card collection, ability to spout baseball stats, and galactic battle scene skteches—might not actually exist.

He couldn't shake the premonition that his family had been conducting involuntary human testing here.

At twelve, while building a model airplane in his room with his best friend, Finn had whispered that his family was doing important, top-secret work on a nearby deserted island. Dave had asked if they were working for the CIA. Just as Finn was clarifying, Rollie had thrown open the door, grabbed Finn by the ear, scolded him for not having helped his mother fold laundry, and told Dave to head home.

That was the only time—until he met Lily—that Finn had mentioned the project to anyone outside his family. In the days that had followed, Rollie's edginess had made Finn wonder if he was afraid of getting caught for something far more severe than trespassing.

Yesterday, after seeing the weather forecast, Finn had hastened his preparations and rescheduled a client meeting. Offering to help her evacuate would serve as the perfect excuse for his return.

Breathing in the stench of the salted, moist dirt, Finn reminded himself that thinking of her only as a victim would put him at greater risk.

The woman had chucked four scalpels at him and might impale him with a fifth any moment. He was a Gettler; nothing she'd said or done suggested that she would spare him again.

Yet he didn't regret his decision to return. If his intuition were correct, he had a responsibility to save her. And even if he was wrong, those scars had been caused by someone.

Although his father's influence now seemed farcical, his parents had instilled in their sons a sense of altruism and purpose. Through his family's dedication to microbiology, they believed their future discovery would save humanity when—not if—a deadly pathogen emerged and spread like wildfire through our densely packed global society. The day his birth mother died, Kristian had accepted Rollie's mandate to study medicine as if it had been his idea. Thirteen years later, upon hearing Kristian describe a cadaver dissection for a premed college class, Finn had declared that he too wanted to become a doctor.

"Finny," Rollie had said, "the sight of blood makes you queasy. You're a round peg; don't force yourself through a square hole."

To show Rollie that a round peg could bust its way through any square hole, at his kindergarten graduation ceremony, Finn proudly raised his sign that stated what he wanted to become when he grew up: "The Incredible Hulk."

While not superhero worthy, he'd turned out to be muscular enough. Though, today, the survival skills he'd acquired in Africa would prove more useful.

A breeze rattled the bushes. She could be watching him now, her throwing arm raised.

Soon it would be light enough for him to begin his search.

From a pocket in his cargo pants, Finn retrieved his Swiss Army knife. Lily had given it to him after he'd completed his master's degree in architecture at Cal Poly. In the past two years, it had traveled with them to four countries. Now it represented his only form of self-defense against a woman he could never bring himself to harm.

While packing for this trip, he'd wanted to tell Lily about her, but Lily would have made the connection between the woman and Finn's worries about his dad. He still couldn't bring himself to share his suspicions. For Lily, growing up fatherless had been like missing an essential vitamin, of which she now couldn't get enough. Rollie, who'd always wanted a daughter, had leaped into that void.

Finn pictured her waking up alone, and a pang of guilt shot through him. To let her know he'd arrived safely, he sent a quick text—a row of *M*'s, signifying their willingness to move mountains for each other. It had started as a joke; now it was simply another way of saying, "I love you." Then he turned off his phone to conserve its battery.

A heron squawked. Another responded and took flight. The ruckus of the colony intensified. The woman had to be awake.

He strapped on his pack and walked within a strip of forest near the meadow he'd sprinted across last time.

At least today he didn't have to worry about running into any city parks workers. Before his first trip, Lily had learned that the parks department wouldn't sanction visits to the island during the heron nesting season, which extended from March 21 through September 21. She'd tried to persuade Finn to wait until the fall, when she might be able to get them both included on an official tour.

Before this second trip, she hadn't even asked to join him. Presumably because she'd expected him to say that he needed to go alone, so he'd promised her that he'd tell her everything afterward.

Finn rubbed his lower back, sore from battling the currents. If the woman were still here, the tuberculosis pavilion seemed the most logical place for her to be staying. From his research in the New York Public

Library's archives, Finn knew the structure had been completed in 1943. Its walls had to be far sounder than those of the buildings constructed decades earlier, and from its top floor, she could survey the entire island.

The cawing of birds drowned out the sounds of the morning rush hour. He would never hear her approach.

Finn glanced back. The forest had blotted out the shore and Manhattan's skyline. The humidity triggered a sense of déjà vu; he was back trekking through the jungle, about to cross one of the Mekong Delta's infamous monkey bridges. He closed his eyes.

And saw her face.

Those startling baby blues.

"Hello!" he called out as he jerked his chin upward to search for her. The leaves blurred as he spun. Dizzy and disoriented, he stopped.

He consulted a small compass on a cord around his neck.

To the northeast, he could just make out an ivy-covered lane bordered by cast-iron lampposts that protruded from the overgrowth. He imagined how cool those lamps would look relit at night. Maybe he would find his sketchbook today. More likely, she already had.

He poked at the dirt with his hiking boot and uncovered cracked concrete, another reminder that this forest belonged to New York City. Wiping his brow, he rotated to face what had to be the maintenance building, the first of three structures that would block him from the view of passing watercraft until he reached denser foliage.

She could be hiding among the grime-coated rubbish that loomed beyond those broken windows.

He squeezed the folded knife and pictured his mother, back when she'd been strong enough to stand up for others. Although she was too ill to handle whatever Finn uncovered today, if she had known about his plan, she would have approved. Before his flight back to Ivory Coast in 2003, Rollie's final words had been, "Don't be a hero. We need you to come home alive." Without echoing the sentiment, Sylvia had given him one last hug and kiss. She understood that someone must take on that role.

Even though his odds of convincing the woman to leave with him today were low, he had to try. Failure meant he'd have to confront Rollie.

The PowerBar he'd eaten on the subway to Barretto Point Park felt like a lump of wet cement in his stomach.

He continued along the ivy lane. A fire hydrant appeared among the brambles, and he shook his head in wonder at this place, forgotten by the world.

In case she was watching him, he called out a greeting: "A major storm's headed this way! You won't be safe here!"

The faint whistle of a commuter train sounded from the Bronx.

Maybe she'd already left. "I've brought food."

A bird took flight.

"Protein, a few oranges"—his voice cracked—"and chocolate."

Still nothing. *What woman doesn't like chocolate?*

"It's a Toblerone," he said to the leaf canopy.

It had been in his bag since his trip to Bryce Canyon with Lily. After each of their treks, financed through a combination of their wages and Lily's trust fund—the only kind thing her asshole father had ever done for her—they gorged on McDonald's cheeseburgers then split a Toblerone. Usually Lily followed a vegan, organic diet. At age four, she'd beaten brain cancer. Thirteen years later, she'd developed myelodysplastic syndrome, a blood cancer her doctors blamed on the original chemo. Convinced she had a genetic predisposition to cancer, Lily treated carcinogens like venomous snakes. Finn's goal for their expeditions was to help her let go of her fears and *live.*

"Lils, I know you'd understand." He propped the chocolate in the crook of a willow oak branch and stepped back.

The peace offering looked paltry, so he worked a tribal bracelet off his wrist and looped it over the bar.

Listening for movement behind him, he continued north, and the roof of the two-story male dormitory appeared. To his left, the sky reflected off a large cistern, its greenish water teeming with bacteria and parasites. In one of his father's journals, he'd noticed a table containing the microorganism densities of samples taken from that tank.

Finn rounded the corner of the building and reeled back at the sight of the tuberculosis pavilion's four-story central tower, jutting above the trees like a Mayan temple.

Finn hadn't seen a single reference to its interior in Rollie's logs, which made sense if he hadn't wanted Sylvia to know what he'd been doing there.

Pocketing his utility knife, he threaded his way through the overgrowth. At the bottom step of the central entrance, he scraped the dirt from the treads of his boots.

Finn touched his phone within his pocket for reassurance and ascended the stairs. He reached the granite doorframe and paused. The crumbling walls and ceiling had left a layer of white dust on the folding chairs and broken furniture scattered throughout the dim, circular lobby. The room looked frozen in time. The scent of plaster was so strong, he could almost feel the grit in his nose.

Short patches of sunlight sliced into the gloom but did little to illuminate the far doorway. He stepped forward to study the structural integrity of the room.

A single, distant clanking sounded from above.

He jumped at the sound.

It could be her.

Or a new occupant.

Or a rat.

The noise didn't repeat. He moved to the center of the room and slowly turned. The walls lining the exterior were decaying faster than those within, but overall, the structure appeared to be sound.

Boot prints, covered in a film of dust, crisscrossed the lobby. None looked recent or small enough to be hers. And the tread marks didn't match the pattern of the orthopedic sneakers Rollie wore to combat his plantar fasciitis.

Curious if his fresh prints would be obvious, Finn scrutinized his tracks and noticed a clean line in the dirt near the entrance.

Crouching before it, he spotted a piece of twine. Visually he traced its path upward through a series of eye bolts screwed into the plaster. The string disappeared into a slit in the ceiling. On the opposite side of the entrance, six inches from the ground, he found a single empty hook. *For a tripwire.*

He tugged on the twine, and the distant clanging sounded again.

It had to be a homemade alarm system. Despite the humidity, a chill brushed the back of his neck.

"Hello!" he yelled, and his greeting echoed through the chamber.

As Finn crossed the lobby, the air thickened with the scent of decay. He took a deep breath and entered a dim room filled with broken desks and filing cabinets. Blue tiles coating the lower halves of the walls gave the administrative office an underwater-like quality. Finn passed a row of rusting mail slots, some still locked, and peered into an open closet. On the floor lay a sheet of paper titled ***Hospital Patients in Seclusion Rooms.

He shuddered.

From his research, he knew there were isolation units above him. By the time the facility's construction had ended, a vaccine for tuberculosis had gained traction, and local hospitals could more safely treat infectious diseases. The building had never been used for its originally intended purpose. Instead, from 1952 through 1963, Riverside had served as an experimental rehabilitation clinic. The clerks who'd worked in this suite had processed admittance paperwork for juvenile heroin addicts.

And his grandfather had been one of their doctors.

A decade ago, Sylvia had whispered to him that his grandpa had been stationed at Dachau. At first, Finn had been shocked. An apple-pie-loving patriot, Grandpa had donated to the local VA and driven his antique Model T in the Port Jefferson Fourth of July parade every year. He'd even given Finn his collection of vintage American flags the day Finn had signed up for Cub Scouts. And he'd regularly stated that the immunological breakthrough they were so close to achieving would help "every single American, no matter how black or dirt poor."

A Nazi past hadn't seemed possible.

Yet his grandpa did have a cruel streak. Most Sundays after church, Rollie had taken Finn on the Long Island Rail Road to visit his grandparents. Kristian, who'd often met them there, would join their father and grandfather behind closed doors, leaving Finn with two choices: find Grandma in the kitchen or head outside. More than once, Finn had wandered too far from their property or "accidentally" smashed one of the little clay gnomes in his grandmother's garden. It had been Grandpa who'd dealt the punishment, with his leather belt.

When Finn broached his grandfather's past with Rollie, his dad hung his head in shame. "Why do you think he's so obsessed with eradicating disease?"

Finn shrugged.

"It's the only way he'll ever forgive himself," Rollie said and changed the subject.

To Finn it sounded like just another outlet for his grandfather's fanatical drive and discipline, but his father's tone had warned him to keep that view to himself.

Trying to stymie creeping visuals of lobotomies and electric shock therapies that had surely occurred here while the facility had treated drug-addicted teens, Finn squared his shoulders and stepped into the main corridor, his eyes widening. The decaying plaster and flooring, patches of blue wall tiles, and streaks of sunlight created a kaleidoscope of human-made and natural effects.

The last time he'd felt this sense of awe he'd been fifteen. His mother had taken him to a cut-paper shadowbox exhibit at the Museum of Modern Art. For hours, he'd stared into the three-dimensional, intricate scenes, each backlit with an LED light. A humpback whale breaching the sea, a boy lost in a haunted forest, a Chinese pagoda atop a mountain.

That day, he'd realized that by studying physics, he could contribute an expertise needed for research on an island with no access to power. Rollie had approved the plan, and for a while Finn had felt like he might live up to his father's expectations.

With his knife and flashlight in hand, Finn entered what must have been the medical wing. From the doorway to an operating room, he bounced his beam from floor to ceiling, where it landed on a framework of lamps hanging like meat racks, their incandescent lights broken.

The odor of antiseptic filled his nostrils, and his stomach contracted. Just as it always did when he entered his mother's hospital room during one of her stays.

Lily, too, detested that smell. After her bone marrow transplant, she'd remained confined to a sterile hospital wing for eight weeks because of life-threatening complications with graft-versus-host disease.

Finn continued down the corridor, halting in front of a closed metal door and turning its knob. *Locked.* The room on the far side of that steel might contain boxes of medical records. Or something far more sinister.

Throughout Finn's childhood, Rollie would bring home patient charts to update while Finn completed his homework. Each file's top right corner had a name scrawled across it that didn't match the patient's. The first time Finn noticed the pattern he'd asked Rollie about it.

Smiling, Rollie set down his pen. "I try to chat with all my patients, and then record the name of the person they each love most."

To an eleven-year-old, the practice sounded lame. Finn grimaced. "Why?"

"To help me see them as people, not just a collection of organs. Your great-grandfather's early records show he did the same. He shouldn't have dropped the habit." He squeezed Finn's bicep. "Make sure I don't."

Now Finn worried that that's exactly what had happened.

Glancing down the corridor, Finn decided that if the woman were on this floor, she would have made her presence known by now.

He climbed the central staircase to the second story and studied a faded, peeling mural adorning the hall. He could just make out a poem, written in cursive:

I hate Riverside
Its workers too
Though some of the
Nurses will fuck for you.

Appalled that his father had grown up in this environment, Finn shook his head.

The heat trapped within the pavilion was starting to get to him. He swigged his water and continued up the stairs, which led to a dayroom invaded by vines. They'd slithered in through the broken windows and strangled the radiators.

Softly, he trod down a hallway plagued with debris. Even on this floor, the smell of antiseptic lingered.

The scent had to be in his head, he decided. Ahead, every other door was sheathed in metal. Finn inspected one. Below a small, eye-level slot, a deadbolt had been retrofitted to the door. He'd reached the isolation rooms.

Pausing at the first doorframe, he peered into the room. Sunlight, filtered through the fenced-over windows, cast an eerie glow. One sidewall contained a window covered in mesh. Beyond it had to be a nurses' station, from which a junkie could be supervised during detox. Penciled graffiti adorned the cell walls. From the hallway, Finn craned to see the nearest marks.

Help me
I am being
held here
Against my
Will

Holy shit.

He wondered where the guy was now, and what role Grandpa had played in his "treatment."

As he turned toward the main stairwell, a succession of shrieks erupted outside.

From the corridor, he strained to see through the grating over the cell's window. In the distance, he could make out a swarm of birds. Either a patrol had come ashore or the woman had disturbed them.

Or worse: Rollie had arrived.

Finn squeezed his utility knife.

This was Tuesday; Sylvia had physical therapy. Rollie always accompanied her. They should be there now.

His father could have instructed the day nurse to take her. But he would have had to kayak here in broad daylight without the Harbor Unit detecting him. Even though he was in excellent condition for his age, his approach to the island, against the currents, would have been labored and slow.

Maybe Finn's entire theory was off-base. Unless Kristian's irritation at Rollie for mothballing the project had also been a ruse and he'd been handling the onsite work.

He glanced down the hall to ensure it was still empty and moved to the grate, where he smelled iron, and beyond it, fresh air.

The herons were taking flight from the trees near where he'd come ashore.

The beach and both decaying docks near his landing spot were empty.

Beyond them, a dark, red form blotted out a patch of the glistening water.

"Fuck." He squinted for a better look at the object, circling in an eddy.

She must have pushed in his kayak. If he sprinted, he might be able to reach it before it became ensnared by a current or was spotted by a patrol.

Finn bolted for the exit, reeling backward just before smacking into the door.

He hadn't closed it. Nor had he heard its rusty hinges as it swung shut.

Blinking rapidly, he pushed, but it didn't budge.

What the hell?

He slammed his shoulder against the metal. The pinched nerve in his neck ignited in pain, blending with a fiery sensation in his bicep.

"Guys much stronger than you have tried that same move," said a faint, raspy voice from the adjacent observation room. "It didn't work for them, either."

Heat radiated from his chest, flooding his entire body with fire.

He'd found her.

Or rather, she'd found *him*.

1902–1904

A period of rapid expansion for Riverside Hospital,
spurred by a series of outbreaks in Manhattan's tenements

February 1902

Heat from the blaze stung Cora's back as cold wind chapped her face. Pushing through the knee-deep drifts, she slogged barefoot toward the seawall. Falling snow blended with the lavender-gray sky and whitecaps of the East River, creating a heavenly illusion. Even if her survival instincts could override her desire to die, hypothermia would render her swimming skills useless.

A scream crackled through the air.

Cora halted.

Although she kept to herself, several in the typhus overflow encampment had been kind to her. Mostly immigrants who'd settled in the squalid tenements of New York City, they clearly understood the pain that death leaves when stealing a family member.

Now she turned to face the burning tent as Mrs. Levitsky staggered from the inferno, flames devouring the back of her gown.

Horrified, Cora scanned the men in the fire brigade, who appeared too busy managing the hose to come to the woman's aid.

"Help her!" Cora screamed, but the wind stole her words along with her breath.

Despite the germs' grip on her frail body, Mrs. Levitsky had been like a mother to the group, telling Russian fairy tales at night, beckoning sleep to each fevered mind. Cora hadn't understood the words, yet they'd still been soothing.

"Damn it!" Cora yelled through gritted teeth before darting back through the knot of makeshift shelters and frantic patients.

A nurse reached Mrs. Levitsky first, grabbed her, and threw them both into a snowdrift.

Even after the smoke had cleared, the old woman continued to wail.

Cora dropped to the ground and helped the nurse pack snow onto her friend's backside as she writhed.

Although she should try to calm her, Cora couldn't bring herself to look at the woman's contorted face. Before Cora had arrived at Riverside Hospital, New York City's most notorious pesthouse, she'd wanted to become a medical assistant. Two months on the island had changed that. These days, she wanted nothing more to do with disease and the doctors' feeble attempts to stop it. She'd rather work at a Macy's counter or sell pickles on the street.

Beyond them, a section of the tarp fell away, creating a window, framed by flames, into the pavilion, where a single ember had jumped from a coal stove to the canvas. All two dozen of the thin pallets were burning. Aside from Mrs. Levitsky's, the only bed Cora could be certain was empty was her own. They'd been so fearful of the silent assassins festering within them; this incarnation of the devil posed an even greater threat.

She detested this prison island.

An orderly arrived to carry the moaning, charred Mrs. Levitsky to the main hospital building, and Cora stepped out of his way. A current of air, packing sea spray and snow, whipped her tunic around her legs before crashing against the burning timbers. Despite its water content, the gust countered the efforts of those manning the fire-extinguishing apparatus. So far, the blaze had been contained to the single tent, but if the staff failed, the devastation would surely spread to the other makeshift shelters and then to the hospital's permanent wards and ancillary buildings.

Behind her, a child coughed the deep, rattling trademark of consumption, sending a shiver through Cora. With no other safe way to comfort the girl, she simply smiled. The child's blue lips remained in a taut grimace. She'd likely be dead within a week.

Dozens of other invalids, cloaked in blankets, joined the vigil. The smoke had driven the typhus patients from their assigned tents, and others had come to gawk.

"*Tretet zurück!* Step back!" shouted a strained voice with a German accent. Though he was holding a rag over his mouth, Cora recognized Dr. Otto Gettler.

Seemingly mesmerized by the fire, most of the onlookers didn't budge. The blaze was alive, more so than anything else Cora had seen here. Two years before, when she'd read about the great Hoboken docks fire in the *Tribune*, she'd secretly wished that she'd witnessed the spectacle. Her name, with a brilliant quote, might have appeared in the paper alongside the other firsthand accounts. What a fool she'd been.

After an orderly shouted that they'd cleared the tent, a cheer reverberated throughout the encampment.

Dr. Gettler whooped in obvious relief and tossed the rag.

Waving his arms, he addressed the crowd: "Return to your pavilions." He spun and beckoned to the nearest staff member, who happened to be head nurse Kate Holden. "You know they must remain segregated by disease. We cannot have the pests mingling."

"We'll see them to their wards at once, sir," she replied.

A prickling sensation crept up Cora's neck. Nearby, a man cleared the phlegm in his throat, and the sound felt like a fog bell pressed to her ear. A woman coughed wetly, and Cora covered her own mouth and nose.

Nurse Holden called to four in her staff, who lined up like soldiers to receive their orders. Only the sodden hems of their Mother Hubbard gowns, tangled around their rubber overshoes, betrayed the women's fatigue as they collected those housed in their respective wards—measles, scarlet fever, tuberculosis, and typhus.

Cora dropped her hand from her face. She should welcome another disease: it would hasten her death.

The typhus patients who'd evacuated the burning tent, barefoot from fleeing their cots so quickly, looked to nurse Holden, who'd personally suffered through a bout with this most deadly of diseases. Although she managed all aspects of the hospital not under the head physician's purview, she often found time to lift their spirits.

Her wit reminded Cora of her dearest friend, Sophia, who lived in her same tenement on West Ninth Street. She wished she were with her now, talking about marriage prospects and the hats they couldn't afford in the shops on Millinery Row. Cora wondered if she would ever again find joy in something as trivial as a green felt headpiece.

Now though, as the nurse, her face blackened with soot, surveyed those remaining, she made no lighthearted remarks.

Even though they'd survived the fire, several wouldn't see another sunrise. The day following the last one in the overflow encampment, Cora had heard two of the nurses discussing the final death count in hushed tones.

"Ladies and gentlemen," the head nurse called, clapping her hands, "I'll be reassigning you to new quarters, where you'll receive medical attention, as well as blankets and tunics. Please give the fire a wide berth so the men can do their job."

Before the loss of the tent, the typhus ward had already been overcrowded. A shipload of Russian exiles had imported an outbreak that had filled the quarantine hospital beyond capacity. Now, to accommodate the newly displaced, pallets would be laid on the floor wherever space remained. Throughout the night, Cora knew, there would be moaning, coughing, vomiting, and periodic final gasps, followed by the removal of a body. By morning, the incinerator would be busy.

She would hear it all; for the past week, sleep had been illusory. Those relying on willpower and prayer to stave off their last breaths wouldn't benefit from her despondent restlessness. She edged away from the huddle.

Beyond the camp, she trudged past piles of construction material for the final five single-story, wood-framed pavilions, their progress halted by the harsh winter. She sunk to her knees and burrowed her arms and face into the snow. Like a coffin, it muffled the distant commotion as well as her sobs. The tears that had refused to surface before now sprung free and froze on her lashes. The darkness felt as heavy as dirt piled on a corpse. She might as well be lifeless. Then, at least, she would no longer be burdened by the stench and specter of death that was so pervasive on North Brother Island. And she would be reunited with her sister, Maeve.

Icy water pricked her exposed skin, and her hospital gown gripped her in a frigid, wet embrace. She rubbed her eyes to break the icicles clinging to her lashes and sat up. Squinting, she noted that she'd fallen to her knees near the edge of the island.

If she stepped off the partially constructed seawall, during her final moments she would be numb. *No!* She wanted to suffer. For letting her sister accept that tin toy train from the boy who'd wandered from the typhus ward over to the measles pavilion.

Ten weeks earlier, as she and her sister were being forced into a Health Department carriage, bound for the reception hospital on Sixteenth Street, Cora had promised their mother that she would watch over Maeve. Born from a different father, Maeve didn't possess the hardiness that Cora had inherited from hers, whoever he might be.

After two days on Hospital Island, Cora had fully recovered from the measles, but the disease had hit her sister much harder. Three intense weeks later, she turned the corner. With both girls anxious to go home,

Maeve's recovery progressed agonizingly slowly. Finally, a month ago, the small red spots covering her body had disappeared and her energy for play had returned.

Cora had been too busy envisioning her mom's joyful tears to recognize the new threat hiding in plain sight. Despite Riverside's isolation rules, she hadn't rebuffed the boy's gift.

As Maeve's body, still weak from her bout with the measles, had succumbed to this second, deadlier disease, she'd been in too much pain to manage more than a whimper. Cora's death should be no easier.

Soon, the blazing tent near the center of the island would collapse into a smoldering heap.

"I'm sorry I failed you, *Mamaí*." Cora stood up and walked toward the flames.

The heat increased; her skin felt like it was blistering.

She didn't even turn her cheek. The air became dense with acrid smoke, her dress began to steam, and the intensity of the light forced her eyes shut. She let the hissing and popping of the wooden timbers and the escalating temperature guide her.

The bone-dry air became unbearable, yet she reached for that fiery gateway.

Her lungs gave out; she collapsed.

But instead of descending to hell, her soul seemed to be rising.

The heat diminished and she became aware of a pair of muscular arms crushing her torso, carrying her away from the fire. Opening her eyes, she recognized Richard O'Toole's red hair, thick with ash.

"Put me down," she demanded, struggling to free herself.

The orderly maintained his hold until they'd reached a safe distance from the inferno and set her on her feet. A nurse wrapped a coarse blanket around Cora's shoulders.

She wiped at the sting in her eyes. "How dare you grab me like that?"

O'Toole flinched, and she shrank away from him. Her mother, Eleanor, would be ashamed of her for being so forthright with a man, even though she routinely ignored the decorum she preached. Long after the murmurs of the head physician bringing "the black bottle" to quicken Maeve's departure, O'Toole had tended to her.

"I'm sorry, I—"

He raised his hand to silence her, softening the gesture with a smile. "I know how hard this is for you, but think of your mum. If she lost you too—"

"*Vielen Dank*, Mr. O'Toole," Dr. Gettler said with a cough, likely to clear smoke from his lungs. "We work so hard to return them to their *Familien*, and now we've lost four already tonight." He rubbed his spectacles with the corner of his ash-stained dress shirt.

"Mr. O'Toole, please see this young lady to Pavilion Five. I'll meet you there shortly." He touched the stethoscope hanging from his neck. It looked out of place without the standard gown, gloves, and rubber overshoes worn by the staff. When the fire began, he must have been on his way to the ferry.

She'd never been treated by this doctor but had overheard the nurses talking about him. They fancied him for more than his resemblance to a Norse god: he knew the names of all the indigent ill he treated, and he always asked who they planned to see first once recovered. Before Maeve had passed, Cora's answer would have been her mother. Now she dreaded even the thought of that visit.

Tonight, the doctor's skill would be better devoted to patients who wanted to survive. "Dr. Gettler, sir, I'm well. Others need your attention more."

He raised his glasses to rub his reddened blue eyes and peered at her. "Miss . . . *deine Name*?"

"Coraline McSorley."

"*Doch*." He dropped his spectacles onto the bridge of his elegantly straight nose. "Miss McSorley, your samples were brought to my attention earlier today. The results are *sehr interessant*. I was planning to review your health history tomorrow. And take a trip to the microscopes in Carnegie Laboratory. For that I'll need additional specimens."

Why would he go to all that effort? she wondered.

There must be something wrong with me. In my blood.

That morning she'd gritted her teeth during the jab from a needle, as thick as a crochet hook, and fought off the wooziness while her blood had surged into four vials. Now she felt equally lightheaded. White spots crowded out the flurries that spun through the gray sky, and she felt herself fading.

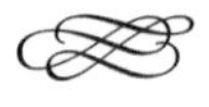

A joyful shrieking rang in her ears.

Maeve.

I must be in heaven, Cora thought. Whiteness enveloped her, and she felt as light as a wisp of wind.

The scolding voice of a nurse interrupted the laughter.

Cora turned her head to the side.

A child, covered in smallpox, stomped in the slush one last time and ducked inside the nearest wood-framed pavilion.

Dr. Gettler's face, his mouth and nose now covered by a mask, appeared close to hers, and a brightness momentarily blinded her. She blinked as he lowered a lantern and held up his hand. "How many fingers?"

"Three."

"Sehr gut."

She met his gaze. The tendrils of darker blue within his irises reminded her of the spokes on the snowflake in her natural history textbook. She'd never been this close to such a handsome man. Her cheeks burning, she looked away.

"How do you feel?" he asked.

"Well. I've always had a strong constitution."

He nodded to O'Toole, who lifted her from the muck and fixed her blanket around her.

The doctor sized him up. "I've heard the saying, 'Nothing can kill an O'Toole.' I hope it's true; I need your assistance. Even though she's symptom-free, I've reason to believe that Miss McSorley is highly contagious."

Cora gasped. "That can't be. I'm not sick."

His expression softened into a sympathetic smile. "I wish that were the case." He turned to O'Toole. "We must take every precaution. You and I shall be the only staff permitted to treat Miss McSorley. Please escort her, and keep her segregated from the others."

O'Toole held out his massive hands. "I think it would be best if I carry you, if that's all right, miss. We don't want your feet gittin' frostbit."

Cora backed away. Aside from the chill that had gripped her core, she felt perfectly fine. "He's wrong. Leave me alone, please."

She wanted to run, away from the disease and death that permeated this callous rock. But if the doctor were right, and a pest was living in her now, that wouldn't do her or society any good. Raking her nails along her arms, she again thought of the river and the end it could bring.

The ferry's horn sounded, signaling its departure without Dr. Gettler. As the families of those under quarantine surely did every night, his would likely spend this one worrying.

"Come now, Miss McSorley," O'Toole said. "Let's get you out of the elements."

She knew he would stop her before she reached the crust of ice at the water's edge.

"If you won't walk, I'll have ta carry ya."

Shaking from fear, anger, and the cold, she followed him to the fifth structure in the line.

O'Toole eased open the door, and a rush of stale air and murmurings of discontent greeted them. An electric lightbulb hanging from the ceiling blinked out intermittently. He pulled back a curtain and she entered a small, secluded area. At least here she would be alone.

She sat on the examining table, and O'Toole wrapped a fresh blanket around her.

"You gave us a real scare, Miss McSorley."

"Us?"

"Me and the doctor. He saw you first but was busy helping Mr. Orlov."

Her teeth chattered, but she'd warmed up enough to realize how frigid she was beneath the wet hospital garb.

"I'll get you some hot tea." O'Toole left, yanking the curtain shut behind him.

For two weeks, Maeve's fevered body had fit snugly against hers on the cot they'd shared. The heat, proof that Maeve was still alive, had kept Cora warm as she'd rubbed her little sister's back and brushed the sweat-streaked hair from her forehead. In the week since Maeve had turned cold, Cora had been so frigid that her teeth would spontaneously begin knocking against each other. Certainly, her temperature hadn't risen above normal.

O'Toole returned with a steaming pewter mug, which Cora grasped with nearly frost-bitten fingers to take a sip. The tangy, bitter liquid scalded her tongue but did nothing to warm the rest of her. She continued to drink anyway.

When the ferry had delivered Maeve and her to the hospital, O'Toole had been waiting on the dock. Later, Cora had learned that the four blasts of the ship's horn had signaled the arrival of measles, enabling nurse Holden to send the right orderly to receive them.

O'Toole's hulking size and protective cloak had terrified seven-year-old Maeve, who'd been too weak to walk. Just as he'd scooped up Maeve, Cora had spotted a golden coin protruding from the sand beneath the pier. She'd tried to give it to her sister, but not even the unusual prize had piqued her interest.

The coin! It was now among the rubble of the burned tent. She would have to retrieve the golden guinea first thing tomorrow morning before someone else did.

As it had turned out, O'Toole had been much more effective at engaging Maeve than any trinket could have been. By the time he'd laid her on a gurney in the lobby of the main building, she was giggling—a sound Cora hadn't heard in days.

After they'd been admitted and assigned to beds, and Maeve had fallen asleep, O'Toole had brought Cora a cup of this same tea. Its aggressive taste had surprised her; he'd explained that he'd brewed it from plants grown in a small garden near the kitchen. When he'd whispered his secret recipe, she'd felt like he'd entrusted her with the location of the missing Kruger millions.

If she hadn't caught the measles from the *Post* newsy, who'd let her read the headlines for free, and if she hadn't passed it to her sister, the man from the Health Department never would have torn Maeve from Eleanor's embrace. Instead, Maeve would be sitting at the table beside the stove in their single room, practicing her figures for school tomorrow.

Button. That's what Cora and her mom had called Maeve when she was a baby, and the nickname had stuck. Because Maeve had been "cute as a button."

Now, because of her, Button was gone forever.

Certain the throbbing in her chest would never lessen, Cora swallowed the scorching tea; a hint of pokeberry lingered on her tongue.

"Thank you, Mr. O'Toole," said Dr. Gettler, who was standing at the gap in the curtain in a Mother Hubbard gown, its hood framing his face.

O'Toole nodded and stepped aside.

"Pray to God we don't lose many *diese Nacht*. He finished putting on a pair of rubber gloves and paused, his hands folded. "Fire is far too traumatic an experience for those already in an unstable condition." He turned to O'Toole. "You can leave now. Vielen Dank."

The curtain fell shut behind O'Toole, and the doctor motioned for Cora to rotate on the table so he could listen to her lungs. If she did have a pestilence inside her, she wondered, would he be able to hear the individual animalcules? Did they growl and gnash their teeth like rabid dogs? She pictured them tearing at her veins and fought the urge to bolt from the enclave.

"I'm sorry for your loss. Maeve, correct? She's in God's hands now." He tugged his hood, covering more of his face, and raised his stethoscope.

Afraid of what that metal disc would reveal, she lowered the blanket from her shoulders.

Wishing she knew a prayer to recite, Cora inhaled slowly. Despite her mother's Irish Catholic upbringing, her mam had never taken the two girls to church. From whisperings in the outhouse line following the death of an old maid in their tenement, Cora had learned that God doesn't allow those who've committed suicide into heaven. Maybe this was her punishment for having marginalized her survival, she thought as the doctor repositioned the cold metal beneath her wet nightgown.

If I make it off this rock, she prayed silently to God, *I promise I'll attend Mass. Please, don't let there be anything wrong with me.*

"Your lungs sound clear."

Cora was overcome with relief. "That means I can go home, right? My mother, she should learn of Maeve's fate from me."

"Soon." The doctor tugged off his gloves. "Your case is . . . what's the English? Peculiar." He washed his hands and flipped open a folder. The fact that he'd taken the time to retrieve her file from the administration cottage meant it must contain something important. Cora felt queasy; maybe she did have typhus.

"On December 17, 1901, you and Miss Maeve arrived here." As he described the events that had followed, Cora wavered against a fresh swell of nausea.

He shut the folder. "Miss McSorley, your specimens from this morning were rife with the bacterium that causes typhus."

Her attention jerked to his chiseled face, writ with concern, and the examining table beneath her seemed to capsize. Dizzy, she clung to its edge. The mutterings in Russian beyond the curtain echoed in her brain. Delirium was a symptom of the fever. So was nausea. A red rash might be spreading across her body now, like a swarm of flies on a freshly fallen horse. She checked herself.

Her limbs were as white as ash, and her forehead still felt cool. She was so cold. "I don't have the fever, sir."

He sighed, looking tired for the first time. "I'm afraid your blood proves that you do."

"No, sir, I meant I don't have *a* fever."

"It is strange, although it may simply be due to an unusually long incubation period. What's odder: three of the patients in your typhus tent have been diagnosed with measles. You're the only person they've had contact with who's recently battled that illness."

"That was two months ago."

"Your body should be free of the virus, I agree."

"Virus?"

He rubbed the bridge of his nose. "A great man, Dmitri Ivanowski, discovered evidence of microbes so small they can pass through candle filters. They're too tiny to be seen even with a microscope, but his research proves they exist. I believe measles is caused by one of these undetectable viruses, and I suspect it's still lingering within you."

Picturing a horde of mangy, feral dogs gnawing on her organs, she shivered and scratched her arms, wishing she could dig them out.

Dr. Gettler finished adding a note to her file and capped his fountain pen. "I'll instruct Mr. O'Toole to draw your blood first thing tomorrow, as well as collect stool samples every three days."

Every three days? She'd already missed nine weeks at Wadleigh High School for Girls. It was unlikely the principal would allow her to graduate in the spring. What if he wouldn't reserve her a seat in next year's senior class until she'd petitioned him in person? With the new building scheduled to open in the fall, girls across the city were clamoring for admission. "When can I go home?"

His chin dropped. "Not until your specimens are free of the typhus bacteria, and we must rule out the possibility that you're still harboring the measles virus—how, I'm not sure, but I'll find a way." He shut the folder. The case was closed. She had no say in the matter.

She was a prisoner, no freer than the convicts working the jail farm on Rikers Island, visible from the upper story of the measles ward. Her mother would find out about Maeve from a health official. Estranged from her older brother, Kieran, the only family who'd immigrated with her through Castle Garden, her poor mamaí would be alone in her grief.

Cora twisted the edge of her damp tunic, but no droplets emerged. "How long will that take?"

He brought his hand to his heart, as if he could personally feel her sorrow. "I know you're homesick, but our priority has to be your health, and equally, the well-being of society. I *will* figure this out. Tomorrow, while at Carnegie, I'll check to see if the world's leading microbiologists have noted any similar cases. An orderly will bring you a cot. Please, sleep well tonight. Your body needs to recuperate."

The doctor departed, and she stared at the swaying curtain until it stilled. Like her, he would be away from his family tonight for "the well-being of society." But tomorrow evening, he would strip off his protective gear, shower as an extra precaution, then ride the ferry to the 138th Street pier and take a carriage to Kleindeutschland on Manhattan's Lower East Side. She'd heard about his darling wife, daughter, and newborn son. By the time he arrived home, he'd kiss his sleeping children on their foreheads and wish them sweet dreams. His wife would then serve him warm schnitzel and cold beer and massage his shoulders while he ate beside the hot stove.

Meanwhile, Cora would be trembling on her isolated cot at the end of a long room crowded with suffering, while mysterious, tiny predators roamed freely through her blood.

Twenty months later

September 1903

The sacrament of Penance drifted through the open windows of the church as Cora bowed her head, shrouded in the hood of a leper's cloak. She folded her hands, encased in gloves to hide lesions that didn't exist, and once again prayed to God for forgiveness and benevolence. If she'd been more alert, or less selfish, there wouldn't now be a five-year-old girl in the main hospital building, slipping into and out of consciousness as Cora's measles germs burrowed their way through her small organs.

How she wished she could go back and undo their encounter a week earlier. From across the central lawn, she'd been so engrossed in watching a game of marbles among three teenagers from the yellow fever ward that she'd missed the telltale sounds of the child creeping up behind her. By the time the girl had pulled back Cora's hood—out of curiosity or as a prank—it had been too late.

She shouldn't have dallied on her way to the northern shore, where she passed many of the hours that seemed to stretch into eternity. There, the gusting winds carried away the deadly air she exhaled. But those kids her own age . . . how she missed having friends.

Please, God, if You let her live, I'll never lose faith in You, I promise. Cora rubbed her crucifix pendant. A month after she'd started attending Mass, she'd found it in the spot on the lawn where she always sat. Affixed to its case had been a note from the pastor:

> And a leper came to Him and bowed down before Him, and said, "Lord, if You are willing, You can make me clean." Jesus stretched out His hand and touched him, saying, "I am willing; be

> cleansed." And immediately his leprosy was cleansed. Matthew 8:2–3

She doubted that God would cleanse her blood, but just in case, she always wore the necklace.

A chorus of greetings broke her meditation.

The Passing of the Peace during Mass had begun.

She twisted to face the rest of the lawn beside the redbrick church by the docks; twenty other contagious invalids dispersed across it came into the narrow view afforded by her hood. By the anguish on their faces and lethargic movements, she knew they were as miserable as she was. To greet them, she raised her hand slightly. Since they couldn't see her face behind the cloth that she wrapped around her head each morning to contain her germs, she didn't bother to smile.

Some waved at her. No one would dare shake her hand, even in its glove. Likewise, none would ever attempt to befriend her. Even if someone tried, she'd have to reject the kindness. Four people in the past year and a half had fallen ill because of her germs. The first three had perished, and Elena, the girl bedridden now, might join them before nightfall.

Whenever the guilt seized her, squeezing her rib cage until she could barely breathe, Dr. Gettler reminded her it could have been so much worse. In hindsight, his decision to falsify her death and recast her as a new patient with incurable leprosy had been prescient. Not only did her hood signal to patients and staff alike to keep their distance, but it also—usually—served as a barrier for her germs while concealing her identity.

During his third examination of her, the doctor had presented this plan in a soft tone, compassion radiating from his blue eyes, and Cora had accepted it without question. He hadn't mentioned that the disguise would enable them to avoid arousing suspicion from the staff if she were to stay for a prolonged period. But Otto must have been thinking it. Otherwise, he wouldn't have instructed O'Toole to build a wooden partition at the end of the typhus ward to give her the comfort of private quarters. Nor would he have written to her mother, notifying her that a "troublesome chronic cough and rash" necessitated a delay in Cora's return.

Every month since, Cora had posted a letter to her mamaí. Not once had Cora received a reply. A year ago, as part of a campaign to alter its reputation as a pesthouse—to curtail the poor from hiding their ill—Riverside had opened its doors to visitors. Watching other families reunite, with tears and squeals of joy: that's when Cora missed her mother the most.

A hymn began, and many of the invalids joined in, their raspy voices collectively thick with foreign accents. Just the sight of their thin cotton hospital shifts made Cora sweat more profusely within the heavy wool. It had been an unusually hot summer and today was no less cruel. How she longed to rip away the shroud, run to the beach beyond the new seawall, and charge into the cool water, racing all the way home.

She'd never make it. Even though a classmate had taught her to swim in the Hudson River four summers ago, she wouldn't stand a chance against the turbulence caused by the convergence of several rivers at Hell Gate, the nearby bend in the tidal strait.

"Maidin mhaith!" O'Toole boomed and dropped to the ground beside her.

Cora planted her hands into the grass. Although she knew it wasn't possible, the ground always seemed to shake when he did that.

To allow the cleansing breeze from across the river to flow between them, she shifted three feet to her right. Having previously suffered from every malady treated at Riverside, he was immune to her pests. Still, she tightened the cloth across her face before returning his greeting, Irish Gaelic for "Good morning."

Although his grandparents had emigrated from Ireland, he hadn't known a lick of the language before he'd met Cora. According to him, during his grandfather's search for a job after reaching the "Land of Opportunity," he'd repeatedly been rebuffed by signs that stated, "No Irish Need Apply." Hungry and homeless, Eamonn O'Toole, with a wife and four small children in tow, had stripped away his brogue and changed the family name to Ogilvy. "On my eighteenth birthday," Richard O'Toole had told Cora, "I marched into City Hall and changed it straight back. Anyone ta turn me down for employment, because of me Irish blood, is a damned *amandan.*"

Fool. She'd taught him that word, too.

While listening to him describe his family's struggles, Cora had found herself thinking of her mam, who'd resorted to a line of work in the Five Points District that required no formal application and that had produced both Cora and her sister. Dreaming of a better life for them, their mother had been adamant that they complete public school. And now Maeve was dead, and Cora's seat had surely been filled a year ago.

"What a fine morning!" O'Toole said loudly, the only timbre his voice contained. "A touch hot, though." He wiped the sweat from his broad, sunburned brow.

Through the sides of her hood, Cora could feel the stares of the other invalids.

"*Shhh*" she hissed, though she couldn't fault him. Early on, she'd asked why he didn't attend St. John-by-the-Sea with his wife, a nurse, and their three children, all of whom were within the chapel now.

"God and I had a little chat," he'd responded. "The Good Lord's okay with me doing His work instead of listening to His word."

Considering no one on the island labored as hard as O'Toole, who assisted both with the patients and the expansion of the hospital, Cora didn't doubt that God approved.

This morning, in addition to the sweat that stained his collared work shirt, he reeked of oil, dirt, and antiseptic. Yet she didn't turn away; she knew she smelled no better.

"Elena. How is she?" Cora asked in a hushed tone.

O'Toole rubbed his temples, which shielded his hazel eyes, too small for his fleshy face. "On my way from the tuberculosis ward, I stopped to help with a tipped coal cart. I haven't been ter the main hospital yet this mornin'."

"What if she's dead?" Cora shuddered.

O'Toole ducked his head so he could look straight into her eyes, beneath her hood. "None of this is your fault. You didn't ask ta have those little buggers crawling inside ya."

"Richard," she said, using his Christian name for the first time, "that doesn't mean I'm not responsible for them. If I'd had the courage to kill myself, Elena wouldn't be fighting for her life now."

"Don't ever say that again," said O'Toole with a growl. He nodded toward the chapel. "Trust in the Good Lord. He has a plan for you."

Cora harrumphed. So far God had given her no reason to trust Him. But, she thought, if He saves Elena, that would be something. *A sign.*

The words of the benediction wafted through the open windows, and Cora realized she hadn't listened to any of the pastor's sermon. With little else to distract her during the weekdays, she often studied the corresponding passages in the Bible she'd received from the Ladies' Home Missionary Society. This week, she would have to search on her own for stories that might give her suffering meaning. Then, as always, she would question whether those miracles had actually happened.

Beside her, O'Toole grunted as he clambered to his feet. Cora sensed that the other convalescents had begun to return to their wards. She stayed put, waiting for Dr. Gettler so she could ask about Elena as soon as they began their customary stroll. Her heart pounded like a caged squirrel knocking its teeth against the bars. If Elena had passed, Cora didn't know what she would do. Five people dead—one her own sister—because of her? How could anyone take another step beneath the weight of that shame and guilt?

The door of the church banged open, and the resident staff's children, laughing and screaming, darted outside.

O'Toole rushed forward to embrace his two boys and girl, all with ruddy complexions and hair as orange as his. Oddly, they'd never contracted any of Riverside's germs.

"Why doesn't he study them?" Cora had asked a few weeks ago while she and O'Toole had been watching Dr. Gettler give the children a drawing lesson.

"Because," O'Toole had whispered, cupping his hands over his mouth and bulbous nose, "I won't let him."

Cora sucked in her breath.

"Darn it." O'Toole grunted in irritation at his mistake. "The doctor's a good man. If anyone can cure you, so you can git home to your mamaí, it's him."

She nodded in agreement and reminded herself of Dr. Gettler's dedication to eradicating her germs. He genuinely cared about her. Whenever he cut her open to extract a much-needed tissue sample, he maintained a nearly one-sided dialogue as a means of leading her thoughts elsewhere. Often, he would tell her of microbiology's daring pioneers, whom he'd studied while at Oxford, and his dream of becoming one. His favorite: Spallanzani, who'd debunked Needham's theory that microorganisms, or "wee beasties," could arise spontaneously from a "vegetative force."

"Similarly," the doctor liked to say, looking at Cora over his spectacles and surgical mask, "your immunities cannot be caused by a vegetative force. I will get to the root of *dieses Geheimnis*—this mystery."

She believed that he would succeed.

Hopefully soon.

Nurse O'Toole, a Clydesdale of a woman whose coal-black mane gave away her Sicilian descent, joined the rest of her family. After a kiss on her husband's lips, so unreserved it made Cora's cheeks feel like they'd just been slapped, nurse O'Toole shepherded them toward the cafeteria for lunch, leaving Cora once again alone.

Her stomach rumbled from envious hunger. At mealtime, one of the line cooks always left her a tray outside the service entrance, beside the pails of garbage that would travel via ferry to the incinerator on Governor's Island. In good weather, she would eat on the western shore, from which she could just make out the triumvirate of high-rises that housed the reporters and editors for the *New York World*, the *New York Tribune*, and the *New York Times*. Across the street from City Hall, "the center of the world," those journalists ravenously consumed events as they transpired, whereas she foraged for secondhand, stale news.

The crowd exiting the chapel had thinned, yet Dr. Gettler still hadn't emerged. The city had mandated that at least one doctor stays on duty at Riverside at all times, and this was Dr. Gettler's weekend. *He should be here*, she thought anxiously.

While she felt terrible that his children lost so much time with him, she couldn't help but look forward to their constitutionals. Away from his lab in the main hospital building, she didn't have to face the apologetic look in his eyes before he penetrated her skin with a needle or knife. Here, beside the river, she could enjoy his stories of Ingrid's and Ulrich's antics, as well as his vision for Cora's future once she could return to Manhattan.

Finally, the doctor's brown boater appeared in the doorway behind a cluster of nurses who served as the church's choir. With an image of Elena's frail little body, as cold as Maeve's, in her head, Cora stood up.

The women, who looked out of place on the island in their slim skirts, smart blouses, and deep-crowned, small-brimmed hats, veered toward the staff house to change into their Mother Hubbard gowns and rubber boots, giving Cora a clear view of the doctor, as well as the man beside him.

Her heart flitted at the sight of Linnaeus Jones, a hospital orderly and the most dashing man on North Brother Island. Aside from Dr. Gettler, he was also the cleverest. From what she'd overheard of the nurses' gossip, only the high cost of medical school had kept him from becoming a doctor. At age ten, Linnaeus had begun working in the Marvin Safe Company's sweatshop to help meet rent for the family's room in a boardinghouse that Cora imagined must have been far more squalid than the Bowery, where she'd lived. It was a wonder he'd managed to obtain his position here at Riverside.

Absorbed in a conversation, the two men shrugged off their suit jackets, rolled up the sleeves of their collared shirts, and walked toward the seawall. Not until Linnaeus returned to his duties could Cora approach the doctor and ask him about the ill child.

Neither man glanced in her direction, which wasn't surprising. Dr. Gettler had an uncanny ability to intensely concentrate on a single subject, blocking out everything else. And Linnaeus: well, to him, she was simply the resident leper, incurable and unapproachable. She doubted he even knew that the person beneath the shroud, whom he graciously waved at each time he extended his route to avoid coming too close, was a young woman. He certainly couldn't be aware that she thought about him every day, timing her movements around the campus to catch glimpses of him.

Even from a distance, she could tell when Linnaeus was speaking; he punctuated his speech with broad gesticulations. His energy, olive skin, and hair the color of black lacquer provided a sharp contrast to the doctor's calm demeanor and fair complexion.

Dr. Gettler pointed at the main hospital building, and Cora fantasized that he was inviting Linnaeus to become his lab assistant. "The research is daunting," the doctor might be saying, "but with your sharp mind, we will succeed." Mere months later—so went her daydream—she would be leaving this hellish place by ferry, hand-in-hand with Linnaeus.

He lit a cigar, his body still for the first time since he'd exited the church.

With false hope, she waited for him to cast his smoldering eyes toward her in shock at what had been hidden within plain sight.

He did no such thing. A schooner sailed past, and Linnaeus tugged on Dr. Gettler's sleeve. The doctor's hobby of constructing ships in bottles for his patients was well known.

When the ship had disappeared, Linnaeus consulted his watch, then nodded to the doctor and hustled toward the staff house behind her.

Cora's heart throbbed. He would pass within twenty feet of her. She stood stock still and held her breath so that none of her germs could possibly reach him.

He waved to her without slowing, and she nearly collapsed from the sudden weight of his attention. Maybe the doctor had let the orderly in on their secret. To find out, she hurried toward him, the first few steps faltering until she'd regained her composure.

"Good morning." Dr. Gettler flashed her a smile as she stopped a safe distance away. "I see the way you look at him."

Her cheeks blazed, and she was glad her hood concealed her reaction. "How can you?" she asked loudly so he could hear her.

He snorted. "Silly *Fräulein*. His features are attractive and his future promising. He would be a great match for you."

Cora bit her lip. "Did you tell him about me?"

He shook his head.

"Maybe . . ." Cora ground the leather of one glove against the other. A barge steamed past, and she spotted its captain, grimacing in her direction. Often, sailors gawked at Riverside, rife with outcasts. To them, the sighting of her leper's cloak must be particularly, entertainingly macabre. She longed to rip it off and show them the girl beneath.

Turning her thoughts back to Linnaeus, she continued, "Maybe he could be of use in the lab."

"Oh, Coraline. I wish that were possible. You're a lovely young woman who deserves to experience romance. But it won't come this way. It can't."

"Why not?"

"Until I find your cure, you cannot go near that man."

The girl. The thought of her now cut through any disappointment Cora might have otherwise felt at the doctor's edict. "How is Elena?"

He grinned. "Her fever broke around three this morning. I expect a full recovery."

Cora squealed in relief, so loud that the noise startled her. She'd forgotten what her voice sounded like when she was happy. A tear welled at the corner of her eye, but wiping it away would contaminate her glove.

"Thank you, God," she whispered. "I will keep my promise. No matter how hard it gets, I will trust in You."

Too far away to have heard her vow, the doctor clicked his tongue. "I'm happy too, but her survival doesn't mean we can be less vigilant. You absolutely cannot go near Linnaeus. Or anyone else, for that matter."

The euphoric sensation evaporated, and Cora dropped her chin to hide her face within her hood.

"During my courtship with Rolene, in Bavaria," the doctor continued, "her parents didn't approve of me. Because I wasn't a Lutheran. I know firsthand that forbidden love emboldens the heart. The patients in the measles ward depend on that man. Riverside cannot lose him."

To prevent the doctor from seeing her despair, she pulled her hood farther down over her eyes.

"Any day now, you could have your breakthrough," she announced through the wool. "Then it won't matter." She pictured herself beside Linnaeus and wondered if she would ever have the chance—or courage—to kiss him the way nurse O'Toole had greeted her husband.

"That would be wonderful. I'm trying, so very diligently." He ran his finger along the ribbon of his hat for good luck—the only superstitious habit the man had.

"Miss McSorley?" He draped his suit jacket over his forearm and peered at her through his spectacles.

The formality of his tone drew a pool of dread into her stomach. "Yes?"

"I must be honest with you: I'm concerned."

"About what?"

"The concentration of *Ricksettia prowaezekki*, the typhus bacterium, in your samples has been increasing. And the laboratory mice have been dying more quickly from *Rubeola*."

A tingling sensation raced through her body, and she pictured angry packs of wolf-like germs marauding through her organs. "What are you saying?"

"I'm worried that the animalcules have been growing stronger and will eventually be able to best even your immune system."

The sound of snapping jaws clattered in her brain. She shook her head, but the din only grew louder. She scratched at her stomach. Somehow, she had to get them out. Whatever thoughts she'd had of suicide, they'd been foolish. With 100 percent conviction, she realized she wanted to live.

"You have to help me." Her voice had sounded husky, and she knew the germs were trying to prevent her from speaking. She forced out the words: "I'll do anything. You mentioned cleansing my blood, running it through a filter? Shouldn't we try that?"

He pressed his hat to his head, and his eyes disappeared beneath the brim. "Let's walk."

She followed him, her legs shaking with each step.

Maintaining their standard distance, they moved toward the whitewashed fence that partitioned off the federal lighthouse. Far too quickly, they would complete their lap, reminding Cora of just how narrow her world had become.

A world that might close to her entirely if the doctor didn't find her cure soon.

Ten Months Later

June 1904

All that remained on the tin breakfast tray was a single crescent of syrupy, canned peach—the brightest object on the island. During her two and a half years at Riverside, the cafeteria food—and her newfound trust in God—had been among her only sources of comfort.

The bitter taste of loneliness heightened her craving for another few seconds of sweet distraction. According to Dr. Gettler, as the pests continued to breed within her, she was becoming even more dangerous to the other teenagers on the island, whom she secretly longed to befriend. With a clammy, gloved hand she maneuvered the morsel onto her spoon.

Her body always felt feverish beneath the heavy wool, yet today she seemed to be radiating heat. Perspiration trickled down her sides.

Now queasy, she dropped her spoon. Ever since Dr. Gettler had voiced his concern that her germs might eventually best her immune system, she'd been watching for this symptom and a host of others.

To assess her throat, she breathed into the cloth wrapped around her head. She felt no rawness, and the Williamsburg Bridge still appeared sharp in her vision.

Cora raised a forearm to bring her veins to eye level. "You haven't beaten me yet," she jeered.

In her head, she could hear their response: low growls, followed by the gnashing of teeth.

In disgust, she lowered her arm and strummed her fingers, sweaty within their glove, against her thigh.

Today, especially, given the heavy winds, she longed for the cool relief that would come with removing the pair. But Dr. Gettler was pacing along the beach. Earlier this morning he'd informed her that his family would be attending St. Mark's annual Sunday school outing. He planned to wave at them as the grand steamboat churned past on its way to a picnic site on Long Island Sound's southern shore.

Even though the doctor hadn't said as much, she was certain he wished he was going with them. As the months had passed, their conversations about his family had become a careful dance, in which both were afraid of a misstep.

"Deficiency of affection." That's what he'd termed the sorrow that felt like a grinding stone against her heart. Presumably out of compassion, he'd stopped referencing the blessings in his own, full life. But those awkward silences, when she knew he was missing his wife and children, made Cora feel even worse. She would ask him to share his thoughts, then regret it as the warmth in his eyes reached his lips in the form of a story. Envy would surge through her as he recounted the time Ulrich had spilled a flour sack while they'd been making *Apfel Kuchen,* turning all four of them into *Geister* (ghosts). Or when Ingrid had convinced herself that a troll was living in the tunnel that was being constructed beneath Kleindeutschland for the new underground transit line.

Cora stared at the peach, which had slipped from her spoon. If she turned to look at the doctor now, his restlessness while he watched for the steamboat would deepen the void she felt. Yet, at the same time, her curiosity begged her to observe this rare exhibition of love. To fortify herself against the hurt she would surely feel, she ate the last wedge, allowing its sweet pulp to linger on her tongue, then pivoted on the wall to face him.

He'd stopped moving, so completely that the shorebirds paid him no heed as they strutted past, plunging their beaks into the shallows for fish. With his body steel-beam straight, his mouth agape, and his hand affixed atop his hat, he stared downriver.

A chill passed over Cora.

She followed his line of sight. An orange orb, far brighter than any sunset, hovered above the waters at the head of Hell Gate. Rising from it, a thick band of black smoke strangled the cornflower blue sky.

It had to be a boat on fire.

Cora flung her breakfast tray and pushed herself off the seawall.

Her shoes met packed, wet sand, and she ran toward the doctor, stopping herself only five feet from him.

"It's headed our way," he said, still motionless, his eyes wider than his spectacles.

The wind buffeted her cloak, nearly knocking her over. She gathered the folds and held them tight at her sides. "Is it theirs?"

"*Ich weiß nicht*," he snapped and swiped the river mist from his lenses with the cuff of his shirtsleeve.

Of course he doesn't know, she thought, and chided herself.

The blaze erupted angrily.

Squawking, the birds in the shallows took flight.

Either the vessel was approaching them, or the fire had spread. Or both.

The brilliance burned her eyes, yet she couldn't look away.

A small hodgepodge armada had formed in the floating fire's wake, and Cora became consumed with the plight of the passengers who must be evacuating the vessel. Most likely they couldn't swim. Twisting the fabric in her grip, she wondered why the captain wasn't docking her along the wharf.

Through the smoke emerged the outline of the ship's white bow, three decks high, topped by a flag. Engulfed now, a bridge and two smokestacks towered over the midsection. A steamboat, Cora realized, designed to hold hundreds of passengers. For day trips to destinations such as Locust Grove. She stole a glance at the doctor, whose narrowed eyes and rigid jaw told her that he'd reached the same conclusion.

Her legs wobbled; her mouth tasted like ash. The stench of burning wood, still familiar from the tent fires in the overflow encampment two winters ago, seeped into her nose.

"*Mein Gott.*" He tore off his boater hat. "The captain. He's going to beach her. *Hier.* I have to mobilize the staff." His feet remained fixed to the sand, his eyes barely blinking.

"Go," Cora said in a commanding tone.

His shoulders jerked and the hat fell from his grip. He spun away from the ship and dashed toward the main building.

Without breaking her hypnotic connection with the approaching inferno, she stooped to pick up the hat, inches from the tide. Although she'd always avoided contact with his personal effects, now she felt a compulsion to run her gloved finger along the blue band.

Praying that this wasn't the ship carrying the doctor's family, she watched the fire, fueled by a strong southerly wind, devour more of the massive, wooden steamboat. Smoke billowed around the paddle wheel, bringing into and out of view the vessel's abbreviated name, *Gen! Slocum*, painted in a large, Old English font. Cora could make out passengers clinging to the remaining railings, and others plunging into the water to escape the devastation. The thought of saltwater eating away at burned flesh was terrifying.

Behind her, frantic shouting signaled that rescue efforts were under way. She turned toward the commotion.

The entire Riverside staff, carrying blankets or medical supplies, appeared to be in motion on the lawn in front of the main hospital building. Nearby, three mechanics were dragging a hose from the physical plant toward the seawall.

"They're almost here!" O'Toole shouted and leaped from the wall, hitting the sand with a thud. He ripped off his shirt and waded into the shallows. Around him, a volley of people, including Linnaeus and several nurses—but not Dr. Gettler—landed on the beach. He must still be in the hospital, overseeing preparations for an influx of patients, she decided, wondering if that meant he didn't believe his family was aboard. Then again, with so many people depending on him, Cora knew he wouldn't shirk his leadership role for even the most sacred of personal reasons.

Those on the strand began stripping down to their undergarments. Cora caught sight of Linnaeus's lean, muscular torso, even finer than she'd imagined. Trying to concentrate, she told herself all that mattered now was his ability to swim.

A thunderous sound invaded her hood and assaulted her ears as waves of scorching heat blasted her skin.

Hysterical screams rose above the hissing and crackling. As she turned to face the steamboat, almost upon her, black spots filled her vision, like she'd just stared into the sun. Scrambling backward until the seawall halted her retreat, she shielded her eyes and took in the chaos. The people jumping for their lives from the decks, landing on others already thrashing in the churning water, were women and children, as were those clinging to the vestiges of railings.

Twenty feet offshore, the bow ground to a halt with an ear-splitting groan, and the spray from the fire brigade disappeared into a wall of flames.

O'Toole, Linnaeus, and the others in the shallows hurled themselves into deeper water and grabbed the nearest victims. Lulu McGibbons, the switchboard operator, ran past Cora and dove in, followed by nurse Pauline Puetz.

The recently married head nurse, Kate White, barreled past, single-handedly carrying a construction ladder. She extended it beyond the shoal, and victims grabbed ahold.

Dr. Gettler dropped to the sand, wrenched open his black physician's kit, and began treating a teenage boy disastrously burned.

The doctor wasn't searching for his family; could it mean her premonition had been wrong? Cora willed it to be.

Heat rolled off the ship like a blacksmith's forge, cooking the shallows. She yearned to throw off her cloak and dive in to join the rescue effort.

Three at a time now, O'Toole pulled children to shore. Linnaeus handed a toddler to a nurse who couldn't swim and sprinted back into the river, thick with screaming, flailing, shocked survivors.

Still, the inferno raged on, feasting on more of those unable or unwilling to jump. Smoke from their burning flesh merged with the billowing black cloud.

At the bow railing, the orange predator was advancing on a cluster of children.

Cora shouted to the fire brigade to redirect their hose, and the spray disappeared into those flames.

Desperate to help, she rocked on her heels. If the doctor saw her pulling someone to shore, he'd be furious.

Hating her body for the vessel of death it had become, she raked her gloved fingertips down her forearms, wishing she could root out the microbes within her. "God, how can this be Your will?!" she shouted.

Again, no answer.

The screams of the young rose above the din: "*Hilf mir*! *Hilf mir*!" Help me! Help me!

Cora recognized the German phrase. All her remaining hope that this steamboat hadn't been the one chartered by St. Mark's evaporated. Her legs buckled, and she fell back against the concrete wall, its sharp ledge digging into her spine.

Dr. Gettler moved on to another writhing, burned body as Cora wondered if he knew. She scanned the survivors on the beach for his loved ones, even though she wouldn't be able to recognize them; so many were charred, and she'd never met his family.

She couldn't just stand there, watching babies, small children, and desperate mothers drown. *I've been kept alive for a reason, and this might be it,* she thought. The water: it would wash away any pests she expelled. Energy buzzed through her limbs; yet, so conditioned to shun human touch, she remained paralyzed in place.

Every minute she wasted, another person would perish.

Her muscles burned with a will of their own, and she caved to their desire.

Simultaneously, she yanked off her cloak and kicked off her shoes. The fire spewed scorching air onto her skin, only partially covered by her thin cotton shift, and she realized she'd just removed the barrier that kept her germs from spreading. She wobbled on the sand.

Passengers were dying by the second, whereas any she helped—even if she infected them in the process—would at least have a chance of surviving.

Filling her lungs with acrid air, she charged into the shallows; a wave knocked a hymnal against her shin. She froze.

The shrill scream of a young girl, calling *Mutti,* jarred Cora into action. She waded into the river until its drag became too great and dove forward. The heat scalded her skin, yet she forced herself to start swimming. All around her, legs kicked to be free of their Sunday best and hands clawed at other frantic parishioners to use their body parts like rungs on a ladder to reach the surface.

Twenty-Five Minutes Later

The thick, strong arm of what had to be a large man wrapped around Cora's waist, and she writhed to free herself from his deadly grip. If she failed, he would drag her to the bottom with him. Already desperate for more air, the surface at least three feet above her, she kicked backward with all her might. Her heel met soft flesh, and the man released his hold. Her lungs seemingly ready to explode, Cora swam to the surface and gulped in the smoky, acrid air. Ignoring the burning in her muscles—already she'd saved ten children, she scanned the chaos for another to pull to shore.

A body plunged into the river inches from Cora, sending a silty wave into Cora's mouth. The woman bobbed to the surface, and a small boy in her grasp spewed water.

Determined to save them both, Cora hugged the mother's waist with one arm and began swimming with the other.

The woman couldn't keep her son's head above water.

Again, and again, they stopped to give the child a chance to clear his lungs and breathe.

The pair seemed to be getting heavier and the shore didn't seem to be getting closer. None of the boats in the rescue effort was coming to their aid.

Saltwater filled Cora's mouth. She coughed it out, but it flowed right back in. Refusing to loosen her grip on the mom, Cora dog-paddled with one arm.

"*Wir sind zu schwer!*" (We are too heavy!) the woman shouted.

She kissed her son, tore herself free, and thrust the boy at Cora, who bobbed upward from the sudden reduction in her load.

Before Cora had finished righting the child, his mother had sunk into the murk.

Cora, terrified that the same would happen to herself and the boy, began to swim toward shore, paddling with one arm while clutching her precious cargo in the other.

Just as her muscles began to seize up, her toes grazed the sandy bottom. Weighed down by the now unconscious child, she kicked hard three more times and allowed her feet to sink into the muck. Holding his head above the hot water, she called for one of the nurses to take him. Although she was too numb to feel it, Cora sensed that her body had reached its limits. But she wouldn't stop. Not with so many on the verge of death.

Nurse Brighton eased the boy, the skin of one shoulder badly blistered, from Cora's grip. With his fate now beyond her control, Cora turned toward the deeper water to locate another survivor to drag ashore.

The surface had calmed.

They'd run out of time. Unable to hold it any longer, she released a single, strangled sob.

In the shallows floated charred debris and bodies, so many of them, sliding toward her with the tide and then receding.

Several members of the staff were standing stock still, shin-deep in the water. At first Cora assumed that they were simply exhausted. Then, when she noticed they were staring at the blazing steamship, she followed their gaze. A little boy was scaling one of the ship's flagpoles to escape the ravenous death sentence beneath him. As he climbed higher, so did the flames.

The flagpole bent beneath the child's weight. And snapped, plummeting the boy into the inferno.

Cora opened her mouth to scream in fury and frustration, but not even a whisper emerged. The smoke-laced air rushed across her open lips and melded with the taste of salt in her mouth.

She staggered backward and dropped to the ground. Waves, thick with wreckage, washed over her cramped thighs. If she tried to stand back up, to find her cloak, her legs would refuse. With her remaining strength, she pivoted her body to take in the carnage strung out along the shore.

The beach was littered with people, some wailing, most silent. Racing to resuscitate at least a few more, pairs of hospital workers moved among the victims. It had to have been at least fifteen minutes since the last person had jumped from the blazing *Slocum*. Dazed survivors, seemingly unaware of their own burns, broken bones, and lacerations, stumbled around as they screamed out in search of their families.

Now helping the staff were city officials and volunteers, who'd arrived in boats ranging from ferries to fishing trawlers—all large enough to manage the fierce currents that bounded North Brother Island.

With such an influx of outsiders, none of the staff would question the presence of an unfamiliar young woman. Certainly, they wouldn't recognize her as a typhus patient who'd supposedly died more than two years ago.

But she still needed the cloak to contain her pests.

A bedraggled, soaked woman, wearing only a bodice and knickers, stumbled past, within three feet of Cora, reminding Cora that without her symbolic shroud, others wouldn't know to keep their distance. She rolled to one side until both knees met the coarse sand, but she didn't rise. Her legs still felt as heavy as anchors.

"Ingrid!" a hoarse, familiar voice yelled, louder than all the others.

Cora twisted her neck to locate the doctor.

Scanning the rescue workers huddled over limp bodies, her heart plunged into the saltwater within her stomach. There had to be dozens—hundreds—of bodies. And most didn't appear to be moving. Praying she would find the doctor embracing his daughter, she continued her search.

And saw the head nurse, Kate White, seated on the sand with a girl hanging over her knees like a wet blanket. Crouched beside them: Dr. Gettler.

"No!" Cora screamed, and this time the sound penetrated the ashy air.

She scrambled to her feet and began running toward them. Remembering her cloak, she veered away, dodging staff, anguished survivors, and lifeless lumps now baking in the sun. Near the seawall, she found her boots, gloves, and pile of fabric, trampled.

A knot formed in her throat, already swollen from the smoke and salt. Forcing it down, she redressed. Momentarily, blackness encased her. The wool chafed her wet skin. She found the hood, and the chaos on the beach reappeared.

A leper to be feared, she wove her way through the throng, maintaining a safe distance, and stopped ten feet from Ingrid, still draped over Kate's knees.

Not even the smoke-drenched breeze could budge the singed skirt of the girl's dress, coated in sand. Dr. Gettler slapped her back, and brine spilled from her gaping blue lips. Still, she didn't gasp or cough. He rubbed between her shoulder blades, attempting to coax life back into her. "*Mein*

Mäuschen, komm züruck. Du musst zurückkommen." My little mouse, come back. You must come back.

Cora twisted the folds of her cloak. Now there was nothing she could do to help the doctor's daughter, or anyone else. The eleven children she'd rescued were not enough.

The doctor tucked a strand of his daughter's hair back into her plait and listened for her breathing. "*Bitte, mein Mäuschen, bitte.*"

A gust of wind blasted the beach. Smoke filled Cora's nostrils and burned her eyes. She coughed and wiped at them, bringing Dr. Gettler back into focus.

"Ingrid's gone, sir." Kate placed her fingertips on the back of his soaked dress shirt, clinging to his slim frame. "She's with the Lord now," she said in her gentlest southern drawl.

Cora hated that string of words. Since Maeve's death, she'd heard it far too often. And now today, it would be uttered over and over. Why would God have let this happen? Hadn't He taken too much from this island already?

"*Nein.*" He sliced his hand through the air. "Lay her on her back. This time you pump the arms, I'll press on her chest."

Kate didn't stir from her seated position. From Cora's vantage point, she could see tears welling in her gentle, brown eyes. She could tell that the nurse would have embraced the doctor if it weren't for the dead child between them.

"*Noch einmal*! Do as I say!" The doctor scooped up his "little mouse" and stretched her out on the sand to try the resuscitation maneuver once more. Her blank eyes stared upward. Too early in the summer to be tan from playing in the alleys of Kleindeutschland, her pale face, beneath the bright sun, had a sheen to it.

The nurse pulled Ingrid's thin arms above her head, and in a quick, pumping motion, brought them to the girl's sides, right as the doctor jabbed her chest. No water surged from her mouth; she remained silent.

He slapped her cheek. "Wake up, mein Mäuschen, wake up."

With one hand, Kate gripped his palm; with the other, she closed little Ingrid's eyes.

The grieving father moaned and pressed his face to his daughter's. Beyond him, the fire on the steamship raged on.

Cora bit her hand to redirect the pain from her heart. She'd never met this child, but that mattered little. She knew the doctor's grief.

The same man, whom earlier this morning she'd watched with envy, was now curled in the sand next to his deceased daughter. His wailing overpowered the desperate cries of those around them.

Kate adjusted Ingrid's arms, her fingers lingering on a silver chain that winked in the sun. "Her bracelet identifies her. Coroner O'Gorman said we should—"

He raised his head. "Give it to me."

Kate tucked the chain into his palm and wiped a tear from her flushed cheek. Her chin dropped, and her buxom chest heaved. The blond strands that had come loose from her chignon veiled her eyes, but Cora could tell she was weeping.

The doctor rolled the silver wristlet between his fingertips. "It was a gift from Rolene." His focus darted to the steamship. "Where is she? And Ulrich?" He scanned the bodies, many child-sized, some not even two feet long, and his eyes glazed over.

Cora's entire being ached in sympathy with this man, who'd been so devoted to helping her. She moved to approach him but then forced herself back against the seawall. Holding the next breath of thick air at bay, she took in the scene. An unnerving calm had descended upon the shore. Time had run out for the drowning victims, and the doctors and nurses were now focused on tending the burns and other wounds of those still breathing.

There were only six doctors on the island, five without him. Cora knew one way she could help the recovery effort, as well as her grieving friend: "Dr. Gettler, sir."

"What?" he moaned without separating from his daughter.

"Look." She pointed to a burn victim writhing in the surf.

"My Rolene?" He raised his head.

Kate, who'd begun stitching a gash in the leg of a boy about twelve, glared at her. Although the person Cora had pointed out was burned beyond recognition, the physique was unmistakably male.

"He needs help," Cora said, and a look of understanding passed over Kate's face.

Still dazed, the doctor rose and lurched toward the burn victim, but his back foot remained rooted beside Ingrid.

Kate tied off the stitches and came to the doctor's side. "I'll find a covering, and write her name on her arm." She wiped her hand clean and pulled a pen from the pocket of her skirt. "Now"—she looked Dr. Gettler square in the eyes—"you must tend to your work, the work the good Lord's given you."

He gave a rote nod, as Cora had seen so many patients do in response to Kate's orders, and grabbed his kit. Single-handedly, he dragged the large figure onto higher ground. After ripping away the remains of the man's pants, he set about cleaning and bandaging the seared skin that barely clung to the flesh.

"Miss McSorley," he said without looking up, "find my Rolene and my boy."

Cora straightened. *Finally, a way to be useful.* Through the doctor's stories, she'd pictured the boy playing with his rubber ball, stealing a pretzel from the jar atop the icebox, laying track for his toy train set. Her image of him couldn't possibly match his actual appearance. The same for Rolene. Ever since their discussion about Linnaeus, he hadn't spoken of his wife except in reference to their children. He certainly hadn't shown her a photograph.

All around her, volunteers were arranging the dead in rows. Nurses followed behind, draping sheets over their faces. How would Cora find either of them? And what if she did, beneath two of those shrouds? She would have to try yet hope for failure. If they weren't here, they might have jumped overboard before the *Slocum* reached North Brother and hopefully had been rescued. "What do they look like?"

"Find my Rolene," he mumbled as he rummaged through his bag, "and Ulrich."

"I'll do my best, sir." She dug the tip of her boot into the sand. "What do they look like?"

He scrunched his face. "Blond, blue eyes, slim."

That description had to match many of the Germans who'd been attending the Lutheran church outing. At least the boy might bear a resemblance to the doctor, and the memory of Ingrid's features would give her a sense of the mother's.

Sweltering beneath the layer of wool, she walked toward the end of the row of corpses on the beach, closest to the water, and pulled back her hood. *These poor souls are beyond the reach of my pests*, she thought as she tugged down her face covering.

As she moved along the beach, waves tugging at her ankles, she thought of the bodies settling into the muck. Rolene and Ulrich might be among them. What if she'd grabbed a different hand, saving Ulrich instead of a stranger's child? Was his life more valuable simply because his father was her doctor? If she'd swum faster, enabling her to rescue a twelfth, it might have been him.

Nearby, a badly burned elderly woman collapsed in the shallows, and nurse Nellie O'Donnell rushed to her. Cora sidestepped them to keep her distance.

"*Du hast mein Baby gestohlen!*" shrieked a hoarse voice.

Cora turned toward the noise and stiffened. A tall, soot-stained woman in a sodden dress was charging at her, narrowly dodging the bodies in her way.

She thinks I stole her baby, Cora realized.

"*Gib ihn mir.*" Give him to me.

Cora winced at the woman's misplaced hope.

The distraught mother tripped over a leather dress shoe, attached to a corpse, and regained her momentum.

"*Ich habe ihn nicht,*" Cora said, using the German she'd learned from Dr. Gettler, and raised her empty hands to show she didn't have him.

"*Meine kleiner Friedrich, wo ist er?*" (Where is he?) the woman asked from within spitting distance. The strands of wet hair wrapped around her neck and intense, beady brown eyes gave her the look of a crazed animal, but Cora knew it was instead herself who should be feared.

Donning her hood, she backed away from the woman. "*Ich weiß nicht.*"

How could she know where little Friedrich was? Most likely, she thought as a sob snagged in her throat, the babe was somewhere within the burned wreckage or the river depths.

The woman howled and reeled toward another female of childbearing age.

Cora longed to run to her room and hide beneath the bedcovers. Instead, she lifted the sheet from the face of the first body and bit her knuckle. The teenage boy's mouth was contorted in agony, his fingers curled as if he were still clawing for the water's surface. She dropped the cloth and moved on to three children and a woman, all with auburn hair and freckles. Surely the father had heard the news by now and was frantically searching for them.

Stop, she warned herself, or she would fall apart and fail at her task. Clenching her teeth, she peeked under the next sheet and backed into the surf, away from a mother, her baby still clutched to her breast.

Unnaturally warm water, thick with debris, sloshed against Cora's calves. She shoved aside a charred plank and turned away from the pair. The heat rolling off the *Slocum* stung her cheeks and dried her tears. Beyond the shallows, men aboard a hodgepodge armada were collecting the floating bodies, adding to the number of faces she'd have to scrutinize.

No, she couldn't complete this assignment. The sorrow would drown her.

But if she quit, Dr. Gettler might abandon the wounded to search for his family. And then others might die because of her. Inhaling deeply, she once again faced the rows of dead.

Under Kate's direction, volunteers had begun moving the bodies to the lawn in front of the main hospital. To avoid seeing any face twice, she decided to restart her search with the farthest row on the higher ground. Climbing over the seawall, she reeled at the lines of tiny corpses.

"You sh-sh-shouldn't be out here," nurse Puetz called to Cora as she trudged past with a tower of blankets that dwarfed her petite frame.

"Dr. Gettler wants me to find his family."

"Oh, dear God." The nurse handed the topmost to a shirtless, portly man, who was staring into the sun and singing a German hymn in a deep baritone. "I'll keep an eye out."

Cora nodded and skirted the dead to reach her starting point. She passed a mother, hugging her howling baby girl to the side of her body that wasn't burned. "*Meine Adella,*" she said with a sob, "*Meine süße Adella.*"

A bedraggled man, wearing the white collar of the church, reached the mother and patted her head. "Your husband, he's alive. Stay here. I'll tell him where you are."

The woman cried harder. "Vielen Dank, Reverend Haas."

"God is with us, even now." His hand slipped from her brow, and he wandered away.

Maybe she would happen upon Rolene and Ulrich in the same condition, Cora told herself and inspected the first prostrate figure on the grass—a girl close to her own age. Quickly, she moved on, passing two full-size bodies in britches and a plump, shrouded woman, without lifting their coverings. Three fewer faces to haunt her dreams. She approached an outline that looked about three years old.

Saying a quick prayer, she flipped back the sheet. With blondish hair and chubby cheeks, the dead boy looked cherubic. His expression was calm, almost smiling, like he'd just seen an angel. Maybe he had. His eyes were shut; they could be blue.

One of his hands was fisted. Cora struggled to uncurl his fingers.

In his palm was a well-worn engineer figurine, cheaply made. She tipped backward with relief. From Dr. Gettler's stories, she knew Ulrich's train set was a finely crafted Märklin, imported from Germany.

But this boy was *someone's* son. She positioned his hands on his abdomen and acknowledged his death with a moment of silence. Continuing on, she passed three primary-school-age children; a teenage boy and girl who might have been in love; a gangly man; and an infant, fully covered by a scrap of cloth meant to veil only a face. Tears burned at the corners of her eyes.

Carrying a lifeless man in a Sunday suit, O'Toole staggered past her on the far side of the row. His face as white as the corpse's, he didn't notice her, nor did she call out to him. Later they would try to find the words.

She bent over another woman, this one slimmer, and lifted the cloth. Her tousled hair was corn-silk blond. On her neck, beneath her right ear, was a birthmark. If this were Rolene, wouldn't the doctor have included such a distinguishing feature in his description? Only if he'd been of sound mind.

The woman's lips were blue and her skin a waxy white, but still she looked beautiful, with a straight nose and dainty, curled lashes on her closed lids. Cora had seen this heart-shaped face before when picturing the doctor with his *Liebchen*. She prayed the eyes would prove her wrong. With an unsure hand, she raised one lid, glimpsed pale blue, and dropped to her knees.

Still, there was no definitive proof. Cora surveyed the woman's crumpled skirt and dress shirt and stopped at her wedding band. It might be engraved. If not, she could show it to the doctor. But if someone saw her removing it, he might assume she was a thief and summon one of the many policemen now present. She would be carted from the island and imprisoned. Eventually, they would release her. But along the way, how many would fall ill because of her?

An escape wouldn't require a pair of handcuffs: with so many good-size boats strung along the shore, she could act like a departing volunteer.

Preoccupied, the doctor wouldn't notice her slip away. She would have to discard her cloak, but she could huddle in a corner of one of the larger vessels and breathe into her hand. Once in Gotham, she would carefully make her way to Bellevue Hospital, home to Carnegie Laboratory. The first microbiology lab in the country, it housed the best microscopes and the brightest minds. Surely, they could cure her.

But if she fled, and the dead woman before her was Rolene, and one of the many small bodies she hadn't yet checked was Ulrich, Dr. Gettler would be left with nothing. Although she hated this exile, she didn't fault him for keeping her here. He was a good man. The patients and nurses loved him. And she loved him, the way she might have adored a father.

On the other hand, his loss shouldn't matter more than her own. He'd gotten the chance to experience love, whereas she hadn't, nor would she as long as she remained confined to this facility. Conflict bubbled up from her stomach, an organ he'd sliced and stitched three times already and would surely probe again. *If* she stayed.

Unsure what to do, she swayed from side to side on her knees. Inexplicably, Cora felt tied to this woman. Her spirit seemed as present as Maeve's right after her body had slackened. If the blonde were Rolene, Cora would stay at Riverside with the doctor, she decided, so that he would not be alone in his grief. For all he'd done for her, she owed him that. Otherwise, she would make for the nearest vessel that looked ready to cast off.

Before her courage could abandon her, she checked to see that no one was watching and wrenched the ring off the already bloated finger.

On the inner side, glistening in the sunlight, were two initials: *O & R*.

The wedding band fell, and she buried her face in the grass, its smell too sharp even through the cotton wrap. *Too alive*. She sat up and pressed the back of her hand against her nose. First Ingrid, now Rolene, and possibly Ulrich, too. How could any man bear such loss in one day? Fighting off the urge to flee this scene, she found the ring and smoothed out Rolene's skirt, stiffened by the salt left behind after the water had evaporated.

"*Steh auf und geh weg*. I need to see."

She tensed but neither stood up nor went away, as he'd commanded. Dr. Gettler's gruff voice had sounded distant. Without his full hospital garb, he couldn't approach the woman, whom he must suspect was his wife, until Cora had moved.

She shifted to block Rolene from his view.

"Your germs. You'll kill her."

The words sliced through Cora, and she scrambled to her feet. These rows consisted of only the dead; Dr. Gettler had to be in denial. Cora's courage fled, and she edged away.

The wedding band, laced with her pathogens, felt like a branding iron, burning her palm. She dropped it into her shoe. Somehow, she would find a way to return it, sterilized.

Dropping his crumpled boater hat, which he must have recovered from the beach, he rushed past her and crouched before his wife.

Tears streaming down her face, Cora braced for the guttural wailing that had followed Ingrid's death.

None came.

She gingerly stepped around two bodies so she could better see his face.

He'd ripped off his glasses. His eyes were squeezed shut, and his mouth was moving.

Cora lowered the cloth wrapped around her head. Still, she couldn't hear him clearly.

He kissed his wife on the lips and grasped her hand.

Now the ring in Cora's boot did seem stolen.

"Mutti!" a towheaded boy yelled as he ran toward them.

She inhaled sharply and looked at Dr. Gettler, who didn't appear to have heard the child's cries.

Just before reaching the doctor, the boy cut across the line of corpses that included Rolene, as well as the next row, and plowed into Cora.

She stumbled backward, and the sun's warmth hit the top of her damp head as her hood fell.

He wrapped his chubby arms around her leg and buried his tear-streaked, grimy face against her cloak. "Mutti, Mutti."

Without thinking—only feeling the crushing grief of the tragedy around her—she rubbed his back, and he pressed himself tighter against her. His hand found the bottom of her robe, and he reached under the fabric and prodded her knee. Cora straightened but didn't brush him away. It had been more than two years since she'd last received any affection, and this boy needed her. He began stroking her skin. She closed her eyes and allowed his self-soothing to calm her, too. As his whimpering faded, the knots in her muscles unraveled.

This warmth: she wanted it to extend into forever. Focusing on his soft touch, she blocked out everything around them, and her breathing fell into rhythm with his. Her eyes closed, she pretended this child was her own, and she gave him the comfort that only a mother could.

You fool, her subconscious chided.

She jerked her face away from his.

At this very moment, her germs might be traveling down his airway. She tightened the wrap that hung around her neck and pulled the hood over her head. Holding her breath, she shifted to pry him off her leg and gasped at his bare, blistered shoulder. He was the final child she'd saved.

Cora wobbled from the fatigue that accompanied the shocking realization. If she'd been stronger, or more determined, his mother would still be alive. She tried detaching the boy from her leg, but his grip tightened, and he began chanting "Mutti."

Exhaustion was beginning to overwhelm her. She wavered, and the grisly scene around her dimmed. If it weren't for the child clinging to her, she would allow herself to collapse.

"*Wie heißt du*?" What's your name?

"Em-em-Emmett." He wiped his runny nose with his hand.

She brushed back his hair, thick with sand. "*Hast du Hunger*?" With all the chaos, no one would notice her sneaking into the kitchen. "*Möchtest du einen Apfel und Milch?*"

"Nein, Mutti," he said, seemingly unaffected by her shroud.

He was calling *her* mother. Although he was clearly in shock, a warm current still passed through Cora. She knelt and hugged him. "It's going to be okay."

He looked at her with his big brown eyes and nodded, though she doubted he understood English. She wondered if the rest of his family had been aboard the ship. If not, they were probably in Kleindeutschland, frantically searching for the pair among the returning survivors. If all his kin had died in the tragedy, maybe he could stay here with her.

She could find a way to mother him from a distance. Just until Dr. Gettler had his breakthrough. The two of them would be a family.

She knelt before him. "If we can't find your *Vater*, I'll take care of you. I promise."

"*Mutti, ich habe deinen Schmuckkasten.*" From his pocket, Emmett pulled a small, nickel-plated box, its lid engraved with a cross, and handed it to her with a shy smile.

He'd been through so much; she didn't have the heart to tell him it didn't belong to her. "*Du bist ein guter Junge,*" she praised him.

Cora tried opening the box and noticed a keyhole. "*Hast du den Schlüssel*?"

"*Im Wasser.*" He sniffled and pointed at the river, where the key must have been lost during their struggle.

She shut her eyes and brought him closer. "That's okay."

Suddenly the boy flew upward from her grasp, blocking the sun; then he was gone.

Baffled, she shielded her eyes from the glare.

Already five yards away, Dr. Gettler was struggling to hold the writhing boy at arm's length. He, too, must have thought at first that the child was Ulrich.

"Mutti!" the boy wailed.

She ran toward them. "Give him back! It's okay, Emmett, I'm coming."

"*Dummkopf,*" Dr. Gettler said so harshly that Emmett stopped struggling.

The admonishment stilled her, too.

"Haven't we lost enough today? This boy now must be isolated." Still holding Emmett, he set out toward the main hospital building, then turned on his heel. "What were you doing with him?" His tone contained a steel edge she'd never heard before.

"*Es tut mir leid,*" she said, hoping the apology sounded more convincing in his native tongue. "He thought I was his mother, and I—"

He laughed cruelly. "Mother? You'll never be this boy's mother, or any other child's." Holding the whimpering Emmett in outstretched arms, he strode across the corpse-lined lawn.

Emmett cried and reached for her.

She wanted to rush after them, rip the boy away, and pummel the doctor with her fists.

But he was right. Within a week or two, some of those she'd saved this morning might be sent back here.

Clutching the small box, Cora prayed that she hadn't just infected the boy.

A man, dragging his injured leg as he perused the dead, stopped and stared at her, reminding her that the unfathomable tragedy around her hadn't obscured the meaning of her shroud. To these outsiders also, she was nothing more than an untouchable outcast.

Dr. Gettler disappeared into the hospital with Emmett, and she realized he hadn't asked her to continue the search for his one remaining family member.

A part of her wished Ulrich were dead, so that the doctor would be as lonely as she was.

Ashamed of the thought, she traced the crucifix etched on the box and decided she'd been meant to receive this trinket. As a reminder of her promise.

She turned toward the *General Slocum.* The popping and hissing of the fire had slackened. All that remained of the steamship in the shallows was its blackened skeleton. She should have slipped aboard one of the rescue boats an hour ago. Maybe she still could. Until dark, the salvage crews would be working to collect the dead bobbing in the waves.

"It's a quarter past one," the doctor said from behind her, startling her.

Based on his muffled voice and the swishing of fabric, she knew he'd donned a Mother Hubbard gown.

Pretending she hadn't heard him, she watched one of the crews use a grappling hook to retrieve a body. Within her, a fire burned hotter than the one she'd just witnessed.

"How can you be thinking of your research, with your son still missing?" She motioned toward the devastation.

"Presumably, he's at the river bottom, considering his mother and sister drowned. If I'd been with them on that steamship, instead of here, studying you, I would have gotten them into a lifeboat. Or persuaded the captain to beach her earlier." He clenched his fists.

"I must give meaning to their deaths. It's time for your weekly blood draw," he said, pointing toward his laboratory within the main hospital building.

Cora considered resisting, but the authorities would believe the doctor over the word of a leper. Furious, she strode toward the building.

Ten paces behind her, he followed, prattling about the latest theories in microbiology as if he hadn't suffered unspeakable loss and didn't have a three-year-old son unaccounted for.

His words faded away. She thought of the ring beneath her heel, disrupting her stride, and how gratifying it would feel to hurl it into the East River.

One Month Later

July 1904

As the scalpel punctured the tender skin an inch above the navel, Cora shut her eyes and tried to picture her mamaí's indigo eyes and wispy red curls. Despite the numbing effect of the eucaine, she could feel Dr. Gettler slicing a small incision to access her pancreas. How she longed to scream, but she didn't dare startle the doctor while he held a knife in her gut. The sooner he determined where the germs resided, which might happen with this tissue sample, the sooner he could remove them so she could return home.

The dissection stopped.

"Your self-control is impressive," he said, exchanging the instrument for a pair of forceps. "Under the new purview of my research, the specimen requirements will be greater. My success will depend as much on your resilience as my scientific acumen."

Alarmed, Cora lifted her head, igniting a surge of pain in her abdomen. "*Purview?*"

"It means *scope*." He began probing her insides.

She bit down on a rag to keep from howling. Delirious from the torture, Cora couldn't comprehend his words. All she understood was fear.

"The organ contains no visible abnormalities, but the microscope may reveal otherwise," he announced through his surgical mask even though he had no medical staff assisting him. Despite the midnight hour, he'd even locked the door.

Shaking from physical and mental fatigue, she watched him prepare a series of slides, each containing a shaving of tissue that reminded her of liverwurst. "What new scope?" The tragedy had hardened Otto so fast and firmly that Cora was still reeling from the change.

"Now the sutures," the doctor said to himself as he began sewing her up.

With panic welling within her faster than her tears could fall, Cora held still.

He can't keep doing this to me, she thought, even though she knew he could and would. His word ruled the hospital, whereas she was a mere woman, and worse: just another indigent—and a "demented" one at that. Two days ago, she'd tried calling out to one of the other resident physicians for help. He'd ignored her. Later that night, Dr. Gettler had informed her that he'd added a list of psychoses to her case file; no one at Riverside would believe her now.

He knotted the thread. "Before, I was thinking too small. The potential hidden within your blood corpuscles is enormous."

From his tray, he selected a roll of gauze. "Almost done." He smiled for the first time since she'd entered the room.

"This isn't right." Her boldness surprised her, yet she continued, "I won't be used for some grand experiment. I'm begging you. Let me go home."

He lifted her torso to wrap her midsection. "*Du bist zu Hause.*" You are at home.

"No, my home is 3C, 21 West Ninth Street. My mother's probably returning from work right now. I miss her." She tried to strengthen her appeal with eye contact, but he'd turned to his equipment, and the hood of his Mother Hubbard gown blocked his face.

"Please," she said, not hiding her desperation. "My mam could visit me here. I need her."

"You think I don't need my Rolene? And Ingrid?" He shifted so his back was to her, and began immersing his instruments in an alcohol bath. The vague outline formed by his protective gear reminded her of a statue only partially hewn from rough rock.

"Every night," he said so softly that Cora couldn't tell whether he was speaking to her or himself, "my hand reaches for mein Liebchen and falls through the air. She's gone. No matter how hard I pray or wish or work, nothing will bring her back. Or mein kleines Mäuschen."

His shoulders began shaking, and Cora knew he was crying. It was the first time she'd seen him break down since he'd left his dead daughter's side. For the past month, he'd seemed as lifeless as the charred remains of the *Slocum,* which had drifted toward the Bronx shore.

Whenever she thought back to the tragedy, she couldn't smother her inferno of what ifs. What if the fire hadn't started in the lamp room and the lifeboats hadn't been wired to the decks? And the Knickerbocker Steamship Company had replaced its life preservers before their cork had rotted to dust? What if Captain William Van Schaick, now standing trial, had run the ship aground right away instead of charging upriver into a headwind? *What if I'd slipped off the island in one of those rescue boats?* Cora often wondered.

If that day had unfolded differently, in any one of myriad ways, the death count wouldn't have reached a staggering 1,021, mostly women and children. Rolene and Ingrid might still be alive. And, as a result, Dr. Gettler would not have been transformed by grief.

Tears tickled her cheeks. Unsure for whom they'd been shed—his family or hers—she sniffled.

The doctor twitched at the noise. With his back still to her, he tore off his gloves and screamed at the ceiling, "How could you let this happen?"

This time Cora knew he wasn't addressing her.

Weeping, he shoved the cart, dropped to his knees, and curled forward to bury his face in his hands.

His coldness since the tragedy suddenly forgiven, she fought the urge to embrace him. *Lord knows, we both need it,* she thought, but her pests would show no respect for his loss.

So instead, she remained on the examining table, his howls echoing in her empty heart.

At last, he quieted, though he didn't rise.

"Your son," she said. "You still have him, and he needs you."

Over the past month, the doctor had spent every night at Riverside while a *Kindermädchen* looked after Ulrich.

"He's probably awake right now, crying for his Vati in the dark. Tomorrow, go to him."

Dr. Gettler slid his hands into a fresh pair of gloves and adjusted his surgical mask. "I can't." His eyes, the only part of him exposed, showed no emotion. "He wants his mother to comfort him, not me. I can't give him that, and he looks so much like her. It's too much to bear."

Cora closed her eyes now and pictured the boy's ash-stained face streaked with tears.

Shortly after the *Slocum* had stopped smoldering, nurse Puetz had found him wandering on the beach. She'd brought the distressed child to Dr. Gettler's lab, where he'd been drawing Cora's blood. Ulrich did have Rolene's delicate, straight nose, high cheekbones, and curls in the blond hair around his crown.

"Vati!" he'd called, and Otto jumped to his feet in delighted surprise.

Shocked that the boy had survived, Cora had sat up suddenly, and the needle within her arm twisted free, spraying blood onto her and the doctor.

"Ulrich, stay back," he'd yelled, "I'll come to you in a moment. Nurse Puetz, don't let him near me." He rushed to the far side of the lab and stripped off the contaminated gown.

The relieved look on the toddler's face had turned to horror at the sight of his father, covered in blood. "*Ich will Mutti.*" I want Mom.

As he was stepping out of the pile of fabric, Dr. Gettler's body turned rigid. All that moved was his Adam's apple as he presumably attempted to swallow the pain of their joint loss.

"I'm here," he said, shaking himself out of his stupor. "I've got you." He lunged toward his son but pivoted to the sink so he could scrub his hands.

"*Nein*," Ulrich whimpered. "*Ich will dich nicht* (I don't want you). Mutti." His desperate gaze swept the room as if Rolene might be hiding beside one of the equipment cabinets.

Trembling, Dr. Gettler leaned against the counter and covered his face with his hands, apparently having forgotten he'd intended to wash them. "Nurse Puetz," he said without looking up, "take him to a private room and have Dr. Fisher thoroughly examine him."

Silently, Nurse Puetz ushered the boy out of the room.

"I'm sorry," Cora whispered to the doctor's hunched over form even though he couldn't possibly hear her over the rising sound of his sobs.

Despite everything else Cora had witnessed that day, Ulrich's reaction to his father had upset her the most. Partially because she felt responsible. If she hadn't risen so quickly, that needle never would have snapped.

Neither Ulrich's initial reaction nor his striking resemblance to Rolene was a reason for the doctor to shun him now. She shook her head. "He's only a little boy, who's got to be so scared right now. And he does love you, so much."

Dr. Gettler straightened to his full height. "We both know that your sister's death happened for a reason: it shed God's light on the potential within you."

Appalled by his abrupt shift of topic and utter cruelty, her mouth fell open. Unable to formulate a response, she simply stared at him. The air drying her lips and tongue felt as thick as a hand clamped over her mouth.

The rubber of his gloves made a *scritching* sound as he interlaced his fingers. "Similarly, Rolene's and Ingrid's deaths were also by God's design. He wants me devoted to pinpointing the source of your immunities, which will benefit all His children. When Ulrich is older, he'll understand."

"Pinpointing? What does that mean?"

He cleared his throat in irritation. "Vaccines that can eradicate diseases; that needs to be my focus. Any effort to destroy your pathogens is time not spent finding a way to harvest and replicate your unique *Antikörper*—antibodies. The lives I'll save will dwarf those lost from the fire. My Rolene and Ingrid, they'll achieve immortality when I become one of the greats of microbiology."

Cora could hardly catch her breath. Her heart pulsing, she squeezed out her words: "No, no, no! I have to get them out of me."

"You must stop this selfishness," he said with a hiss.

She flinched. But even if he were right, she doubted he would succeed before the increasingly potent germs overwhelmed her body's defenses. "Let the Carnegie Lab help you."

"They would only slow me down. I've made so much progress already."

"What progress?" she huffed.

He rolled his eyes, suggesting she was too simple to understand.

He wants all the glory for himself, she realized and inhaled sharply. The smell of antiseptic fueled her anger.

"I'm not your prisoner," she said through gritted teeth.

Surely, after reading about the tragedy at North Brother, her mam would open a letter from her. "At first light, I'll write to my mother and tell her what you've done to me. You'll lose your position."

"Coraline, you must put this nonsense out of your head. Eleanor has moved on. She thinks you're deceased."

"What?" She tried to sit up, and the dressing bloomed bright red. "No. You wrote her. About a chronic cough."

He sighed heavily. "Unfortunately, because I filed your death certificate so soon after Maeve's, the Health Department notified her during a single visit that both daughters had succumbed to typhus."

The operating light above Cora began to sway, and its electric buzz grew louder. Although she knew it must be a trick of the mind, she ducked her head.

"But my letters. She must have known I was—" Pain shot through her abdomen, and the room blurred. "You filched them before they were posted, didn't you?"

He swung the cart back beside the operating table. "Can you imagine the social unrest if your mother had gone public with a campaign to remove you from isolation? Cora, you're a germ carrier. Rumors spread faster than typhus in those tenements, and we've tried so hard to stifle their fear of this sanatorium. When they hide their ill, we cannot prevent contagion. Do you really want an epidemic on your conscience?"

Of course not. Cora felt dizzy and nauseated. She covered her eyes with the crook of her elbow, trapping her tears against her flushed skin. Eleanor's silence hadn't resulted from her unwillingness to forgive. Although Cora should have felt relieved, an image of her mam, crumpling to the ground upon learning of both girls' deaths, pinned her to the metal.

Her mother's trade required the keeping of secrets; she could have been entrusted with this one. Also, Eleanor was a sensible woman; she would have understood the need for Cora to remain at the hospital until cured. If the doctor had consulted Cora, she would have explained this. How could he have done this to her? Especially *before* he'd lost his wife and daughter.

She pictured Rolene's wedding band, now hidden beneath her mattress, and knew that tomorrow she would bury it. "Why didn't you tell me?"

He exhaled. "I felt awful keeping it from you, but it was my cross to bear. I feared you'd be upset with me and wouldn't cooperate."

"You were right," she spat. "I'm done being your patient."

The doctor shook his head. "You're all I have left. I will not lose you, too." He grabbed her shroud from a hook near the door and tossed it onto the foot of the examining table. "To the rest of the world, you're dead, and so I'm all you have left. Don't you see?"

A scalpel, wet with her blood, gleamed from his tray, and she imagined grabbing its ivory handle and driving the blade into his heart. No, she decided, she would stab him in the pancreas so the animalcules would have time to ravage his body before he died.

"Linnaeus will help me, or one of the nurses."

He laughed, and the sound skittered across her bare skin. "Is that part of your fantasy, that he saves you?"

Cora dropped her gaze to the floor tiles. She hadn't once mustered the courage to return Linnaeus's greeting from twenty feet away as he strode past.

"Presuming you could manage a full sentence in his presence, you would risk infecting him?"

"None of the children I saved from the *Slocum* caught my germs." Every evening she'd been watching the staff direct the new patients and hadn't yet recognized a single face from the tragedy. Also, Emmett had been released to his father following two weeks in quarantine, during which he'd showed no signs of infection.

The doctor harrumphed. "That we know of. They could have been admitted to one of the hospitals in the city. Or died in their homes. After what they'd been through, why would their families have allowed them to be sent back here?"

Cora scrunched her eyes shut. For the past month, she'd been trying to block out those scenarios.

"Miss McSorley, I know you're lonely, but you cannot give in to temptation," he said as he cleaned his instruments.

"Then I'll kill myself." Even as the words passed her lips, she longed to draw them back.

His shoulders slumped. "That would be such an elegant end to this torture, for both of us, wouldn't it? But we can't take that easy path." He packed up his physician's kit, his daughter's silver wristlet looped around its handle. "Because if we do, Rolene, Ingrid, Maeve—their deaths will have been in vain. You loved your sister. You still do. So, because of her you'll endure, as will I."

A tear seared her skin. She didn't wipe the tear away. *Let him see what he's doing to me.*

"I know the sacrifice is great." He extended his gloved hand. "Mine is no less."

Too weak to rise on her own, she begrudgingly accepted his assistance.

Her shoulder blades skidded along the cool metal, and her feet met the ground. To steady herself, she leaned against the table.

"Oh, I almost forgot," he said, reaching into his bag, and set a magazine beside her.

He stripped off his protective gear, leaving it in a bin near the door, and donned his boater hat. Without another word, he left the room.

Only after the door had clicked shut did she look down. *The Lost Cache. A Tale of Hid Treasure*. Otto had given her the ninety-first installment in Beadle's Dime Novel Series as recompense for his ninety-first procedure on her. Cora gripped two of its opposing corners, ready to tear its pages, yet she couldn't bring herself to do it. She cherished these stories. Without them, what would she have left to love?

Squinting to hold back more tears, she pulled on her covering.

The garment landed on her shoulders; through the hood, she glimpsed the bloodied scalpel, forgotten in the corner of the medical cart.

2007

More than four decades since solitary confinement was last prescribed for Riverside Hospital's drug-addicted teens

AUGUST 7

"What the hell?" Finn said loudly enough to be heard through the glass observation window. "Unlock the door!"

"Chill out," the scarred woman said from beyond view. "Yelling won't do you any good. Just like it didn't help the teenage junkies who were locked in here during the fifties—man, did they scream. So will you."

His vision blurred, and for a moment he could almost see the rebels surrounding him and his interpreter. That day in 2002, when he'd convinced their leader to allow Finn's civilian relief team to evacuate Ferkessedougou, still caused him to wake during the night.

Slowly exhaling, he reminded himself that those diplomacy skills could help him here, too. And his street smarts—a trait that had helped him make friends at his New York City public high school.

"You certainly know your local history." He whistled.

"History was one of my favorite subjects," she replied, still out of sight. "That and grammar, which you already know—knew."

If I could make eye contact, this would be a hell of a lot easier, he thought. Casually, he moved closer to the glass—the first unbroken pane he'd seen since stepping ashore seven hours ago. "I think both are right."

"I know that," she snapped.

"Or *knew* that?" he said, smiling.

She didn't respond.

"Irregardless," he said to even the error count, "you outwitted me. I thought you were by the docks."

"It's *regardless*. And it's called a diversion. That canoe washed ashore in a storm years ago. I'd been saving it for—" She coughed, that deep, hacking sound.

Years ago? If that were the case, she could be the woman in my mom's note, Finn thought. Prolonged asbestos exposure would explain the cough.

He had to get himself out of this shitstorm before Lily became so worried that she called Kristian. To buy himself more time, he should text her that the river was becoming too choppy so he'd have to stay until the following night. He slid his phone from his pocket.

"No," the woman said as if addressing a dog, "I'll take that, and the knife."

Finn flinched. Although he could never harm her, the corkscrew would be perfect for digging through the wall if it came to that. "It's got sentimental value."

"The dead have no need for sentiment."

His muscles tensed, and he refused to show any reaction.

Her face appeared in the window.

This close, he could tell that the white marks speckling her tanned cheeks were scars. Yet somehow, they didn't detract from her beauty. Those spots, coupled with the burned red tinge to her brown hair and slightly upturned nose, gave her an Irish air. And, those eyes. Even through the mesh, he could make out the long lashes that framed them.

The fact that she was so pretty unsettled him. He knew that he would have been equally concerned for her if she weren't as attractive, yet he still felt guilty for the urge to protect her that swelled within him each time he looked at her.

"Put everything by the door, now," she said as he noticed a smudge of dirt on her chin. Or chocolate.

"Did you like the Toblerone?"

She responded with a rap on the window.

Without his gear, he would be completely at her mercy. Banking on the fact that it had been a while since her last real meal, he shrugged off his pack. "Sure, but first: I brought you—"

"My scalpel?"

He flinched. It was sitting in the back of his desk drawer. "Sorry. You have so many."

"That one with the ivory is special."

Of course it is, he thought, trying not to roll his eyes. "*That* ivory is why African elephants are endangered."

She furrowed her brow. "I've got nothing to do with that, if it's even true. For twenty-five years, it was my only one. To get the rest back"—she shook her pouch, and the metal within jangled—"I had to kill."

He sucked in air through his teeth. Although she obviously couldn't be that old, he did believe her capable of murder. "If you let me go, I'll return it, I swear."

"So, you're willing to barter." She crossed her arms over her chest, and Finn averted his gaze from the gaping neckline of her tank top.

"If you tell me where the tunnel is, I'll let you go. Then you can drop my blade off on the dock."

"A tunnel? Here?"

"You think I'm that stupid?" she spat and ducked out of sight.

His finger found the power button on his phone.

"C'mon," he whispered as it stirred to life, his eyes darting.

A dark, hooded figure appeared at the observation window, and Finn reeled backward.

She was wearing a World War II–era gas mask; his heart thudded faster.

I'm too late. This woman had been damaged beyond repair. And now he would suffer the retribution.

The panic rising in his chest demanded air. Finn allowed himself a shallow breath, which triggered a need for more.

"Maybe now you'll take me seriously," she stated in a mechanical voice.

The bug eye windows and snout-like mouth filter, connected to a tube that snaked down her chest, made her look alien. Even more disturbing was the wholesale absence of emotion in her eyes as she stared him down.

"I told you, I don't know anything about that," he said, sliding the phone back into his pocket as a creeping realization solidified. He did know: when he'd been twelve, the night before July Fourth, he'd visited their storage unit in the basement to retrieve an American flag and had run into his dad. "Get back upstairs!" Rollie barked. Finn bolted, but not before glimpsing what looked like bundles of fireworks—or explosives.

The following day, Rollie left for North Brother Island before sunrise and returned after midnight. Kristian had gone with him, for the first time. Sylvia had taken Finn to the riverfront to watch the fireworks display. Devastated that he'd again been excluded, and irritated that he had no idea what they were doing with that dynamite, he'd barely noticed the fireworks. Sylvia must have been feeling equally distraught; she'd gripped his hand throughout the entire event. Although too old to be holding his mom's hand in public, where he might run into a classmate, he'd done just that. Because he'd known that she needed him.

Finn hadn't seen any evidence that they'd used the explosives aboveground. But nothing in the records he'd found supported her claim. "I've seen my dad's map. There's no tunnel on it."

"I don't believe you." She raised a canister and tapped the glass, indicating he should look up.

Attached to the ceiling was a spigot. *Holy shit.*

He rushed to the fence that blocked him from the broken windows and gulped the humid air. Frantically, he tugged on the grate, but it wouldn't budge. The gas would fill the room faster than it could escape through the latticework.

"There's a major storm headed this way. You won't be safe here. I brought a raft to get you out of here."

The woman laughed, and the sound whistled through the tube of her ventilator. "Is that supposed to scare me? Hurricanes are my favorite weather." She put her face to the mesh, and her ice-cold expression, through the bulging eye windows, lacked humanity.

A pins-and-needles sensation seized his limbs.

"There's got to be an entrance near the shore," she clipped. "I know it connects to their secret laboratory, probably under one of the ruins. I've searched everywhere. It makes no sense."

The journals hadn't referenced an on-site facility, although it would be a safer destination for the bats than his father's lab, in the back room of his medical practice.

She pressed the pages in his sketchbook with the map against the window. "Show me."

To alleviate the tingling in his legs, he shifted his weight from one foot to the other. "If I'd known, don't you think I would have marked it on there? Or better yet: used it?"

Clicking her tongue, she tilted her head. "Fair point, but it's not my style to quit." She strummed the canister. "You've got ten seconds to put everything, including your hat, by the door. Then put your hands on the fence, facing the forest."

He touched his lucky cap. Lily had bought it for him during one of the Subway Series games they'd attended, and the Mets had won.

A pinging sounded.

She was tapping the canister.

Reluctantly, he set his stuff beside the door.

“Hands on the fence. Now.”

Clenching his jaw, he pressed his palms to the metal, hot from the direct sunlight.

When that door opened, he would charge her. Out of the corner of his eye, he watched for her to leave his line of sight.

She tapped the canister once more, a clear warning, and vanished from view.

Finn tensed, ready to spin and pounce.

Behind him, the hinges groaned, and he dove toward the exit.

The door slammed shut, and his shoulder met metal. He yelped in pain and frustration.

“I came to help you,” he said in a tone more bitter than he’d intended.

She didn’t respond or reappear.

With nothing else to do, he stalked over to the windows.

Outside, the herons had resettled, and the tree canopy rippled in the gathering wind. He might never walk back through that forgotten world. He might never leave this room.

Finn listened for her footsteps but detected nothing.

From the floor above came rodent-like skittering and squeaking.

If he died here, he suspected his bones would be picked clean before he could rot away.

MIDAFTERNOON

A rotten stench filled Finn's nostrils, and he gagged. Expecting to see the isolation room shrouded in a green vapor, he opened his eyes. The verdant forest beyond the grate taunted him with its proximity. Clutching the metal, he gulped the breeze through the broken windowpanes. The smell had been only in his head. Yet the risk that she would gas him remained real.

Again, he considered screaming for help. Soon he might cave to the impulse. For now, however, he still had the presence of mind to know it would be pointless—the only person near enough to hear him would be her.

His gaze raked over the bolts that pinned the fence to the wall. If he could rip the barricade free, he would attempt the three-story drop. No doubt she'd hunt him down. He'd rather take his chances, slim as they were, than stay here, completely at her mercy.

Finn yanked on the fencing, and his muscle fibers fired like a semiautomatic weapon.

The grate barely rattled.

He crouched in front of the locked, rusty access panel to the windows. Its blood-like smell hung thickly in the air. He wrenched the chain, and it scraped across the fence with a screech. Cringing, he glanced at the nurses' window.

So far, his efforts to escape hadn't elicited her return. Either she knew he wouldn't succeed or there'd been a development with his phone. If Lily had texted that she'd asked Kristian to check on him, the woman could be lying in wait for his brother now. Or she might have answered a call from Lily. Finn knew his girlfriend wouldn't take shit from this woman, which wouldn't improve the situation.

Fucked. That's what he was.

If Kristian did arrive, maybe his dry, intellectual commentary would disarm her. Then again, he could be somewhat of an elitist. More than once, Finn had seen him turn his nose away from the smell and outstretched hand of a beggar as Finn was opening his wallet. Similarly, Kristian might look down on this vagrant, despite her poise, and she would sense his disdain.

Finn rubbed his forehead. For all he knew, they'd already formed their opinions of each other. In which case, her hatred of his family suggested that it hadn't gone well.

If Finn and Kristian both died here, Sylvia would have only Rollie left to care for her. And Lily wouldn't have Finn there to keep her safe the next time she had an epileptic seizure, a latent side effect of the radiation to her brain.

God, he missed her already. When they'd started dating, he'd thought it was so cool that she had zero interest in marriage. Two months later, she'd disclosed that her treatments had stolen her fertility. It had taken another three years for her to admit that she would never be ready, despite his reassurance that he was okay with not having children. In a tearful voice, she'd explained that she feared the arrival of a third cancer that would leave him a widower.

Lately, she always seemed to be planning his "Life After Lily," or LAL. While they were at a restaurant or on the subway, he'd catch her staring at another woman. When he pulled her attention back to him, she would make an offhanded comment such as, "Her nose is lovely. I bet she's down-to-earth. You need someone like that." Or, "The way she just wiped the rim of her wineglass: you wouldn't have to worry about toothpaste marks in the sink."

Just thinking about the potentiality of LAL now made him ache.

Exhaustion tugged at the edges of his brain. To stay awake, he knocked the back of his head against the fence and pictured his girlfriend in bed beside him. He imagined running his fingertips over her smooth skin, interrupted by cotton shorts and a tank top. She would be twirling a lock of her unruly hair, as black as the Mariana Trench. Too soon, she would try to slip away. At the last second, he would catch her ankle and pull her to him.

With his head resting against the fence, Finn conjured the aroma that came home with her from work—tree sap and soil. He breathed in, and the smell of decaying drywall obliterated her scent.

If he made it back to Brooklyn Heights, he would tell her all about his suspicions and this woman. Several times over the past week, he'd tried broaching the topic but had lost his nerve. Despite Lily's reservations about marriage, he viewed her as part of his family. As a result, he didn't want her to despise his father. But, if he really thought of her as family, didn't that mean she had the right to know what he'd found? *Absolutely.*

Finn wiped at the sweat on his brow. The heat dragged down his eyelids like lead weights, and he blinked to keep them open. A short nap would make him more alert later. He set the timer on his watch for thirty minutes and stretched out on his side, facing the door.

Finn swatted his Timex to silence its chirping and sat upright.

Across the room, a metal cafeteria tray winked in the sunlight.

While he'd been sleeping, that door had opened. He'd missed his chance. Finn smacked the wall.

He moved to study the tray's contents—a plate of weeds, a tin cup with a brownish liquid, and—he clasped his hands—his moleskin sketchbook, marred by the puncture from her scalpel. The elastic loop still held his pencil.

If she'd simply wanted him to mark the tunnel, she could have torn out the map on the first set of pages. Quite possibly she wanted to see what else he might draw.

Finn set aside the book to examine the dark liquid. Assuming it was potable, she'd either brought with her clean water or had a desalination kit. If Rollie had somehow compelled her to stay here as he tested the impact of different chemical reagents on her immune system, access to clean water might be one of his manipulation tools. Finn raised the cup and frowned. Its herbal smell could be masking a poison.

There were a million more satisfying ways she could snuff him out, Finn concluded, then took a sip. A bitter taste overwhelmed his mouth, so he quickly chugged the rest.

Turning to the salad, Finn noticed chunks of meat perfectly cooked. It had been forty-four years since New York City had disconnected North Brother from its power grid. And the smoke from a campfire would have alerted the Harbor Unit to her presence. Maybe she had a portable generator or sun oven. He poked a piece of meat that looked like chicken but likely wasn't.

His stomach soured at the thought, but he needed the calories. He grabbed a strip and tore off a chunk with his teeth. It tasted surprisingly flavorful. He might as well try to savor this meal, considering it might be his last.

The insides of Finn's cheeks felt brittle. The fuzziness in his brain had returned an hour ago, along with a headache.

Through the fence, he searched for a rustling treetop or burst of herons taking flight. Anything that might reveal her location.

A few broken rooftops poked through the leafy canopy, like mountain peaks among the clouds. Lily would love to paint this scene. That's how they'd met: at a studio while he'd been on a date with a fellow grad student more interested in her wine than her canvas. Before he'd even noticed Lily, standing before her oil painting, he'd fallen in love with her talent.

He pictured her alone, pacing in their apartment, the mounting stress making her susceptible to a seizure.

"It's stunning, isn't it?"

His pulse quickened. Without turning, he knew the woman was standing beyond the observation window.

"It's crazy this is in the middle of the city," he answered. "So much . . . green."

"I was referring to the Manhattan skyline."

"Really?" Finn was always planning Lily's and his next escape from that jumble of strangers, concrete, and foul-smelling garbage. Yet, from this caged view, he had to admit it did look stunning. "At sunset, when the steel glows orange, sure, but it doesn't compare to this place."

He shifted his gaze from the buildings jutting from the forest to the ivy-draped structures near the docks. In the shallows off the southwestern shore: that's where his great-grandmother and great-aunt had drowned.

Each time he'd passed through those waters, he'd felt their presence. In his parents' Long Island home hung an opalotype portrait of Rolene and little Ingrid in a pinafore dress. As a child, Finn had been fascinated by their ghastly deaths.

He made a mental note to add a cross to the shoreline on his map.

Then he should sketch one of the distant high-rises for this woman. "Which is your favorite?" he asked loudly.

"The nurses' residence," she said in a wistful tone, free of its earlier hostility.

With renewed hope, he touched his compass. "I'd meant in the city."

"Oh, then the Astor Hotel." She closed her eyes, and Finn guessed she was picturing it at the heart of Times Square.

Considering that the landmark had been razed in the late 1960s, it was an odd choice. He pointed at the roof of the nurses' home. "I can see why—"

"No, he can't. He can't possibly."

Startled by her forcefulness, and that she'd referred to him in the third person, Finn spun to see if someone had joined her.

Her attention fixed outward, she appeared to have been addressing the island itself.

In the waning light, her sharp features looked softer. In her cerulean eyes, Finn detected sadness.

Convinced that she hadn't meant to reveal that emotion, he averted his gaze to her braided hair, tied off with a piece of vine. "I want to help you, but I can't if you won't tell me what's going on here."

"You? Help me? Yeah right." She backed away from the window and bumped into a counter, her head almost hitting the bottom of an empty hanging cupboard. It was the first clumsy move he'd seen her make. Her first sign of weakness.

"My dad's using you in his research, isn't he?"

Her eyes widened. "Your *dad*? You do look like him. But he's never mentioned you. *Why would he do that?"* she asked herself, or the island. "Because he felt guilty," she answered.

Unsure how to interpret that, Finn wrinkled his nose. "He didn't tell me about you, either."

"Your family always has loved secrets." She coughed.

His stomach twisted, but he had to know: "I found an old note that my mom had written to my dad. She wanted him to leave a woman alone, who'd suffered." He stepped toward her. "If you're that woman, and he's still hurting you, I'll make him stop, I swear."

She arched her eyebrows. "How noble."

"Not at all. Anyone faced with this same set of facts would do the same. My mom would have made sure he'd followed through if she could."

Her eyelids fluttered shut, and she lowered her head. "How is Sylvia?"

Does she know about the Lyme? Finn wondered. "Hanging in there."

"Your father called," she said, her expression hardening.

Finn groaned at his bad luck. Rollie rarely called him during the workweek.

"He was surprised, to say the least, when I answered. Naturally, he threatened me. So, I chuckled sinisterly." She groaned. "That was an adverb. I really try not to use those. Great, I just used another. Anyway, I told him to be here at exactly two o'clock tonight. Your family always has been obsessed with punctuality."

Finn pictured Rollie methodically preparing for the trip, his worry, as well as his anger that Finn had defied him, completely bridled. "My dad claims he hasn't set foot here since 2001. That's not true, is it?"

"His most recent visit was"—she looked upward—"two nights after I caught you peeping."

Furious, Finn balled his fists.

"Don't worry," she said, smiling, "I didn't mention you."

"Did he give you those scars?"

"No."

"Has he harmed you in any way?"

She rubbed her breastbone. "Yes."

The veins in Finn's temples throbbed. "Let me go, and I'll make sure he leaves you alone."

She laughed. "You really are clueless. I love that word, by the way, especially in this usage."

"That may have been the case, but I'm catching on pretty quickly, and I'm not going to let him hurt you again," Finn said, trying to hide his anger. "There are shelters that can help you. I'll find a good one."

"I can't leave here, okay?"

"I don't see any chains."

"They call it *VZ*. The day it was injected was the worst of my life." She looked past him. "It's a weaponized pathogen. My own personal—what do you call it? Electric fence. It'll kill me if I clear the shallows."

Speechless, Finn couldn't believe Rollie had duped her with such a twisted subterfuge. Yet a part of him did. To keep Finn in his room at night when he was little, Rollie had told him the monster lived in the hall closet—not his bedroom's. To compel Finn to get his chemistry grade up, his dad had dangled a formula for a compound that would boost the muscle shakes Finn drank each night after baseball practice. Rollie always had been good at mind games.

"So anyway," she said as if they'd been discussing the weather, "I've got something for you." She ducked out of sight, and Finn's heart pounded.

A moment later, a magazine protruded from the slot in his cell's door. Grabbing it, he caught a whiff of antiseptic. He hadn't imagined that smell earlier. The worn cover depicted a cowboy shooting a Native American. Embellished letters stated that this was number 1,004 in the *Dime Library*: "Buffalo Bill's Death-Deal."

"I've got the full series," she said, reappearing at the nurses' window. "Each one cost me dearly."

"I can't keep this." Nor did he want to, given its glorification of the genocide of America's indigenous peoples, though he sensed now was not the time to raise that issue.

"It's only to borrow, until Rollie arrives, when you'll either die or scurry home." She tossed her braid over her shoulder and turned toward the exit.

"Wait." He racked his brain for a way to keep their conversation going. "How'd you pull off that trick with the birds?"

"I suppose there's no harm in it," she said, clearly not to him, and took a sip from her canteen bottle. "The raccoons love anything shiny. I knotted the foil wrapper from the Toblerone around the end of a rope. Then I strung the rope over a branch and tied its other end to a log."

As she described the rest of the mechanics, Finn thought his own death might occur in a similarly complex fashion. "Apparently physics is another of your strong suits."

"I do have a Rube Goldberg cartoon collection."

"I'd love to see it sometime." It had sounded like a lame pickup line, whereas he simply wanted to give her another reason to keep him alive. "How do you move so fast in the treetops?"

"Basically, I use a network of boards and branches." She smiled shyly. "I stick to the treetops to stay clear of any vandals that make it ashore. Obviously, I dismantle the boards before each winter because if I didn't, the park workers would notice them. Those months, I hunker down to stay warm. Each spring, I rebuild. Mostly I move around at night."

"Yet you shower after daybreak," he blurted out. Embarrassed, his cheeks flushed.

"That was reckless." She bit her lip. "I used the fact that it was summer as an excuse to let down my guard. The only visitors during the nesting season shouldn't be here and thus won't report me. I have had a few run-ins. In most cases I was able to convince them I wasn't alone."

Finn bit the inside of his cheek. He didn't want to know what had happened to the others. Only through winning her trust would he stand a chance of getting home, he reminded himself. "Let me help you prep for the storm."

She rolled her head as if considering the offer.

"Come to think of it, Kristian never mentioned you, either," she said, glancing toward the window.

"So, you do know my brother."

"Yes," she said, staring into her right palm, "though I wish I didn't."

The muscles in his chest tightened. Once free, Finn would confront Kristian. "He can be a little socially awkward, but he's all right."

"What was he like," she asked, clearing her throat, "when he was little?"

"I wasn't around then."

"Oh, right. Sorry."

"I know he was a curious kid, who loved taking things apart to see how they worked. His old toys came to me in bins full of pieces, which was fine by me. I liked putting them back together."

She hugged her middle. "Kristian's a good man, to have helped those 9/11 survivors the way he did."

Finn cocked his head. He knew his brother had been working at the hospital that day, but he hadn't mentioned treating any of the victims. If he had, he would have been too proud of that fact not to have shared it. "What do you mean?"

"He told me what happened to those poor, trapped people after the aliens crashed their spaceships into the top floors. It's terrible. I hope they never return."

Incredulous, he wagged his jaw. Although Kristian could be a smart-ass, disrespecting the 9/11 victims didn't sound like him. Even more disconcerting: she hadn't seen through his con, which meant she actually might have been living here since at least 2001.

Quite possibly, Finn thought, his biceps tensing, *their discontinuation of the project had been nothing more than a brief pause.* They could have used both Sylvia's illness and SARS, which had killed almost eight hundred people during 2002 and 2003, as justification for furtively resuming their work.

No longer could he believe anything they'd told him about this island and their research.

"Yeah, those poor, *trapped* people." He waved his hand at the dead-bolted door.

She chuckled. "Irony can be a bitch, huh?"

"Can you at least tell me your name?"

Reflexively, she patted her pouch of scalpels. "It's obvious what you're up to, but it's pointless. Everyone who gets close to me dies," she said, grunting, "one way or another."

A breeze tickled the back of his throbbing neck, and he shuddered. "How about I guess it? Is it . . . Elle? As in E-L-L-E. Not *L*, as in 'lovely,' though you are. Lovely, I mean." *Where did that come from?* Suddenly the room felt ten degrees hotter.

"No, I'm hideous," she said, crossing her arms to hide her scars. "And the inside's even worse."

She jumped back from the observation window.

Bewildered, he listened for whatever new threat she'd perceived.

Detecting nothing, he looked down and realized that he'd stepped toward her, but didn't retreat. His throat ached. Over the past three weeks, he'd been so fixated on what she'd been through physically, he hadn't considered the abuse's impact on her psyche. Suddenly, he felt compelled to counter the negative self-talk she'd just revealed.

"You must have noticed I can't stop staring at you," he said in a gentle voice.

"Of course I did. Who wouldn't stare at a freak?"

"I don't know how you pull it off, but the scars make you look more beautiful." He moved his foot in an arc along the dust. "It's sad that you wear pain so well."

He looked up and noted the glisten of a tear on her cheek.

"Coraline," she said through the glass, "but all my friends call me Cora." She laughed, and he could tell by her hollow tone that she'd meant it as a joke.

"Nice to meet you, Cora."

Her eyes narrowed, and he felt their connection snap. "No Gettler is a friend of mine."

"Then think of me as Finn. Just Finn."

"Why didn't your father give you a German name?"

"My mom wanted to name me after Huckleberry in *Tom Sawyer*. Her second love is American lit."

"Ulrich must have hated that her Romanian genes muddied his perfect line of Aryan descendants," she said nonchalantly.

How could she know that? Playing it off, Finn laughed. "He never seemed to mind that I was a mutt. Gramps was good to me, aside from when I was causing trouble."

Her face had darkened.

Sensing he'd hit a nerve, he backtracked: "Irregardless," he flashed her a smile, "I like my name. It fits."

"I loved that character. The way he helped Jim . . ." she said, a lightness returning to her eyes.

He grinned.

"That doesn't mean I like you," she said, glowering, then looked toward the exterior. "I gotta go."

His heart thudded. "Why?"

"The sun's about to set." She stepped out of sight.

"Wait."

"I never miss a sunset," she said from the far side of the wall.

The sound of footfalls echoed in the corridor.

Finn darted to the door and yelled through the slit. "When will you be back?!"

"Not sure I will." Her voice had sounded faint.

1907

The beginning of Typhoid Mary's exile on North Brother Island

October

Concealed against the church, Cora pulled back the hood of her cloak and searched the blackness for an unlit boat. The flashing beacon at North Brother's southern tip was little help. Downriver, the star-pocked night faded to an indigo hue as it neared the Gotham skyline. The mansions along Fifth Avenue and Broadway were illuminated by electric streetlamps—she could just make out their orange halos—and an occasional taller building glistened with nocturnal activity. Of the million lights in that city, only one mattered to her. Only one had her weighing the risk of a gruesome death while trying to reach it.

At this early hour, the kerosene lamp in the McSorleys' apartment would be dark. But if she were to attempt—and survive—the river crossing, and the microbiologists at Carnegie Laboratory were able to cure her, within weeks she could be eating a hot bowl of her mother's potato and leek soup beside its familiar glow.

If instead Cora remained here, her future as Dr. Gettler's property would be unavoidable. While he'd been floundering through various methods to isolate her antibodies, the bacteria counts in her specimens and the death rate of the lab mice had continued to increase. With each day she became more lethal.

And more despondent.

Three years ago, she'd pleaded with Dr. Gettler to allow her to fill her days with a purpose. Stumbling over her words, she'd pointed out that he'd devoted himself to his research as a means of blunting the pain from his loss. She needed a similar analgesic. Also, others would be less inclined to object to a leper who'd become a permanent resident if she earned her room and board.

He'd worked out an arrangement with the head gardener, John Canne, whom Dr. Gettler described as "the only man on this island as trustworthy as O'Toole," and secured her a small wage and a room in the nurses' residence.

At the end of each day, she threw off her shroud and collapsed onto her cot. The labor itself, she relished; the constant fear exhausted her. Anytime she raised her gaze from the dirt, she might meet the doctor's expectant stare, summoning her to his laboratory.

Once a week, she had to lie upon his examining table, at the mercy of his latest hypothesis. Only the rodents, in cages stacked against one wall, had it worse than she did. Even now, she could almost hear their squeaking and smell their foul odor.

She tried not to think about what he'd last done to her there, but the two-inch-long, sutured incision on her abdomen throbbed, refused to be forgotten.

If she stayed here, at least she would remain alive—until the microbial monsters prevailed. And she did believe in the doctor's work; if he found the source of her immunities, there would be no need for contagion hospitals such as this one.

Conversely, if she risked the choppy waters, she'd likely drown. A chill seeped through her and settled in her chest. She blew onto her palm and concentrated on the sensation of air, not water. When the nightmares had first begun, Cora would be so out of breath when she woke that she thought she was actually submerged. As a result, she believed she knew exactly how that death would feel.

When Cora's new friend Mary Mallon had mentioned her beau's plan to rescue her, Cora had called them both crazy. To which Mary had responded, "That crackpot doctor treats you like a lab rat. Personally, I'd rather drown a free woman than live here a caged animal."

It had been an easy claim for Mary to make. An asymptomatic carrier from New York City, who'd been vilified by the dailies for purportedly causing multiple typhoid fever outbreaks, she'd been banished to Hospital Island only seven months earlier.

Cora didn't like to talk about that hellish day in 1904. No one who'd been there did. So, she'd left Mary's comment unanswered.

As hard as she tried to recall the eleven she'd saved, those she hadn't were the ones who floated through her memories, their limp bodies suspended around her like a school of jellyfish.

No way could she die like that. Not once since then had she stepped into the East River.

On the beach below, Mary paced, her tall silhouette visible in the glow of the crescent moon. With its reflection, the strait looked like obsidian, though Cora wasn't deceived by its elegance. Beneath its shiny surface were riptides; she could hear them breaking against the two piers.

The wind, particularly sharp today, slapped her cheeks. The waves had to be equally fierce—either bad luck or a sign from God.

"He's late," Mary muttered, and a gust brought her voice to Cora.

An early riser, Cora's boss, John Canne, would be roving the grounds soon. He, or a physical plant worker who'd stepped out for a smoke, would alert the staff to the escape of the "Germ Woman," as the papers had nicknamed Mary. If either spotted Cora, no one would believe that she hadn't intended to flee as well. Undoubtedly, Canne would head straight to the doctor's cottage and wake Dr. Gettler.

Cora willed the boat to appear, though its arrival was far from certain. Alfred Briehof might have gone on a bash last night, or perhaps the savage waters had already claimed the vessel, which had to be small given his meager wages as a coalman. At this very moment, it might be settling in the muck at the bottom, somewhere near the *Hussar.* If a British frigate laden with gold and eighty shackled Revolutionary soldiers couldn't navigate these waters, what chance had a little rowboat?

Eventually she'd shown O'Toole the golden coin she'd found in the sand. After identifying it as a guinea, he'd speculated that it had come from the *Hussar.* To keep herself from impulsively deciding to risk the crossing, she'd intentionally left her satchel in her room that morning.

A gust buffeted Mary's blouse and full skirt. She tucked a loose strand of hair into her coif, raised a covered lantern, and lifted its sheath three times to signal her location.

Cora scanned the water for Alfred. Although Mary couldn't possibly hear her, she tried to be as still as one of the corpses waiting to be transferred by ferry. The dead had an easier way off this island than she did.

Her breathing too loud, she slowed its pace.

Last spring, the day "Typhoid Mary" had been assigned to the hut they'd built for her, Cora had asked Canne to leave a bouquet of primroses on the small porch.

Amid a stream of Irish curses and proclamations that her cooking had never sickened a soul, and that there was "no goddamn way" she'd listen to "that *eejit*" Dr. Soper, Mary had thrown the flowers to the ground.

From against the tennis court fence, Cora had removed the cloth that covered her face and explained that she, too, was a prisoner at Riverside.

Smoothing her strawberry blond hair and starched skirt, Mary had beckoned for Cora to enter and take a seat.

Daily, Mary had ranted in her heavy Irish brogue about her rights, need for a solicitor, and "gittin' the hell outta here."

Always keeping her gloved hands in her lap and her nose and mouth shrouded, Cora would quietly listen to the sentiments that echoed those lodged in her heart, like a keg of gunpowder she was too timid to light.

Even while she'd been praying for her friend's release, a small part of Cora had been hoping it wouldn't happen. Finally, she had a confidante who understood her plight, someone to take the edge off the crushing loneliness.

According to Mary, Dr. Soper and the doctors at Willard Parker Hospital, where Mary had first been admitted, believed the germs resided in her gallbladder. Remove the gallbladder, remove the germs; so went the theory.

When Cora had asked Dr. Gettler if curing Mary could be that simple, he'd deemed it possible.

"Would that work for me?" Cora had asked.

By then a third pest had invaded her body; she'd pocketed a novella discarded by a woman with smallpox. And Cora had likely acquired typhoid fever from Mary. An ex-chef for wealthy families, Mary had struggled with Dr. Soper's edict that she was not permitted to so much as boil an egg. She'd cajoled Cora into stealing ingredients from the shipments unloaded at the ferry so she could cook for the two of them within the privacy of her bungalow.

In response to Cora's question, the doctor had launched into the story of Edward Jenner's discovery of the smallpox vaccine.

Little good the advancement had done her, or the woman who'd owned the book. As far as Cora knew, none of the immigrants in the tenements of New York had received the inoculation. She doubted they would benefit from any vaccines made from her blood. *If* it could even be done.

She had to get away from him.

Still pacing on the beach, Mary cursed, and Cora wished she could again caution her friend to keep quiet. Cora sniffed the air for the scent of Canne's tobacco but detected nothing. She pressed her spine against the wall.

Above the tidal strait, lamps dotted the deck of the Williamsburg Bridge. Beyond it, she could just make out the pearl necklace lighting of the Brooklyn Bridge. If only she could reach Gotham simply by walking across a trestle.

If she joined her friend and the dinghy capsized, a riptide—or one of the others in the group—would drag her under before she could swim to land.

Her body would become lodged between the pylons of a pier. Crabs would eat away her face, and once bloated, she would emerge unrecognizable—just like the sixty-one unidentified dead interred beneath the *Slocum* monument in a Middle Village, Queens, cemetery. Far less grand, she would be buried in Potter's Field on Hart Island, the same site as her sister, yet nowhere near her.

But what if the boat did make it across the river? And the removal of her gallbladder eradicated the germs?

She would be able to hug her mamaí at long last.

Cora longed to be with her now. She'd clung to the memory of the Ambre Royal perfume her mother spritzed on her wrists and décolletage before leaving each night, as much a part of her uniform as the low-cut dress. By now its scent had been reduced to words: amber, orange blossom, vanilla. Oh, to smell her perfume again . . .

She also had a hankering for the pastries in Mrs. Meade's bakery, three buildings down from their tenement. Each night, Cora stared out her window and imagined the velvety feel of buttered soda bread on her tongue. When she closed her eyes, she could almost hear the clatter of horse-drawn carriages along the cobblestone street and the happy racket of children playing "Come with Me" in the alley.

This was Cora's chance to return to that life—to feel alive again.

But what if that place existed only in the past?

The city had changed so much in the six years since she and Maeve had been exiled. Cover to cover, she studied the daily newspapers that Canne passed along. But seeing a photograph of the new Plaza Hotel, or reading another headline on the bankers' panic that was roiling Wall Street and Main Street alike, couldn't prepare her for the changes that must have occurred within her district.

The bakery might have closed, its aromas replaced by the chemical smells of a laundry. The sounds and scents of horses had to be fading with the arrival of automobiles. Without a single car on North Brother, Cora couldn't conjure the rumble of an engine or the smell it produced.

And worst of all, Eleanor might have left their once-cramped apartment with its painful memories, taking with her the kerosene lamp, the Gaelic quilt her great-aunt had stitched, and the sole opalotype of the two girls.

With such uncertainty awaiting her across the river, Cora couldn't overcome her fear of drowning. Yet her hope that the dinghy would suddenly appear felt like a stone in her lungs, keeping her short of breath.

She reached under her shroud and pressed her blouse to her abdomen; warm blood seeped into the cotton. The wound needed to be cleaned and redressed.

Just then, a rowboat with two figures materialized in the dimness. Cora's legs wobbled as if she were already aboard.

"Well, I'll be gobsmacked," Mary said. "The git actually got himself out of bed." She fixed her windblown hair and flashed the lantern three more times.

Blue tinged the black sky. Soon Cora would stand out against the red bricks. Silently, she eased along the wall. While they were preoccupied with the landing, she should slip away.

A scraping noise signaled that the keel had hit the pebbly bottom, and the man she assumed was Alfred jumped out, soaking his trousers. While his mate fought the current with a set of oars, Alfred shoved the boat farther aground. He wiped his hands on his wool coat and fixed his attention on Mary, who'd backed against the seawall.

"Mary Mallon, I've come to take you home," Alfred announced with a German accent, not nearly as thick as Dr. Gettler's, and waded toward her.

From her vantage point, Cora could barely distinguish among his thick eyebrows, dark eyes, and the circles beneath them. Although his features appeared to have sagged with age and alcohol abuse, he was still handsome, and he was staring at Mary as if she were a Broadway starlet. Cora understood why she'd stayed with him through the drinking and joblessness.

Mary raised the pillowcase that contained her boots and other meager belongings. "I was beginning to think you wouldn't show. Before your last, only two letters in six months. Two!"

"I'm not much of a writer, but I'm here, aren't I?" Alfred unfastened his life preserver and tossed it into the boat.

Cora half expected Mary to hurl the sack at him. Instead, Mary hiked up her skirt and splashed through the surf. She dropped the lantern in the boat, and Alfred scooped her up and twirled her. They leaned inward for a kiss, and their faces merged in the gloom.

Cora looked away, her heart breaking.

She'd imagined a thousand scenarios of being embraced like that by Linnaeus Jones. In all, his smooth hands, separated from her skin by only a cotton shift, pressed her body against his broad chest, and his lips tasted like a mix of tobacco and the black licorice he often chewed while walking between wards. Afterward, he would whisper in her ear that he was only one promotion away from a salary that could support her as his wife.

A few times, while she'd been planting alone, Cora had even attached his surname to her first in elegant cursive letters scrawled in the dirt, erased forever with a swipe of her boot.

But the doctor's refusal to focus on eradicating her germs—and the needs of a young man—had worked against her. Two weeks ago, from the stairwell of the nurses' residence, Cora had overheard nurse Carlton coyly describing to nurse Puetz a midnight rendezvous with Linnaeus.

No, she'd thought, her body stinging like she'd landed in a thicket of nettles.

Cora believed that as long as she remained confined to North Brother, no more relevant than a single period in a world the size of the Bible, she would never meet her soulmate. Whereas across the tidal strait, once the doctors at Carnegie cured her, she would walk among two million men.

Even if the scientists at the lab couldn't quickly rid her of all four animalcules, there might be at least one bachelor in New York whose immune system could best whatever germs remained. Mary had found a companion who appeared to be resistant to typhoid fever, and Richard O'Toole's three children hadn't contracted any of the diseases treated at Riverside.

If Cora didn't join the escape party, she would never have the chance to find her soulmate.

Overhead, a seagull cawed, signaling the imminent arrival of the sun. If the boat didn't leave now, they would be discovered.

She ground her gloved palms into the brick wall. Behind her stretched a precarious existence filled only with pain, yet before her raged almost certain death.

Daybreak

A damp wind rushed past Cora, leaving behind a brittle emptiness. Seemingly unaware of the brightening sky, Mary and Alfred remained locked in their embrace.

Attempting to knead out the knot in her heart, Cora rubbed her chest and looked from the couple to the Gotham skyline.

Love was worth dying for. If Cora could have, she would have swapped places with Maeve during those final days of the fever. And without love, life wasn't worth living. Two weeks ago, she'd learned that firsthand as well.

The memory of nurse Carlton's giddy tone, as she'd described Linnaeus's fevered kiss, invaded Cora's skull. As their romance bloomed, Cora wouldn't be able to avoid signs of it. The envy, worming through her bones, would rot her entire core. But if she made it to Gotham, she would be spared that torture, too.

Clutching her cross pendant, Cora scrambled down the seawall. "Excuse me," she said, keeping her voice low, "we should go."

"A leper?" Alfred sloshed backward. "What's it doing here?"

"Ha! I knew you'd come!" Mary said too loudly. "Cora's my friend and not a leper. She was . . . burned in the steamboat fire, while saving dozens of children. And she's right: we'd better skedaddle."

Alfred looked from Mary to Cora and back again.

Cora tugged the head wrap tightly against her nose and lips. Sitting so close to the others would jeopardize them. *No,* she thought, *the wind will carry away any germs that escape my shroud.*

The barrel-chested, hired sailor, resting over the oar handles, shook his head no at Alfred, who nodded in agreement.

"I won't leave without her," Mary announced.

The grimace on Alfred's face settled into resignation.

"Helmut, get ready to row like a madman." He lifted Mary into the dinghy.

Clutching her boots and the hem of her cloak, Cora stepped into the water. Its bite took her back to that day. Submerged in the muck, her feet refused to take her deeper, where she might step on the remains of *Slocum* passengers melded with the sediment.

"Cora, what's wrong with ya?" Mary asked. "Hurry up."

Startled by the rebuke, Cora waded deeper; the stinging water ascended her legs and saturated her shroud. While Alfred held the vessel steady, she hoisted herself over the edge. Her hipbone smacked against the wooden hull and several inches of standing water soaked her rear end. She gasped and sucked in her stomach. Making herself as small as possible, she folded herself into the corner.

Crouched in the other corner of the stern, Mary was wearing a life preserver. So was Helmut, seated on the vessel's only bench.

Alfred reached into the boat for his and fastened it around his neck.

"Have you got an extra?" Cora asked, her teeth chattering.

Helmut fished a flask from his raincoat and took a swig. "We weren't expecting a fourth." The look of derision on his bearded face suggested he hadn't fully believed Mary's claim.

Alfred shoved the rowboat free of the river bottom and threw himself in, disrupting its balance, and Cora yelped.

"You're a skittish one, aren't ya?" Mary asked.

Cora didn't answer. She doubted her friend was as complacent as she'd sounded; Mary's knuckles were white from gripping the gunwale. Cora wiggled her fingers. Beneath the already sodden leather, they felt numb.

Pushing off the bottom with an oar, Helmut turned the bow toward Manhattan. He began rowing, and the boat plowed through the chop.

Cora stared at the campus, bathed in an azure glow creeping up the eastern horizon.

Only once had she seen the island from afar. As the ferry had approached the hospital, she and Maeve had stood at the bow railing, arms wrapped around each other.

Despite a new facade on the main ward, additional wood-framed pavilions, and the specimen trees she'd helped plant, the facility still looked bleak. At its core, Riverside hadn't changed a bit, but it *had* changed her.

Ensnared by an eddy, the boat spun.

The sailor grunted as he worked the oars, and the dinghy lurched free of the vortex.

Alfred and Mary cheered and hungrily eyed each other. If they weren't seated at opposite ends, Cora was sure they would have kissed.

A wave struck the top of Cora's hood, and she squealed in surprise. Runoff streamed down her face, and the terror of drowning gripped her. She held the soaked face wrap away from her mouth and gulped in air.

When the burn in her lungs subsided, her breathing slowed.

Shivering, she settled into the standing water in the hull. With each swell they rode, her stomach heaved, and more brackish water splashed over the sides. Even if they managed not to flip, they still might sink. And Cora's heavy cloak would drag her to the bottom.

A bucket attached to the bench by a rope rattled against the side. Cora grabbed the container and began bailing. More poured in faster.

Ignoring the aching in her arms and the sting as her thinly covered knuckles banged the wood, she scooped faster. "Please, Lord," chanted Mary, an Irish Catholic who never attended church, and Cora matched her tempo.

Maybe this was God's way of preventing the two from leaving Hospital Island. Cora had been arrogant to believe she could walk a mile through a bustling city, where she couldn't wear her leper's shroud because of the attention it would attract, without infecting a single soul. And there was no guarantee that Carnegie's microbiologists could cure her. Instead, they might die trying.

The boat rode up a swell, and she spotted North Brother's ferry dock, diminished in size. They must be nearing the worst of Hell Gate.

Ahead, the whitecaps rose higher. Alfred took the oars from Helmut and yelled, "Brace yourselves."

The boat tossed, and Mary bobbled.

Reflexively, Cora reached for her friend to keep her from falling overboard, but Mary lunged out of reach. The boat rocked, and everyone scrambled to balance it.

Mary's lips curled into a grimace, and she pointed behind Cora.

Cora twisted to check for a ferry charging toward them. Distant sailboats and barges dotted the waterway, but none appeared concerned with their small party. "What is it?"

"Your face," Mary stuttered. "It looks God-awful."

Suddenly Cora's cheeks felt like they'd been scraped with a razor blade and doused in saltwater. A gust seared the raw skin, and she realized her headwrap now hung around her neck.

She dropped the bucket and covered her face, which stung as much as her hands. She wiped sea spray from her eyes, peeled off her gloves, and yelped.

Her fingers looked like sausages and felt like they were in a frying pan. *It has to be from the saltwater*, she thought, looking for something to dry them with. The pain intensified, and a wave of wooziness rushed over her. She brought her hands to her mouth to blow on them.

They weren't cracked; they were blistered. Flat, red boils covered her skin. She tried to bring one of the sores into focus. Her head throbbed, and she felt like she was aboard the *Slocum*, the fire closing in on her.

The blisters resembled smallpox. *No!* she screamed inside her head. *Not now!* They couldn't be real; the stress of the passage must have driven her mad.

But Mary—not Cora—had first noticed them.

Though she could have hallucinated Mary's outcry. Nausea swelled in her stomach, and she turned just in time to vomit over the side of the boat.

Helmut swore and grabbed the oars from Alfred. "Move!" he yelled, and Alfred toppled into the bow. "She's no burn victim! She's got the pox!"

Alfred righted himself. "*Scheiße,* Mary, you lied. How could you let her come?"

"I didn't know, I swear," she cried, her hand covering her mouth.

"I'm gittin' the hell off this boat and away from that vile creature." Alfred began rowing with panicked vigor.

Compressed into the far corner of the stern, Mary kept her hands in front of her chest, clearly ready to ward off Cora if needed.

This can't all be a hallucination, Cora decided. Touching her cheek beneath the wrap, she cringed from the pressure of her fingertips on the bumps.

A sharp pain seared her abdomen. She reached for the incision, but the cramping had originated farther down.

Her immune system must have finally succumbed to the vicious beasts. Scratching her arms beneath the cloak, she howled in frustration.

A wave slammed into her back and she fell toward Helmut, who shouted and dove to port, driving the boat onto its side. Alfred threw himself to starboard, and the vessel righted, but only until the next swell pounded them.

Despite being drenched, Cora felt fever hot. Yet at the same time, chilled to the core. Her throat and head ached. And her muscles. She peeled back the wool; between the welts, her skin had turned the shade of Maeve's typhus rash. Or the red could be a symptom of the measles.

She pulled her hood over her face and drew her hands beneath the tent of fabric. In the darkness she pictured an angry pack of wolves swarming her organs. A communal strengthening over the past five years, as Dr. Gettler had feared? Or a spontaneous uprising? Caused by . . . *a vegetative force. No,* she thought, *that was a fairy tale told to me by a deranged doctor.*

Still, she couldn't risk causing an outbreak by returning to Manhattan.

In her current condition, she belonged under quarantine. She knew that.

Her heart—the one organ that hadn't yet turned against her—thudded.

Returning to the hospital meant facing Dr. Gettler. A fierce cold gripped her body, providing no relief from the fever. Shivering and wet, she huddled in the corner of the stern.

She had to go back. For a chance at preserving the antibodies within her, Dr. Gettler would do all he could to aid her body's fight against the infections.

But at least one of them should gain her freedom, and Mary had already promised to contact Cora's mother.

The water looked furious and unforgiving. In those waves, she would never reach North Brother. And who knew what sea creatures lurked below? When she was younger, she'd read in the newspaper about a great white shark caught in the harbor.

Out of habit, she blew into her reddened, bare palm, quickly realizing that the calming technique wouldn't work. She hadn't just woken from a nightmare; she'd entered one.

Cora tried to swallow a sob, but her swollen throat thwarted her effort.

She had to jump. *Now.* Cora shifted to a crouch.

Helmut stopped rowing. Joining with the other two, he stared at her.

"I'll swim," she said through what felt like shards of glass lodged in her tonsils. "Life jacket?"

No one responded.

"Can I have . . ." *Of course.* Not even Mary would give up her preserver: they still needed them, whereas Cora was practically dead already.

She clasped her hands, and the skin between the pustules turned white. Jumping out now would be suicidal, but remaining in the boat would be equivalent to murder.

By Mary's and the men's horrified expressions, Cora knew that they thought so, too.

She coughed to clear the glass from her flaming throat. "Mary, remember your promise."

Mary's grimace relaxed into a sad smile. "You're a strong lass. You'll make it, and I'll find a way to git ya free, I promise."

Despite everything Cora had told her about Dr. Gettler, Mary still didn't understand. "Don't forget my mam." If only she'd brought the golden guinea, Mary could have passed it along to Cora's mother.

"Ta, absolutely."

Cora pulled off her face wrap and dropped it into the river, then her cloak. She knew she should remove her shift and bloomers as well but couldn't bring herself to do so in front of the men.

"Jump!" Mary barked. "Git on with it!"

Cora covered her ears, but the shrill sound continued.

Seagulls circled overhead. Cora looked at Mary, who appeared to be sobbing.

"Jump now!" the seagulls shrieked.

Delirium. Another symptom of smallpox. And measles. And typhus and typhoid.

The pests were quickly overwhelming her. If she didn't reach shore before they completely stole her wits, she'd drown for sure. *Please, God.* She pressed her crucifix pendant to her lips.

Gripping the gunwale, she pulled herself upward to stand. The sky and river merged, and she swayed as the boat jounced in the waves. If she didn't throw herself over now, she'd topple onto Mary, so she took a deep breath, closed her eyes, and . . .

Pain shot through her lower back, followed by a suffocating coldness.

Moments Later

Tidal water flooded her mouth as a rushing sound filled her head. The water seemed to be getting heavier, pressing against her skull. She tore at the churning river, but the darkness deepened. Her ringing ears felt ready to explode.

The surface should have appeared by now; she must be pointed down. *Air.* She needed air. Up had to be in the direction of her feet. She folded at the waist to reach for them, but a riptide spun her.

The fire of the fever: that had been nothing compared to this burning in her lungs.

Suddenly light appeared. She refused to believe it was anything but the sky.

With both arms, Cora pulled toward it and kicked hard.

The current's force lessened, and she reached for the brightness. The wind hit her face, and she inhaled and gagged. *Too fast.* She coughed out water and sucked in air. Her body tingled, and all she could see was blinding white.

Slowly her lungs ceased their wailing and her vision returned. An intense ache replaced the numbness; the incision on her abdomen stung. In her struggle, the stitches must have ripped free.

Sculling with her hands, she searched the horizon for a boat that could rescue her.

No. She had to let go of that hope. If a ship came to her aid, she would have to drown herself before they could haul her aboard. Her arms slowed with the realization, and her legs felt like sacks of coal, pulling her down.

"Keep your head above water. Don't panic: it'll tire you out."

Mary. They'd come back for her!

Searching for the boat, Cora thrashed in a circle.

"Find the lighthouse, and swim toward it. *Cruadal*, my friend, *cruadal*."

The voice, urging courage, had to be in her head.

Still, she should heed it. She cleared her eyes and cast about for a familiar landmark.

The Williamsburg Bridge appeared on the horizon. She pivoted and found North Brother's lighthouse, and to its right, South Brother Island. They were shrinking; the current was dragging her away. She had to swim hard, or she'd be carried into the harbor. Her bloomers billowed around her legs, so she yanked them free.

A swell knocked into her, and she hacked to clear her breathing passages.

The whitecaps made the front crawl impossible, so she dog-paddled. After a few awkward strokes, she managed to establish a rhythm. Her muscles burned, and her stomach felt like it was ablaze. To keep the spray from her eyes, she squinted, and every few pulls swiped at them.

The horizon blurred and the lighthouse refused to stay in view. She stopped and treaded water while reorienting herself. Blood ran from her nose. Farther away, everything seemed both light and dark. She blinked to clear her vision.

Beyond the Williamsburg Bridge rose Manhattan.

Her mother would continue to wake up alone. Cora's tears vanished with her blood into the tidal strait as she kicked her legs to spin away from the city.

The physical plant's smokestacks came into view, and she began swimming toward them. Yanked by a current, she struggled against it. Her muscles were cramping, and she had a side ache. Soon she wouldn't be capable of staying afloat.

Something grazed her leg.

Shrieking, she peered down but couldn't see even her hands, just below the surface.

Another delusion, she hoped.

She grasped for a calming thought: Maeve's giggle after she'd beaten Cora at Old Maid.

The creature banged against her thigh, and she screamed. As it glided past, it maintained contact with her skin, giving her a sense of its length.

Only she could hear her desperate, terrorized cries.

She sprinted toward North Brother. Within a few strokes, the cramping had reclaimed her muscles.

Again, something scraped against her thigh; panic locked her limbs as she imagined the long outline of a shark.

Far worse than fluid filling her lungs, her body would be shredded and consumed. The sea devil must be circling her now. At any moment its jaws would pierce her flesh. Now hyperventilating, she broke into a coughing fit. Her legs felt exposed, like bait dangling from a hook.

Again, she made for the lighthouse.

A current repelled her; she fought back. Her shoulders felt like meat beneath a butcher's cleaver. She was tired, so tired. She craved sleep as her head went under, and she began slipping downward.

The light faded.

Soon it would brighten, and she would be with Maeve again.

The creature bumped her thigh, then her other, thrusting her upward. Her face reached the air, and she gulped it in.

That same rough skin. How could it have simultaneously hit her from both sides? Unless there were two.

Oh no! Panic seized her like a pair of jaws. They would fight over her like dogs with rotted meat.

As her mouth filled with water, she began to sink.

One, and then the other beast, prodded her. Too tired, she didn't fight back.

Suddenly light hit her closed eyelids.

This was the end—not the one she'd envisioned, but equal in suffering to her little sister's and those she herself had infected.

Maeve's face appeared, with its pinched nose and playful, big brown eyes.

Acute pain shot through Cora's bicep.

She thrashed, but whatever had grabbed her wouldn't let go.

Her body rose, and bitter wind blasted her wet skin. Her chest hit something hard, forcing out the remaining air.

She fell into the hull of a boat and realized that she'd been dragged over its gunwale.

A blanket landed on her lower half as she collapsed.

The back of her head met the wooden bottom.

Once again, her ears were submerged in water. This time the rushing sounded gentler. Sunlight prickled her eyes, so she kept them shut. The craft seemed to be rocking less than before, though anything would feel steadier than that undertow.

This peace, was it another delusion?

She blew into her pocked palm, the crystalline vapor assuring her she was still alive.

Had that voice urging her to stay strong belonged to Mary? They shouldn't have returned for her. Cora wanted to admonish her friend, but her head felt too heavy to lift.

The rhythmic smack of oars penetrated the whirring in her ears.

As much as her body welcomed the respite, she couldn't allow it to last. The boat couldn't reach Gotham with her still in it. As soon as she caught her breath and stopped shaking, she would have to dive back overboard.

Blinking away the droplets that clung to her lashes, Cora raised her head.

"She's breathing!" a familiar voice yelled. "Praise *Gott*!"

Cora's remaining scraps of strength disintegrated at that sound. Shivering, she pulled the blanket around her.

A face, enshrined in the hood of a Mother Hubbard gown, blocked the sky. Dr. Gettler's eyes widened, and his lips parted just far enough to reveal the tips of his impossibly white teeth. His attention fixed on her, he dropped his oar handles and fumbled for his spectacles. "*Mein Gott. Variola.*"

"They've finally won," she said with a sob, pressing herself into the stern. "Stay back."

He leaned away, and Cora noticed Mary, Alfred, and Helmut huddled in the middle of what appeared to be a vessel twice the size of their original. A hulking form in hospital garb, whom Cora knew to be O'Toole, was sitting on the bench behind them, grunting as he labored. It must have been he who'd pulled her over the gunwale. In the bow, the much smaller Canne was rowing in sync with O'Toole. Cora wasn't sure if his face and arms, exposed below the rolled sleeves of his soaked shirt, were red from exertion or anger. Most likely both.

They were taking her—all of them—back to Hospital Island.

The pulsating in Cora's skull intensified, and the germs seemed to be tearing her innards apart. Out of the frigid water, the poxes, now whitened with pus, once again felt like they were searing her skin. To resist the urge to gouge them, she shoved her hands beneath her.

"What happened?!" she shouted to Mary.

"We were taking on too much water." Mary shuddered and covered her eyes, and Alfred pulled her closer. "They came up alongside, and we climbed aboard. Alfred almost fell in. If he'd died because of me . . ."

Cora's legs slumped, and her knee banged against an oar in the bottom of the boat. Today her mother wouldn't learn the truth, or that Cora loved and missed her.

A sob lodged in her swollen throat, and she began coughing.

"Take my oars and start rowing!" Dr. Gettler shouted to Helmut. "We need to get her to my lab." He motioned for her to lean over the gunwale, then whacked her on the back, forcing the water, tinged with bloody sputum, from her lungs.

As she watched the ruby-red trail dissipate into the river, he continued rubbing the space between her shoulder blades.

The motion calmed her, and the choking fit subsided. She crumpled into the hull.

Holding the edge of his hood over his mouth, he inspected her abdomen, where blood was flowing in rivulets from her incision site. "*Macht Schnell!*" he shouted to compel the men to speed up the boat.

"Thank you," she croaked.

"*Bist du verrückt?*" (Are you crazy?) The doctor scooted backward. "Or just insanely selfish?"

"I'm sorry. I didn't know this would happen."

"I've been warning you about this for years. Good God, Cora, imagine if they'd overpowered your system just one hour later." He thrust his index finger toward Manhattan.

He didn't need to chastise her; she was already angry at herself. To avoid his probing glare, she closed her eyes and willed unconsciousness to arrive. Listening to the staccato slap of the oars, she sensed that the boat had accelerated.

"Cora," the doctor said softly, "once we reach my lab, I will not leave your side until you've recovered. You know that God has greater plans for us. These symptoms are a test for both of us. And through our perseverance—and sacrifice, my breakthrough, by the will of God, will happen."

Sick of hearing the creed he'd used to justify every violation of her body, she wilted.

The three men working the oars shouted as they outmaneuvered the currents. The vessel had to be nearing the docks.

Afraid to open her eyes, she imagined the campus with the glow of the sun at its back. Only an hour ago, she'd thought she would never have to face the facility again. Now, most likely, Riverside would be the last place she'd ever see.

The pounding in her head and cramping in her stomach subsided. Her throat was no longer excruciating and the fever had slackened. Only the chills remained. Either her spirit had already separated from her body, or her ability to feel had shut down.

"Our Father, who art in heaven, hallowed be thy name," Mary said in her brogue.

Surprised, Cora peered at her friend.

Alfred was gawking at Cora, too. He crossed himself and joined Mary in her prayer.

I must be dead.

Helmut and O'Toole stopped rowing to gape at her, leaving only Canne in the bow to battle the currents.

The doctor's face appeared above her. She reached out to swipe her spectral hand through him, and her fingertips grazed the slick surface of his gown.

"Ahh." He rocked back. "Foolish girl."

"You felt that?"

"Of course."

She'd never noticed her sister's touch, though surely Button's spirit had stayed close to her. Maeve could be nearby now. Cora looked around. "But I'm dead."

The doctor grabbed her wrist, and she recoiled at the familiar texture of his rubber glove. Her surgical wound throbbed, and she wrested her hand away.

"Cora," he said in a stern tone, "*gib mir deine Hand.*"

The saltwater in her stomach churned like she'd swallowed the rapids themselves. She must be alive, though she wished it weren't the case. She extended her arm and yelped. The pox had flattened and faded.

Instead of checking her pulse, as she'd anticipated, he probed the sores. She didn't even wince. Their tenderness had subsided.

"*Unmöglich,*" he whispered.

He was right: such a fast recovery from *Variola* was *impossible.*

She lifted her other hand, and a water droplet from her hair fell onto it and rolled unobstructed off the skin. If it weren't for the spattering of fresh scars, she would have assumed that she'd imagined the blight. She exhaled, and the air flowed through her throat. All her symptoms had abated, except for the fatigue, which could be attributed to the swim.

As quickly as her immune system had failed her, it had returned and squelched the rebellion within her. Amazing.

Hope thrummed through her veins.

Dr. Gettler lowered his hood and brought her hand closer to his face. "Mein Gott. The pustules have healed further within the last minute. Either the germs have returned to their dormant state, or your immune system has finally defeated them. Either way, this *will* lead to my first big breakthrough in five years." He looked up. "Thank you, God."

"You've been here that long?" Mary dropped the lock of hair she'd been refastening.

Cora nodded.

"You said you missed your last semester of school." She tapped a hairpin against her teeth. "That means you were about eighteen at the time. My child, you don't look a day older."

Everyone turned to Dr. Gettler, who shrugged. "In the words of Jacob Riis," he said, plucking at one of his gloves, "North Brother Island is unique. There is nothing like it anywhere in the world."

"What does that mean?" Mary snapped. "The island's keeping her young?"

"Don't be absurd! That's scientifically impossible."

He'd said it too quickly.

"Holy Christ," Mary said, crossing herself, and Helmut swigged from his flask and handed it to Alfred.

"Freak," the oarsman said in a low, guttural tone and took a long pull from the bottle.

Shrinking away from them, Cora ran her fingers over the skin of her face, now marred by pox scars. Only a few times, in an empty communal bathroom in the nurses' residence, had she glimpsed herself in a mirror.

But the doctor had seen her face every time she'd disrobed for another of his medical procedures. She scowled at him. What else about her condition had he been hiding?

The prospect of eternal youth should have thrilled her. Instead, all she could think about was how it must have been feeding the doctor's obsession. Even if he succeeded in cultivating vaccines from her blood, his experimentation on her would continue until the day he died. Or achieved eternal life.

The boat bumped against the dock, and the rowers collapsed over their oar handles. Alfred scrambled out to tie up the vessel.

From the pocket of his soaked trousers, Canne removed a pouch of tobacco, examined it, and tossed it overboard.

Alfred helped Mary onto the pier and they hurried toward the shore.

O'Toole nudged the doctor.

"Miss Mallon," Dr. Gettler called out, "return to your cottage at once. Your guests can wait for me at the staff house. If you cooperate, I'll consider keeping this out of your file. But if there's any more trouble, I'll have the dispatcher connect me to Dr. Soper's office immediately."

"You can't keep me here," Mary said with a snarl. "I'm not sick, and I've never infected a soul. That eejit wants to cut out my gallbladder. I'm not some cow to be butchered."

Shushing her, Alfred linked his arm through hers and led her to the path.

Seated on the pier, Helmut dangled his legs into high tide. "I'm not setting foot in that pesthouse. Or near that freak again," he said with a growl. "When's the next ferry?"

"In two hours," Dr. Gettler said, not bothering to hide a smug smile. He turned to O'Toole. "Please help Miss McSorley. Quickly now, to my lab, before someone sees her."

O'Toole offered a gloved hand to Cora. "Let's get you dry."

Even though she'd accepted the adage that nothing could kill an O'Toole, she still feared being the one to prove it wrong. Holding the sopping blanket around her waist, she shunned his outstretched hand and climbed onto the pier. "I'm sorry I put you in harm's way."

"You know that's not possible." O'Toole removed his gloves to emphasize his point. "You're safe now. That's all that matters," he said, rubbing an arrowhead that hung from a piece of twine around his neck.

It reminded her of the grayish-green slate bird stone tucked within her satchel. In 1905, O'Toole had found it at the excavation site for the nurses' residence and had given it to her on her twenty-first birthday.

Could that talisman be the source of her oddities? Or the golden guinea? She'd left both behind when she'd boarded the boat. If either of them were enchanted, it very well could mean that the germs still lurked within her.

The locked crucifix box from Emmett; could her strength have come from it? Or the cross pendant from the pastor? One of them seemed far more likely to possess a miracle power than relics related to ancient spirits or Revolutionary War ghosts. But, unlike the bird stone and coin, both the tin and the necklace had arrived on the island after her immune system had silenced the typhus and measles germs. Those Christian trinkets, however, could be keeping her from aging.

She hated not knowing what was happening within her body. The conflict beneath her own skin was no more visible to her than the current unrest in Russia.

But at least her blood samples and their impact on the mice would reveal the status of her monsters.

With the blanket wrapped around her, she let O'Toole escort her down the dock.

They reached the gravel path, and Dr. Gettler stepped in their way. "As soon as you reach the lab, draw four vials of blood. I want to determine her white blood cell count before it's had a chance to normalize."

O'Toole nodded and steered her toward the lab.

"Once she's rested and fed," the doctor said, following them, "I'll conduct another interview. Her extraordinary immune system may be dependent on this island; I need to reevaluate all environmental influences."

Another interrogation, during which the doctor would demand that she "think harder!" Cora longed for a soak in a tub, both for its heat and the privacy it would provide.

Yet she had no choice but to cooperate. Unless Dr. Gettler completely deconstructed the mysterious workings of her cells, she would never hug her mother again. Her days, stretching into eternity, would be spent reading about the world rather than experiencing it firsthand. She would never ride the IRT, see a silent picture, or go to Coney Island.

The doctor darted ahead to open a side door for them.

O'Toole stooped to enter. His hulking figure receded, and Cora felt utterly alone.

"You've a brilliant mind, for a woman." Dr. Gettler eyed her. "But perhaps I've overestimated your ability to act in the best interests of the common good."

He must have assumed that she'd been bound for her tenement. Although her plan to head straight to Carnegie would make her seem far more responsible, he would never forgive that betrayal.

Rather than defending herself, she apologized by stepping over the threshold.

"You've sacrificed a lot, I know," he said, reaching out but not touching her. "Just as Leeuwenhoek toiled all those years, studying the microscopic world through lenses he ground himself, just as Spallanzani refused to accept the notion of a vegetative force, I will find the cause of your abilities. That is my vow to you. In exchange, I expect you to follow my orders."

Goose bumps formed on her damp neck, and she yearned to run from him, not stopping until her legs gave out.

Instead, she stalked toward his laboratory, where she would lose yet another piece of herself.

Summer 2007

August 7

Lily finished another lap around the rooftop deck of the walk-up in Brooklyn Heights and peered north. Millions of city lights, yet not one of them shining from North Brother. Even while there'd been daylight, she hadn't been able to make out the small island that far up the strait.

Although Finn had told her not to contact Kristian unless he hadn't returned by morning, she didn't know if she could wait any longer. To keep herself from caving, she punched the speed dial button for Finn—the hundredth time that day.

On the fourth ring, the call connected.

Lily's heart pounded.

"Hello," said a raspy female voice.

Shocked, Lily hiccupped.

"Who is this?" the woman asked sharply.

"Who are *you*?" Lily fired back.

Husky breathing assaulted her eardrum. Filled with dread, she strained to hear Finn in the background.

"Coraline. McSorley," the woman answered at last.

"Well, I'm Finn's girlfriend," Lily stated hostilely. "Why do you have his phone?"

"Do you plan to marry him?"

"Excuse me?"

"You'll regret it. Every woman that marries a Gettler does."

"Who the hell do you think you are? Where is he?" The wind from the approaching storm whipped her hair, and she gathered it away from her face. "Put him on."

"He needs to rest. I know it won't seem this way, but what I'm about to do to him: it's to save you, too." The call disconnected.

Screaming, Lily flung her phone and it ricocheted off the brick wall.

Afraid she'd broken it, she rushed over and flipped open the glowing screen.

Instead of feeling relieved, a sudden heaviness pulled her to the ground, and she began sobbing.

Almost every night since Sylvia's birthday party a week ago, Finn had stayed late at his office. Apologizing for needing the time alone, he'd repeatedly reassured her that he would explain everything once he knew more, after this second visit to the island. She'd assumed he'd been researching how those bats and syringes related to his family's work. Secretly, Lily had done the same.

She'd learned that bats are ideal hosts for deadly pathogens. In their search for food, they cover vast areas, dropping feces that can land on other animals' food sources. In 2004, scientists from China's Wuhan Institute of Virology found a cave in the wilderness of Yunnan Province that was home to bats carrying hundreds of coronavirus strains. One of those strains matched the virus responsible for the SARS outbreak. Only about half a mile stood between that cave and the nearest village. Its exact location: a well-protected secret.

Lily hoped to God that those bats in the Gettlers' shed hadn't come from that cave, via the black market. Regardless of their source, their presence was problematic. During her Internet searching, she'd read about three subsequent smaller SARS outbreaks. The World Health Organization believed that they'd all originated from failures in safety procedures at virology laboratories. If even those top institutions' containment procedures had been flawed, then the security of the Gettlers' off-the-grid operation couldn't be ironclad.

Where did those bats wind up? Lily wondered for the gazillionth time. She'd assumed that Finn's determination to return to North Brother related to that very question. Dread that Rollie was using the abandoned island to secretly house lab animals pooled in her stomach.

If those bats were carrying a coronavirus, or another disease, such as Ebola, and one escaped . . .

Considering her and Sylvia's medical issues, the notion of a respiratory disease outbreak in New York City freaked her out.

To fend off a panic attack, Lily forced herself to breathe slower. She was jumping to conclusions, she told herself. Then again, maybe Rollie was crazy, and a threat to public health. Clearly Finn was concerned about that possibility.

Long before she'd glimpsed that cage through the shed window, Lily had suspected something was off with his family. It didn't require a psychology degree to realize that any family who believed it had been ordained to unearth a chemical compound that would lead to a universal vaccine or cure had serious problems. But it had been more than that.

Rollie's questions about her medical history, values, and commitment to Finn, seemingly whenever the two of them were alone, had begun the night they'd met, when Finn had stepped away to use the restroom during dinner at a Cal Poly restaurant. The covert looks, too, made her feel like Rollie was constantly assessing her suitability for his son.

She knew that his father's approval mattered a great deal to Finn. So, for Finn, she'd tried to win Rollie's favor. And, admittedly, for herself as well. All her life, she'd been longing for a dad, and she'd found one in Rollie by disregarding her gut instinct to stay clear.

Two years ago, Leonard had finally confessed that having a toddler with brain cancer had been too much for him. As if that justified his relocation to Los Angeles before she'd finished her third round of treatment. "I thought you were going to die," he'd informed her while asking for forgiveness twenty years after the fact. She'd told him she'd think it over. As long as she had Rollie, it had been easy not to.

But had she really been ignoring her instincts? Lily wondered. Her stated reasons for refusing to commit to Finn were legit; he deserved a healthy wife and biological children. Yet, if she truly believed that he'd be happier with another woman, wouldn't she have already forced him to move on? There had been another factor at work within the shadows of her subconscious, fueling her fear of commitment.

Cora's ominous words had given her permission to recognize a feeling she'd smothered for years. The notion of marrying into a family so tightly bound by loyalty, secrecy, and reverence for its patriarch frightened her.

While she liked Kristian, whom she knew genuinely cared about her health and happiness, she had been quietly observing his wife. Hannah always seemed on edge around Rollie. Even Milo showed an unusual amount of deference to him.

That same man would likely find out that Finn had broken his edict to stay off the island if she did call Kristian, which was beginning to look unavoidable. Regardless of any possible truths behind Coraline's insinuations about marrying into the Gettler family, Finn was in danger.

Picking at her nails, she considered notifying the police instead, which would land Finn in jail.

Rising, she began another lap. To solve this, she needed more information. The only way to achieve that was by calling the woman back.

Holding her breath, she pressed the speed dial button and waited.

With each ring, her heart rate accelerated.

The call connected with a click.

"You need to stay away from them." That same, hoarse voice.

Lily's stomach clenched, but she wouldn't be pushed around. "Put Finn on."

"No," Coraline breathed heavily. "This project poisons their souls. I can see Finn's a good man, but he won't stay that way."

"You're wrong," Lily said with a snarl. "You don't know anything about him."

"I'm sorry, for what I'm about to do."

"What the fuck does that mean?!" Lily shouted into the phone.

The line had already gone dead.

Two hours later

August 8

To relieve a muscle ache in his back, Finn curved his shoulder blades, inward and away from the window fencing. According to the woman, Rollie should be arriving in fewer than two hours. Assuming he could make it here.

The water looked like a smooth, asphalt path from his third-story vantage point, but Finn knew the chop had to be severe.

Compulsively, Finn yanked on the grate. If he could reach Barretto Point Park within the hour, he could borrow a cell phone and call off his dad. Then, tomorrow morning, he would show up at Rollie's practice and demand an explanation. If his father gave him the runaround, then Finn's voice might have to get a little too loud near the patients' waiting room. Rollie would view such coercion as a direct violation of their sacrosanct family rules, but at this point Finn didn't care.

"You ready?"

Startled by her sudden return, he jerked his head toward the dark observation window. "For what?"

"To leave. I'm letting you go."

In disbelief, Finn tried to shake away the dizziness caused by dehydration.

"Your kayak's still on the western shore."

"I'm surprised you didn't steal it."

Cora snorted with annoyance. "She's exactly where you left her, poorly hidden in the marram grass."

Unsure if she'd meant that as an insult, he asked, "What happened to waiting for Rollie?"

"Change of plans. Your girlfriend called."

Finn swore under his breath.

"The name Lily kept appearing on the screen, even when the phone didn't ring. Kinda like a telegraph. Anyway, two of the times she called, I did answer."

"And . . . what did you say?"

"That I plan to execute you for your family's crimes."

Finn winced, then reconsidered.

"I don't buy it," he said, shaking his head. "Lily's got nine-one-one on speed dial. This place would be crawling with police by now."

"Nine-one-one?"

How could she not know about that? Unless she had spent her first decade here, too. *Impossible.* "What did you really say?"

"That I'd snuck onto the island to photograph the ruins and found your phone. She was so worried about you. Apparently, she's in love. It made me feel guilty, so I'm letting you go. But if you'd rather stay . . ."

It had to be a trick. Allowing him to walk out, then slicing one of his major arteries, would save her the effort of dragging his body. Or this related to her scheming to find the entrance to the supposed tunnel. Regardless, his odds of survival would be better outside the cell.

"I'm good with leaving." He stooped to pick up the dime magazine. The story hadn't ended well for the Native American.

"Did you call off my dad?"

"I left him a 'voice message,' like the recording told me to do." She rapped the pane. "Now pay attention. If you don't follow my instructions precisely, you will get a knife in your spine."

Finn gritted his teeth. "I'm a good listener even without a death threat."

"Open the door. It's unlocked."

Surprised, he twisted to check. Before entering the nurses' station, she must have silently slid aside the deadbolt—another reminder that this was her terrain. Cautiously now, he crossed the room. The door squealed as he eased it open.

"Your gear is on the floor. Take out your flashlight, then sling your pack over one shoulder. I want to have a clean shot at your back."

In the darkness he groped for the main zipper. The interior reeked of antiseptic. He slid the magazine—a valuable bargaining chip—along with his sketchbook into the pack and reached for his phone, to no avail.

His knuckles banged against his canteen bottle. He finished it off and tucked the container into the cording that crisscrossed the front of his bag.

"Did I say you could drink that?"

Her voice had echoed from the blackness down the corridor.

"You didn't say I couldn't." The reprimand had come after he'd finished. Maybe she did intend to let him leave.

He found his tactical flashlight and nudged its switch.

The beam illuminated the swaying corpse of a baby, hanging from the top frame by a vine.

Finn yelped and jumped back.

Wrapped tightly around her neck was the tribal bracelet he'd left with the Toblerone.

Did she strangle that infant? With his eyes squeezed shut, he could still see its small, battered form and open, crystalline blue eyes.

Those haunting irises: his light had reflected off them like they'd been made of glass.

Maybe they are, he thought, forcing himself to return the beam to the tiny body.

An antique baby doll, Finn realized and exhaled heavily with relief. Yet, still, he felt nauseated. The whole thing was gruesome and sick.

"Why the fuck did you do that?"

"It's a warning," she said from the gloom. "And a test. Your reaction was surprising, considering you're Ulrich's grandson. He would have appreciated the gesture, more so if it had been an actual Jew or Gypsy."

"How do you know so much about him?"

"I know everything about your family."

The statement had sounded like a threat.

"What he did was heinous. I would change my last name, but what good would that do? The Jews he murdered would still be dead. I'm nothing like him."

"People change. I'm not going to sit around and wait for that to happen to you."

I have to get out of here.

He flicked the beam in the opposite direction, and she appeared near the end of the wing, a respirator mask shielding her face.

She pointed at his bag. "You need more bug spray, a good, thick coat."

"Why?"

"Just do it. Then take the stairs in the dayroom. Once you're outside, take your same route as before." She strummed the tiled wall. "In reverse, obviously."

Fending off a recurrence of the light-headedness, he sprayed his entire body, the cloud of chemicals nearly choking him.

"I'll give you a thirty-second lead," she said before the air had cleared, "then the hunt begins."

Finn raced along the corridor and down the two flights of stairs. Hurdling overturned chairs and dodging file cabinets, he charged through the dark administrative suite and lobby.

As he passed through the entrance, the fresh air hit him, and he inhaled its briny scent.

Across the narrow clearing loomed the wall of dense foliage. Searching for where he'd punched through this morning, he swept his light along it. With each second he wasted, his adrenaline surged.

A bolt of lightning fractured the sky, and he spotted a cluster of broken branches. To reach them, he would have to cross the open space, where he'd be entirely at her mercy. Despite her command, he shifted his bag to shield his spine.

Halfway to cover, he glanced back. She hadn't yet emerged. To buy himself time, he could Frisbee-throw her dime novel. With a storm coming, he doubted she'd leave it there. But even with the detour, she'd catch up. And then there'd be hell to pay.

Instead, he plowed through the thicket. Brambles scraped his arms. The buzzing of insects merged with the groaning of the trees in the wind.

His light lurched from one shadow to the next as he searched for the male dormitory, the last structure he'd passed on his way to the tuberculosis pavilion.

The air trilled, and a blade sank into the earth five feet ahead of him, immediately lost to the undergrowth.

She had to be among the branches above. Instinctively, he hunched his shoulders and covered his head with one hand.

"Keep moving!" she barked.

Lightning streaked across a gap in the tree canopy, flooding his retinas. The toe of his boot caught something hard, shrouded by ferns, causing him to stumble.

"That was a street curb." This time her voice had come from ahead.

He directed his beam at the trees bordering the ivy-covered lane.

"There must be hundreds like it in Gotham." She coughed, that gritty sound.

This nightmare was getting more bizarre by the minute. "Come down, where I can see you."

The air whistled.

He jumped to the side, and a faint *chink* sounded, barely wide of where he'd been.

Shuffling his feet, Finn continued moving.

The cistern sparked with the reflection of lightning. "One-one-thousand, two-one—" A rolling boom reverberated in his chest. Ahead, he could just make out the maintenance building that flanked his escape route. Launching his kayak in this weather would be reckless, but he liked those odds better than his probability of staying alive here.

He reached the path through the trio of buildings by the docks. The Harbor Unit wouldn't patrol during an electrical storm, but someone in the Bronx might notice his flashlight and call the police, who'd likely arrive too late. Also, he couldn't risk tipping them off before fully understanding his father's connection to her. He turned it off.

A *ping* sounded from close behind him. He whipped around just as a surgical knife skittered across the cracked pavement. It must have bounced off his canteen bottle.

"What the hell was that for?" he asked, addressing the forest.

"The road at your back, between the two buildings: take it."

Gladly, he thought and hurried toward the city lights on the far shore. The seawall came into view. Soon he'd be within sprinting distance of his kayak.

"Stop!"

He halted and clenched his jaw to hide his irritation.

"You see that building ahead, with the arched windows? Head in there."

The morgue and pathology building. Originally, it had been a church, though God had abandoned the structure long ago. "No way," Finn stated even as he memorized the placement of its windows and door, which would orientate him once inside.

A scalpel sailed past his right shoulder.

"That was intentionally long."

As soon as he entered that building, she'd once again have him cornered.

He turned to face her.

Just visible from the light pollution, she was standing at the edge of the ivy lane.

"Move it, Gettler!" she barked. "Your dad will be here soon."

"You didn't need to lie; you already had me by the balls."

"I didn't lie. Not entirely. I did speak to Lily." She motioned toward the foreboding, two-story brick structure.

Blood rushed to his ears. "So, what did you really say?"

"That she'll have to find a new boyfriend," she said, tossing a scalpel toward the brooding sky.

Horrified, Finn reflexively shielded his chest and face.

Catching the knife, she continued, "It may take her a while to realize it, but she'll be far better off without you. Now get going."

Clenching the flashlight—his only weapon—he strode toward the dark doorway, suddenly less confident in his conviction that he couldn't possibly hurt a woman who'd been as damaged as her scars suggested.

1910–1915

May 1910

Cora hugged her shins over her shroud and tried to ignore the water lapping the dock below her. Only because of O'Toole, seated beside her with his fishing rod, had she ventured this close to the river in which she'd almost drowned two and a half years ago.

The bacteria density of the specimens collected after her and Mary's failed escape had almost matched those taken the day before. She hadn't needed the doctor's "scientific mind" to deduce that her immunities worked only while on the island. Something—or some being—was keeping her here. She was still trying to figure out what, and why, but she did have a theory too audacious to voice.

Knowing the cause wouldn't make her existence any less lonely, or the doctor's procedures any less agonizing. But it might make it easier not to give up. Lately the temptation had been strong.

Three months earlier, after three years of forced quarantine for Mary, the new health commissioner had granted her permission to return to the city, provided she find employment that didn't involve cooking. Ever since Mary's solicitor, Francis O'Neil, had taken on her case pro bono a year earlier, Cora had been steeling herself for the loss of her friend. Yet every morning since their tear-streaked good-bye, while drinking her tea alone, Cora had still felt as hollow as the stem of a joe-pye weed.

Similarly, Canne, who'd tossed them a newspaper each morning, then left a shell or flower on Mary's windowsill each evening, had been acting like a dogwood that hadn't sprung to life with the rest of North Brother's ornamental trees and shrubs.

His feelings for Mary had bloomed last winter when she'd learned that Alfred, who in twenty years as Mary's beau hadn't asked for her hand, had instead proposed to another woman. While Cora had been fleeing the bungalow to avoid being inadvertently hit by a kettle, tea box, or hairbrush—all items Mary regularly hurled against the walls of the one-room shack—she'd passed Canne. Halfheartedly clearing away the dried stalks of pansies and snapdragons, which he planted in front of Mary's porch each spring, he'd looked more hopeful than sympathetic.

Occasionally, the two women had chatted about Canne's obvious fondness for Mary, who'd made it clear that she had no interest in "that little man." Watching him try to win Mary's heart had pained Cora. For his sake, she was glad Mary had left. Over time, Canne would forget her, whereas Cora still saw Linnaeus Jones seven days a week. A year ago, he'd married nurse Carlton at St. John-by-the-Sea. From the lawn, Cora had listened to the ceremony. She wished she hadn't.

Afterward, whenever she saw his sleek, black hair and broad shoulders from afar, she ducked her head to hide her eyes—the only outward evidence that she was as human as the rest of them.

Also, she'd given up on the possibility that Dr. Gettler's humanity would return with the curative passage of time. No longer did he attend the church services, despite now being on the island every Sunday. And he limited his interaction with the staff and patients to the bare minimum required to maintain his position. Not even for his son could he rouse the compassion that had once made the nurses and patients adore him. As far as Cora could tell, he rarely visited the now nine-year-old boy, still living with a nanny in Kleindeutschland.

O'Toole had become her only friend.

Now he jerked the pole twice. "*Feck.* It got away." With a groan, he heaved his body to a standing position and reeled in the line.

Whatever he caught today, nurse O'Toole would fry in the cafeteria kitchen for their children. In two hours they would return on the same ferry that delivered them each morning to the Lower East Side, where they attended Public School 188. According to O'Toole, it was the largest in the world, occupying an entire block of Houston Street. To spend just one day as a student there, Cora would give up her golden guinea.

An empty hook rose from the river.

"Bad *cess*, that's all I've caught today," O'Toole muttered, moving to the end of the pier, where the wind carried away the stench of the small fish he'd sliced as bait.

Bad luck is right, Cora thought. Her gaze fell from the Queens shoreline to the whitecaps of the river, and she shivered. "Maybe the sharks have eaten all the striped bass." She bit her lip. Not once since her battle with the currents had she mentioned those beasts.

He laughed and rubbed his ruddy nose with the side of his fish-juiced hand. "Sharks? The ship traffic chased all those away a century ago."

Would he think I'm mad? She inhaled the salty air and raised her cheeks to the sharp wind. Here on the southeastern dock, the farthest accessible point from the hospital, she could safely remove the wrap that shielded her breath. As the days had carried her farther from that encounter, she'd begun second-guessing the creatures' existence. Maybe she was insane. O'Toole would tell her the truth.

She waited for him to cast his line and sit back down.

The reek of his sweat permeated the air once again. Cora didn't mind; she cherished being this close to another human.

"O'Toole?"

"Yes, my sweet lass?"

"That day I almost drowned. If I were to tell you that a pair of sharks . . . saved me. Would you . . . Am I crazy?"

O'Toole bellowed, the deep sound echoing off the water.

Humiliated, she reached for her hood.

He quieted and gripped her arm. "Hold on, I didn't mean to make you feel bad."

"I must have imagined it. I must have been delirious from the fever."

O'Toole stuffed his fishing pole under his armpit and twisted his massive torso to face her. "People say I laugh too much for an orderly at a contagion hospital, but laughter—and me family—are the only things that get me through each day on this godforsaken rock. The idea of guardian angel sharks: it's thrilling." He put his paw on her glove. "I hope they weren't an illusion. You need a few angels on your side."

She peered at him through her lashes. "Why would they help me?" she asked despite having her own idea. In her satchel she carried the pastor's note with the Bible verse about Jesus cleansing the leper. Although time and wear had faded the ink, and she was no leper, its potential application to her had been gathering strength deep within her.

O'Toole motioned to the campus behind them. "I've always thought there's something mystical going on with you and this place."

Reflexively, she touched the wool covering her chest, beneath which lay her crucifix pendant. "Mystical?"

"I don't mean no disrespect to the Good Lord," he said, crossing himself, "but I don't think He's all that exists. The Indians, who used this island as fishing grounds, they have their own set of spirits. Maybe those sharks were making sure you stay put on what may very well be sacred land."

She clutched her bag and thought of the bird stone within it. "Why me?"

"Who's ta know?" He raised his line and cursed the empty hook. "Though 'chosen' you clearly are."

"I don't want to be," she snapped, standing and turning inland. She'd seen more than enough of the river to last a lifetime, however long that might be. "I'd rather be dead than live like this," she said, sweeping her hand across her cloak.

Her cheeks felt hot, and she realized she was crying. "I should jump in now and let the current carry me out to sea. Then we'll know for sure about those sharks."

O'Toole glanced toward the outbuildings, presumably to ensure that no one was watching, and grabbed her shoulders. "You can't do that," he said, his voice hitching. "I can't lose one of my best friends."

Overwhelmed, and flattered by his characterization of her, she replied, "You're one of my best friends, too. Actually, the only one I've got left," she finished bitterly.

He ruffled her hair. "Then I guess you'll stay put so I don't have to dive in after you." He smiled, his full cheeks nearly swallowing his eyes. "The amount of meat I've got on me bones . . . those sharks of yours would have a field day."

She mirrored his smile. "They wouldn't stand a chance against you."

"Perhaps. Seriously, though, I don't understand your circumstances any better than you do. But I'm certain that you will bring good to mankind."

Cora squirmed at his sudden change in demeanor.

His hand returned to her shoulder, gripping it more tightly than she knew he'd intended. "I'm here for you, in any way you need. Always have been, always will be. You know that. I understand that your blessings are also a curse. But if you don't let the doctor finish his work, then your sister's death will have been in vain."

She leaned away. "You sound like him."

O'Toole shrugged. "Whatever greater force that's at work here, perhaps Rolene's and Ingrid's drownings were by its design."

The possibility made her sick to her stomach, and she curled forward.

He rubbed the top of her head, and his touch sent a wave of warmth through her.

"Trust in God. And yourself. Miss McSorley, that leper's cloak may fool others, but I know who you are: the descendant of a great Celtic warrior. And no one of that bloodline—not even a woman—would ever give up."

Cora looked up at his fiery orange hair, cresting this mountain of a man. *Far more likely*, she thought, *he's the one of warrior descent*. But O'Toole was right in one regard: she had to carry on. For Maeve's sake. And because of her pact with God.

She looked at the watch that Dr. Gettler had given her for her nineteenth birthday. In ten minutes they had their standing appointment for her weekly blood draw.

"I need to go. The doctor hates it when I'm late."

O'Toole sighed and cast his hook. "As long as you walk tall, with your head high, he can never own you."

Smiling weakly, she rewrapped the cloth around her head and pulled on the hood.

As she neared the building, her feet began to drag.

Who was O'Toole kidding? She was no warrior.

March 1915

The musty air within the bungalow felt like a second layer of wool pressing against Cora, yet she resisted the urge to step outside. Mary had unpacked most of her suitcase, without chucking a single one of her possessions across the room. After five years of freedom, Cora's friend had been forced back into isolation permanently, as the newspapers had proclaimed, but not with her spirit intact.

"Dr. Soper was right," Mary whispered in the Irish brogue that reminded Cora of her mother. "Disease and death follow me everywhere I go." Keeping her back to Cora, she arranged her comb, jar of hairpins, and hair powder on the tray beneath her mirror. "I was wrong. In so many ways."

There were no words of condolence that wouldn't ring empty. A month ago, a typhoid fever outbreak at Sloane Maternity Ward had infected twenty-five patients, two of whom had died. Unbeknownst to health authorities, Mary had been working there as a cook.

Mary stared into the mirror. By her furrowed brow, Cora could tell that her friend abhorred the person she saw.

"Sixteen years ago," Mary said, pinching the far corners of her eyes, "I was the cook at the Kirkenbauer estate. Little Tobias, he used to love my peach ice cream. He died from typhoid fever. His mom and the butler too."

"I'm so sorry," Cora murmured, her friend's loss echoing through her own hollow spaces.

Mary turned away from the mirror and began unpacking the blouses and wool skirts she'd laundered and ironed herself throughout her last stay at Riverside.

Cora understood: all these years, Mary had been refusing to believe she was a germ carrier because that would have meant accepting responsibility for the little boy's death. As a result, how many more had been lost? Cora wondered if Mary knew, or had even tried to guess.

"Sour milk," Mary muttered and shoved a stack of shirts into her small dresser. "I feel like I've drunk a pitcherful."

Cora knew that sensation; she'd often felt it herself. Frequently she'd wondered how many people she'd inadvertently infected despite her isolation. In addition to the five people she'd sickened in the first year following Maeve's death, she suspected that she'd been responsible for at least six other cases, including two deaths. Once, she'd asked Dr. Gettler if he could figure it out from the hospital records.

He'd replied that the potential benefit for the greater good far outweighed any isolated casualties; tallying the *sacrifices* would be an unproductive distraction.

Cora loathed that word.

"I know how you feel," she said softly to her friend.

"Aw, *shite*." Mary tugged the other wooden chair to the far side of the room and flopped onto it. "We're a sorry pair, aren't we?"

Cora raised her head so Mary could see her eyes beneath the overhang of her hood. "If I tell you I'm glad you're back, will that sound selfish?"

For the first time since Cora had watched her step off the ferry that morning, Mary smiled. "No, it would sound human. I'm equally glad you're stuck here." She inspected her hands, roughened from twenty years of plying a trade that involved scalding water. "You're all I've . . . My Alfred, he's dead."

Cora jolted upward. "What? When?" For the past five years, she'd been assuming that Alfred had remained married to Liza Meaney.

"A heroin overdose. My fault, just like the others."

She's been through so much, Cora thought, and she'd been oblivious to it all. Suspecting that Mary would pass along messages intended for Eleanor, Dr. Gettler hadn't allowed Cora to write her, even after Cora had declared that she'd rather have her mother think her dead than know the truth.

"How could that possibly be your fault?" Cora asked, still agitated that she hadn't been there to support her friend.

Mary exhaled and turned away from her reflection. "About four, five years ago, just before Christmas, he was burned something terrible when a lantern exploded in his hands. When the doctor refused to give him more morphine, I started buying him heroin—it was cheaper. To get the money, I sold pies to the other tenants in our . . ." She hiccupped loudly and put her hand to her mouth.

Cora longed to cross the room and hug her friend.

"They wouldn't even let me attend his burial," Mary said, sobbing. "And I can never cook again. I've got nothing left."

Cora's insides twisted at the statement. She reached into her satchel for the envelope she'd kept safe throughout Mary's absence. "It's not much, but—"

"Miss McSorley," Dr. Gettler called through the open window, and her shoulders stiffened. "I need you in the lab, disrobed and ready for surgery. Now."

The scars from her past incisions seared with the dread of whatever he had planned.

"They still want to remove my gallbladder. I won't let them . . ." Mary pursed her lips.

Although Mary had stopped herself, Cora knew the rest of the refrain: ". . . split me open like a pig on the butcher's block." During her first stay at Riverside, Mary had said it more than once. Often Cora had recalled the line as she lay beneath the doctor's scalpel.

Maybe someday Cora would explain why she wished she could have her gallbladder removed, and why she could never go through with it. But not today. Not with Dr. Gettler standing impatiently outside and Mary still so chafed by her mistakes.

"I'm coming!" she hollered.

Mary groaned. "If you're not gointa stand up for yourself, I'll have to find a way to do it for you."

Cora bit her lip. She didn't want to argue with her friend, not on their first day together again. From the envelope in her gloved hand, she shook out two dozen flecks.

"Whatcha got there?"

"The makings of your next crop."

Mary inhaled sharply.

After their failed escape, Alfred had sent her a packet of tomato seeds, and each summer Mary had tended the resulting plants with the care of a nursemaid. At Cora's request, Canne had preserved the seeds from the tomatoes that had ripened after Mary's departure. Often, Cora had recalled the sweet tang of the succulent vegetable, fresh off the vine, but she'd never felt tempted to plant the seeds herself. They wouldn't have tasted as good without Mary beside her. "I kept them, not in the hope that you'd ever be back, but as a remin—"

"Miss McSorley!" Dr. Gettler barked from the lawn.

Cora glanced out the window. Beyond the doctor stood John Canne. He'd put on a fresh collared shirt and was holding a bouquet of gardenias.

"I'd better go. Should I tell Canne you're resting?"

Mary groaned. "Please do." In their old custom she opened the door for Cora and stepped aside.

Cora paused. "I'm sorry. About everything."

"Liar." Mary flashed a weak yet toothy grin.

"You're right. Isolation Island wasn't the same without you." Cora adjusted her cloak and headed toward the doctor, his arms crossed.

"This renewed female companionship is a fantastic development," he said as he began walking. "I'll see that she's treated well."

Surprised, Cora squinted at his back. Maybe his old self hadn't been entirely lost. "How kind of you," she said, following him.

"I'd hoped—expected—to have made a breakthrough by now," he said, glancing back at her. "I'm disappointed in myself. I hate putting you through so much pain. But every day that I fail to replicate your antibodies is another day that thousands of people die from disease. For the sake of those who fall ill tomorrow, and the day after, we have no choice but to double our efforts. The recovery time between procedures, it's been delaying my progress."

Goose bumps shot down her arms. "What does that mean?"

"It means you won't be able to fully heal from one surgery before the next. I'll do everything I can to eliminate your discomfort, but your dedication will be tested. You'll need the support of a friend now more than ever."

They reached the morgue, and her feet refused to carry her over the threshold.

O'Toole's words, after her admission about the sharks, jimmied their way into her consciousness.

Fighting her body's rising cry, she straightened her spine and lifted her chin.

"For Maeve," she whispered and lifted one foot, then the other.

August 2007

August 8

"The door's open," Cora called from behind Finn as he approached the morgue and pathology building. "Don't touch anything. The place is a hot zone."

The notion of a deadly virus, lying in wait, made his skin tingle. Though her claim couldn't be true: Riverside hadn't housed patients with communicable diseases since the 1930s.

"There's a sealed N-Ninety-Five mask at your feet. Put it on, and—"

Thunder rumbled; she waited for the sky to quiet.

"Leave your bag. Then go left, down the hall, and take the stairwell to the roof."

Challenging her claim would only exacerbate her ire, so Finn set down his pack and put on the mask. Almost immediately, the air trapped against his face felt steamy. Adjusting his grip on his flashlight, he stepped inside.

The smell of rot aggressively invaded his nostrils. Pushing the mask against the bridge of his nose, he took in the decomposing, cavernous hallway.

As he passed the nearest room, his flashlight beam landed on a rusted examining table at its center. Vines nearly covered its articulated panels and wheel crank for raising the footrest.

"Keep moving!" Cora shouted from the entrance. "You're at risk!"

He could almost see bacteria crawling on the corrugated tiles and virus particles suspended in the dank air. Her paranoia was getting to him.

Her concern could mean that she intended to let him leave, Finn reasoned. Unless she simply wanted to maintain her leverage.

Watching for debris that could send him flying, he made his way down the hall. Through an open doorway, he spotted what might have been a laboratory. Another led to a room with rusting metal drawers: the morgue.

In the stairwell, he climbed without touching the handrail.

As he neared the top, her footsteps below echoed upward through the chamber and clashed with the wind, howling through the open door to the roof.

Switching off his light, he stepped outside and wrenched off the mask. A gust battered his face, and he breathed in its refreshingly cold fury.

Holding back his hair, he stared at the Manhattan skyline, glittering like a gemstone collection behind glass. Down that river, near the Brooklyn Bridge's eastern tower, Lily had to be a complete wreck.

Whenever her anxiety spiked, Finn would remind her of the statistical improbability of something terrible happening to one of them. The approach had never worked. Tonight she might be proven right.

"Do you see the chain and open cuff?" Cora asked from within the stairwell. "Fasten it to your ankle."

Tethered to a stake, he'd be no better off than a stray dog about to be put down.

He turned on his flashlight to quickly survey the rooftop. To his left, a scattering of bricks and wild grass surrounded a hole. With one of those blocks, he could knock her out.

"Throw the flashlight over. Now."

Since it should withstand the fall, he dropped it over the side of the building where he'd entered and planned to exit.

She cleared her throat menacingly, so he picked his way over to the manacles and pretended to snap the open ring around his ankle.

Lightning sliced the sky, illuminating the two smokestacks across the road from the morgue. The top of the taller flue resembled a crown of thorns. It must have been struck, with the energy surge having thrown the topmost bricks here. His stomach churned. This was a stupid place to be during a storm.

The hinges of the door squeaked, and he wheeled toward the noise.

Cora stood with her gloved hands on her hips. "I didn't hear a . . ." She inhaled sharply and adjusted her respirator. "Idiot. Put your mask back on."

His skin crawling with imagined microbes, Finn shoved the shield onto his face.

"Your father had better listening skills when he was four." She locked the door and stuffed the key ring into her shoulder bag. "I bet Sylvia used some sort of new-age parenting philosophy on you." The corners of her eyes crinkled. "Ulrich absolutely detested her."

The way she spoke about him was eerie, considering he'd died when she'd been just a child.

Her eyes narrowed. "The click." She pointed at his ankle. "I need to hear it."

He groaned but fastened the cuff. The chain was tethered to a metal eyehook embedded in the asphalt roof. To test its strength, he took a subtle step back. The bolt didn't budge.

She huffed. "I got those cuffs from an escaped Rikers convict; you think I couldn't handle securing that pin?"

Finn appraised her bare biceps. "I wasn't underestimating you; I was overestimating myself."

She sniffed—a weak attempt to conceal a chuckle—and sat with her back to the wall, the gaping hole between them.

The sky sizzled and a bolt snaked down the lightning rod atop the Empire State Building. Almost instantaneously, a sharp crack followed the billion-volt electrical surge.

Nonchalantly, he kicked a rock into the crevice. "Did you know it's a myth that lightning always strikes the highest point? We're—you're—not safe here."

"Really? Then how do you explain that?" She pointed at the smokestack.

"If there's a tall object within the small area at the end of a stepped leader's trajectory, that's where it'll hit. But when the discharge is initiated, miles above, it's 'blind' to whatever's on the ground."

"Interesting. I haven't—hadn't—learned anything new in years."

His pulse quickened. Maybe he *could* talk his way free.

"You said you're an architect?" she asked. "Not a doctor?"

He shifted his feet, and the cuff jerked his ankle. "That's right."

"Ulrich didn't give your dad a choice, but I know Rollie would have picked medicine anyway. He loves to heal. I have to give him credit for that. The fact that you didn't follow family tradition is surprising though. Unsettling, actually."

"How so?"

"Every Gettler has a role to fill."

One of his father's pet phrases, from her tongue, made him shiver. "What's that supposed to mean?"

"Never mind."

By her clamped shut lips, he knew not to press her. To regain the casual tone their conversation had lost, he sat down. "I've always been fascinated by light waves and electrical currents."

Cora straightened. "Right," she said to herself. "Ulrich would have approved of that."

"Hardly: I'm an exterior lighting designer."

"A what?" she asked, her brow furrowed.

"Essentially, billionaires hire me to light their estates."

"Rollie's okay with that?"

"He thinks it's a waste of my talent, but I fell into the opportunity through a friend. It pays better than civil work."

By the arching of her eyebrows, he knew she was intrigued.

"This place could look amazing. Wherever I go, my brain automatically thinks about placement, voltage, lumens. I've already outlined a rough plan for this island in my head. Completely within the interior so that nothing would be visible to the patrols. And the lamps would be concealed. Once I'm back in my office, I can whip up a design in CAD."

He let the idea of his release linger.

"There's no power source." She coughed softly. "It wouldn't work."

He could tell by the yearning in her tone that she'd envisioned the effect.

"They could be solar powered."

"I don't understand," she said, her brow furrowed in frustration.

She really had been living under a rock. Or, rather, on a rock. "We could wire photovoltaic cells—"

She scrunched her nose. "Forget it. Your father's on his way, and what I need from him is far more important than some pretty lights in the trees."

Pretending to feel slighted, Finn cast his eyes down.

"That was mean. I'm sorry."

"You'll let me go—unharmed—once my dad tells you about the tunnel?"

"*If* he tells me. In this case, that subordinating conjunction is quite conditional." She twisted to face a hole in the wall. "No sign of him yet."

"About that lightning: you shouldn't be up here. It's not safe."

"It won't kill me."

"Statistically speaking, that's true. But it could."

"No. It *won't*." She shifted to look at him. "Usually, during electrical storms, I climb the taller smokestack. You can't see it, but I built a platform within its crown."

His eyes widened. "That's ridiculous. No offense."

Cora sighed. "I can't believe I have to explain this to a Gettler." She drummed her fingers against her frayed khakis. "The lightning won't kill me. Neither will any other act of nature. Through all these years, the island's kept me alive for a reason. Whatever greater force is at work here, it has a purpose for me. It's given me a gift that someday will save countless others. If I die, the gift dies with me."

"Where I come from, that's called a 'Jesus complex.'"

"Actually," she said, clutching her necklace, "to the contrary, I know that I'm just another one of God's children. I have to believe that He'll reward my devotion by cleansing me. After the *right* virologists figure out how to use my blood to cure others."

Despite the madness of her claims, Finn had a sinking feeling that she was connected to his family's research.

If he gave any indication that he was aware of their mission, his chances of getting off this roof alive would plummet. He pointed at the jagged top of the flue. "Were you up there when it was struck?"

She shook her head. "That day, it was your . . . But someday, once the right man—not a Gettler—has figured out how to harvest and replicate my antibodies, it will be me that lightning strikes." She looked up. "Then I'll see Maeve and my mother again, and meet my father."

"You think God will let you stroll through his pearly gates if you kill me?"

She folded her hands. "There'll be plenty of time to atone for that sin." In the dim light from the city, her blue eyes looked like ice blocks.

Reflexively, he pulled his knees to his chest, and the chain jangled. "If my dad didn't give you those scars, then who did?"

"The other men in your family." She ran her finger across one of the displaced bricks. "By far, Rollie's always been the kindest. But he, too, has used me. And treated me like I'm their property." She rapped the brick against another, then tossed it aside. "I'm their human guinea pig. Did you know George Bernard Shaw coined that phrase?"

"No, though it doesn't surprise me. My mom's a big fan."

"He's one of my favorite writers," Cora continued, "and not just because he was a vivisectionist." Thunder crackled almost directly overhead, yet she didn't flinch. "Unfortunately, that movement didn't benefit me. For the past hundred and five years, four generations of your family have been experimenting on me."

Laughter erupted from his closed lips. The release felt good, so he let it flow until he had to catch his breath. "That's impossible."

"I wish that were the case."

"There's no way you're that old."

"Thus, your family's obsession." She checked the spy hole behind her, then tilted her head from side to side, as if carrying on an internal debate.

Fearful that whatever Rollie and Kristian had done to her had driven her mad, Finn waited for her attention to return to him.

With a heavy sigh, she stood up.

"I suppose it's nothing he hasn't already seen," she said aloud but to herself—or the island.

Her gloved hands shaking, she removed her scalpel pouch and messenger bag and set them beside her.

"Please, don't," he begged.

Facing away from him, she unbuttoned her pants and let them fall to her ankles.

He ducked his chin, but his reaction hadn't been fast enough: he'd already glimpsed pale, sinewy thighs below her tank-top hem. "Why are you doing this?"

"You wanted proof," she said, her voice muffled by her shirt as it passed over her head.

This felt wrong, even more so than when he'd come upon her showering. Yet the awareness of this naked woman before him made his groin throb. He sensed that she wouldn't redress until he'd looked, so he raised his gaze.

She'd removed her tank top.

Her torso resembled the scarred earth of a battlefield.

Looking him square in the eyes, she touched her midsection. "Dr. Otto Gettler, pancreatic tissue removal, 1907." Her hand moved upward. "Dr. Ulrich Gettler, lung tissue transplantation, 1950." She fingered the base of her throat. "This one, too, Dr. Ulrich Gettler, thyroid tissue sample, 1982."

She ran her finger along a horizontal scar below her belly button. Trembling, she bit her knuckle and looked to the sky.

If she started to cry, he didn't know what he would do.

Her attention snapped back to him, and she pointed to her lumbar spine. "Dr. Kristian Gettler, spinal tap, 2000."

Finn gasped.

"Your father's not aware of that one," she said, arching her eyebrows. "Kristian bought my silence."

Blackness swallowed her; he thought he must have passed out. Then everything flashed white. Rumbling filled his ears, and he shook his head to clear his vision. She was pointing at a series of scars on her thigh. "Dr. Ulrich Gettler, bacterial battery, 1936."

His esophagus heaved, and he clamped his hand over the N-95. This had to be a sick nightmare. Maybe he was still asleep in the cell. No, he couldn't have dreamed this up.

"Put your clothes back on, please."

"Why? You can't handle what your family's done to me?"

It can't possibly be true. Yet the memory of one of Sylvia's old poems suggested otherwise. As a teenager, he'd found it in her desk drawer. So disturbing, the verses had stayed with him. He'd asked her why she'd written about men hurting a scarred woman. Sylvia had answered that it was a metaphor relating to the women's rights movement.

Now Finn wished he could dismiss those stanzas as coincidence. The history she was describing didn't jibe with an effort to generate and harvest "super" antibodies. Either she was lying about the source of those scars, or he knew far less about the true nature of his family's work than he'd thought.

Cora rotated ninety degrees, and he gaped at the silhouette of her body.

"Dr. Ulrich Gettler," she clawed at the patch of thick whip-mark scars on her back, "pain tolerance testing, 1959."

Feeling suffocated, he tore off the mask.

She jerked up her pants, grabbed her top, and sprinted to the far wall. "The air I've breathed: it's not safe for you."

Willing to do anything to appease her, he covered his face again.

She began to put on her tank top, so he stared at the shackle around his ankle. He had to convince her that he was on her side, which would require playing along with her wild claims. "Why haven't you flagged down one of the patrols?"

She settled onto the ground. "The police would never believe my story. They'd haul me away, and as soon as we reached deeper water, I'd be dead. Shortly after that, so would they."

"Right. Because of *VZ*."

"And my seven other pests."

"Pests? Like rats?"

"As in *pestilences*. I have to stay here because of them." She wrapped her arms around her middle. "For whatever reason, they only turn on me when I leave this island. There's a force here that keeps them dormant. I think it's God, though it could be another spirit, an element in the air, magnetism in the rock, or something buried deep within the schist. Whatever the source, it's real."

"I believe you," he said, not sure that he did.

"I used to love swimming, before the *Slocum*." Cora briefly covered her eyes. "Those waves, crashing on the beach." She motioned for him to listen. "They're like prison bars that never stop clang—"

She tensed, and he could tell she'd detected a foreign sound. Wondering if it was Rollie, he listened.

Cora army-crawled to the wall and looked through a chink. "They're here."

"They?"

"I specifically told Rollie not to bring Kristian," she said, scowling. "Let them see you."

Finn scrambled to his feet. "I'm up here!" He lunged toward the wall, and the chain jerked him back. Leaning forward, he caught sight of two figures in front of the physical plant, dressed in black . . . bio hazmat gear.

Holy shit.

This *was* a hot zone. Crushing the respirator mask against his face, he backed as far away from Cora as the chain allowed.

"*Now* you believe me," she said with a sneer.

His forehead burned, and the low, Queens skyline wavered.

"Let him go!" Rollie yelled.

Cora rose slightly from her crouched position. "Not a chance. He's a Gettler."

"What do you want?" bellowed Kristian.

"Where's the tunnel?"

"Slightly southeast of 'Fuck you,'" Kristian replied.

Shocked, Finn grunted with disgust. He'd never heard Kristian speak that way to anyone before, aside from when he and Finn were ribbing each other. "Dad, just do what she says."

"The mutt takes orders; she doesn't give them," Kristian said, and Rollie raised his hand to silence him.

Appalled by this new side of Kristian, Finn strained to see his brother's face behind his visor.

"We think her antibodies can help your mom!" Rollie yelled.

Had they succeeded in isolating the chemical reagent from the ruins? But then why would they need Cora's antibodies if they could directly give Sylvia the immune system-boosting compound?

Raindrops landed on Finn's forehead. He wiped them away and looked at Cora questioningly.

She grabbed a brick and tested its heft. "They've never been able to replicate this island's effect on anyone else. So they want to use me. To find a cure for her Lyme."

A ringing sounded in Finn's ears, and vertigo seized him. His mother lived with these same sensations. He spread his arms to steady himself. *Could this woman hold the key to curing his mom?* he wondered.

Suddenly Cora seemed a lot less crazy and a hell of a lot more vulnerable.

If she did possess special immunities, there might be some truth in her other claims as well. The fact that Rollie had kept her existence hidden from Finn certainly supported that possibility. A surge of pain shot from the pinched nerve in his neck. He shuffled closer to the wall. The whole thing was bizarre, and as even the slightest detail became plausible, Finn was feeling spooked. "What have you been doing to her?"

The wind howled.

"I need to know."

As he waited for Rollie to respond, her list of his family's transgressions cycled through his mind. Reality was proving to be far worse than anything he'd imagined after finding that note in their shed.

"She's an asymptomatic carrier," Rollie said. "I was working to eradicate her pathogens. Until 2001, when she asked me to stop."

"But you didn't listen to her, or Mom." Finn thought of the bats and Kristian's obsession with how woefully underprepared the world was for an "inevitable" mass pandemic. Curing Lyme couldn't be their only objective. With so much at stake, they wouldn't have allocated any of their time or resources to Cora's welfare. "I don't buy that your research has been at all for her benefit."

"That's not true," Kristian said. "We've made several advancements with her case. We're so close to getting her back to Manhattan."

"They keep feeding me that line. Please! Maybe Otto originally wanted to fix me, but that hope died with his wife and daughter."

Unsure what to think or whom to believe, Finn pivoted to face Rollie, who stretched his arms toward Finn. "I did suspend my work, for a year. But then your mom, the arthritis, and ongoing nerve damage . . ."

"You think Cora's antibodies can cure her?"

"Yes," he said, stepping closer to the building so Finn could better hear him. "If we can harvest Cora's autoimmune T-cells. And inject them into Mom. It should wipe out the Lyme bacteria in her synovial fluid."

Finn pictured Sylvia gripping a pen, her slanted cursive flowing across a journal page. It had been almost four years since she'd written her last poem.

He studied the woman whose blood might be able to save Sylvia, the same woman who'd apparently been the subject of his mother's note.

Cora shifted forward onto her knees. "I won't let him inject me with a ninth microbe," she said, glaring at Finn. "They claim they only want blood samples, but I know Kristian would cut me open again if given a chance." As she rose, she pulled Finn's utility knife from her shoulder bag and extended its blade.

"Rollie, tell me where your tunnel is or I'll"—she nicked her finger with the blade—"infect your son with all eight of my germs."

"No!" Rollie shouted.

"Tell her," Finn demanded, kicking to yank free the bolt anchoring the chain.

Kristian raised a sleek gun, and Cora ducked down against the brick wall.

"Empty that tranquilizer, now!" she screamed, taking a step back, closer to Finn.

Adrenaline and fury surging through his blood, Finn tried to lunge away from her, but already the chain contained no slack.

Rollie snatched the air gun from Kristian. "I'm removing the dart," he called to Cora, and she popped her head up just high enough to watch.

"Store it with the others," she yelled, "and throw me the case, or Finn dies now."

Kristian pivoted away from Rollie, who sidestepped to close the gap. Their heads came together, and Finn could tell they were arguing.

A moment later, Kristian fiddled with the dart case and hurled it toward them.

It landed on the roof, near Cora, with a *crack*.

Her eyes gleaming, she snatched the container with her clean hand and shoved it into her messenger bag. "I'd been wanting a few of these," she said, getting to her feet.

Her voice had held that same gleeful yet menacing tone as when she'd been wearing the World War II gas mask.

With the knife raised, she glanced at the pair below, then took a step toward Finn.

Behind her, the eastern sky, almost overtaken by the storm, had lightened to a midnight blue. Soon the sun would rise unseen.

"Dad, just tell her!" He tugged on the chain, but the eye hook remained lodged in the concrete.

"*Ricksettia prowazekii*!" she shouted. "You've got till I've finished naming the other seven. Then my blood meets his."

Rollie rocked on his heels, and Kristian grabbed his arm. "We're micrometers away from Pasteur's dream of eradicating disease—Otto's dream, too. If you give in to her, a hundred years of progress will be wasted. Otto wouldn't have wanted that."

Finn stared at his brother. Kristian couldn't possibly have meant . . . yet his words had been crystal clear.

"*Rubeola.*" She dodged a tangle of bricks.

Rollie shook his head. "He wouldn't have wanted me to sacrifice his great-grandson, either."

"Sacrifice," Kristian said. "That was his motto."

"That's enough," Rollie snapped. "You may be in charge at the hospital, but here, you remember your place."

"Kristian," Finn yelled, "have you gone nuts?! What's wrong with you? I'm your brother."

"Half brother. But Sylvia's just as much my mom as yours. We're so close to her cure."

"*Variola major*!" Cora shouted, seemingly oblivious to the light rain spattering her forehead and chest.

To maximize the distance between himself and any air that escaped her mask, Finn dropped to the ground. Wildly, he searched for an errant brick.

"Zagazig 501."

Finn grimaced.

Cora smirked as blood ran in a rivulet down her finger and smattered on the ground. "What, you haven't heard of that one? It's a deadly strain of Rift Valley fever. The mosquitos here seem to love my blood, which I why I insisted you put on my bug spray." She smiled coldly. "Though surely the rain's washed it all off by now."

"Stop!" a new, higher-pitched voice shrieked from the path.

Lily. Finn sprung to his feet. Although the cloud cover had lightened to an angry gray, the rain still obscured his view. Shielding his eyes, he spotted her yellow life vest.

"You need to leave!" Finn shouted down to her. "Now!"

"No."

He spun eastward. "Kristian, get her out of here."

"I'm on it!" Kristian shouted, rushing to her.

Finn couldn't hear their dialogue over the rising wind, though Lily's excited gesticulations suggested it was a heated exchange.

Lightning tore across the sky, and Finn worried that the bright flashes would trigger a seizure.

Kristian put his arm around her, and she wriggled free.

Rollie joined them, and his hand motions suggested he was attempting to placate her.

"Trust you?" Lily shrieked. "Look at you! In that suit, with your son chained to the roof!" She backed away from Rollie. "She's about to murder my boyfriend. I'm not leaving without him."

Cora whistled. "Quite the spitfire, isn't she?"

Unsuccessfully, Finn tried to stifle a smile.

"Why didn't you call me for help?" Kristian touched Lily's shoulder.

"She warned me about you Gettler men. She may be a crazy bitch, but there's usually some truth in crazy." Backing away from him, she called up to Cora, "Let my boyfriend go."

The expression in her eyes as unyielding as rock, Cora strode to the northern end of the roof and waved the utility knife. "His family has maimed and tortured me, and they will ruin you, too. Leave him while you still can."

"No." Lily's right shoulder jerked.

"Then you're weak," Cora spat.

"Strength is what got me here. He's my soulmate, and I won't leave without him."

Longing to run to her, Finn turned toward the locked stairwell door.

"Your *céadsearc*," Cora murmured, standing stock still. "Who am I to get in the way of such love?"

Afraid to break the spell that had transcended her anger, he stayed silent.

She twisted the handle of his utility knife, and the metal blade sparked with light. "'Sentimental value.' That's what you said. She gave you this, didn't she?"

Finn sensed the loneliness that had gripped her body. A walking biological weapon, she would never experience such a bond.

He nodded.

"Kind of like with the scalpel you took from me. So now we're even," she said, wiping the blade clean, then folding it closed and dropping it into her scalpel pouch. From her shoulder bag she pulled a strip of cloth and bandaged her finger.

"A fair trade," he said, trembling with relief that she'd decided not to use it on him.

Suddenly, sheets of rain pummeled them.

Finn felt as if he were suspended underwater. He ripped off his mask.

To block the deluge, he put his arms over his head. Still, he could barely see Cora. He wanted to do something for her, but offering friendship would seem like an empty, desperate gesture.

"The key to your cuffs," she said, seemingly unperturbed by the downpour, although she too had removed her mask. "It's under a small, flat rock, two feet from the bolt."

He flinched in surprise, both at her revelation and her sudden magnanimity.

She leaped over the hole and dashed across the roof. In front of the stairwell, she dug through her shoulder bag, removed a key from her ring, and shoved it into the lock but didn't turn it.

Then she lifted one end of a wooden beam from flush against the eastern wall. Working her hands down the wet wood, she raised the end skyward.

A catwalk. To avoid Rollie and Kristian on the ground, she clearly planned to cross over their heads to the physical plant's roof. From there she'd be able to reach the tree canopy, where she would disappear.

"Thank you," he said.

Preoccupied, she didn't respond.

Before the rain could sweep away the debris, he had to find that rock and the key beneath it. He raked his fingers through the standing water.

A splash sounded from below.

Finn shot upward and lunged forward to catch a glimpse of Lily.

On the ground, she was convulsing, her hands slapping the mud, her mouth dangerously close to a swelling puddle.

He swung along the arc allowed by his chain.

His dad and brother weren't within his limited view of the street. "Dad! Kristian! Lily needs you!" he shouted.

Finn strained to hear their response.

None came.

"Where are they?" he called to Cora, who'd frozen with her hands above her head, supporting the beam.

She let the wood fall, and it hit the roof with a sharp *bang*.

Gripping the wall, she leaned over its edge and peered at the street. "They must be inside the morgue." Her back straightened, and she grabbed the plank again. "They're planning to ambush me."

He swept his fingers along the flooded asphalt. The water had shifted the rubble. "I'm on my way," he called to Lily, even though she'd likely blacked out.

An echoing *boom* signaled that the far end of Cora's beam had landed on the neighboring building.

"Wait," Finn said, scrambling to his feet.

Standing atop the wall, one foot already on the catwalk, she turned toward him, her hand shielding her eyes from the rain.

"The key. I can't find—Lily—she'll die."

Cora looked from him to the physical plant. "I don't have another."

"But they can save her." He peered into the dark, gaping hole and called to them. The wind swallowed his voice.

He clasped his hands. "Please."

She gazed longingly at the forest.

"Lily's innocent."

"I know that." She raised her face toward the thunderheads, and the rain lashed her cheeks. Her lips were moving.

If she were consulting God, Lily might have a chance, Finn concluded. "We're running out of time."

Her eyes snapped open, and she hopped off the wall and unlocked the stairwell door.

"What are you doing?"

"Letting myself get ambushed. *Obviously*."

Her hand fluttered to the pouch on her hip. "No, too risky," she murmured and hung her sack of scalpels and messenger bag on a makeshift hook within the stairwell. "It's the fastest way to get their attention," she said and began her descent. "I'll tell them . . ." Her voice faded.

Finn stared at the dark doorway. He couldn't believe she'd martyr herself for a woman she didn't know after all his family had done to her.

Moments later, a high-pitched scream echoed from deep within the morgue.

A sharp *thud* echoed upward, and Finn pictured his brother slamming Cora's body against a wall.

Either they'd knocked her out before she'd had a chance to speak or she was too big a prize. No, they would never intentionally leave Lily to die.

His fingers connected with jagged metal, and he whooped with relief.

While the wind roared with hurricane force, he unlocked the cuff and scrambled to his feet.

Lily's face might already be submerged, he knew.

Through the water, he sprinted to the stairwell. A gale banged the door shut, and he fought to open it.

Swiping at his eyes, he looked toward the heart of the storm south of the harbor. His mouth fell open.

Beyond the farthest bridge, a funnel was tearing its way across the horizon.

A tornado. In New York City.

Moments Later

The twister swirled over Brooklyn. Despite the distance, the air racing past Finn howled. Shielding his eyes from the deluge, he watched the funnel long enough to confirm it wasn't headed their way. Not yet at least. If Cora had conjured the freak phenomenon, it would be no less astonishing than her other superhuman abilities.

He darted inside and almost slipped on the slick stairs. Reaching for the wall to steady himself, his hand brushed against her messenger bag, hanging from a piece of rebar. The satchel had gaped open, revealing the dart case, which he jammed into a pocket of his cargo pants.

Avoiding the handrail, he stepped forward into the darkness and tested the traction on the steps. Guided by memory, he worked his way down.

"Dad, Kristian!" he shouted.

Only his echo responded.

If Cora had failed, Lily might be dead already.

Picturing water, thick with sediment, pouring past her clacking teeth, he made a beeline for the patch of weak daylight that marked his exit, and burst outside.

Rain flew at him sideways. Shielding his eyes, he reoriented himself and charged through the mud.

"Let me go!" Cora shrieked from behind him.

Unwilling to waste even a second, Finn didn't look back.

He rounded the corner.

Partially submerged in a puddle, Lily's body lay motionless, her limbs splayed.

Shouting her name, he ran to her.

Driven by the wind, small waves were breaking against her mouth and nose. He hooked his arms under her armpits and dragged her from the water.

Crouching over her, he shielded her face from the rain and checked for breathing.

No, God, please no.

Desperately, Finn began chest compressions. *Rollie or Kristian should be doing this*, he thought. Without disrupting his rhythm, he yelled for help.

The windstorm drowned his plea.

If he stopped to find them, Lily could lapse into brain death. *If she dies, because of their obsession with that woman . . .* He would never forgive them.

Grunting out each number, he reached thirty and put his ear to her face. *Nothing.*

He pinched her nose, twice infused her mouth with air, and resumed the compressions. "Come on, Lil. Come back to me."

Abruptly, the downpour began to abate.

An eerie, cobalt glow permeated the gray sky, and the wind had weakened to an angry whisper.

Yelling for help, he started another round.

"Finn, come here," Kristian called from the side of the morgue where Finn had exited.

His heart pounding with renewed hope, he straightened but kept the compressions going. "I can't. Doing CPR. I need you!"

"Come help me, and Dad will go to Lily."

Help with what?

The thought of leaving Lily alone chilled his cold, wet skin. What if Rollie didn't reach her in time?

"Now!" Kristian demanded.

With no alternative, Finn gave Lily two final mouthfuls of air and raced around the corner of the building.

From behind her, Kristian was bear-hugging Cora.

In response to Finn's calls for help, Kristian must have carried her this far, Finn surmised.

"We thought it was a trick," Kristian grunted as Cora thrashed. "Hold still," he hissed and shook her hard.

"She lies all the time," he said to Finn. "We didn't believe she'd give herself up. Certainly not to help one of ours."

Twenty feet from the struggling pair, Rollie was stripping off his hazmat suit. "I'm going to Lily." He tossed a syringe case near Finn's feet.

Rollie sprinted past them, giving Cora a wide berth.

Longing to join his dad, Finn swayed. There, he would merely be watching, praying, as Rollie tried to resuscitate her. Whereas if he stayed here, he could try to compel Kristian—through reason or force—to free the woman who'd selflessly attempted to help his girlfriend.

"Let her go!" Finn commanded.

"Not till you inject her with that." Kristian jerked his chin toward the ground.

In the mud near the case, Finn spotted his flashlight. He scooped up both objects and clipped the flashlight to his belt loop. With the bottom of his soaked T-shirt, he swiped clean the thin plastic container to read its label: *BBSCV-112.*

"What is this?" Finn asked.

"*Borrelia burgdorferi.*" Kristian tightened his grip, and Cora gasped for air.

"That can't be all," Finn said, just as Cora raised both legs and drove her boots backward, kicking Kristian's shins.

He yelped in pain but didn't loosen his hold.

Twisting, she jabbed her elbow into his collarbone, and her wet braid smacked the shield in his hood.

"I can't hold her much longer," Kristian said, attempting to wipe the visor. "Do it now, so I can help Dad."

"This is wrong." Still gripping the syringe case, Finn put his hands to his hips, and his free hand brushed against his flashlight. His biceps fired, and he felt a sudden urge to clock his brother with the military-grade tool. "I won't let you hurt her," he warned through clenched teeth, his fingers squeezing open the hook.

Cora stopped struggling, and her body slackened against Kristian's chest.

"This is Mom's only hope," Kristian pleaded.

Suddenly Finn saw the brother who often sat beside their mom's wheelchair for hours, simply holding her hand, and he wavered. He knew that each time Kristian lost a pediatric patient in his neurology clinic, he closed his office door and bawled—once, Finn had arrived early to join him for lunch and caught him in the act.

That same man stood before Finn now, plainly desperate to save their mother, and convinced that this was their best shot at doing so.

"If we can eradicate the drug-resistant bacteria," Kristian said firmly, "it'll be easier to reverse the nerve and arthritic damage."

He'd made it sound so easy, so *plausible* for their mother to be once again pain free.

Torn, Finn shifted his focus to Cora's face and took in her sheer terror.

It can't happen this way, he knew, and certainly not along with whatever else that serum contained. Shaking his head, Finn released the flashlight's clip from his belt loop. "Let her go."

Cora pitched her head and shoulders forward, clearly preparing to bolt if given a chance.

Kristian clutched his forearms to strengthen his viselike hold and stepped toward Finn, bringing Cora with him. "Give me the needle."

Raising the flashlight in his right hand, Finn shifted the case in his other hand to behind his back. Any blow he could land would disable his brother long enough for Cora to flee.

Kristian exhaled loudly through his respirator. "What do you think you're gonna do with that? Hit me?" He jolted Cora upward—a human shield.

He couldn't risk striking her, Finn decided. But one of the tranquilizer darts wouldn't require the same accuracy-reducing windup. A puncture, however, would potentially expose his brother to Cora's germs. Finn sucked in his breath. With a woman at Kristian's mercy, did he even have a choice?

He dropped the flashlight and syringe case, his body shielding their fall from Kristian's view. Subtly he reached into the side pocket of his pants for the dart container.

Certain that from ten yards away his brother wouldn't be able to distinguish the two cases, he removed a dart. Holding it up, with just the tip exposed, he approached the struggling pair. "Hold her steady."

"How dare you?!" Cora screeched. "I trusted you!"

"What did you expect?" Kristian jerked her hard, stilling her. "We're family."

Finn kept walking, his hand with the dart trembling with rage.

Visibly devastated, Cora remained inert.

"Silly me," Kristian continued. "You can't be expected to understand. It's been more than a century since you've known that kind of love."

Unleashing a piercing, primal shriek, she slammed the heel of her work boot into his rubber overshoe. He grunted and shook her. "Hold still, mutt, it's almost over." He pivoted so her shoulder faced Finn. "Do it now."

Finn raised the needle, and the look of terror and hatred in her turbulent eyes almost froze him.

"Run," he said with a hiss before bringing the dart down into the Teflon of his brother's suit.

"Ahhh," Kristian roared and flailed his arm.

Cora sprang free.

"You . . ." Kristian twisted his arm to inspect the puncture, but obviously consumed by rage, he couldn't direct his attention away from Finn. "You've betrayed us."

"You've got to be fucking kidding me!" Finn screamed inches from Kristian's visor. "You're the one who said my life would be an acceptable loss."

"I was bluffing!"

"Bullshit," Finn snapped, even though he knew it could be true. While Finn had been in middle school, Kristian had been living at home to save money. More than once, Kristian had taken a black eye for him as he'd tried to defend Finn from some asshole teenagers who hung out on their block. At the moment, that didn't matter. It might take as long as two minutes for the drug to knock him out. Finn turned to Cora, who was watching them, stunned. "Go."

Her lips moved, but no sound emerged.

Kristian lunged for her; she sidestepped him and made a beeline for the trees.

Seconds later, her figure merged with the foliage.

A heavy *thump* sounded, and Finn turned toward his brother, who'd landed in the mud.

Frantically, Finn checked to ensure that air could still enter through the filter in Kristian's suit.

Lily. He scrambled to his feet and sprinted toward his girlfriend. Taking the corner so tightly he almost clipped his shoulder, he reached the path beyond the northern wall of the morgue.

In the same spot where Finn had left her, his father crouched over her limp body.

Suddenly, the wind seemed to cease. The chop of the East River softened. Even his dad's form stilled.

Finn couldn't lose her. He just couldn't. While the rest of the world hung suspended in time, he raced to her.

1926–1938

June 15, 1926

In a long, gray woolen suit and Panama hat, the young man could have passed for a city official. But the bouquet of lilies, cradled in one arm, his other hand fisted, told Cora otherwise. She knew why he'd come. The anger-infused sorrow, rising viscerally from him like steam, seemed to merge with her own.

From the church's roof, she watched him descend the ferry gangplank. The last to have disembarked, he stopped halfway down the pier. His head bowed, he seemed to be waiting for the day staff to disperse across the campus before stepping ashore.

Today marked the twenty-second anniversary of the sinking of the *Slocum*. Earlier this morning, Cora had stood on the seawall with Mary, O'Toole, and his wife and prayed into the wind as it scattered their white rose petals. Below her, on the sand where Dr. Gettler had tried to revive his daughter, fluttered a cluster of edelweiss. Every year on this day, he visited the site at sunrise to mourn alone.

By this evening, the beach would be dotted with garlands and small, wooden crosses, though their count had been dwindling. Each year, fewer of the staff who'd helped that day remained at Riverside. Even Linnaeus and his wife had left; eight years ago, he'd filled a prestigious administrative position at Tisch Hospital after its previous occupant died during the Spanish flu. Only then had she realized that seeing him with another woman had been better than not seeing him at all.

Most of the families of the deceased, their hurt assuaged through a new generation of births and marriages, had stopped making the annual memorial visit. Grief had broken that community; Kleindeutschland no longer existed. And with its dissolution, as well as anti-German sentiment following World War I, New York's collective resolve to never forget the *Slocum* had disintegrated.

Finally, the man lifted his face to survey the island, revealing fair skin; a nose as straight and steep as the Alps; and short blond hair, barely visible beneath his hat brim.

Gawking at the familiar look of his Norse features, Cora strained to better see him through the spyhole she'd drilled between two bricks a year ago. Resembling a younger version of Dr. Gettler, the man could be Ulrich, she thought, now twenty-five years old.

Cora wondered if Otto knew. For the past year, since they'd faked her death a second time, burned her cloak, and reintroduced her to Riverside as Canne's new, equally reclusive assistant, she'd spent much of her free time people-watching from this roof, where she couldn't spread her germs. In the nearby hospital building, Mary was cleaning the bottles in Dr. Gettler's lab. She'd threatened to expose the nature of his work unless he made her his technician.

Now Cora peered through the fissure.

Dr. Gettler stood rooted to the footpath, staring in the direction of the pier. Often, when a new theory struck him, his body would become stone still, all his energy seemingly rerouted to turning the wheels of his mind. But, in this moment, Cora could tell from the rapid blinking of his eyes that he was not thinking of his science. The young man had to be his son.

During the past two decades, Otto had not once brought Ulrich back to the island, and he'd rarely mentioned him. Five years ago, Otto had stated in a stiff tone that his son had begun his training to become a surgeon. From his silence on the topic since, Cora figured that the two had become estranged.

His attention on the shallows, Ulrich strode down the dock.

Almost imperceptibly, the doctor raised the heels of his black cap toe shoes; she guessed he was contemplating greeting him.

"Go on," she whispered, "this is your chance to say sorry."

Ulrich noticed him and halted abruptly.

Ten feet apart, they eyed each other, their shoulders squared, arms at their sides, jaws locked shut. The back of Otto's dress shirt had darkened with sweat.

With her hand pressed to her heart, she waited. Throughout the years of specimen collections and unexplained surgeries, she'd repeatedly attempted to divert his attention from her to his former hobbies. Rekindling his interest in building ships in bottles had been out of the question, but she'd hoped he might rediscover the joy he'd once found in either sketching or the Pigs in Clover marble maze games he used to make for the quarantined children. Nothing had worked, so Cora had prayed that someday, through his son, the doctor would find his former self.

"*Willkommen*." The wind carried Otto's stiff voice to Cora. "I'm . . ." He removed his hat. "Did you have a smooth crossing?"

"Tell him you love him," Cora whispered, even though she knew Otto had forgotten that phrase.

"I'm not here to see you." Ulrich turned his shoulder to his father and faced the beach.

The doctor lowered his gaze to the lilies, burning white against his son's smoky gray suit, and said nothing.

"*Sie gehörten auch zu mir*," Ulrich stated, his tenor lower than Otto's.

"You're right; they did belong to you, too." Otto returned his hat to his head with an extra tug that brought the brim in line with his eyes.

"All you cared about was your own sorrow."

"*Es tut mir leid*." Otto raised his hand in an apology but stopped short of touching his son. "I didn't handle it well. I should've—"

"I lost my entire family that day."

Otto's shoulders jerked, and Cora closed her eyes to block the tears. For both Ulrich's and her sake, she wished she'd been more assertive—and relentless—in reminding Otto that he still had a son and a responsibility as his father.

"I'm here for you now." Otto reached for him.

Glowering, Ulrich stepped back. "What need do I have for you *now*? When I was eight years old, terrorized by nightmares, *that's* when I needed you. Not a Kindermädchen who didn't believe in 'coddling' boys." His fingers were gripping the flowers so tightly that the stem of one snapped.

Although they'd been living worlds apart, she'd developed a bond with her imagined version of this man, who'd been just as lonely and scared as she was. She too knew how it felt to be fatherless. But, thank God, she'd had her mamaí. A sudden longing to be enveloped in her mother's warm, fleshy hug gripped Cora so intensely it felt like it was crushing her windpipe.

"Without any help from a father," Ulrich continued, "I put myself through medical school."

"I tried to transfer funds." Otto grasped at the emptiness between them.

"I know. I instructed the bursar to refuse payment from you." Ulrich brushed a speck from his sleeve. "I don't need your money: I've accepted a surgical position at Bellevue."

"Congratulations," Cora murmured, and the bricks absorbed the sound. She'd often wondered what would become of the boy. During the second wave of the Spanish flu, which had blazed across the country in the fall of 1918, killing healthy people his age within twenty-four hours of the first sign of infection, she'd prayed for him. Despite Otto's lack of relationship with his son, the doctor's fear that Ulrich would fall victim to the virus had driven him to insomnia. One night, well past midnight, Otto infected Cora with the deadly strain. Throughout the dark hours of the months that followed, he feverishly attempted to extract from her an antibody that could end the pandemic. Oblivious to his father's efforts, largely on his behalf, Ulrich had presumably been braving the streets each day to attend his college classes until they'd been canceled. Surely the mass misery he'd witnessed had served as a calling for him to the medical field.

"A surgeon," Otto finally said. "*Wunderbar.*" Wonderful.

Cora tensed. In addition to awe and regret, his tone had been laced with something else. *Hope*, she realized.

"*Jawohl,* top of my class. So, you see, I'm doing fine without you," Ulrich said, his chin high. "I came here today only to honor meine Mutti und *Schwester,* whom I know almost nothing about, thanks to you."

Otto put his fist to his mouth, and Cora sensed that he was stifling a sob. She'd seen him do it before, while bent over his microscope or work papers.

"All I know of them, I learned from our neighbors." Ulrich stroked one of the lilies, and Cora realized he was no longer addressing Otto. "Since my own *Vater* wouldn't share even a single memory."

"Weißt du," Otto sang slowly, the timbre of his voice rising as he found the melody, "wieviel Sternlein stehen an dem blauen Himmelszelt?" Can you count the stars that brightly twinkle in the midnight sky?

Cora's mouth hung agape. She'd never heard the doctor sing before. *And his voice!* So clear and strong, yet vulnerable. Maybe the man he'd once been still did exist.

Ulrich was staring at him, and Cora could tell that he'd recognized the song.

"*Deine Mutter,* she used to sing that while cradling you in the rocking chair near the stove. That's how you fell asleep each night, even when you were three. Even the night before . . ." Otto stuffed his hands into his pants pockets. "I'll show you to the site."

"No, I came alone. I'll mourn alone." Nearly choking the flowers, he strode along the seawall.

Wringing his hands, Otto took a step forward, then pivoted to look at the church roof, where he knew she often hid.

Cora held her breath.

The doctor spun toward his son. "Wait, Ulrich."

The younger Gettler halted but kept his back to his father.

"When you're done, stop by my lab. I'd like to introduce you to my *spezielles Projekt.* Just one hour, and you'll understand why I had to stay here."

Without acknowledging that he'd heard the plea, Ulrich continued toward the beach.

Otto hurried after him.

TEN YEARS LATER

OCTOBER 1936

Cora tried to keep the noisy hedge trimmers to a whisper so that she could hear the nurses gossiping in the parlor of their residence. Silence would cause them to suspect her of eavesdropping and hush their voices. She searched for another errant branch, but the shrub blurred into a tangle of thorns. Since Otto's sudden absence three days ago, she'd been able to see straight only with her eyes closed, while imagining what might have happened to him, and what would become of her now that Ulrich was in charge.

"Maybe he fell in love again." The woman's voice had drifted through the open window.

From her crouched position, Cora stretched toward the conversation. She was certain Otto hadn't abandoned his life's work for an affair, but at least the ladies had turned to the only topic she cared about. If anyone at Riverside knew of his whereabouts, it would eventually be dissected over tea and wafers in this lounge.

Each afternoon, the construction crew renovating the nurses' home and dormitories took their break and the women gathered to enjoy a half hour of tranquility.

"More sugar, dear?"

The nurse sighed. "Aren't we almost out?"

"Dee says that with the patient count so low, she's got extra. Eggs, too."

"Mmm. A nice country omelet."

"Wouldn't that be nice?" A plume of cigarette smoke wafted from the window.

Cora willed them to return to the matter of Otto's disappearance. In retrospect, she should have seen it coming ten years ago, when Ulrich had first arrived.

Initially, he hadn't believed his father's claims. But by the time Ulrich had finished interrogating Cora and studying specimens under the microscope, his blue eyes had gleamed with curiosity. Mere weeks later, he'd requested a transfer from Bellevue to Riverside so he could serve as Otto's assistant in his free hours.

Unable to stifle his proclivity for grandstanding, a trait not tolerated by his father, Ulrich had resorted to sharing his theories with "the mutt," as he often called her. He'd explained that he thought she might have inherited her unique abilities. He was fascinated—and frustrated—by the question mark of her father, and he believed that if they could map her "impure" bloodline, they could "breed" her with other descendants. According to his hypothesis, offspring with a more concentrated version of the attribute would be able to safely leave the island.

Once, she'd summoned the courage to ask him if removing her gallbladder might eradicate her pests. He'd scoffed at the hypothesis, calling it scientific chicanery. "Mary may be an obtuse, ornery broad, but she was right to refuse the procedure. You, on the other hand, have no rights."

Around the onset of the Great Depression, Ulrich became equally obsessed with testing her resilience at a cellular level. Over the years, the uncomfortable silences between father and son had morphed into hushed academic arguments that could span several days. Although Otto's experimentation on her had been torturous, his research had always maintained its noble purpose, and he'd never derived pleasure from her pain. The same did not hold true for his son.

Recently they'd become so absorbed in their ethical debates that they'd stopped bothering to even lower their voices in her presence, as if she were just another lab mouse who couldn't understand.

And then, last Friday, before the pair had left the lab to board the ferry, Otto had given Ulrich an ultimatum: either adhere to the project's original objectives or quit.

Through what they'd left unsaid over the years, Cora had surmised that they spent their time away from Riverside apart. Yet they'd always returned together on the Monday morning ferry. Except this last time.

Ulrich had stepped onto the dock alone, carrying his father's black medical kit with Ingrid's wristlet still looped around its handle. He'd informed the head nurse that Otto had quietly retired to avoid a big send-off party, then he'd shown her the papers from the Health Department that outlined his promotion to chief resident physician.

Concerned about what Ulrich's new position would mean for Cora, Mary had vigorously stirred the rumor pot from her sickbed.

Although Cora couldn't prove it, she'd always suspected that Ulrich had somehow caused the stroke that had paralyzed Mary in 1933. Frequently Mary had threatened both Gettlers, but the way she growled at Ulrich had reminded Cora of a mastiff who could sense evil in a man. Worried that he might similarly hurt O'Toole or his wife, she'd stopped confiding in the man who'd been so good at repairing her confidence and bolstering her inner strength.

Yesterday one of the mechanics had approached Cora to ask if the doc had gotten mixed up with the Mafia. Because of her routine visits to the lab, the staff assumed she was caring for the animals in addition to her responsibilities as sole gardener following Canne's retirement four years earlier. And so, the machinist, like all the others, was oblivious to the germs she exhaled with each breath, trapped by the wide-brimmed hat and neckerchief she always wore across her lower face as a "sun shield." Leaving her spade and shovel in the planting bed, she'd run from him, further cementing her reputation as the island hermit.

With Otto gone, Cora expected Ulrich to begin conducting the experiments he'd so carefully mapped out in the journals he kept within a locked filing cabinet in the lab. *Did he kill his own father?* she wondered again.

Careful not to bump any of the raw incisions that ran down her thigh, she disentangled the clippings from the bush.

Monday evening, after his first day as head physician, Ulrich had summoned her to his father's lab, tied her to a table, and roughly taped her mouth shut. Without first giving her local anesthesia, he punctured her skin, like he was marking a yardstick, and smeared a different emulsion onto each of the wounds. He'd said he was starting small, with everyday microbes that most any immune system could handle. "Not yet should you worry."

Now, cowering in the dirt, hoping to catch tidbits from the nurses, Cora was worried.

A stray tabby, which often trailed her while she worked, sidled up to Cora. Purring, he nosed her bag in search of scraps of meat.

"Jeepers, get lost." She shooed him away to prevent the women from turning their attention outward.

"He might have been arrested," said a silky voice. "Those animals in his laboratory; the Gettlers have been doing terrible things to them."

"Or he has—had—a gambling problem and his debts cost him his life."

Cora shook her head. Otto had viewed gambling as a sin. She tugged on her trousers to air the wounds. While she still had to be careful, advances in germ prevention theory and antiseptics allowed her slightly more freedom.

"Maybe he's simply *Gone with the Wind.*"

This was pointless, Cora decided, slumping to the ground. Through her neckerchief, she inhaled the brittle smell of the browning leaves. Soon even the island's plants, her greatest sources of comfort, would desert her for the winter.

In a vain attempt to relieve the burning in her thighs, she rocked on her heels and thought about the collection of scalpels she'd been amassing over the years. They were hidden beneath a floorboard in the gardening shed. While Otto had been in charge, the sense of power they'd given her had been reassuring, but she'd never actually used one. Now they would need to serve as more than a psychological crutch. It was time to scrub off their rust and learn to wield them.

"True, he's handsome," said a high-pitched voice from the parlor, "but the way he eyes me, it gives me the creepy crawlies. And so full of himself. Claire, would you like a top-off?"

"Yes, please. His father may have been a loner, but at least he was a gentleman, a per—"

"Did you ladies read about Jesse Owens?"

The sudden shift in conversation made Cora tense.

"He's claiming that our very own president—and not Hitler—was the one to snub him."

To appear industrious, Cora raised the pruning shears, but the tremors in her arms prevented her from locking the blades onto a branch.

"The way they treated him at the Waldorf, after that ticker-tape parade..."

The smell of Foster's hair gloss, mixed with antiseptic, soured the breeze, and Cora stifled her gag reflex.

The nurses had stopped their chatter.

She lowered the clippers.

"Miss McSorley, the rosebushes by my cottage are diseased," Ulrich said from the road in front of the residence. "Let's have a look."

Slowly she gathered her tools.

Since he wasn't wearing protective gear, she fell into step her standard ten paces behind him. Hoping, irrationally, that Otto would suddenly appear, she kept her gaze fixed on the dock.

Halfway across the central lawn, Ulrich swerved away from the site of the future tuberculosis pavilion, where the main hospital building had previously stood, and toward the morgue and pathology building, confirming her suspicion that the plagued roses had been a ruse.

He entered, and she watched the door swing shut behind him.

As instructed long ago, she waited outside while he put on a gown and mask. She felt the itch to run, but where could she go? The complex was too small to hide her for long, and the river—well, that simply wasn't an option.

A rapping on the far side of the door signaled that she should enter.

Rocking on her heels, she couldn't bring herself to do so. Yet she knew that the consequences of disobeying him would be far worse than whatever awaited her within the lab, its arch windows papered over when converted from its original use as a church.

She mustered the courage, took one last deep breath, and entered the house of the dead.

The corridor was empty; he'd already returned to preparing his instruments.

Dawdling a moment longer, she stopped in the doorway. "Where's Otto?" she asked over the squeaking of caged rodents. To deflect their scent, she kept her breath shallow.

"The mutt's got a new master," he said without looking up from his mortar and pestle. "Take off your trousers and lie down so I can check for infection."

She tried to swallow, but the lump in her throat had swelled to the size of a peach pit.

He looked up. "This isn't a breadline. Get moving. I've got two more pavilions to visit before I need to leave for an NSDAP dinner."

The pit in her throat dropped to her stomach, and she did as he'd directed.

Humming Bing Crosby's new tune "Pennies from Heaven," he removed the dressings as tears slid down her temples.

"No sign of infection, as I'd expected. Apparently only the more potent germs can coexist with your immune system. It's a shame your unique cellular abilities don't include accelerated healing, but we cannot let a little discomfort slow our progress, can we?" He leaned over to inspect the incisions at the top of her thighs, and she spat on his protective goggles.

"You disgusting bitch," he said, methodically setting them in the sink designated for contaminated glass, then donned a clean pair.

When he turned to face her, an Erlenmeyer flask, now in his hand, glinted beneath the operating light.

Cora's stomach clenched, and she whimpered. *Just like a mutt.*

He raised the object above his head.

"No, please!" she cried and slid to the far side of the table.

A rush of air hit her eyes, driving them shut, and glass shattered against her crown.

"Excellent. Another test site." Carefully avoiding the shards, he placed a bedpan on the floor to catch the dripping blood.

"If your old master hadn't gone so easy on you, mankind might already be rid of disease. Tens of millions died from the Spanish influenza. Because of your weakness, and Otto's lack of resolve, those corpses sit squarely on your conscience."

His accusatory stare pierced her, sharper than the sting of the split skin on her forehead, and she fought the impulse to curl away from him.

"The next time that foreigners bring a novel disease to our shores, we will be ready for it. I'll let you go back to your work, digging in the dirt. But know this: if you ever resist; if you tell anyone; if you attempt to harm me, I'll destroy what matters most to you."

"You don't know what that is," she taunted.

Ulrich grinned. "Sure, I do. Otto's records—the ones relating to curing you, so you can leave this island. Without those files, you'll never be free."

He despised her, to his very core, she knew. Throughout the past ten years as Otto's assistant, he'd been making offhand remarks that had amounted to an obvious conclusion for Cora: Ulrich blamed her for his lonely childhood, absent of love. To some extent, his view was merited. If it weren't for her, Otto would have eventually returned to Kleindeutschland to comfort his son. The incident with her blood spraying onto Otto's gown, after Ulrich had already witnessed so much trauma, had also been her fault. Those first moments during their reunion following the tragedy had been so crucial, and her impulsive reaction had destroyed any chance of them uniting in their grief.

Fortunately, Ulrich appeared to have no memory of the encounter. For if he had, she would have heard about it, and directly experienced his pain. Whenever she thought back to those moments, the guilt overwhelmed her. So, she tried not to.

"I'll find another doctor, a smarter one," she said, bracing for a second blow.

Ulrich lunged, stopping just shy of her, and laughed at the way he'd made her flinch.

Backing away, he removed his mask. The strap had riled his short, blond hair, and the sides of his broad forehead bore red indents. "Do you know what happens to dogs who bite their masters? They're euthanized. Since I need you alive, your consequences will be inflicted upon others. Do you understand?"

She closed her eyes to blockade the tears. The knives hidden within the gardening shed would do her no good.

"Do you understand?" He picked up a scalpel.

Cora nodded.

"Good doggy."

November 1938

In the hallway outside the laboratory, Cora inhaled deeply to calm her nerves while keeping her gaze on the watch Otto had given her. Since his disappearance two years earlier, whenever she checked the time, a wave of sadness crashed down on her, quickly replaced by fear.

During Ulrich's first week in charge, she'd arrived late to her long-standing weekly appointment. That night, he tied her to a chair and forced her to watch as he sadistically dissected Jeepers. Her eyelids held open by a pair of surgical sutures, tears streamed down her cheeks as he sliced the tabby like a melon. Aside from Mary, who was currently suffering from pneumonia, the cat was her only remaining friend. "Next time you're late," he said, "it'll be a child."

The dial reached twelve with a *tick* that seemed to reverberate down the corridor. Clutching the brown bag with her urine and stool samples, she inhaled and opened the door.

The stench and chittering of the rodents didn't greet her as usual.

The hair on her arms rose; something was wrong.

"Stay in the hall," Ulrich said without looking up from the carton he was sealing. Nor did he consult the clock.

Even more astounding to Cora: he wasn't wearing protective gear. And the drawers of the file cabinets along one wall stood open and empty. The room smelled of musty paper instead of mouse droppings.

He's leaving, she realized, and her heart pounded so hard she worried it might crack her sternum. "What's going on?"

"The Fatherland needs me, but don't worry, I'll be back."

She bit her lip to keep from screaming with joy.

As his praise of Hitler's ideology had intensified, she'd fantasized about him joining the movement. During his first month on the island, she'd perceived his internal struggle to establish a sense of identity.

Cora had understood exactly how he'd felt; she, too, didn't know where she belonged. Seven years later, when Hitler became the chancellor of Germany, Ulrich swore his allegiance, and in doing so, found himself.

Five weeks ago, the Germans had marched into Sudetenland, and Ulrich's gait had become almost a goose-stepping march. Yet, still, Cora hadn't allowed herself to hope that his patriotism would translate into freedom for her.

He lifted the box and let it fall atop another with a *thump*.

All her lab reports were in those towers. Without them there would be nothing to show for the torture she'd endured. And any new—kinder—doctor she convinced to help her would be forced to start from scratch.

"Where are you taking those?"

Ulrich smiled and rubbed his clean-shaven chin. "They're going with me to Germany."

"They should stay," she said, not daring to raise her gaze from the floor. "They're mine."

He made a tutting sound. "You know that's not true. I'll return, and we'll pick up where we left off."

"But what if you get killed?"

He laughed. "I'm sure you'll pray for that to happen. Go ahead, beg that God of yours to drop a bomb on me. He didn't listen to my father; why would he listen to you?"

Cora balled her hands. *If I strike him in the eye, how fast will my germs kill him?* she wondered, then realized that they likely wouldn't succeed before he'd boarded the ferry, where he might infect others.

Eyeing her fists, he cracked his knuckles. "Unfortunately for you, Hitler is the only god that exists. And his SS Medical Corps, with their microbiology aspirations, won't risk an asset like me near the border." His lips curled into a smug smile. "Trust me."

That she would never do.

"Now run along, little animal. Go play in your dirt," he said, then kicked the door shut with his boot.

Late Summer 2007

After the Tornado

August

Stupid. Lily clicked the remote to change the channel on her hotel room's boxy television. *Gettler.* She jabbed the arrow again. *Men.*

Because of their collective stupidity, any minute now she might feel the creeping onset of a headache, weakness, runny nose, or cough. Then her temp would begin to climb, reaching more than one hundred four degrees as chills raked her body, followed by vomiting and diarrhea and an excruciating stomachache. Lesions could form on her tongue and palate, followed by macules on her face, with more popping up by the minute on her abdomen and chest, then her extremities. In the final stages, her liver and kidneys could fail. She'd become delirious. Blood might flow from her eyes, nose, and mouth.

As her condition worsened, the Gettlers might take her to a hospital. Or, more likely, Rollie would treat her in his lab to avoid tipping off the Health Department to Riverside's resident "Patient Zero."

Even if she made it to the ER, she'd probably die. From as little as one or as many as seven infectious diseases. Only measles was covered by the immunizations Lily had received.

Same with Finn, now quarantined in the adjacent room.

She'd become habituated to the possibility of her own death, but the notion of Finn falling ill practically paralyzed her. To prevent that ball of dread from unraveling again, she concentrated on her hand. It was shaking. And her throat felt raw. *Initial symptoms?*

To check her face, she moved three feet into the bathroom. Already a yellowish pallor had replaced her tan. But no rash. Yet. Although her acorn-brown irises weren't rimmed by red, dark bags had settled beneath them. And her hair, the color of rich potting soil, clung limply to her neck.

Her forehead seemed warm, which could be attributed to the ninety-degree room temp, thanks to the crappy air-conditioning unit sputtering in the window frame.

From Finn's phone conversations with his dad over the past four days, he'd learned that Kristian, two doors down, had better odds of survival, despite his punctured suit. As Rollie's research assistant, he'd been vaccinated against typhus fever, smallpox, typhoid fever, measles, and *VZ*. Lily shuddered.

She paced across the room, not much bigger than a coffin.

According to Finn, inoculations didn't exist for Cora's three other contagions: Ebola, Rift Valley fever, and Spanish influenza, all of which Gettler men had intentionally infected her with.

Neither Ebola nor RVF were airborne, but RVF could be transmitted through any mosquitos that had first bitten Cora. That rainstorm had washed off their bug spray, leaving Finn—and herself—fully exposed for over an hour.

Even worse: Spanish influenza was airborne, and could kill within a day of symptom onset. With a 10 to 20 percent death rate, if one of them had caught the highly contagious disease and passed it to someone in this hotel, it could decimate the world population within weeks.

Furious, Lily punched the remote control's off button.

Even Rollie, secluded in his lab while running tests on their samples, might have been infected; he'd removed his suit to save her. Her heart hadn't been beating on its own for a solid minute before he'd managed to bring her back. Ever since he'd finished drawing her blood on the shore of North Brother Island, as Finn secured her to a raft, she hadn't spoken to him. Until she knew whether she'd contracted a lethal cocktail of diseases, she had no interest in his outlandish scientific theories.

Feeling a tickle in her throat, she coughed. *Typhus?* Breathing slowly, she listened to her lungs but detected no congestion. Yet. Rollie's effort to revive her may have only prolonged her life by a few weeks. If so, he'd also inadvertently caused her death to be far more protracted and miserable.

Her bad gut feeling about the Gettlers hadn't even scratched the surface.

On the walk to this seedy hotel, she'd been too agitated to speak to Finn. The Gettlers' wild claims about Cora had been swirling through her head, as aggressively as the tornado that had cut a nine-mile path from

Staten Island to Brooklyn. Finn must have been just as overwhelmed, for he'd also remained silent.

Only after she'd taken a long, hot shower and slipped on pajamas, from a package of necessities left by a delivery boy outside her door, had she called him.

"I get why you didn't want to tell me," she'd said quietly, wishing she could hug him. "Whatever your family's done to her doesn't make me love you any less."

In response, he'd cried. Although his sobs had been practically inaudible, Lily could feel them reverberating in her chest. Only once before had he lost it in front of her, while still within view of the restaurant they'd left mid meal because his mom's pain had been unbearable.

For a good half an hour, she'd stayed on the line with him, neither of them speaking. Simply being together had been enough.

The following morning, he'd told her about his mother's note and the bats, and she'd admitted she'd seen the cage while spying on him. "If we live through this week, we'll find the truth together," they'd promised each other.

With nothing else to do, she rapped on Finn's wall.

No response. He must be napping. The night before, they'd talked until three a.m.

She moved to the window and craned to see the sky, obscured by a building five feet away. After settling into this temporary prison, she'd secured a leave of absence at work due to "a death in the family." More than anything, she wished she were outside right now, in the fresh air at the Conservatory Garden, pruning the Japanese holly.

Her cell phone rang.

Rollie must have their test results, she realized.

Unable to break the quick-spinning sensation that suddenly gripped her, she dropped to the sketchy bedspread.

Her phone continued to ring.

Pushing through vertigo, she flipped it open to check the caller I.D.

Kristian.

What does he want? The brothers were furious at each other, and she had no desire to get caught in the middle. So far, she'd followed Finn's request not to answer Kristian's calls.

The ringing ceased.

Pushing through the dizziness, she concentrated on the red digits on the alarm clock.

The way Kristian had treated Cora, as described by Finn, disgusted Lily. She didn't know what to think of him anymore, or her ability to judge character.

The phone rang again.

This time she answered it.

"Lily, I've got news."

"Okay," she said, gasping.

"You're free. The tests were all negative."

"Oh my God," she choked out. "Are you sure?"

"Rollie ran them all twice."

Shaking, Lily lowered her head to her knees. *You're cancer-free!* Suddenly she was in a hospital bed, wearing a royal blue gown, a port in her chest.

"You still there?"

Kristian's faint voice pulled her back, and she returned the phone to her ear. "What about Finn? And you and Rollie?"

"He ran your tests first."

Finn had traipsed all over that germ-ridden island, and had been near Cora . . .

"Lily?"

"Yes."

"He might be fine. She's always been hyper diligent about containing her microbes."

"Okay."

"But Lily . . ."

"Yes?"

"I have to tell you . . ."

She blinked rapidly. "What?"

"The way Finn looked at her . . . and defended her . . . a woman who's already killed one Gettler and won't be happy till we're all dead."

"She did what?"

"Never mind. That was a slight exaggeration."

"What do you mean, the way he looked at her?"

"Listen, I don't want to cause any trouble between you two."

Bastard. She'd been so wrong about him. That fact that he would imply that Finn felt anything but concern for Cora . . . The insinuation had to be Kristian's way of getting back at Finn for freeing the woman. Finn was devoted to her; Lily knew that. Yet she herself had done a double take at the ruggedly beautiful woman—exactly Finn's type.

"Anyway, you're free to leave. Tomorrow you can go back to work. I'm sure being cooped up here has been especially miserable for you."

Vicious bastard.

September

As the seal on the door marked "Patient Files" wheezed open, the sharp smell of antiseptic hit Lily, knocking her back to her junior year of high school.

Eyeing her nervously, Rollie flicked a switch; a halogen light illuminated a wash station, bins of PPE, and a neon-red biohazard waste container.

Lily's oncology nurses had worn purple hazmat suits when dispensing her chemo. The memory triggered the fiery sensation of a blood-orange chemical coursing through her veins. She shook her head. Right now, she couldn't afford to be burdened by the past. Beyond the plastic sheath at the end of this air lock lay the Gettlers' secret laboratory. And her boyfriend.

"We'll take it slow." Rollie smiled at her, briefly revealing his coffee-stained teeth, and shut the outer door.

Before all this, the way his grin stretched from his loose jowl up to his eyes had always melted away the discomfort she'd felt after one of his offhand remarks about the influence of family structure on child development. Although he'd never said it, she knew her upbringing as an only child, raised by a single mom, concerned him. Now that she had some understanding of their secrets, it made sense why he'd always seemed to be evaluating her fit for inclusion in his family.

To be fair, however, Rollie had always been supportive. Through his praise and questions that showed his genuine interest, she knew he was proud of her for finishing in the top 10 percent of her college class, as well as for her work with the Central Park Conservancy. "Oh. You're a gardener." That had been Leonard's reaction after asking how she planned to use the degree paid for by the trust he'd established shortly after her birth.

Now Rollie's disarming smile made her skin crawl. A part of her longed to tell him that she'd had her own reservations about joining their fucked-up family cult. But she loved Finn, and right now he needed her.

"Let's get going, please. I want to see him."

"You will, but we need to follow protocol, starting with your jewelry." He pointed to a tray next to the sink. "It could puncture the suit. And Lils, you—"

"Don't call me that."

Rollie rubbed his jaw. "I understand I've lost your trust for now. But that's why I brought you here." He reached for her but quickly withdrew. "You're like a daughter to me. And always will be, even if you and Finn—"

"Don't," she said with a scowl.

He rubbed his heavily lined forehead. "I invited you here so you can see the full magnitude of what's at stake. This isn't just for Sylvia; it's for you, too."

"Is it also for Finn? Because you don't seem to care what happens to him."

His hand drifted to a scar at the corner of his jaw, his "Zugzwang Tell," as Finn called it. Whenever the two played chess, Rollie's fingers rested there when he'd run out of moves that wouldn't put him at a disadvantage. The only other time Lily had seen him do it was while discussing Sylvia's therapies.

"He's the world to me," Rollie said in a stern tone, his voice stretched thin by age and exhaustion. "My—and Sylvia's—greatest accomplishment."

Lily picked at a nail. Finn had once told her that Ulrich had pressured Rollie into marrying his first wife, a woman of pure German descent. Although Rollie had loved Sylvia more than Petra, it had been Kristian—not Finn—who'd received preferential status.

"Let's see how he's doing," she said curtly as she tied back her hair.

She let Rollie help her into a Teflon suit and rubber boots. Following his lead, she raised her hood and put on a respirator and face shield, then elbow-high rubber gloves.

He unzipped the plastic tarp and held it open for her.

At the sight of medical equipment, she suddenly felt like her boots were bolted to the floor.

Reminding herself that Finn needed her, Lily envisioned a plant—this time, a bougainvillea. Slowly, the tension in her muscles dissipated and she stepped into the lab.

Searching for Finn, she took in the long row of metal cabinets, computer desk, industrial freezer, incubator, centrifuge, and five microscopes arranged across three lab stations.

From a cot at the far end of the room, Finn grinned at her through his face shield. "Hey, gorgeous."

She beamed back at him, and a kaleidoscope of butterflies agitated the queasiness in her stomach.

Distantly, behind her, she heard Rollie sealing the air lock.

Finn began to rise, then wavered. He grabbed the rim of the folding bed for support.

Lily rushed toward him, but he motioned for her to stay back. "I got it."

"Take it easy." Rollie helped Finn up.

"You said he wasn't sick," Lily said.

"He's not. He's had some minor, common reactions to the vaccines, but nothing serious."

Just three weeks after Rollie had declared all three Gettler men disease-free, he'd asked Finn to return to the island to convince Cora to help Sylvia. "You now have a rapport with her," he'd said. As if that were reason enough for Finn to reengage with the deadly woman.

Lily had considered begging him to say no, but she would do anything for her own mother, even this. So she'd given him a deep kiss good-bye before he'd left to receive far too many inoculations at one time. They'd had no choice: the heron nesting season would be over soon.

"So," Finn said, crossing the room to Lily's side, "now you have us both here." He squeezed her hand through the rubber, and she immediately felt safer. "How about that tour?"

Rollie made a sweeping gesture.

Lily surveyed the long, narrow room for a second time. There were no animal cages. So where had the bats gone?

"It's not much," Rollie said, "but it's everything to our family, and will be to humankind. I pray to God that our breakthrough comes before the next pandemic."

"You're right," Finn said. "It's not much. *If* I decide to talk to Cora, I'll be sure to bring her a stack of books. She's got a long wait ahead of her."

Rollie cleared his throat. "Without the resources that Ulrich had at Lab Two Fifty-Seven, our progress has, admittedly, been slower than we'd like."

"Then why don't you call the CDC? I hear they're pretty good at this sort of thing."

"They'd never believe that her immunities are influenced by a local factor. Those out-of-touch wonks would have her on a plane to Atlanta within an hour. She'd be dead before they landed."

It was obvious to Lily that Rollie had constructed this scenario decades ago as justification for his family's actions. Even though the CDC might respond precisely the way he'd outlined, it didn't give him the right to decide Cora's fate.

Finn snorted. "As opposed to your humane tactics?"

"I told you: that was Ulrich," Rollie said, nonchalantly leaning against the desk, one side cluttered with loose sheets of graph paper, the other side—presumably Kristian's—perfectly organized.

"So you've said." Finn looked at Lily, and she sensed his confidence wavering.

To signal her support, she moved closer to his side.

"How could you not tell me that the cure you're searching for is already inside a human being?"

Rollie's face darkened, and he straightened to his full height. "Are you questioning my judgment?"

"To think, during all those days you missed with us, I'd been picturing you sifting through hospital remains. Those baggies of dirt and plant samples you'd bring home were just a ruse, weren't they?"

"Not at all. There's got to be a chemical compound there, that she's ingested, that's triggered her immune response."

Unwilling to let his father reroute the conversation, Finn continued, "Throughout all those sermons about loyalty, you were lying to me. And when Mom asked you to stop—I found a note she wrote in 2001, demanding you leave Cora alone—instead of listening to her, you lied again."

"For good reason. Your mother's in constant, excruciating pain!"

"How does that explain the cage of bats I found in your shed? They're infected with a coronavirus, aren't they?"

"What are you talking about?" Rollie reached to remove his face shield but stopped himself. "I didn't . . ." His eyes clouded over.

"You know something," Finn said, shaking his head. "I can tell."

Rollie raised his hands, palms out. "I'm as baffled as you. Wait—we do use a pest control service. The exterminator probably put a trap there."

Lily sensed that his ignorance might be genuine. She turned to Finn.

"Then they must belong to Kristian," he stated, folding his arms. "The label on the syringe you handed me by the morgue included the letters SCV—I'm guessing that's short for SARS coronavirus. You had that case in your hand. You knew he was planning to infect her with more than Lyme."

"Not until that moment," Rollie said, shaking his head, "when it was too late."

"It wasn't too late," Lily stated coldly. "It wasn't in her veins yet."

Rollie glared at her. "'Too late' will be an apt summary the next time a coronavirus emerges from a rainforest in China. *If* I don't allow Kristian to think bigger than Lyme. A large-scale pandemic is not just science fiction fodder; it's an inevitable outcome for our global society."

A rush of claustrophobia pressed against Lily from all sides, and her shoulder began to spasm. Suddenly the inside of her mask smelled like a hot glue gun.

Darkness invaded her vision, and she reached to rip off her hood.

Finn stopped her by clasping her hands in his own. "You okay?" he asked, studying her face.

She nodded with too much vigor.

He turned to Rollie. "We need to get her out of here."

"No, I'm fine." She edged away from him.

Ever since her blackout on North Brother, Finn had been treating her like the last of an endangered species. Eventually, she would tell him to chill out, but that crazy morning, and the tense days of waiting that had followed, had scared her, too.

The pungent scent dissipated.

"I'm good." She rotated, bringing more of the room into view, and the claustrophobia subsided.

"We should still go," Finn said.

If they did, Rollie would be spared from Finn's interrogation. To keep the pressure on, she said, "'Too late' will also be a fitting description if one of those bats, wherever they are, does manage to escape."

Rollie aligned a microscope with its neighbor on the table, and Lily could tell he was attempting to hide his frustration.

"If those bats did belong to Kristian, you can rest assured that he's been following all the proper containment protocols." He looked up. "Frankly, I'm having trouble understanding why you would object to Kristian studying coronaviruses. Obviously, Sylvia's health is my number one priority. But if another novel virus does leap from bats to cats to humans, and we have an effective technique for producing a safe therapy from Cora's antibodies, it would cut years from the vaccine development process." He looked straight at her. "With most viruses, the fatality rate is significantly higher for those with pre-existing conditions. A vaccine would protect you and my beautiful wife."

Lily glanced at Finn, who blinked hard before meeting her gaze. Neither spoke.

"I truly care about Cora," Rollie continued. "All we need is a few units of her blood—once she's injected herself with *Borrelia burgdorferi* and developed an immunity to it. If our current theory works, we should be able to reproduce her unique antibodies in the lab. We can use it to develop vaccines, but also to cure her. And cancer," he said, glancing at Lily, then back to Finn. "If you can convince Cora to cooperate, we can have her back in Manhattan within a couple of years."

"How am I supposed to believe that the work that happens here"—Finn made a sweeping gesture—"will ever be for her benefit? She certainly doesn't. By the way, where are your logs for all those trips after you supposedly called it quits?"

Huffing, Rollie unlocked a cabinet. "See for yourself. Ever since she told me to leave her alone, in 2001, we haven't collected a single unit of blood. We haven't so much as touched her."

"Until last month," Finn countered, "while Lily lay in a puddle, convulsing."

Rollie clasped his hands sheepishly. "That whole night was awful. I was so upset that she'd threatened you, but there won't be another lapse in my judgment. For the past six years, we've exclusively been collecting environmental samples. That's it."

He handed Finn a stack of journals and rolled back the desk chair so Finn could sit down to read. "You cannot mention any of this to your mother."

The request rankled Lily. According to Finn, Rollie believed that Ulrich's unhinged scruples were the direct result of growing up without church and family. Determined to prevent Otto's legacy of neglect from ever being repeated by another Gettler, Rollie championed the importance of both. And the values that came with them.

"I don't like the idea of keeping this from Sylvia," she said.

Fiddling with a microscope, Rollie cleared his throat in obvious irritation.

A *Mensch*. That's how she'd described him to her own father, admittedly to make Leonard envious. Now, away from Sylvia's guiding hand, Rollie had strayed from that characterization.

"Please," Rollie said, and she realized she'd been shaking her head.

He unlocked the freezer, exposing a vast blood databank, toxins surely sleeping within the pouches, and removed a slide. After placing it under a microscope, he indicated that she should look through the eyepiece.

To show she couldn't be manipulated, she turned her attention to Finn, hunched over the desk, seemingly oblivious to their conversation.

"You've seen how Lyme has debilitated her." Rollie peered through the eyepiece and twisted a knob. "If you tell Sylvia, she'll make me stop. Or worse, kill herself, so I'll have no reason to continue. The antibiotic-resistant spirochete that caused her Lyme will go unchallenged. And so, too, will this disease." He backed away from the microscope.

Without looking, Lily knew the slide contained a cancer cell. Her stomach churned. He could have planted it there before her visit, or begun work in earnest on a therapy.

During her elementary school years, she'd wanted to become an oncologist. Even if she'd had the genetic goods to make it through medical school, all that radiation to her brain had stunted her critical thinking ability. And, most likely, her dyslexia had been caused by those treatments. That's why she loved plants and painting. Aside from the occasional tremors, her hands worked perfectly. From her touch, life and beauty bloomed.

Yet always, in the back of her mind, she'd felt like she'd let herself down. Along with so many others. Sure, she'd raised money for cancer research, but the sum would never be enough, no matter how many miles she raced for a cure.

Standing in this lab, mere feet from a microscope, was the closest she'd ever been to "the front line." *If* the Gettlers' work had any validity.

"You really think you can cure cancer?"

Rollie cocked his hooded head. "Cancer cells are crafty—they often evolve and become drug-resistant, but we'd like to try."

"Billions of dollars have been spent, and you think . . ." Suddenly, overcome with irritation at his arrogance, she couldn't complete the thought.

The steamy air within her hood felt like it was about to suffocate her. She wanted out—of this room, and away from yet another tantalizing path of false hope.

"Lily," he said in the same pleasant tone he'd always used with her, "none of those big pharma companies has Cora."

"Then why don't you share her? They'll succeed where you've failed, and I can stop worrying, and Sylvia will be cured, and Finn and I can get married, and . . ." Finn was staring at her, but she couldn't stop. "You'll get to meet the president, and they'll turn this pathetic room into a stop on the national heritage tour."

Out of breath, she inhaled stale air.

No one spoke.

Tears traveled down her face.

She wished she could wipe them away, and maybe take back her diatribe. Not because she hadn't meant it. Only because they now might exclude her from future discussions.

"You know they would kill her," Rollie said, "one way or another."

Lily closed her eyes and pictured Cora on the morgue roof. In her heart, she knew Rollie was right. But conceding that would condone his choices.

"Let's go." Finn rose from the desk, and the name of the file cabinet behind him came into view. *VZ.*

"Does your wife know about that one?" Lily asked, pointing to the label.

"No."

She shook her head. "I'm not surprised."

Finn rapped the metal cabinet. "You're asking me to meet with her; I deserve to know."

"Why does it matter? You've been inoculated against it."

Finn glared at him.

Rollie squared his shoulders. "*VZ* is our—no, society's—safeguard. It's what ensures that Coraline can't survive away from the island long enough to spread her germs."

"Conveniently, that strengthens your excuse for why we can't involve the CDC," Finn said, "but it sure doesn't jibe with your supposed goal of returning her to the city."

"First of all, it wasn't my doing. Secondly, it doesn't have to be permanent. Theoretically, the vaccine could be used to develop an antidote."

"Theoretically," Lily muttered. That word had been helping the Gettlers rationalize their actions for more than a century.

"You still don't trust me," Finn said, and she sensed that he was thinking of Kristian. Although Finn had claimed he wasn't hurt by the fact that they'd excluded him for so long, his recent sullenness suggested otherwise.

Rollie tugged on the file drawer to ensure it was locked. "This isn't about you." He put away the journals, securing that cabinet as well. "I haven't told your brother what it stands for either. We're done here." He ushered them toward the exit.

Lily stole one last glance around the room, her gaze settling on the microscope, its stage clips still gripping the slide with the malignant tumor cell. The notion that this lab could produce a magic bullet for cancer seemed absurd. Yet the impossible did happen—somewhere—every day. She stepped into the transition space, and a sterilizing agent cleansed her biosafety suit.

Maybe it could happen here, she thought. And the speck of hope she'd been harboring, initially the size of a single cell, divided in two.

1946–1963

September 1946

Otto.

Cora dropped her gardening hoe. From the field beside the coal house, she strained to see the man in the brown boater who'd just stepped off the gangway. At his feet rested a suitcase and a black physician's kit that made Cora tremble.

The Bronx skyline behind him swayed.

To steady herself, she sat back on her heels. Ten years had passed without a single credible detail regarding his whereabouts. During the first two, when Ulrich had dominated her, she'd scrutinized every male who'd stepped off that ferry. Back then, Otto's return, with his more humane methods, would have been akin to salvation. Following Ulrich's departure, however, she'd been thrilled to be rid of them both, her exhilaration marred only by a nagging concern about her missing files. And she hadn't yet found a new doctor she could trust.

Following Germany's surrender, Cora had read in the papers about Ulrich's role as a doctor in Hitler's Schutzstaffel. Either through his imprisonment or hanging, she would be beyond his reach forever. Yet she hadn't celebrated the news. For weeks she'd lain in bed, wishing that, back in 1938, she'd convinced him that he could better serve the Fatherland by advancing his research on her.

Now abandoning her effort to weed the field, Cora buried her face beneath her neckerchief and pressed her wide-brimmed hat farther down her forehead. Still, she felt too exposed.

Otto's resumption of their project could assuage her guilt, she told herself. Especially if he succeeded in creating a cure-all for disease. Her stomach, however, heaved in disagreement.

Grasping her crucifix pendant, she studied the man.

No, it can't be him, she realized, exhaling slowly. At seventy-eight, his stature would be stooped, whereas this man's chest bulged in his white dress shirt.

A flaxen-haired boy of about four years ran down the gangplank, and the man swung him onto the dock.

Just another veteran and his family, she decided. For the past few months, they'd been carrying out a full-fledged invasion of the island. To accommodate the influx of ex-soldiers studying at New York City universities under the GI Bill, Riverside had been rezoned for student housing. Even the rooms in the tuberculosis pavilion, completed only four years earlier, had been converted to apartments. Thankfully, the colleges had retained her as a groundskeeper, which allowed her to continue living in the nurses' residence.

The man hugged the child and offered his hand to a statuesque blonde. Hampered by their luggage and the spirited boy, the couple progressed down the pier, the man walking with a slight limp that favored his left side.

The back of Cora's neck prickled.

He was staring at her.

Reflexively, her shoulders rounded forward.

He grinned.

Ulrich.

No, she thought, *it can't be. His war crimes...*

Had he escaped from Nuremberg?

She clutched the grass, which suddenly smelled repulsively sweet. Like chloroform.

The blonde squeezed his shoulder and whispered into his ear.

He laughed, the harsh wind bringing the familiar, grating noise to Cora. And the revolting scent of his Foster's hair gloss.

How Ulrich had persuaded President Truman to allow him reentry she couldn't fathom, though she should have expected it. After all, she was convinced that he'd murdered his father and then worked the system to fill the empty position himself. *He must be using a fake identity.*

The pokeberry tea in her stomach felt like it was fermenting.

In her nightmares, she'd often contended with the prospect of his return, but he'd always arrived alone. Not with a ravishing wife and child, while Cora remained achingly single. Now, not only would he resume the torture, but he'd torment her with his happiness as well.

The child squirmed free of his mother's grasp and ran toward the meadow. He was heading straight for her.

"Rollie," Ulrich shouted, "*halt*!"

The boy reeled toward his father, a mischievous grin filling his chubby face.

"*Dieses Fraulein ist nicht gut für dich. Bleib weg.*"

Ulrich was right: she was a danger to the boy. Hastily, she tossed the tools into her bucket. As much as she despised the father, the child was innocent.

Gently, Ulrich rotated his son and instructed him to run to his mother.

Cora slung her satchel over her shoulder and rose to flee.

"Miss McSorley, I didn't dismiss you," he called out as he strode across the field, seemingly unslowed by his limp.

Rollie reached his mother, who clutched him against her lipstick-red skirt.

A safe distance from Cora, Ulrich stopped and folded his arms.

Now that he was closer to Otto's age at the time of his disappearance, Ulrich's resemblance to his father was striking. A twinge of sorrow gripped her heart.

He stood there, she knew, expecting an apology.

It had been eight years since she'd last heeded him as her master; the required submissive demeanor no longer came automatically. Plus, now that he was a war criminal, why should she cower before him? She straightened her shoulders and looked him in the eyes. "I'll tell them who you really are."

He grinned, revealing his straight teeth, still pearly white. "They're fully aware."

At a loss for words, she stared at him.

"The US government has absolved me of all *alleged* crimes." He tipped his hat at the American flag, fluttering above the morgue roof. "They've recruited me for Operation Paperclip."

Her temples pounding, she pinched her trousers to keep from putting her gloved hands to her eyes. None of the four newspapers she subscribed to had ever referenced a Project Paperclip. "What's that?"

"Our new enemy is the Soviet Union."

"What's that got to do with the hundreds of people you exterminated during those immunization experiments at Dachau?" she asked loudly, hoping a passing veteran might overhear. Even if the US government had condoned his Nazi past, the soldiers who'd won the war would not.

"*Allegedly* killed, and if you speak of those false allegations to anyone, I'll turn your files over to my new employer. Germ warfare has become one of the biggest threats to our national security. If I were to tell the government about you, this entire campus"—he arced his hand— "would become an army base dedicated to studying you. And dissecting you. In a theater operating room with dozens of observing scientists, each concocting new ways to extract your secrets. The rest of the time they'd keep you in a glass observation box—your home for eternity."

Her fingers tightened on a trowel, which she'd instinctively pulled from the bucket.

He nodded at it. "At least while I'm in charge, you can keep your little hobby."

"I don't believe your lies."

"The army's recruiting the brightest minds to help our country shore up its defenses against the Commies. You don't think they were eager to have me, given my alleged immunization experiments?"

Yearning to gouge out his eyes, she pressed the tool against her leg. Her body shook with rage for all the wrongs he'd committed against her; for everything he'd done to the concentration camp prisoners.

"Uncle Sam's even paying for our housing, and they've set up a lab for me in Building Two Fifty-Seven. That's their research facility on Plum Island, off of Long Island. It's even got a storage room for 'my' files." He grinned, showing those piercing white teeth. "I can't let them down, now can I?"

"Certainly not," she said, keeping her chin high, "or they might deport you."

His ice-blue eyes narrowed. "Get a good night's sleep. Tomorrow we'll pick up where we left off. My work has progressed nicely, thanks to all the Juden who sacrificed for the cause. After all, *sacrifice* is the core tenet of this project. I learned that from my father." He nodded and winked.

She scrambled to her feet to charge at him.

"Ulrich!" his wife called from the far side of the field.

Cora froze.

"Don't you think we should be on our way?" the blonde asked with an almost imperceptible German accent. "It's suppertime."

"Yes, darling," he called to her as he backed away from Cora.

Cora studied the gorgeous woman. "How can she stand to be with a monster?"

"Angelika—I call her Angela now—is a devoted Lutheran who believes that Jesus died for the forgiveness of our sins," Ulrich said, gazing at his wife, and Cora recognized genuine love in his expression. It sickened her. "She's been teaching Rollie the Bible stories, in English, which will help him assimilate."

A knot formed in Cora's throat, and she looked away from Angela, now rubbing Rollie's back as he continued to cling to her.

"Otto would be so pleased," Ulrich added with a chuckle.

Refusing to give him the satisfaction of seeing her disgust, she kept a straight face. "Does she know about me?"

"Of course not. She thinks we're living here while I teach microbiology at NYU."

He turned and strolled toward his son, who broke free of his mother's hold. They met halfway, and Ulrich scooped Rollie up and spun him. Giggling, with the sun shining upon them, they fell to the grass.

Against her will, Cora pictured little Emmett and Linnaeus, roughhousing as she watched with amusement from a nearby picnic blanket. Each would grab one of her arms, pulling her into a heap with them. Over the years she'd reworked their images into her perfect, imaginary family. One that would always remain beyond her reach.

And while she was destined for eternal and utter loneliness, here was Ulrich: wholly undeserving. And deliriously happy.

She dropped the trowel into the pail and hurried to the gardening shed, where her knives were once again rusting away.

Cora pried the floorboard free and removed the dirt-covered case. Before her, secured by loops she'd sewn in herself, ran four rows of tarnished surgical scalpels. She slid one from its lodging.

Surrounded by rakes, hoes, and potting jars, she raised the blade and vowed to drive him from the island. Alive or dead.

But, as she schemed, the memories of his cruelty broke through their sealed chambers, and her strength began to erode. Like the onset of a new disease, fear crept into her bones and raked her body with chills.

Her grip loosened; the knife fell to her feet.

On the floor of the shed, she curled into a ball, allowing the dread to overwhelm her.

Seventeen years later

July 1963

The *chrrr* of the physical plant died. With the throw of a lever, all power to Riverside had ceased. The Beatles song that had been blasting from the Emerson radio near the dock cut off at midrefrain and with it the commotion of the workers loading the ferry for its final departure.

"The Day" had come. Far too fast. Within an hour, everyone but Cora would be gone from this godforsaken island, and she would be left to endure on her own. Except for the promised assistance from the man who'd been torturing her since his return seventeen years ago. Those visits would simultaneously keep her alive and destroy her.

Sweat trickled down Cora's forehead, and her blouse clung to her back. Beneath the late afternoon sun, the enclosed roof of the morgue was acting like an open-air oven. The rooms below had to be cooler, but even if she army-crawled to the stairwell, the door's movement might give her away.

Riverside had sat dormant before, but only for brief periods. She'd survived those transitional times with food stockpiles and her victory garden. According to the recent gossip, this closure was permanent.

Cora shimmied to her eastern spy hole so she could see the silent physical plant across the street. Soon the ferry would leave, and she could refill her canteen at the cistern. That morning, the city had shut off the flow of clean water through a pipe beneath the river. The notion of drinking dirt and algae made her shudder, but at least the microbes couldn't harm her.

From Ulrich, she'd learned much about her abilities. And limitations. Because of his first experiment after Otto disappeared in 1936, she knew that her body could wipe out most common infections. Over the two years that had followed, he'd continued to probe her physiology. And then, after the war, Ulrich had further expanded the scope of his work.

He'd employed the methods developed by his colleagues during their transplantation experiments on the "Ravensbrück rabbits"—eighty-six female concentration camp prisoners. Unbeknownst to the world, Cora had become the eighty-seventh *lapin*. Seeking to pinpoint the source of her immunities, Ulrich inserted tissue from her organs into infected hosts. Since he no longer had access to a pool of expendable human subjects, he used the livestock at Lab 257.

When that effort produced no conclusive results, he reversed the process by implanting bovine and swine tissue into her. After a month-long incubation period, he removed the samples and returned them to their original—subsequently infected—hosts, in the wild hope that the animals would acquire her special traits.

Months later, undaunted by failure, Ulrich moved onto other hypotheses influenced by his Nazi colleagues.

In 1950, the veterans received their diplomas, and the idyllic island community departed with them. Forced to relocate, Ulrich moved his family to Long Island to split his time more easily between Plum Island and North Brother. During those two years, with no one around to hear her cries, he'd ruled over both Riverside and her.

On July 1, 1952, the day the hospital reopened, Ulrich, with his family in tow, became a resident doctor, while maintaining his affiliation with Lab 257. The very next day, he registered Cora as an addicted juvenile whose treatment plan required isolation. And whose "heroin-induced schizophrenia" meant no other doctor would believe her "fantastical claims."

In addition to testing environmental influences, he embarked on a side project to determine the effects of trauma on her vitality. While installing apparatus that enabled her isolation cell to double as a gas chamber, he explained that he'd observed a correlation between stress and accelerated aging in the Jews. "I began collecting data," he said as he secured his mask, "so they could serve as my control group for you."

Gas flowed into the room, and she choked backed her screams to keep from inhaling the poisonous vapors. Each time her body began to convulse, and she was sure that death had finally arrived, he would turn off the spigot.

After seven stints in solitary confinement, Cora still looked eighteen years old, which taught them both something: her cells were tougher than her psyche.

Now, a whole new form of isolation—and torture—was about to begin. Cora shook her canteen, and the last few drops landed in her mouth.

The American flag, affixed to a pole in the corner, flapped in the wind.

Two years ago, she'd watched Kennedy's inauguration on the television from the doorway to the crowded commons room in the staff house. She would have voted for him, but the island hadn't contained a polling station. Not that she could have registered: she'd lost her citizenship with the filing of her death certificate. The convicts on neighboring Rikers Island had more rights than she did.

During the ceremony, Ulrich had sat near the TV with Angela and their young daughter. Every time the camera panned to the crowd blanketing the National Mall, they searched for Rollie, who'd volunteered in Kennedy's grassroots campaign.

When the president had implored, "Ask not what your country can do for you; ask what you can do for your country," Ulrich had winked at Cora and grinned with those straight, pure white teeth. Otto had viewed his ability to resist tobacco, coffee, and liquor as a testament of his faith, whereas Ulrich abstained simply because not doing so would be a sign of weakness.

Although Ulrich had never said it, she knew he wanted to use her to develop a biological weapon for which the United States—or he alone—would possess the antidote. With her in complete seclusion, he could extend her deadly disease count without fear of triggering an outbreak.

The door to the physical plant banged open, and two mechanics exited the building. They didn't bother to lock up, which would save her the trouble of having to break in.

For weeks, she'd been hoping that the moving crew would leave behind the large backup battery stored there. The unit could power her space heater on the cruelest of days. The *Farmers' Almanac* had predicted the winter of 1963–1964 to be brutal.

The taller of the technicians tossed a cigarette to his greaser partner, and they lit up. "About time they pulled the plug on this shithole."

"Where'd they take all them junkie teens?" The greaser took a drag.

"Some other shithole." He chuckled. "You got a new gig yet?"

The shorter one pulled a pair of shades from the breast pocket of his jumpsuit. "A lead or two, but what I'd really dig is another place like this, with easy chicks."

Guffawing, they ambled toward the dock.

Cora pressed her fingernails against the cement bordering one of the bricks and wished she could hurl it at them. Some of the girls sent here had been keen on messing around, but others had been raped by staff or other patients. Or both.

When she'd first learned that Riverside would specialize in treating teenagers, she'd fantasized about making friends. Out of the couple hundred that would come, she'd hoped that at least a few would be willing to hang out with her from a safe distance.

The teenagers who'd been treated for communicable diseases hadn't prepared Cora for how different these addicts would be from Sophia and her friends at Wadleigh High. How she missed them! By now they were nearly eighty years old, if even still alive.

Riverside's cold-turkey treatment approach had seemed to make the kids crave heroin even more. A few had been friendly, and one handsome, sweet fellow had taken an interest in her. To keep him from coming too close, she'd had to pretend that she wanted nothing to do with him. Repeatedly. The sting of those memories still felt as fresh as the day they'd happened.

Cora released a single, strangled sob of self-pity.

Come on, woman. Get a grip. You. Are. Strong.

Mary. Cora closed her eyes and imagined her old friend beside her. If she were here now, she'd make sure neither of them starved. Cora should have paid more attention to Mary's chatter about the foods she'd once prepared or preserved.

Far more than her cooking, though, Cora missed her companionship and bold spirit.

Mary would have thrown a brick at those technicians.

But Mary was dead, Cora reminded herself, and an intense wave of sorrow and loneliness deluged her.

She brought her palm to her mouth and concentrated on the coolness of her breath against her skin. *It's only air. Not water.*

She visualized the supplies in her two secret caches, which she'd accumulated over the past three months. The food, toiletries, and batteries would make her less reliant on Ulrich initially, and the tools, clothes, blankets, and kitchenware should last for decades.

The iciness within her receded. Once again, she could feel the sun baking her backside. She returned to the spyhole facing the ferry. Most of the two dozen laborers were awaiting the "all aboard" call. Many were smoking, and almost all were shirtless.

"We forgot the flag!" hollered a guy with Coke-bottle glasses.

She dropped her head to the asphalt. The hot, rough surface pricked the side of her face, and its stench filled her nose.

If they found her, they would make her leave with them. She'd be dead within days, and shortly thereafter, a large portion of Gotham's population would join her. The spread wouldn't stop there: the passenger planes that thundered overhead from LaGuardia would carry her invisible assassins to England, France, and every other country on her atlas.

The sound of muffled conversation interrupted her thoughts. Cora raised her head and heard laughter.

"No way I'm setting foot in there, no matter who fought in Korea. It's full of spooks."

"Don't be such a candyass."

"Boys!" said a sharp voice. "The scheduled departure's in . . . three minutes."

Cora's mouth felt like it was filled with sand. She put her eye back to the gap and located Ulrich, in a white lab coat, which had to be for her benefit alone.

Last night, from this same roof, she'd watched him stroll aboard the ferry to spend the night with Angela and Greta in their new apartment on the Upper West Side. He hadn't arrived with the crew this morning. So how had he gotten here?

"Boss says I have to fetch the flag," protested a man whose large biceps were covered in tattoos.

"Until that ferry's unloaded in the Bronx, you work for me," Ulrich declared, waving a clipboard authoritatively. "The flag stays."

She wished she could believe that Ulrich had inadvertently saved her, but everything he did was premeditated. He must know she was up here. How long had he been avoiding her surveillance? Likely long enough to have made his own preparations before the movers began boxing up the medical supplies.

"Grab a dolly and two of your buddies," Ulrich said. "There's a backup battery in the plant that needs to go. We leave on schedule."

She spat out a curse. Ulrich had helped her, only to increase her suffering. He'd told her about the hypothermia experiments his colleagues at Dachau had conducted on the Jews, and so he knew exactly what that battery meant to her.

The McSorleys' apartment hadn't been wired for electricity. Cora's mother had heated their watery soups, rarely containing meat, over a coal stove, and the three had eaten beside a kerosene lamp. At the time, Cora hadn't known life could be better.

Now that she'd become accustomed to those luxuries, she didn't know how she would go without. And Ulrich knew that. He wanted her entirely dependent on him. Her head burned fever hot, and her muscles twitched. She despised that man.

If for no other reason, she would survive to spite him.

I know who you are: the descendant of a great Celtic warrior.

O'Toole. Expecting to see him, Cora whipped her head around. "No," she said, sharing her anguish with the empty rooftop. "He died fourteen years ago."

But maybe he'd been right.

Fisting her hands, Cora decided that she would do more than endure: she would best Ulrich. Instead of agonizing over the ways he might torture her with no one around to intervene, she should be viewing the island's abandonment to her advantage. If she fought back, there would be no one nearby for him to harm in retaliation.

Her grip tightened on the shaft of an imaginary javelin. She would love to drive a spearhead into the back of his graying head the first time he returned, but that would be akin to killing herself. Her revenge needed to be carefully crafted.

First, she would get through a full cycle of the seasons, which she couldn't do without his assistance.

Second, she would figure out how to survive on her own.

Third, she would exterminate him.

Fourth, Cora unclenched her fists. Rollie was nothing like his father. As far as she knew, to him, she'd been merely a groundskeeper, part of the island's scenery. Whenever he'd passed her, he'd smiled and waved. Since she'd always worn a wide-brimmed hat and kept her distance, he couldn't have noticed that she hadn't aged as he'd grown.

But now that he was a premed student at Columbia University, she had to assume that Ulrich had shared with him the details of their family's spezielles Projekt.

A thud, followed by the vibration of metal, drove Cora's attention back to the physical plant. Three of the laborers were maneuvering the battery, strapped to a dolly, toward the dock, with Ulrich snapping commands to keep them lumbering in the right direction. With age, his limp had worsened. Ever since learning that he'd sustained the injury to his right knee while at the concentration camp, she'd fantasized that a Holocaust prisoner had fought back, and wounded him—proof he wasn't invincible.

Cora moved to the other wall now to watch Ulrich and the last of the crew climb aboard. The captain blasted the horn, and the men cheered as the ferry began backing into the currents.

Through the crowd at the bow railing, Ulrich emerged and stared at the morgue roof.

Even though he couldn't possibly see her, Cora sensed those arctic eyes fixed on her. If she tried to murder him and failed, his rage would be animalistic. And to punish her further, he could find victims in Manhattan who wouldn't be missed.

Ulrich put his hand to his mouth and then left the bow.

He just blew me a kiss, she realized. An urge to dry-heave rose from her stomach, and she forced the sensation back down.

"I will kill him," she said, her attention fixed on the receding ferry. Until the ship disappeared, she couldn't be certain he was truly gone.

How and when he would return, she had no idea. The sensation of heavy water, pressing down, stole her breath. In staccato gasps, she sucked in air.

When the boat passed under the Hell Gate Bridge, she was alone. Truly alone.

Her breathing slowed, and she stood up. A breeze whipped her hair across her face, its whistle filling the silence. Riverside Hospital existed no more.

Eventually New York City would reclaim its land. Whether the campus would house the sick, the insane, or soldiers preparing to fight a third world war didn't matter. For now, North Brother Island belonged to her, Coraline McSorley.

"Cruadal, my friend, cruadal," Mary seemed to whisper inside Cora's head.

Repeatedly over the years, Mary had told Cora that it wasn't her fault Ulrich had turned out the way he had; Cora owed him no compliance or forgiveness. In response, Cora had always nodded to appease her friend. As hard as she'd tried to believe Mary, a niggling doubt had remained.

Now, fully understanding her deceased friend's often repeated advice to muster courage, Cora nodded as if Mary were standing beside her. "You were right," she whispered.

Turning toward the abandoned grounds, she yelled, "I *do* have the blood of a Celtic warrior. And I will show no mercy. Ulrich Gettler, you are not my fate: I sentence you to death."

The wind blew her voice across the island, and Cora cringed at her boldness.

Reflexively, she curled inward to protect herself from a beating. The first time she'd rebelled against him after their reunion in the meadow had been her last.

The memory of Susie's small fingers, frantically clawing at the tiny air holes drilled in the wood, and at Cora, throughout the hour that Ulrich had kept them locked in a coffin together, still made her squirm. The girl had been the six-year-old daughter of a World War II Medal of Honor recipient, whom Cora had beseeched for help.

Cora pressed her hand against the pocket of her satchel, where she kept the bunny barrettes Susie had been wearing that day, then looked across the river. Somewhere behind the glare of the sun stood the Gettlers' new brownstone, which she suspected had been paid for with Ulrich's share of the valuables stolen from the prisoners at Dachau.

She knew he was relying on the lasting trauma from Susie's death to keep her in submission. Picturing an armored Celtic chieftain, she decided to instead use that memory against him.

Cora turned to face the four-story tuberculosis pavilion. Although the building had become the wellspring of her disgust with this island, avoiding it would be shortsighted. The most modern of the structures, its ventilation would make it the coolest place during the summer's peak heat, and in winter, without that backup battery, she would have to rely on the thicker insulation within its walls.

Also, she needed to control the pavilion so that Ulrich couldn't. She would make it so that he could never operate on her in there again.

She rotated to survey the rest of her twenty-acre domain. The campus had become a ghost town.

Wistfully, she stared at the fenced-in tennis courts across the street from the nurses' residence. The shouting of players and thwacking of balls had practically been constants on the island. Their absences now were deafening.

In 1916, O'Toole had taught her the game, and she'd picked it up quickly. She could still remember the exhilaration of beating him for the first time. From the porch of her nearby bungalow, Mary had shrieked in celebration.

After Mary's death in 1938, her "germ-infested" hut had been razed.

Now even the nets were gone. Cora turned away from the clay courts and headed down the stairwell.

Moving through the gloomy hallway, she passed the pathology lab, stripped of equipment, and recalled the original Dr. Gettler, bent over his microscope. Cora could almost hear him repeating his favorite quote from Pasteur: "It is in the power of man to make parasitic maladies disappear from the globe!"

While he'd been operating a centrifuge or cleaning his equipment, she'd often kept him company in the hopes of hearing an update that would enable him to shift his focus to ridding her body of the germs. Occasionally, using a pair of forceps, Otto would dip a chocolate bar in honey and give it to her. He never kept a piece for himself: protocol dictated that he didn't eat in the lab.

Her mouth watered at the memory.

She might never taste chocolate again.

Cora hurried past the morgue and stepped outside. She shielded her eyes from the brightness and leaned against the wall. With too few trees to conceal her from passing ships, she would have to limit her movements between buildings to dusk or night.

The setting sun's reflection danced on the river, in sync with the sound of water lapping on the beach below the seawall. Without the bustle of human activity, it seemed much louder—and more grating on her ears.

Across the river, a train rattled past. When its clacking subsided, Cora registered the rumbling of truck engines and beeping of horns.

Civilization was so close, yet it might as well have been on the moon. NASA had a better chance of achieving President Kennedy's goal than she had of ever walking a Manhattan street again. Not that she would hear of a lunar landing. Yesterday's newspaper, discarded by the foreman, might have been the last she would ever read. The batteries she'd stolen for her transistor radio would die within a year, and updates from Ulrich would bear a steep price.

At least she wouldn't have to fully rely on him for food. Four years ago, after Ulrich had broken her seemingly beyond repair, he'd "prescribed" gardening. At first the excruciating memories tied to the seeds kept her from planting them, but then she'd found herself kneeling in the dirt, and a tendril of happiness had sprouted within her.

Since learning of the facility's planned closure, she'd spent her evenings doubling the size of her plot.

What if Ulrich had trampled her plants while she'd been watching the workers from the roof? She would have to wait until dusk to check. No, she'd had enough heartache for one day; she would look tomorrow. Even if he'd destroyed her crop, she still would have her stash of seeds and tools.

A tugboat appeared, and she ducked into the doorway and watched it head toward Gotham, whose towers had spread across the horizon like a steel garden grown wild. The image of her mother, cooking in their apartment, refused to form: Eleanor had died in 1930. Of what, Cora didn't know, though she had learned that her mother must have reconciled with her brother; the obituary mentioned Kieran's two sons.

Canne, too, had died, seven years before O'Toole. Everyone Cora cared about, including Otto, was gone.

Her only remaining companions were the characters in her complete set of the *Beadle's Dime Novels* and the abandoned library books.

A heron alighted on the beach. *And the birds.* She smirked. The service building had an auditorium with a film projector. Every Sunday afternoon, the administration had shown a different flick—a big hit with the junkies, who used the dark, close quarters to trade contraband. Watching through a crack in the velveteen drapes, Cora had been mesmerized by the animation in *Snow White.*

Cora was no Snow White; she had zero intention of befriending the birds that shared her island. Rather, she planned to eat them.

And she had no expectation that a prince would arrive and save her with a kiss. *A kiss.* She would trade a thousand backup batteries to experience just one.

Somewhere in that metropolis across the river lived her céadsearc. Cora still believed it, even though he couldn't be the same man she'd imagined while climbing into Alfred's boat.

American engineers were developing the technology to reach the moon; the tiny mysteries within her blood, right here on earth, couldn't be unsolvable. They just couldn't. All she needed was the right person working on them. That man wasn't Ulrich.

She slid down the wall to a seated position. Accustomed to an evening nap before embarking on her night raids, she tucked her chin behind her knees and closed her eyes. Worn down from worry, her mind didn't resist.

Cora woke to a purple horizon. The skyscrapers dazzled with light. She sucked in her breath and noticed the usual twinge in her heart at the sight of *her* city.

Never again, she promised herself, *will I miss a sunset.*

Motionless, she watched the colors of the clouds deepen. By the time full darkness arrived, she wanted to be inside the nurses' residence. Two weeks ago, after the last of the women and patients had left, Cora had moved back into her former space. Although she would have to make the tuberculosis pavilion her permanent home, for now she wanted to be somewhere that contained happy memories. And she needed to be close to one of her two caches.

"Good night, Gotham," she whispered, stepping away from the security of the wall.

Rounding the corner of the morgue, she halted at the sight of the physical plant. It looked like an abandoned fortress, its thick smokestacks a pair of turrets. The back of her neck tingled with a warning that someone could lunge from the shadows. She reminded herself that all the male patients and staff were gone, and she'd watched Ulrich leave only hours earlier.

Her stomach rumbled; she hadn't eaten since morning. For the last time, in what had become a nightly ritual, she gathered the paper sacks the movers had discarded on the beach. As usual, they hadn't left much, but it would be enough for one meal.

She filled her bottle at the cistern and took a swig. Her neck prickled again.

Cora spun.

The morgue stood motionless. Aside from the river, lapping the shore, and the chirring of crickets, the island was silent. *Too* silent.

She began to run.

Normally by this time of the evening, the iron streetlamps would be glowing. Instead, illuminated by the nearly full moon, they looked like rigid corpses.

Goose bumps speckled her skin like the pox. Finally, she reached the nurses' home, yanked open the front door, and locked it behind her.

In the darkness, she fumbled behind a radiator for her candle and matchbook, then introduced a meager light into the foyer.

She doubted she'd ever become accustomed to the newly acquired emptiness that seemed to radiate iciness throughout the building. Even though she'd been an outsider while living there, she'd enjoyed listening to the women socializing.

Now the only friendly voice would be her own. "Hello!" she shouted, and her greeting reverberated up the spiral staircase. "Race you to the top," she murmured.

As she climbed, the candlelight cast spindle-shaped shadows on the walls of the lobby, and her footsteps echoed. The air became hotter and thicker. Already the building smelled of disuse. With only one warm body left, all the spirits that must be lingering around Riverside now had space to drift. Cora reached out and imagined her fingers meeting Maeve's. "Hey, Button, you'd better not leave me like the others."

She reached the third floor, and the candle's glow ended partway down the hall. Ulrich's departure could have been a ploy; he could be lying in wait for her.

To calm her nerves, she pictured the crowbar stored in the supply closet adjacent to her room, along with gardening tools, seed envelopes, and other critical provisions.

If she had her scalpels with her, she could chuck a few into the gloom. Unfortunately, she'd hidden them with the other half of her supplies in the deserted lighthouse. Tomorrow she would retrieve them and begin perfecting her throw.

Holding the candle at arm's length, she inched down the hall. Each time the flame illuminated another set of opposing doors, she braced herself for his sudden appearance. The heat, trapped beneath the roof, pressed into her. A skittering sound came from above, and she paused. Too light to be human steps, the intruder must be a rodent in the attic.

Passing her bedroom, she retrieved her key ring from her satchel. With shaking hands, she selected the one for her closet and unlocked the door.

Candlelight flickered against the walls of the now bare room and she gasped in shocked horror.

Closing her eyes, she spun, hoping that when she stopped and looked, everything would be where it belonged. It had to be a trick of her mind after a long day. Dizzy from the motion and heat, she cracked open her eyelids and saw only black. Her flame had gone out. She dug into her pocket for the matchbook. The first match wouldn't light, nor the second or third. At last, the sulfur sizzled, and the room reappeared, still empty.

All that canned food, the sacks of sugar and flour, the tools, warm clothes, and pots and pans. Half of everything she'd squirreled away. Gone.

Cora screamed, and her rage resounded throughout the empty space.

Snarling, she smacked her hand against the wall, and darkness returned. Cursing, she used a fifth match to relight her candle.

This couldn't have been the work of the movers. She'd checked the grooves of her key against all of those on the board in the maintenance building. With 100 percent certainty, she'd been sure she possessed the only one to this room.

Ulrich must have hired a locksmith. Evidently, when he returned, he wanted her to be on her hands and knees, begging like a mutt.

Thinking of Mary and O'Toole, she vowed never again to plead for mercy from that monster; never again to roll over when he wished to slice into her.

Even though her new existence had just gotten much harder, she would not let him break her. After all, she still had the other half of her supplies. *The lighthouse!* But what if he'd cleared out that stockpile, too?

She lunged toward the hall, and her foot slid forward. Caught beneath her shoe's tread was an index card, which she grabbed.

Written in his thin, slanted cursive were two words: "Trust me."

Cora curled her fingers into a fist, crushing the note.

Fall 2007

October

The rubber bow bumped against the rocks as Finn jumped out to secure the raft. Rollie flashed a penlight to help Finn get his bearings. They'd chosen this night for its waning crescent moon—just enough light to see by, but not enough to be seen in their black wetsuits.

"Watch yourself," Rollie whispered as Finn teetered on a moss-covered slab of granite.

If they woke the herons nesting in the nearby mulberry trees, Cora would be upon them in minutes.

Finn hopped down to the packed sand. The island felt no less foreign than it had the first time he'd beached his kayak.

A thick mist hung in the grove. Despite the neoprene, he felt its bite. This cool damp was nothing like the heavy air that had preceded the deluge six weeks ago.

The memory of those moments, when Lily hadn't been breathing, still sickened him. During the quarantine that had followed, he'd dwelled on how close he'd come to losing her, and just how shitty Life After Lily would be.

Rollie grabbed Finn's shoulder to keep his balance, and Finn helped him onto the sand.

"We need to get out of sight and into PPE," Rollie said as he hoisted one side of the boat. Finn grabbed the other, and they dragged it over the rocks and into the thicket.

After removing two large pouches from the raft, Rollie sprayed a cloud of insect repellent around them and began peeling off his wetsuit.

As Finn quickly stripped down to his Speedo jammers and put on a hazmat suit, it occurred to him that Cora might be watching them. From her perspective, he would look no different from the other Gettlers who'd used her. So easily she could have killed him on the morgue roof. Or any time before then. Hopefully she wouldn't do so today, either.

He exhaled slowly through the respirator. Last night, Lily had been on edge. To calm her, he'd outlined his dad's protocol for operating in this hot zone. And for interacting with the most diseased human who'd ever walked the planet.

That was the perfect description to keep in his head as he prepared to meet with Cora. There was something about her vulnerability that he couldn't shake. Unless Rollie and Kristian cured her, she would never have the chance to experience a relationship or even a one-night stand. If her old-fashioned morals would allow for such a thing. Then again, she'd been around heroin addicts in the early 1960s; she had to know that times had changed.

Regardless, she deserved a chance to *live.* If they were as close to perfecting her antidote as they claimed, then convincing her to tolerate a few more of their requests might make the difference.

The knotted muscles in his upper back tightened, and he rolled his shoulders. Only once had he spoken to his brother since their altercation here. Kristian had denied knowing anything about the bats. Irritated and not in the mood to deal with his brother's attempts to wear Finn down through esoteric, scientific jargon, Finn had hung up on him.

Rollie flicked his penlight at Finn. "Do we need to review the plan?"

"You wait in the lighthouse while I attempt to undo a hundred years of mistrust."

"You're new to Cora," Rollie said, drumming his fingers against the Teflon covering his thigh. "Spend enough time around her and you'll lose that cockiness."

Not dignifying the comment with a response, Finn continued, "If I'm not back by sundown and haven't texted that I need more time, you call in Kristian." He had no intention of letting it come to that. "It's pretty straightforward, even for someone without a medical degree."

Rollie grunted. "You need to get that chip off your shoulder."

Finn glanced at his shoulder. "There's no chip; I like my job. Besides, why would you need me when you already had Boy Wonder as your lab assistant?"

"Your mind works differently than Kristian's, and mine. Maybe you'll see things that we've been missing."

If Rollie really thought that, he wouldn't have kept him in the dark, Finn thought, twisting the toe of his boot against the dirt. "Let's get this done."

Careful not to puncture their suits, they covered the boat with loose branches and made their way to the collapsed lighthouse.

Rollie crawled into the cave-like shelter.

Now hidden from the river by the mulberry trees, Finn took out his flashlight. "She'll find you here. We should be using your tunnel."

"You've only got a chance as long as she believes you're not one of us. With that maneuver outside the morgue, you certainly went a long way in proving that." He rifled through his bag, and Finn decided not to start a debate about loyalties.

"Besides"—his dad looked up—"I wanted to give you two space. This is the farthest structure from her home."

"That pavilion isn't her home."

Rollie sighed. "You're right. It was a tenement on West Ninth Street that was razed in 1925, five years before her mother died in an almshouse in Queens. On that same block Maurice Sendak wrote and illustrated *Where the Wild Things Are,* which was published in 1963—the year the city shut off power to Riverside." He found the plastic case containing a syringe filled with the antibiotic-resistant strain of *Borrelia burgdorferi.*

"You think I don't know what her 'gifts' have cost her? Every day I work on this puzzle so she can have her life back. And so, her misery won't have been in vain."

He handed Finn the container. "This is just *Borrelia.*"

"You swear?"

"Yes, I swear." He gazed down at it. "Hopefully, with this injection, we will save the human race."

Finn coughed. "Your bullshit lines won't work on me anymore."

"At the least it'll help your mother."

Finn shut his eyes. Two weeks ago, Sylvia had begged him to assist her in ending her life, since neither Rollie nor Kristian would. To give her a reason to hang on, he'd told her that he was confident Lily would be ready to commit by next summer. He planned to propose on the Fourth of July, he'd confided, and the conversation shifted to wedding rings.

If he hadn't convinced Lily by then, there would be a new reason for his mother to hang on: she would understand that he couldn't simultaneously lose both the women he loved.

He shoved the case into his backpack.

Now that he understood Cora's situation, he'd brought her an array of supplies, including a tactical flashlight with extra batteries, mosquito repellent, and vitamins. He'd wanted to include a radio, but Rollie had made the case that it would trigger culture shock. And increased feelings of isolation. Finn wasn't sure he agreed, but for now he didn't push the issue.

Lily had jammed in a large box of tampons, which made him uncomfortable. Last, he'd added a book. Apparently, the *Twilight Saga* was a big hit with teenage girls. Despite Cora's actual age, he couldn't stop thinking of her as young.

Eyeing the forest, Rollie beckoned for Finn to crouch in front of him.

With the aid of his penlight, he slipped Finn two clear cylinders. "Find a safe place for these."

"What are they?" Finn asked, inspecting the ring of colored tape below each of their stoppers.

"Plan B," his father whispered. "The orange one contains a dozen black-legged ticks, infected with your mother's strain of *Borrelia burgdorferi*. And the red one: cotton dipped in an analgesic."

Finn grimaced. "There's no way—"

Rollie raised his hand. "I understand why you took her side over Kristian's. But now that you've seen our lab and how close we are . . ." He steepled his gloved hands. "Please. If she won't agree to help us, see if you can't set them loose on her clothes. Or, if she skips her nap, use the gas."

Finn stood up in protest. "You can't be serious."

Rollie pursed his lips, his silence saying it all.

"This is so irresponsible. If they bite other animals, they could spread this strain across the Northeast."

"By then we'll have developed an effective treatment and hopefully a vaccine."

Exasperated, Finn groaned. No way could he do this to Cora—or the general population—but he knew that engaging in a philosophical argument with Rollie now would be pointless. He studied the tiny arachnids. During the tour of his father's lab, he would have noticed a tick colony. "Where'd you get them?"

His dad motioned for him to talk more softly. "If I hadn't needed Kristian, I think he would have become an entomologist."

"From where?" Finn repeated, waving the cylinders. "His own laboratory?" That would explain where the cage of bats had been headed.

Rollie's gaze darted to the trees. "Put those away."

Finn tucked them into his backpack. *So Kristian does have his own lab.* "Funny you never mentioned that he's been moonlighting."

"That's a good word for it. I don't know how he gets by on so little sleep, but I do know I can't run this project without him. There's too much data for one man to process. He uses his lab near their apartment after joining Hannah and Milo for dinner. It's just hobby equipment. Besides the Lyme, he doesn't keep any pathogens there. And no bats, since I know that's your next question."

"When's the last time you've been in it?"

"I see all of the analyses from his time there. Your brother's always needed space to think. As long as I'm still around, he wouldn't dare conduct any experiments on her without my permission."

Finn thought of Cora's revelation about the spinal tap. If he told Rollie now, and Cora found out, he'd lose any chance of gaining her complete trust. "You sure about that?"

"Positive. I put up with his attitude toward her because I can't afford to lose his assistance, but Kristian knows that if he ever crosses the line, I'll tell Sylvia." Rollie signaled for Finn to hold out his arms so he could check the seals on his gloves.

Finn nodded. He knew that Kristian cared a tremendous amount about Sylvia's opinion of him. According to Rollie, Sylvia had delicately honored Petra's memory while easing into the role of Kristian's mother. Kristian had learned to look forward to the folded, clever riddles in his lunch box long before he realized how much he adored Sylvia.

Finishing the inspection, Rollie leaned back. "There's something I need to tell you."

Finn's pulse quickened. "Shoot."

Rollie inhaled deeply through his respirator. "Cora killed your grandfather."

Finn recoiled.

Everyone had told him that Ulrich had died of natural causes. Though, now in retrospect, the closed-casket funeral had seemed odd.

Clenching his fists, Finn pondered if it could be true. The more he learned about his family's involvement with this woman, the more he sensed that he still didn't know. The fact that he'd been the only one kept in the dark was infuriating.

"It's true," Rollie said softly. "Kristian was there."

Finn ran his tongue along his teeth. Lily had mentioned Kristian saying something to her about Cora murdering someone in their family. She hadn't taken him seriously, nor had she remembered his exact wording.

Considering Kristian had also lied about 9/11, when it had suited his needs for their project, Finn believed him capable of twisting the circumstances of Ulrich's death to vilify Cora.

"Where did it happen?"

"There." Rollie pointed toward the buildings by the docks.

"You took Kristian's word for it?"

"I did the autopsy."

"From what I've heard, Gramps deserved it," Finn said, thinking of the whip mark scars on Cora's back. Also, an offhand comment that Grandma Angela had once made now had him wondering if Ulrich had played a role in his great-grandfather's disappearance.

"Did he deserve 'overkill'?" Rollie asked. "At age ninety-one?"

"Seriously?" Finn asked, wrinkling his nose.

"Kristian brought your grandpa here, one last time, because Ulrich had found religion and wanted to beg Cora for forgiveness. Finn"—his voice cracked—"she showed no mercy. The way his frail body looked: no God-fearing person could have done that."

Finn didn't know what to say. He'd witnessed her hatred of his family, so intense she'd wanted to kill him simply because of his last name. Suddenly less confident that she would spare him a third time, he fished from his backpack the scalpel he'd pocketed after their first encounter, which he hoped to trade for his utility knife. Rubbing the small crucifix etched in its ivory hilt, he surmised that Ulrich must have said something that had made her snap. His stomach soured with the realization that the possibilities were endless.

"Why are you telling me this now?"

"So, you understand how dangerous she is."

"Our family made her this way."

Rollie exhaled heavily. "That may be the case, but it hasn't been a one way street. Did Ulrich influence the way Kristian treats her? Absolutely. But the hatred: that came only after Kristian witnessed Cora slay his grandfather."

Still processing this new information, Finn balanced her scalpel on his fingertip. His father's admission had been well timed—an obvious effort to reinforce where Finn's loyalties should remain during his upcoming encounter with her. Did he believe that Cora was capable of the act Rollie had described? Yes, but that didn't make it true. Or her fault.

"You should keep that knife handy. Give me your arm," Rollie said, flashing the roll of duct tape. "Low, out of sight."

Reluctantly, Finn agreed. But what could one scalpel do against an entire pouchful, wielded by a woman skilled in the art of throwing them?

The pair shifted, so their backs faced the opening in the lighthouse remains. Finn held the knife to the underside of his left rubber glove as his dad secured it.

"The way Ulrich treated her changed her," Rollie said, tucking the roll back into his duffel bag. "She's no longer a rational, feeling human being. If she shows any signs of aggression, get out of there. She's killed one of us; she'll do it again."

Great pep talk, Finn thought as he stood and faced the interior of *her* island.

"Tell me you heard me."

"Got it," Finn replied, his attention on the tree canopy. Taking a deep breath, he waded through the wild grass, toward the woman who'd viciously murdered his grandfather.

Fifteen Minutes Later

Finn stepped into the shadow of the nurses' residence, and a chill passed over his skin. Sapling limbs stretched from the first-floor windows, and kudzu vines covered the facade. Within a few decades they would tear the building apart. Would Cora still be trapped here to witness its collapse? Not if he could help it.

Glancing around the gloomy wild, he still couldn't believe she'd survived here alone for forty-four years. If she didn't announce her arrival by piercing him with one of her scalpels, he could offer to install a few "pretty lights in the trees." Then again, her list of more practical needs had to be a mile long. Not that she would accept any kindness from a Gettler. Returning had been a mistake, yet not doing so hadn't seemed like an option.

He should continue moving farther from Rollie, but he wanted Cora to find him here, near her favorite building.

To appear nonchalant, he studied the interplay of shade and deeper shadows on the brick façade. If he made it off this island, he would sketch this scene.

The squawking of the herons made it difficult to concentrate. She had to be awake; no one could sleep through that racket. Perspiration was pooling between his shoulder blades, and it would only get hotter within his suit as the sun rose.

"I knew you'd be back."

Instinctively, his hands flew upward to shield his head, and he peered into the tree canopy, his visor limiting his field of vision. If he couldn't see her, the scalpel taped to his glove would be useless, even as an empty threat. Rotating, he searched for her.

"You Gettlers don't know when to quit, do you?"

The sound of his breathing roared in his ears. "I wanted to apologize."

"Well, that's a first." She coughed. "I'm guessing that wasn't in Daddy's instructions."

She *had* been watching them. "Do you ever sleep?"

"I rest."

"Of course you do," he muttered, continuing to turn. "Can you please come down?"

"Am I making you nervous?"

"Yes."

An upper branch of a nearby tree bobbed, and a blue jay alighted on a pokeberry bush entwined in the tennis court fence.

If she's as brutal as Rollie claims, why hasn't she finished them off, too? Finn asked himself. His dad claimed that the sheer volume of her medical records, stored in his Upper East Side lab, kept them safe. Given all his family had done to her, data alone didn't seem like a compelling reason for her to spare them. Or him. If the files were so important, why hadn't she demanded they hand them over when she'd had Finn chained to the morgue roof?

There had to be another reason. Finn sensed that Rollie was withholding something. If Finn could gain Cora's cooperation today, he would use his influence with her as leverage to get answers from his dad.

"How's this?"

He whirled toward her voice.

In the middle of the ivy-covered street that led to the staff house, she was standing with her hands on her hips. His cheeks heated at the memory of her showering there. Today, in another pair of cargo pants and a tank top, she looked dangerously alluring. In the early morning light, filtered through the trees, he could just make out the faint scars that dotted her face. Again, her hair was braided and tied off with a vine.

"Much better."

"At first, with that suit, I thought you were Kristian." She examined the palm of her olive-green work glove. "But you're taller than him. And thinner."

"Better-looking, too." He grinned to show he was joking.

She didn't return the smile. "But not smarter."

"Ouch. I thought you hated him."

"'Hate' isn't the right word. Is he with your father in the lightkeeper's house?"

"Really? You missed our landing?" he asked, raising his hands in mock surprise.

"Just tell me." Cora hugged herself. "Please."

Finn lowered his arms. "No, he's not."

She really must be afraid of him, Finn thought. "Seriously, though, you should consider rigging those rocks so some hooligan from Brooklyn Heights doesn't catch you by surprise."

Her face crinkled into a smile. "Firstly, the herons are my alarm system at this end. And secondly, as it turned out, I arrived too early. I could have gone without seeing you in your drawers."

He cringed. "You mean my jammers—they're a swimsuit. By the way, these days the cool kids use a's and b's."

Her smile winked out. "You think I'm old-fashioned." She edged around a street curb, upended by the roots of a cottonwood. "It's not like I've been completely cut off from the world. When people sneak onto this island, they think they're alone. They're not. I'm always listening from above. And I pay attention to their diction. *Capiche?*"

His ninth-grade math teacher had loved that word. "Sorry, that was thoughtless." He sighed. "I'm sorry for a lot of things."

"I know why you're here, and the answer's still no." She reached for the lowest branch of the cottonwood, and Finn could tell he was about to lose her.

"You don't know me as well as you think." He patted his overstuffed backpack.

"I don't need your charity," she said, eyeing the bag.

"I get it. You don't want to owe a Gettler."

He unzipped the main compartment and located the encased dime magazine. Between two of its pages, he'd tucked an illustration of the Astor Hotel at the height of the Great White Way's popularity in the early 1900s. If she contemplated the hours of billable time he'd forfeited to draw it, she wouldn't accept the gesture. Not that it would matter; he planned to be long gone by the time she discovered it.

"The supplies are repayment for letting me borrow this." He waved the booklet.

Cora dashed across the clearing and snatched it from him.

Before he'd fully registered her proximity, she'd returned to her original spot, the story clutched to her chest.

His pulse pounded in his temples. "The library would never let something that rare go into circulation."

"*This* is nothing. I've got something here far more valuable. Follow me." She tucked the booklet into her shoulder bag and darted into the foliage.

Wavering, Finn decided that if he wanted her to trust him, he first had to prove he was willing to do the same. At least this time he had backup.

With his gloved hands outstretched to ward off the branches that threatened to snag his suit, he followed her.

Ten yards ahead, she moved as lithely on the ground as she did within the trees. He struggled to keep her in sight while staying afoot.

A massive spider web, stretching between two trees, suddenly came into focus and he ducked to miss it.

Ahead, a two-story, utilitarian brick structure, which had to be the service building, appeared through the vegetation. Cora stopped at its front entrance.

She opened the door and motioned for him to enter.

He hesitated.

"Don't worry, I've no intention of harming Lily's *soulmate*."

He knew she'd meant it to sound mocking, and that she didn't want his pity, so he said nothing and stepped inside. His boots crunched on dried leaves and plaster. Poorly ventilated, the lobby had to be at least ten degrees warmer than outside. Given the insulating effect created by his suit, the temperature of the air trapped against his body would quickly rise.

She strode down a hallway, one of its walls skewed from the weight of the metal support beams.

He hustled to catch up.

They passed an open door marked Principal's Office.

"I bet you wish you could've been a student here," he said.

"In a way, I was, for four years. After the war, I would tend the shrubs below the windows. On all but the coldest days, the teachers kept them cracked open. High school English was on the first floor."

"Ah, your love of grammar."

"My favorite was sentence diagramming. I'd use a stick in the dirt to complete the exercises along with the class."

Finn pictured her crouched on the ground, biting her lip in concentration, and felt a sudden urge to kiss her. Shaking his head, he dispelled the unwelcome thought.

Although it would make his task easier, he couldn't lead her on. Feigning interest in the deteriorating papers underfoot, he bent to decipher their markings.

She turned away and continued down the corridor.

Conversely, he realized, acting like he didn't care about her would get him nowhere. "It must have been tough, being on the outside," he said, hurrying to catch up.

She shrugged. "There's a theater in here. I used to watch their films from outside. I'd love to see a real cinema, and another movie."

"It'll happen. Have faith."

"In your family? Yeah right."

She opened a stairwell door, and he hurried to catch it. "Where are we going?"

"The roof."

He raised his hand. "Based on our last rooftop experience, I'll take a pass."

"Fair enough, considering I'm passing on exposing myself to Lyme." She began climbing.

"That's not why I'm here." He followed her. "Well, it's not the main reason."

"But you do love your mom?"

"I do."

"I loved my mother, too. In 1902, she was told I'd died from typhus. How do you think that felt?"

"My family's done a lot of shitty things to you." They didn't deserve her altruism. "I will make them stop; I swear."

"Sure, you will. Right after I give you Borrelia antibodies. You'll become just like them. It's just a matter of time." She rapped on a door to the second-story hallway. "The science classrooms are that way. It was hard to hear those lectures."

The men in his family had always known so much more about her body than she had. No wonder she'd lost conviction that any of their theories would work. "Next time I'll bring some medical textbooks."

"Next time?" She resumed her ascent. "The nesting season ends in two weeks."

Finn wasn't sure why he'd said that. He'd informed his dad that if she said no to the injection today, then he was done. And that he'd do everything in his power to ensure the same held true for them.

Regardless of today's outcome, Finn knew that every time he glimpsed the East River this winter, he would think of her, cold and alone. At least he wouldn't have to worry about his family antagonizing her then; Rollie had explained that even with the tunnel, there was far too much at stake to risk being caught trespassing by authorized visitors during the winter.

She stopped at the door to the roof. "Don't you think it's a little ironic, your mother having Lyme?"

He narrowed his eyes. "How so?"

"Before Ulrich started his research on the black-legged deer tick, the disease didn't exist in North America."

"That's ridiculous."

"They really did keep you in the dark," she said with a sniff of disdain. "One of his projects at Lab Two Fifty-Seven was studying the tick as a vector for *Borrelia burgdorferi*. It was separate from his work on me, since, back then, *Bb* wasn't strong enough to coexist with my immune system. The first documented cases in the United States occurred in Lyme, Connecticut. Interestingly, that town happens to be right across Long Island Sound from Plum Island." She clicked her tongue. "I guess he should have been more careful with those little buggers."

Finn pictured the cage of bats so haphazardly positioned on that old, wooden spool. Considering how paranoid Kristian was about the inevitability of a global pandemic, such a reckless action from him didn't seem plausible. Yet there was no one else they could have belonged to.

Not to mention, Finn now knew Kristian had at least one other host species in his lab. He thought of the vials buried in his pack. As soon as he'd distanced himself from the lighthouse, he should have destroyed those ticks. It seemed farfetched that Ulrich could have brought the disease to America. Then again, Finn's recent reeducation in the seemingly unthinkable made it difficult to dismiss it as coincidence. "You're saying my mom deserves to be miserable?"

"No; I like Sylvia. She kept your dad in line. And while I feel bad that Petra died, I can't help but think that Kristian turned out better because of Sylvia."

She threw open the door, and bright light flooded the vestibule.

"I love it up here," Cora declared. "If I could be anyone in the world, it would be Amelia Earhart." She scrunched her face. "Before she vanished."

"Have you heard of Nikumaroro?" he asked, shielding his eyes.

She shrugged as she stepped outside, and Finn guessed that she felt insecure about how little she knew about the world today.

"It's a remote island in the South Pacific. They've found evidence that Earhart was marooned there. Apparently, she wasn't as good at survival as you."

Stifling a smile, Cora signaled for him to join her.

He exited the stairwell, and a strange sensation washed over him. For the first time while on North Brother Island, the surroundings felt familiar. He was standing in a rooftop garden similar to the co-op Lily participated in above the corner supermarket.

Lily would never see this firsthand, but he could describe it to her. Better yet, he decided, committing the scene to memory, he would draw it.

Despite the suit, he could almost smell the nearby tomato plants, their leaves rippling in the breeze. "You were right: this is far more precious than your story collection." His stomach growled. "Or any pile of gold."

"Who says I haven't come across one of those as well?"

Finn raised his eyebrows. As a kid, he'd dreamed of becoming a shipwreck archaeologist. He'd always been fascinated by the fact that the *HMS Hussar,* potentially laden with hundreds of millions of dollars' worth of golden coins, still lay at the bottom of the East River.

She didn't elaborate, either by design or because the hood had blocked his reaction.

"It's beautiful."

"I know."

He chuckled and set down his pack. "No modesty, I see."

"Why would there be? I've worked hard."

"I can tell."

"What I don't eat fresh, I store in root cellars."

"So that's how you survive winter."

"It's how I survive. Period. God, the earth, and my plants; they're my only solace."

She sounded like Lily, Finn realized. That's what Cora needed: a girlfriend, and Lily would be perfect.

"I'm sorry you've had it so rough."

Cora stroked a corn stalk leaf. "The original seeds came from Ulrich. Want to guess how he gave them to me?"

Finn didn't but felt obligated to hear it. "How?"

"By that point I was too wrecked to walk, so one night he came to my isolation cell in his Nazi hazmat suit—the same one you saw me wearing—and hauled me out behind this building. He dropped me and shoved my face into the mud with his boot. 'You've got two weeks to get well,' he said, tossing a bag of seed packets out of my reach. With no covering to shield my germs, and thus nowhere I could go, I spent the rest of that night in the muck, wearing only a shift."

If Ulrich were still alive, Finn would kill him himself.

The fact that she'd tolerated Finn this long was nothing short of a miracle. "Why did you bring me here? Aren't you worried I'll tell Rollie or Kristian?"

"You won't."

Because I harmed my own brother so that you could escape. Rollie had been right: Finn's act of defiance had put him closer to Cora than any Gettler had been since Otto had first become her doctor. "How do you know?" he asked to test the theory.

She strolled over to a strawberry patch and bent to pick a few. "*A*, you're not yet obsessed with this project. *B*, your dad didn't bring you through the tunnel, which means he doesn't trust you. That's a positive in my book. And *C*," she raised her eyebrows as she bit into a berry, "this place is booby-trapped."

Finn froze, ramrod straight.

She wiped the juice from her lips with the back of her hand. "Don't worry: as long as you step only where I do, you'll be fine."

"Sounds simple enough," he said, trying not to imagine a volley of arrows spraying his chest. Or what it would be like to kiss those lips. "Do you want help?"

"Why else would I bring you here?" She tossed him a cracked bucket and put on a straw hat and gardening gloves.

"It's noon," Cora said, studying the ground. "Time to eat. Then rest."

The heat within Finn's suit was insufferable, and he was thirsty and hungry, yet he didn't want to look weak. "Since I can't take this gear off, I'll keep working while you eat."

"We should rest in one of the classrooms for an hour so you don't faint," she said, arching her eyebrows.

Given that might happen if they kept working, Finn had no comeback. He grabbed his pack and followed her to an empty second-floor room, where she rolled out a shabby quilt.

From the doorway, he eyed the rubbish scattered across the tiled floor. The safest way for him to rest would be with his feet jutting into the hall so she couldn't lock him in if he did drift off. To avoid puncturing his suit, he would need to sweep a space clear.

Crouched beside her blanket, Cora smoothed out a wrinkle. "This is an awkward question," she looked away, "but would you mind lying next to me?"

He took a step back, knocking his elbow on the door frame, and an electric jolt surged up his arm. Grimacing, he clutched his funny bone to avoid answering.

"It was a dumb idea." She examined her glove. "Forget it."

"No, I . . . it surprised me, that's all," Finn said, searching her expression for any indication that this was a ploy to get him fully into the room.

"I didn't mean it inappropriately. It's just that a person needs other humans to feel fully human herself." She stood up and moved to the window.

"I'm a cold monster, too selfish to save your mom, and mankind," she said, staring out the broken window, the caramel streaks in her hair glowing with sunlight.

"No. You're a good person, who's been put through hell. That's not your fault."

"Yeah. Right." She touched the inner corners of her eyes, and Finn noticed a small scar on the outer edge of each eyelid, mirrored by another below each eyebrow. He couldn't imagine what heinous act had left those marks.

"You get why I can't help, don't you?"

"Absolutely."

Her finger traced Manhattan's skyline. "I know I've told you *this* is my island, but it's not true." She jabbed her hand through the opening. "*That* is my island. I want to go home, once I've fulfilled my purpose here. But every disease you Gettlers add to my blood is another shackle."

Even if she offered to inject the bacteria, Finn couldn't let her do it. Sylvia would feel the same way. But an assisted death? That couldn't be the alternative. If she hung on until Lily had agreed to marry him, then what?

"I get it." Finn pulled the syringe from his bag, snapped the needle against an exposed pipe, and returned the pieces to the case. "Let's be human together." He straightened the quilt.

She smiled, though it didn't reach her eyes, and dropped down beside him.

With a narrow divide between them, Finn settled onto his back. Self-conscious of his hands at his sides, he folded them over his stomach, which also felt clumsy. He reached over and clasped her hand.

She squeaked in surprise, and he realized how novel this must feel to her.

"You sure this is okay?" she whispered.

No, he thought, *this is far from okay*. "More than sure. Now *shhh*. Go to sleep." He knew she wouldn't. But neither would he.

To stay awake, he began rattling off in his head the names of the US presidents.

He was feeling woozy, like he'd just popped a pain pill. The heat within his suit made it impossible to keep his muscles tense, and his mouth was parched.

Monroe.

Her breathing slowed and became almost a sighing sound, its rhythm lulling.

Adams.

His eyes drifted closed.

Finn reached for Lily's backside, and his hand landed on a worn, patchwork quilt. He bolted upright.

Near the door, Cora sat, the contents of his pack spread around her.

He scrambled to his knees. "What are you doing?"

"You said you brought this stuff for me." She popped the last slice of an orange into her mouth and wiped her hand on her pants. "I don't know what it is about vitamin C. I've never been able to get enough. This book is excellent, by the way. Thank you."

Twilight lay open on the floor. She had to be twenty-five pages in.

Fending off a wave of dizziness, Finn blinked hard. "I thought you were asleep."

"I was, just not as long as you."

The ticks! Encumbered by the suit, he scrambled to retrieve his now-empty bag.

"Looking for these?" She held up the two vials.

He swore under his breath.

"I assume this one's chloroform." Cora raised the tube ringed with red tape. "Your family always has been infatuated with this chemical." She flicked the other, marked with orange. "These are deer ticks."

"They're not mine."

"I'm not an idiot; obviously they're from Rollie. But now they're mine."

"You should destroy them, like I was planning to."

"That would be foolish. Like every other resource I come across—including you—I'll have to evaluate their best use." She tucked the vials into her messenger bag, and he swore under his breath.

By allowing her to get her hands on those tubes, he'd just reached a whole new level of familial betrayal.

Refusing to let her keep them, he reached for the edge of the duct tape that held the scalpel in place.

"Whatcha got there?" She leaned toward him.

He peeled back the tape and raised the instrument so she could see it.

"That's mine!"

"It *was* yours, *before* you chained me to a roof! *And* pocketed my phone and Swiss Army knife."

"The phone doesn't work anymore. And what can I say? I like knives." She eyed the scalpel in his grip. "If you think you can kill me with that, go ahead and try."

Finn shook his head. "How about a trade?"

Staring at it wistfully, she rocked on her heels, then looked at the vials and back to the scalpel.

He studied the cross on its ivory handle. "You said it's got special meaning."

"How's this for a trade?" She patted the pouch on her hip. "Give it to me, and I'll let you live."

"Sure, if you throw in those two vials."

"No deal."

"Then it can't be that special to you," he said, positioning the scalpel against the pipe he'd used to break the syringe.

"Then you must not value your life."

Hoping she wouldn't call his bluff, he grinned. "You won't kill me. Not after I tranquilized my brother for you."

"You're right; not today. But just like the dead"—she slipped the vials into her bag—"I have no need for sentiment."

So much for trust being a two-way street, Finn thought and reattached the scalpel to his glove. "I'm done here," he said, looping his arm through the strap of his pack.

"For today. I don't blame you. When you do return, though, along with the textbooks, bring me the next in this"—she inspected the cover—"*Twilight Saga*. Please. And the latest edition of the *New York Times*."

"If you're so hell-bent on revenge, why should I return?" He moved to the doorway.

"Because." She picked up the book to continue reading. "You're the kind of cat who likes a challenge."

"These days we're just called 'guys.'"

"Fine. The meaning doesn't change."

Finn stalked down the hall, hating that she was right.

1964–1965

January 1964

Cora pulled the hood of her parka tightly around her face, as much to shield her from Ulrich's view as to ward off the frigid air. The snowflakes clinging to the crate were only a precursor to the blizzard that he'd claimed would arrive by dusk. From the morgue roof, she'd overheard him instructing the owner of the fishing trawler to return at three o'clock. His time constraint did little to settle her: Ulrich could accomplish plenty in nine hours, and based on the contents of this latest bimonthly installment of provisions, he had something special planned.

"You've dithered long enough," he scolded from behind her as she crouched before the row of crates.

The shadows of the physical plant's machinery shifted, and Cora knew he'd raised his lantern to strike her.

To keep him from seeing the fear on her face, she didn't look up. Still, she could sense his hulking form, enlarged by the winter weather gear layered over his hazmat suit and mask.

Everything she'd requested appeared to be here: canned food; a jar of lard, which she would use for cooking over a small open fire on moonless nights; candles and matches; wool socks; toiletries; vitamins; and gasoline for the portable generator that powered her space heater on the coldest days. In November he'd surprised her with it, and she'd grudgingly thanked him—only because not doing so might cause him to take it back.

The complete fulfillment of her latest list wasn't what had her worried. Rather, it was the extras he'd included. The goose down comforter, winter boots, fresh fruit, and parcel of beef couldn't have come from the goodness of his heart.

A click sounded, signaling he'd shut the padlock that secured his dolly to a pipe in the boiler room. After his first delivery, he'd left it untethered, and she'd used it to blockade all the first-floor windows of the tuberculosis pavilion with furniture.

They'd both been learning from their mistakes. Once he left today, she would move these provisions to hiding places dispersed across the campus. Last July, not only had he emptied her second cache in the lighthouse, which had included her scalpels, but he'd also trampled her vegetable patch. Thank God he hadn't recognized the resilience of the plants or the seeds hidden within their fruits. This spring, using a rusty trawl left behind in the supply shed and an old bucket to carry up the dirt, she would create a secret garden on the roof of the service building.

The tapping of his boot on the concrete warned her to finish her inventorying.

"I didn't ask for this stuff"—she lifted a fur-lined mitten—"so I don't owe you for it." The lantern's glow brightened, and she flinched in anticipation of a crack to her skull.

"Your comfort is my utmost concern," he said, his mask not softening his voice nearly enough.

Ulrich never used sarcasm. She rounded her shoulders inward and remained in her crouched stance. Since Riverside had been abandoned the previous summer, he hadn't experimented on her once. And now this: genuine interest in her well-being. She didn't understand the behavior change. And she didn't like it.

"I do appreciate your thoughtfulness," she said because he expected it.

"I trust I've been including enough feminine hygiene products?"

"Yes," she mumbled.

He brought the lamp closer to her face. "Your last menses: it began . . . ?"

Wishing she had her mother's strength, she pictured the calendar he'd given her for just this purpose. "The thirtieth, of December."

Through her jacket hood, she could hear the scratching of a pencil as he recorded the date in his journal.

"*Sehr gut.*" He snapped shut the book and picked up his doctor's kit. "Daybreak's almost here, and the river traffic will be heavy this morning before the storm. Get up."

She slid on the new mittens and followed him outside.

Instead of crossing the street to his laboratory in the morgue, he turned east.

"Where are we going?"

"The male dormitory."

The toe of her boot caught on the pavement, and she almost fell. The last time she'd entered that building had been three weeks ago, and then only to get a few books from the first-floor library. For all she knew, he'd recently sneaked onto the island and installed a new laboratory there, which to her would be just another torture chamber.

Ulrich had kept walking, still unhindered at sixty-two by his uneven gait. She sped up to reestablish her standard trailing distance.

As she followed, she fantasized about smashing a rock against his skull. Despite the ease with which she could hurt him, he never seemed concerned with having her at his back. Because he knew that without him, she couldn't survive. Yet.

I will kill him, she thought with even greater conviction than the first time she'd made that vow.

She rounded the corner of the physical plant, and the male dormitory came into view. One of the original Riverside structures, it had witnessed more than its share of misery. She scooped up a pebble and tossed it into the nearby cistern, one of the many pointless routines that now filled her long days.

He would take pleasure in any agitation she showed, so she refrained from asking for details. During their last session, after collecting the standard vials of blood, he'd probed her about her family tree. How long had her relatives lived and had they been healthy? Who'd had blue eyes, a widow's peak, fair skin, and brown hair, like her? How had her sister differed from her, and what did Cora know of Maeve's father? Absolutely nothing—the same as with her own.

At the end of the previous session, after measuring the distance between her eyes, the angle of her nose, and the height of her forehead, he'd said, "Your Irish lineage is unfortunate, but you appear to possess traces of Aryan ancestry."

Biting the inside of her cheek, she'd refrained from mentioning that he'd missed the conclusion so obvious to O'Toole. Cora wasn't merely *Irish.* Even though she hadn't yet harnessed its fearlessness and savagery, she could feel her Celtic warrior blood coursing through her, as real as her microbial monsters. The previous autumn she'd found a book about the Roman dynasty, which had referenced Brunnus, the great Celtic war chief who'd led the sacking of Rome. If she were his descendant—and it was possible—any Aryan ancestry she had would have yielded to these Celtic genes.

A gust of wind stung her face. Already the flurries were thickening into a more substantial snowfall. Ahead, Ulrich stopped five yards shy of the dormitory.

Apprehensive about what this delay might mean, Cora reeled to a stop. *This could be the day he finally infects me with a new, weaponized virus strain,* she thought, her knees shaking.

Motion in a maple tree beyond him caught her eye.

A gray squirrel scurried down its trunk.

Even though his back was to her, she knew Ulrich was mesmerized by the animal. Having grown up in a city with only rats, cockroaches, and pigeons, he'd remained fascinated by the few rodents that had managed to reach this island.

Abruptly he strode through the main entrance without a backward glance and propped the door open for her.

Cora glanced back at the cold, cruel river. She could sprint there now and dive in. Hypothermia would shut down her body long before Ulrich found a way to rescue her. That, however, wouldn't be the act of a woman of warrior descent. Nor was it her destiny. Over the past six decades, the island had been speaking to her through small miracles. This spit of land had given her the stamina to go on.

I won't let you down, she whispered back to it.

Making the sign of the cross, she entered the foyer.

Ulrich beckoned for her to follow him to the second story. From the main hallway, the rooms within her view looked untouched.

He barked at her to hurry, so she began climbing. Out of habit, she refrained from touching the handrail.

"This way," he called from the first of the communal sleeping quarters.

Cora peered into the room, which didn't contain any medical equipment. Her insides felt like they were trying to dig their way out of her, with the hope of escaping even if the rest of her couldn't.

"Macht schnell." He crossed to the far wall and set his bag on a dresser. "The probability of success will be lower if I'm rushed."

She stayed in the doorway, near the stairs. Already this building smelled of decay.

"Did my father ever tell you the story of old professor Pettenkofer of Munich?" he asked as he wriggled out of his coat.

Back when Paul de Kruif's book *Microbe Hunters* was first published in 1926, Otto had read her that particular passage. Shortly after, she'd sneaked into the laboratory to thumb through the tome herself. Mesmerized by that first glimpse of the "wee assassins" lurking within her, she'd read the entire history of microbiology in one night. But she couldn't tell Ulrich that. The only time she'd inquired about Otto's absence, Ulrich had threatened to remove her vocal cords if she ever mentioned him again.

"Tell me about the old professor, please," she said, humoring him.

"Professor Pettenkofer was a skeptic. Today he would be laughed out of scientific circles. But in those days, he was one of many who viewed germ theory as hogwash. When the brilliant Dr. Robert Koch returned from Calcutta, he claimed that deadly cholera doesn't arise spontaneously in its victims. Rather, it's caused by a comma-shaped microbe. Pettenkofer scoffed at the theory. Now I've told you about Koch's earlier work with *Bacillus anthracis*—Anthrax—through which he discovered that microbes are the root of disease . . ."

Cora nodded, eager to further delay whatever Ulrich had planned for her. Whereas the microbiology greats had inspired Otto, Ulrich idolized Josef Mengele. The Asian flu outbreak that began in 1956 did little to reignite Ulrich's desire to prevent a global pandemic. But it did solidify his disdain for the Chinese. Surely the appeal for him in developing a universal antidote from her blood now centered on the exclusive access he would have to it, and thus control over its distribution—both in the case of germ warfare or a naturally occurring outbreak.

"Pettenkofer was aware of these findings," Ulrich said with a flourish of his hand, "as well as Koch's discoveries of *Tubercle bacillus* and *Streptococcus*. Foolishly, he demanded that Koch send him a tube of the supposed cholera microbes so he could prove they weren't the cause of the disease. Koch obliged, and much to the astonishment of the scientific community, Pettenkofer swallowed the whole damn vialful. He should have died a terrible death. But he didn't," he said, shaking his head. "That old codger didn't so much as run a fever. I'm not telling you this story, Cora, to make you feel less special. Instead, it's to help you understand that the super immunity trait also exists in the Aryan race. And thus, quite possibly in my bloodline."

"Have there been others?" she stuttered. Consumed with horror about what awaited her, she wanted this discussion to last forever. "Germans, I mean, that can't get sick."

"Enough. Story time's over," he said, opening his kit.

The next morning, white blanketed the campus. The snow's brilliance overwhelmed her, yet Cora didn't look away. Huddled on her cot on the fourth story of the tuberculosis pavilion, she tugged the new comforter tighter around her. Her lower region throbbed, more from the memory of the heinous "medical" procedure than from the act itself.

"You're to spend the next month resting," he'd told her while unbuckling the leather straps he'd used to tie her wrists and ankles to the corners of one of the beds in a long row within the communal sleeping room. "I'll have fresh produce, meat, and dairy, as well as other supplies dispatched to the coal dock weekly, which I expect you to eat—not squirrel away." He eyed her. "When they arrive, you are to remain out of sight."

Not even tempted to disobey this command, Cora had nodded. She knew the man who would bring those goods would be the same thug who operated the fishing trawler that always delivered Ulrich to her. No doubt Ulrich was paying him handsomely to look the other way.

"In one month, I'll return. And continue to do so until you're pregnant."

"Why?" She'd wailed.

"You haven't figured it out? That's disappointing. Even if immortality isn't possible for me, I can at least try to establish it for the Gettler lineage."

Gazing at the dazzling snow, she sipped her pokeberry tea, flavored with the last of the cinnamon and cloves from her stores within the pavilion. The crate she'd opened yesterday was still sitting in the physical plant. Her abdomen was radiating heat, and she wondered if it could be from more than the steaming liquid.

Hugging her middle, she imagined a baby growing within her. For so long, she'd been yearning to experience motherhood. The hope of an antidote that would lead to her eventually having the chance to fall in love and start a family had sustained her through Otto's and Ulrich's experimentation.

If a cure never came, this could be her only chance to have a child.

But *his* child, conceived in such a vile way?

If it were possible for a baby to inherit her immortality, then reason stood that it was equally feasible for it to possess Ulrich's cruelty. At least with Ulrich, his ability to harm would end one day.

In all likelihood, the Gettlers' lineage hadn't crossed with Pettenkofer's. If that were the case, the baby's only unique immunity genes would come from her, which would likely mean that his ability to coexist with germs would also be limited to the island. If he couldn't safely leave Riverside, would Ulrich let her raise him? She bartered with him for supplies; could she do the same for rights to a child?

But what if the infant were normal? She wouldn't be able to touch her baby. Through six decades of contemplation, she'd recognized that Otto had been right: it could never have worked for her to raise Emmett.

Her love could have killed that little boy, just as it might any child she conceived.

Fourteen months later

March 30, 1965

As another contraction seized Cora's abdomen, she gritted her teeth to suppress a scream. Attempting to combat the pain that wrapped around to her back, she bent at the waist and clutched the balcony railing. Everything but the metal in her grip blurred away, yet still she could feel Ulrich watching her.

The cramping subsided, and her body slackened. Behind her, she could hear the tapping of his finger against his Eberhard watch, followed by the scraping of pencil on paper.

"Three minutes and thirteen seconds. Excellent."

Without losing her hold, she lowered her head between her arms and rocked to comfort her baby, who, she imagined, was terrified of these tremors. She hadn't felt her—or him—move since before the labor pains began.

Despite his kindness during the pregnancy, she couldn't admit to Ulrich that she was concerned. All those affectionate phrases and creature comforts: she knew better than to believe they'd been for her.

It had taken him six miserable months to impregnate her. Following his first attempt, she'd decided to flee before he could drag her back to the male dormitory—to hell with her greater purpose and whatever spiritual force had ordained it. She'd even constructed a makeshift raft. He must have guessed that she would try to escape; two days before she planned to push off, he arrived alone in a small motorboat and instructed her to climb in. They'd just cleared the eddies that clung to North Brother's shallows when she felt the onset of a fever. A minute later, pustules competed for space on her skin. With a smug smile, his eyes twinkling, he returned her to her prison.

By the time she missed her period, all she'd been able to feel was relief. Upon his next arrival, he'd promised that she would never have to enter the male dormitory again, provided she gave him a healthy baby. During the months that followed, his visits weren't any longer than an appointment she would have had with an obstetrician in the city. Although he never mentioned it, she knew he understood that the stress caused by his presence was felt by the baby, too.

A month ago, despite the bitter winter weather, he'd taken up full residence in the doctor's cottage. In case she went into labor early, he'd explained. Cora had a different theory: he'd finally told Angela about his research and this latest "experiment," and she'd been furious. Though if asked of her, she would presumably come around to raising the baby. While the Gettlers had been living at Riverside, Cora had never seen the woman act anything but compliant.

Undoubtedly, all he'd invested—and sacrificed—had made him even more committed to ensuring the endeavor's success. But also, Cora knew he'd fallen in love with her baby. At the end of each exam, he placed his gloved hand on her belly and waited to feel a kick, no matter how long it took. "I think it's a boy, no, a girl." Surprisingly, he seemed equally excited by the prospect of a daughter. When the baby did move, the smile in Ulrich's eyes, visible through his mask, made Cora forget for a second who he really was.

Another contraction squeezed her midsection, and she went through her motions. The desolate campus, gray in the late afternoon light, blurred away.

At last, it passed, and she exhaled again.

"Three minutes, seven seconds."

To get away from Ulrich, she waddled farther down the balcony. The nip of early spring felt good against her flushed skin, partially exposed by the hospital gown.

He isn't the only one in love with this baby, she thought, cradling her belly. Over the past eight months, the days he'd been absent had been the happiest of her life. Then it was just her and "Peach." Night and day, she prattled to her little one, filling her tiny ears with all the good that Cora knew of in the world and none of the bad. Always, at the back of her mind, a voice that sounded a lot like Mary's warned her that Ulrich's seed might have contained his cruelty.

But even that hazard couldn't dampen the exhilaration of experiencing firsthand the miracle of life. Despite the perils of it, Cora dreamed of raising her child.

Now the muscles in her pelvis and abdomen ignited, and she clenched her jaw. Long ago she'd decided to deny him the pleasure of hearing her agony, though at times the pain had been greater than her willpower.

The moment he deemed Peach sturdy enough to attempt the river passage, Cora was sure that he would take her away. Unless the baby's immune system had the same dependence on the island as hers. Then, he might decide that it would be safer—for the public and Peach—to keep her on North Brother Island.

If Ulrich's hypothesis was wrong, and the baby had no special qualities, Cora feared he would allow the newborn, no longer worthy of a place in his lineage, to die. As an atheist, he had no qualms about breaking the Ten Commandments. Conversely, Cora had already begun planning the repentance that murdering Ulrich would require.

The contraction ended, and she sank to her knees and sobbed. Once she gave birth, this child would no longer be hers.

"Did your water break?" Lurching to compensate for his bad knee, he ran to her. "Are you okay?"

"No, yes."

"Which is it?" He checked the ground, presumably for her fluids, and then placed his stethoscope on her abdomen and listened. "The heartbeat's faint. We're losing her! We must get to the OR."

Horrified, she let him help her up.

On her feet, she felt even less steady.

A fall could cause more trauma than the baby could sustain. She swallowed her pride, and disgust, and hooked her arm through Ulrich's, protected by the slick sleeve of his hazmat suit.

"This way," he said, pointing with his other hand. "I shouldn't have agreed to you laboring up here." He stooped to pick up his doctor's kit and glanced at her. "I suppose we should bring your satchel, too."

Surprised and genuinely grateful, she nodded and tightened her hold on him. They crossed the balcony to her bag, and he slung it over his shoulder.

Together they made for the stairwell, pausing whenever a contraction gripped her.

Each time her muscles slackened, she pulled her mind inward until everything but her womb disappeared. Hypersensitive, she waited to feel the slightest of movements.

Not once did she perceive life.

If the baby were stillborn, the true Ulrich would return.

Most likely, he would kill her on the operating table. That would be fine with her: without Peach, she would have no will to go on.

If instead he let her live, she didn't know if she could withstand another series of that "procedure," followed by pregnancy with a child that could never replace this one.

They reached the stairs. "We'll take it slowly," Ulrich said as they began the descent. A spasm hit, and he rubbed her back. Although she despised his touch, she didn't shake him off. He alone, through God's grace, could save her baby.

The contraction abated, and she lowered herself to the next step. "Please, Lord, let her live."

He held her steady. "Please, God, please."

Ten Minutes Later

"The baby's breach." Ulrich withdrew his hand from inside her pelvis.

"What does that mean?" She pushed herself up on the pillows piled behind her and looked at him between her legs.

"He's feet down. I'll have to perform a C-section." Ulrich ripped away her gown.

"Wait! I don't—" The cramping intensified, and the yellow tiled wall blurred. The contractions were on top of each other now, the valleys barely more manageable than the peaks.

Ulrich came around the operating table. "It'll save the baby and you. Trust me."

She jolted at those last two, familiar words.

"I must act quickly." His hand skimmed the instruments on his tray. "Where did I . . . No matter, I've got these." He reached into his black kit and pulled out a case that Cora recognized.

"Those are mine!" she yelled.

He eyed her through his mask. "Nothing is yours." He caught his breath, and his eyes softened. "Though if this baby lives, and you prove to be a nurturing mother, I will be generous." He flipped back the folded cloth, and the three rows of her blades now gleamed. He must have sterilized and polished them.

A pain seized her, so sharp she had to shriek.

"We need to get this baby out." He grabbed a scalpel.

Bracing for the incision, she wondered if she'd heard the "we" correctly. Angela must be more stubborn than Cora had surmised. She stared across the room at the bassinet, lined with the friendship quilt she and Mary had made four decades ago. She'd thought she'd lost it forever when Ulrich stole her cache from the supply closet. But after first detecting the fetal heartbeat, he'd returned it to her.

Rather than cutting right into her abdomen, he injected local anesthesia. "Tell me when it's numb. We can only spare a few moments."

"Do it now."

Without hesitation, he carefully sliced through her skin and muscles, then pulled out the baby.

Straining to hear those first cries, Cora bit her hand to silence herself.

Even Ulrich, holding the newborn with his back to Cora, didn't speak.

The room remained as quiet as a crypt.

Stillborn.

"No!" Cora screamed, trying to sit up, but the severed muscles couldn't engage.

She toppled back onto the pillows, which felt torturously soft.

A dark, bottomless hole, that's what she needed. The earth, it should break open beneath her. Then seal itself shut above her. No longer caring that Ulrich could hear her, she bawled with abandon.

A resounding wail joined Cora's.

Afraid it might have been an echo, she choked down a sob.

The reedy cry continued.

"Let me see."

"It's a boy." Ulrich twisted to show her their child, and the red of her babe's face deepened with a howl that could only come from a healthy set of lungs.

The sweetest sound, she thought, sobbing anew.

"Weißt du," Ulrich sang to the baby in a baritone deeper than Otto's, "wieviel Sternlein stehen an dem blauen Himmelszelt?"

Cora blinked rapidly in disbelief. It was the first German she'd heard him speak since his return from the war. Despite all the years that had passed, she'd recognized the lullaby Rolene had sung to him. He must genuinely love this child.

He laid the infant beneath a warming light powered by Cora's small generator. "Weißt du," he crooned, his face close to the baby's, "wieviel Wolken gehen weithin über alle Welt?" Can you count the clouds, so lightly o'er the meadows floating by?

Tears slid down her temples. A heart-wrenching sadness—for Ulrich's loss of his mother, and the resulting absence of warmth and love throughout his childhood. Often, Cora still thought back to that tragic day, and those moments when such a young, traumatized boy had shunned his father's solace. There were so many ways that outcome, which had translated into so much pain for her, could have been avoided.

Despite all that Ulrich stood for and had done to Cora, she could hear in his tender tone now a promise to this child that his upbringing would be nothing like Ulrich's own. From afar, she'd observed his devotion to his other two children, and she wept with gratitude at this early indication that he loved this baby too.

He cut the umbilical cord and cleared out the baby's mouth and nose.

The newborn cried louder. Cora stretched toward him, and blood from her abdomen sloshed onto the floor. "Give him to me."

"The crying's good. It means he's strong." Ulrich swaddled him and placed a knit cap over his head.

"I love you, *mein kleiner Mann*," he said in the same soothing voice she'd heard him use with Rollie and Greta when they were young.

Cora could only guess—and pray—that Ulrich was speaking German to their child because it would be safe to do so with him living here on the island.

"Say hello to your Mutti while I stitch her up."

He placed the wailing newborn on Cora's chest, and she gasped at the sensation of his cheek against her skin. He was so warm, and wet. Afraid he would slip away, like so many of her hopes, she awkwardly held him to her.

The baby squirmed, so she tightened her grip. *I'm hurting him*, she worried.

"How do I do this?"

Smiling, Ulrich looked up from his needle and thread. "Put him to the breast."

Of course. She was, after all, his mother.

She repositioned him, and of his own accord, he rooted for her nipple. The silence was equally exquisite to his wailing. Stroking his tiny head through the cap, Cora tried not to let her weeping disturb him, but she couldn't hold it back. *This* was why she'd never given up.

Ulrich tied off the stitches, bandaged the wound, and stepped back to appraise their son.

Reflexively, she tightened her hold.

"Don't worry. I need a moment to catch my breath." He dropped onto a stool and watched their baby nurse. "I still have to administer some tests to determine his Apgar score, but he appears to be healthy. A beautiful boy. We did it. And you'll make a great mother."

Mother? You'll never be this boy's mother, nor any child's. Otto's declaration after ripping away Emmett sounded in her head.

Tears, tainted with deadly germs, slid down her cheeks, and a warning sounded within her: the more she loved this child, the more it would hurt when Ulrich took him.

Cora blinked away the thought and gazed at her cherub's face. Almost nonexistent, his eyebrows and lashes would surely come later. Tufts of black hair peeked from the edges of the cap. His lips, hugging her skin, looked pinker than a tulip, and his nose: impossibly tiny.

"What's his name?" Ulrich asked.

Shocked, Cora looked up. Had she misheard?

"I wish I could hold him without my suit." He folded his arms. "Unfortunately, I have many trials to conduct before that's possible. It may never be."

She bit her lip to hold back a smug reply and stroked her babe's cheek. If he were also an asymptomatic carrier who couldn't leave North Brother, she wouldn't want Ulrich to forget the attachment he now felt to the boy. She knew what she had to do: give him a German name.

One that was good and kind. Daily, she'd prayed for God to bless this baby with a gentle soul.

She wrapped his fingers around her pinky. "His name is Kristian."

Fall 2007

The heron nesting season draws to a close

October

Lily lowered the piece of sushi to her plate with almost-inhuman restraint. The lingering, sweet taste of yellowtail turned bitter in her mouth. "What do you mean," she said, punching out each syllable, "you're going back?"

"I have to." Finn leaned away from the folding table in their apartment.

A week ago, when he'd returned from his failed attempt to convince Cora to cooperate, he'd been beyond frustrated. Biting her knuckle to stymie a volley of questions, she'd let him rant, then listened without judgment as he voiced a series of impractical solutions. Not once had he mentioned the possibility of another trip—so soon.

"No, you *don't* have to," she replied.

"That place is like a keg of dynamite," Finn said too loudly. "Between those bats, their obsession with injecting her with Lyme, and now the fact that she's got chloroform, it's not going to end well. For who, I don't know. Maybe everyone. My brother's being a total ass, but I still love him."

Lily pushed her plate away. "I don't want anyone getting hurt, either, but she's just too insanely dangerous."

"Lils, she trusts me. She wouldn't have shown me her garden if she didn't."

A knot formed in Lily's throat, and she tried not to imagine the two of them on that rooftop. The days that Finn helped Lily at the co-op were her favorite. Somehow, he managed to be entertaining and productive at the same time. She didn't want to picture him acting that same way with Cora. "Maybe that's true, but she didn't strike me as particularly sane. There's got to be another option."

Finn stared out the window at the adjacent building, barely visible in the waning light. Usually, Lily's heart skipped at the sight of his profile, with a nose so straight it almost made him pretty. This time she had to clench her teeth to keep from demanding that he concentrate on her instead of a brick wall.

"What do you suggest we do?" he asked.

She rose to pace across their kitchenette. "I care about her, and your family. But"—her voice cracked—"I care about you even more."

He kneaded the back of his neck, and she knew he was thinking of her unwillingness to marry him. She considered admitting that her misgivings about Rollie had always been a factor, but Finn was a problem solver. Especially right now, she didn't want him attempting to engineer a workaround to what her instincts were telling her.

To keep him on topic, she spoke first: "Promise me you won't go before the nesting season ends. We should figure this out together over the winter."

Finn nodded. "Okay. She'll be safe from them during the winter anyway."

Lily studied the potted cacti on the windowsill, the most recent of which she'd added for Susan, whose second bone marrow transplant had failed last spring. Two years earlier, they'd met at a summit for young adults with cancer and became steadfast virtual friends. Hating the unfairness of life, Lily scrunched her eyes shut. Her grief didn't disappear.

The flowering Echinopsis next to Susan's represented Elisabeth, who'd lost her seven-year battle with metastasized breast cancer. They'd developed a bond during a kayaking camp for cancer survivors, which Finn had encouraged Lily to attend. Elisabeth and Susan, along with the others represented in her memorial garden, had understood her in a way people who haven't had cancer could not.

Except for Kristian, who'd accepted her anxieties as rational. But it was looking like she'd lost him as a friend, too. The fact that he viewed Cora akin to a lab rat was appalling.

Over the past two months, he'd repeatedly tried contacting Lily. Each time, she'd silenced her ringer. How could a man who showed endless compassion to his patients and their families treat another human so inhumanely?

Because Cora had killed his grandfather.

But one sin could not justify an endless series of other sins, which would eventually spur Cora to retaliate, maybe even during Finn's next trip.

The cycle had to be ended. But with it, the potential for a cure? Lily hesitated.

Unquestionably, Cora could defend herself now. The abuse—of her body, her rights, and her trust—had largely occurred before Finn had stepped onto North Brother Island. Perhaps they could find a way for the research to continue with the two of them advocating for Cora as Sylvia once had. Startled by the boldness of the idea, and unsure of its morality, she dropped into her seat.

"What're you thinking?" Finn swigged his beer.

Lily scraped her fingernail across her lower lip. "Isn't that my line?"

"Hopefully I'll have better luck with it." He raised his eyebrows to implicate himself.

"I should stay quiet, so you know how it feels."

"Sure, you could do that. But we're in this together, so I need to know what's going on in there." He leaned over the table and tucked back a lock of her hair.

Gazing at her cacti, she thought of all the friends she'd made who were still battling their cancers. With their immune systems weakened by their treatments, they were even more susceptible than she was to a novel virus. As Kristian had stated during one of his voicemails: on any given day, a highly lethal and contagious new strain could emerge from a cave, rainforest, or wet market—a mere trek and plane ride away from New York City.

She wondered if all maladies, including cancer, really could be eradicated someday with Cora's gift. It didn't seem possible. *Yet maybe . . .*

Cora, too, had a garden, Lily reminded herself, for a vastly different purpose.

An idea struck her like a slap on the back, and she straightened. "I should be the one to go."

"What?" Finn spat.

Leaning forward, she propped her elbows on the table. "She'll trust a woman—not related to your family—far more easily." Plus, they'd be able to relate: they each feared what lay beneath her own skin. "She risked her life for me; that tells you something."

"Out of the question," he said, slamming down his bottle. "I almost lost you there once."

The reference triggered a cascading of spots in Lily's vision. To steady herself, she pressed her palms against the table.

He gripped its edge, clearly trying to maintain his composure. "It's like you think you're fated to die early and just want to get it over with."

"So now you're admitting it's too dangerous?"

"I don't have epilepsy. And my organs haven't been—"

Fuming, she glared at him.

"I'm sorry. I didn't mean—"

"Whatever," she said, knowing he hated that expression. "But you bring up a good point: I'm already damaged goods. So my life is less valuable."

Finn's eyes narrowed, and he chugged the rest of his beer.

She knew he was planning his words carefully, so she changed course: "She's worried about you becoming like them. The same doesn't hold true for me."

He tossed his empty bottle into the recycling bin by the door, and it thudded against the plastic bottom. "You're still one of us, though, and if you'd seen her scars, you'd understand how deep her hatred runs. It's too risky."

Flinching, she dropped her gaze to hide her hurt. Twice Finn had seen that woman naked. Cora was untouchable; Lily knew she shouldn't feel envious. Yet she couldn't dispute the woman's allure. Even from two stories below, during a downpour, Lily had felt her magnetism. And the heart tends to want what it can't have.

Finn nudged her foot with his. "I love you."

She wrapped her legs around her chair.

From across the table, he was staring at her with those intense, earthy green eyes. She could tell he was waiting for her to return the gesture and that he knew it wouldn't happen.

Lily gathered her dishes. "You know it's the only way."

He touched her arm. "I can't lose you."

The words closed in on her, and she slouched to bring her ears between her shoulders. Comments like that were too much pressure. Twisting, she set her plate in the sink. Whenever she needed to be alone, she headed for the promenade at the end of their street. From the front closet, she retrieved her running shoes and iPod.

Finn blocked her. "Your whole life, you've been running from yourself. My dad and brother are smart—maybe brilliant—but I don't want you getting your hopes up. There's nothing they can achieve in that dippy lab that can undo what cancer—and your dad—did to you."

She ducked past him and into the hall. "I have to believe in the impossible. Because . . ." This conversation was pointless: Finn was too pragmatic. To him, the probability of them finding a cure for cancer was so slim, it was irrelevant. To her, a single iota of possibility meant everything.

She started to run and tripped on one of her untied laces.

Finn rushed to her.

"I'm fine." She wriggled away from him, and with shaking hands double-knotted her sneakers.

"I know; you're tough," he said, backing away from her. "I couldn't just stand there, not helping someone I love."

"I get that. But you don't love Cora, and I'm the one who owes her," she said, then hustled down the open-air stairwell and onto the sidewalk. Dodging an older man pushing a lapdog in a stroller, she sprinted toward the esplanade.

From the balcony of the vestibule seven stories above, Finn had to be watching. She knew he wouldn't chase after her—not because he couldn't catch up, which he couldn't, but because he too would have concluded they'd reached a dead end.

Running with the East River and the Lower Manhattan skyline at her side, she made for the Brooklyn Bridge. Once across it, she would keep going until exhaustion hit her. Only then would she turn around.

Two months later

December

Slabs of ice blockaded the docks that jutted into the East River. Soon the entire strait might crust over. Lily shivered and gazed toward Randalls-Wards Island, barely visible from Kristian's office on the hospital's eighth floor. Beyond it and Hell Gate lay North Brother. Somewhere on that island huddled a woman, surrounded by eight million people ignorant of her plight.

Lily didn't know if Cora was still capable of accepting anyone as an ally, but she had to try. Even if it meant going behind Finn's back.

Usually, she avoided hospitals because of the visceral memories they triggered. She'd steeled herself against them to meet Kristian here, yet she still felt sick to her stomach. For multiple reasons.

"It's so good to see you again," he said from behind his oak desk, a genuine smile on his face.

A lump in her throat fought to block her from betraying Finn, or saying anything that Kristian might construe as forgiveness.

"As long as you're here," he said, evidently used to ending the charged silences that must frequently occur during his meetings in this room, "I've been wanting to tell you something. I had nothing to do with those bats out at the summer house. That had to be a trap cage left by my parents' exterminator. They were probably roosting in the shed, and bats are one of the main carriers of rabies."

Trying to picture the cage, so that she could refute his claim, Lily closed her eyes.

"Think about it," Kristian continued. "If they were instead for our research, they would have needed to be handled according to Biosafety

Level Three guidelines. It's inconceivable that I would have put them in that shed, no matter how temporarily."

Glancing out the window, she reminded herself that mentioning the syringes that Finn had found near those bats would derail her plan. "I believe you."

"Good," he said, adjusting a spray of candy canes in his pen holder. "So why are you here?"

"I need vaccines, a hazmat suit. So I can go back to North Brother this spring to talk to Cora."

"It's too dangerous for you."

"Me? It's your family she hates!"

"What happens if you have another seizure?" Kristian tilted back in his chair.

"The lightning triggered that. This time"—Lily shrugged—"I won't go in a storm." She strummed her fingers on the radiator.

Sighing, he removed his stethoscope. "As a doctor, and your friend, I'm advising you against it. You mean a lot to me, and you mean everything to Finn."

Blinking, she inhaled slowly to keep her emotions in check. "What if I can convince Cora to start giving you blood samples again? Isn't that worth a shot?"

"Why would she listen to you?"

"I'm not a Gettler. She wants off that rock, and you have all her files. Plus, I'm"—Lily's voice wavered—"weaker than her. More vulnerable. She won't fear me."

Slowly, Kristian leaned forward. "You're the fiercest among us, but I understand your point: she doesn't know how strong you are."

Unwilling to let him think he'd won her over, she allowed herself only a thin smile. "I want you to find that cure for your mom."

"This is about helping you, too."

"I know." She leaned against the windowsill, its sharpness feeling oddly therapeutic.

"I have to admit." He cleared his throat. "I was surprised Finn failed so completely, considering she clearly has a thing for him."

A jolt of pain raced along Lily's sciatic nerve.

He pushed the bridge of his glasses against his nose, the top of the frame merging with his thick, dark eyebrows. "At first, I thought we could take advantage of her interest in him, but now it concerns me."

"Why?" She rested her elbows on the sill. "She's just starved for affection. I feel bad for her. I can't imagine being that lonely."

"Lily, if she falls hard for him, what do you think will happen when he rejects her?"

A chill swept over her, leaving an ice dam in her stomach.

"It's probably for the best that you go instead of him." Kristian cocked his head. "He doesn't know you're here, does he?"

"No. He can't know."

"Hopefully the fact that she stole those vials has clued him in to her real nature. He should give me a chance to clear up a few major misconceptions."

She looked down at her chinos and noticed a streak of dirt from the city greenhouse where she'd spent the morning. "I'm sure he'll come around."

"I'll keep trying until he does." Kristian turned to the bookshelf behind him, then handed her a small, framed photograph.

Lily appraised the pale toddler with soulful, brown eyes. That had been her once, though her mother hadn't kept a single picture from that wretched period. "Who is she?"

"The first patient I ever lost." Kristian gazed out the window.

Bombarded by recollections of her own past trauma, Lily let him dwell in the memory as she struggled to tamp down her escalating anxiety.

His shoulders straightened, and his deep blue eyes locked onto hers. "Do I think one woman should be willing to endure a little discomfort to save thousands—millions—of children like Simone? Yeah, I do. Does that make me a bad person?"

"No," she replied without meaning to. "Could Cora's immunities—I mean, could her cells really . . . ?" She wondered how many parents had sat here waiting for Dr. Gettler to pronounce the odds of survival for their child.

He folded his hands. "Once we've had that final breakthrough, we'll achieve Pasteur's vision." He took the frame from her and returned it to the shelf. "I know it in my heart."

She perched across from him. "What makes you so convinced you're close?"

He drew a comma-shaped circle on a notepad. Within it he scrawled *NBI*. "Location is the key to her immunities," he said, tapping the figure with his pen. "My great-grandfather conducted all stages of his experiments while at Riverside, but his equipment was crude and his knowledge elementary. Rollie and I have had the tools to replicate her antibodies, and we've been doing so onsite. But just like Ulrich with his livestock at Lab Two Fifty-Seven, we were conducting our animal testing—"

"Offsite, where her cells had lost their special properties."

"Exactly. Or, in our onsite lab, deep within the bedrock. My theory is that the schist blocks whatever on the island influences her cells."

Lily's arms tingled. If he were right, a cure could be close. "Can't you test that theory with her existing pathogens?"

"I'll admit: my top priority is healing my mother."

"I won't ask her to inject the Lyme bacteria," Lily said, shaking her head.

She reached for her coat and purse, and he came around the desk and touched her shoulder. Although the brotherly gesture had never bothered her before, her entire body tensed.

"Your reasons for wanting this puzzle solved are not as selfish as you think."

Lily shifted out of reach, yet waited for him to continue.

"I know why you've been holding out on Finn."

You are so wrong. She busied herself with putting on her jacket.

He slung his stethoscope over his shoulder. "You'll make a great mom, regardless of whether your children come the old-fashioned way. If we can harness Cora's immunities, you won't have to worry about leaving them motherless."

To cover her ears, she zipped her collar to the top. "I gotta get back to work."

"Likewise." He motioned for her to go first.

She hurried past him, and her stomach lurched at the antiseptic smell and polished floor of the corridor.

"Promise me one thing," he said.

The glow of the fluorescent lights bounced off the metallic garland and ornaments hanging from the ceiling. She spotted the sign for the elevator and sped toward it.

His footsteps sounded behind her.

She jabbed the down button.

"There will come a time when you'll question my loyalties."

The elevator dinged, and she stepped inside and swiped at the panel.

"Please remember"—he reached to prevent the elevator from closing—"that I always put family first."

The doors met; Lily was finally alone.

1966–1967

Invasive species begin their slow strangulation of the island

October 1966

The rock struck Cora's finger instead of the nail. Ignoring the sting, she continued bolting the plywood to the two doors she'd taken from the nurses' residence. Soon dawn would arrive, and with it enough light to chance the voyage she'd begun plotting seventeen months ago, the day after Kristian was born. Although she'd longed to believe that everything would be fine, *trusting* Ulrich was something she would never do.

A tugging on the cord tied to her waist shifted her attention to Kristian at its far end, playing among three cartons in the tall grass. By sunrise, their makeshift raft needed to be at the edge of the dock, with those provisions lashed to it.

He climbed atop one and clapped in self-praise.

"Good job!" To please Ulrich, she usually spoke to Kristian in her rudimentary German. But from now on, she vowed, her son would hear only English.

"*Sehrrrrr groß*." He raised his arms above his head and wobbled. She tensed, ready to scoop him up in a hug if needed, but he regained his balance.

"Soooo big," she translated and grabbed another nail.

"Mutti," he whined, and she knew that in addition to wanting her, he was missing his blankie.

To create the impression that a patrol had picked her and Kristian up, she'd left it on the ferry dock near a US Coast Guard cap. Ulrich wouldn't be fooled so quickly; she knew he would search Riverside. So she'd packed enough provisions for them to hide in the small forest on South Brother for three days. Hopefully, by then, Ulrich would have concluded that the coast guard had taken them. Any longer than that, even with sustenance, she wouldn't have the strength for the return journey. Measles, typhus, smallpox, and typhoid fever hadn't taken pity on the thousands of indigents sent to Riverside; they would show no kindness to a mother protecting her young son.

Kristian ran to her and pointed at the amalgamation of boards. "*Boot. Im Wasser.*"

Barely a toddler, he already loved the river as much as she detested it. "We'll push the boat into the water as soon as Mommy's done."

A month ago, he'd ridden on one for the first time. Afterward, when Ulrich set him on the dock, he'd cried. Cora, who'd been pacing along the seawall, had rushed to him, expecting—hoping—to see fading symptoms of her illnesses. Instead, she'd learned that their perfectly healthy boy hadn't wanted the excursion to end.

Kristian wedged himself between her and the raft.

Although she would love to cuddle him, there was much to do. She found a stick and set him in the grass. "Dig for night crawlers, my little bear," she said, using the English version of her nickname for him for the first time. She tousled his blond hair and tried not to think about what would happen if her plan failed.

During Ulrich's last visit, she'd overheard him telling Kristian that next time Vati came, Kristian would get to ride in a boat to the big city.

Naturally, the statement had meant nothing to the boy, but it had meant everything to her. Ulrich had said it while kicking a ball with him on a patch of lawn shielded from the river by the buildings. *Grab your baby and run!* her instincts had screamed. After Kristian's fourth clean blood test, Ulrich had stopped wearing his containment suit around their child. Without the mask that usually concealed his face, it had become even more evident to Cora that he coveted the boy.

But she did so even more. *Du bist mein Ein und Alles.* You mean the world to me; you are my everything. Daily she'd repeated that simple German phrase to her son.

In the week since his pronouncement, she hadn't wept once. There was no time for tears. Ulrich always visited on Tuesdays, when he wouldn't be missed at Lab 257, so she knew he would return today.

She rose to drag the raft onto the dock, and Kristian toddled toward her, the knees of his corduroy trousers already dirty and his arms outstretched.

"Just a few more minutes."

"*Decke*," he whined. His hand, lost without the threadbare blanket usually in its clutch, fluttered along his side.

Unable to bear the preview of how he'd react to losing her, she pulled him close and lifted her shirt. He latched onto her breast, and they settled onto the ground. Although they could barely afford the delay, a full tummy should subdue him for the crossing, she decided.

His fingers traveled from scar to scar on her abdomen. Stroking his cheek, she marveled at the feel of his skin against hers and kissed his forehead. *This* was why she was about to risk both their lives. They belonged together.

And not with Ulrich. He would warp their son's mind with his ideologies. She couldn't let that happen.

Each night since Ulrich's last visit, she'd stared at her sleeping baby, then at the Gotham skyline, second-guessing her decision to hide Kristian. Her son deserved a normal childhood. Why should her condition keep him from growing up in the greatest city on Earth? Each night she'd reached the same conclusion: with Ulrich he wouldn't have a normal childhood.

Someday, when he was old enough to navigate his way back to her, she would help him become a true New Yorker. In the meantime, she would homeschool him, using the textbooks that had been left behind.

With Kristian cradled in her arms, she could no longer use busywork as a distraction from her fears. Today they both might die. If she became too sick to keep paddling, or the raft capsized in the chop, they would join the victims of the *Slocum*.

And then, she allowed her tears to fall.

Occasionally, nightmares of drowning still ripped her from sleep. Drenched in sweat, she would breathe into her palm, her old trick for proving it had been only a dream.

Hazarding that fate for Kristian seemed incredibly selfish, yet she couldn't compel herself to hand him over to a monster.

If Ulrich did catch them, her punishment would stretch on for years. Kristian would go unharmed; he loved the boy. There was no risk to her son. She tried to hold back a sob and failed. Her fingers wove through the curls at the back of his head, and she brushed her lips across his cheek. "I love you, my little rascal." Wishing this moment would never end, she pressed their bodies closer together.

He looked up at her, and the blue of his eyes matched the early light. Even though he didn't say it, she knew he loved her, too, and needed her. The tears flowed faster.

His lips parted, and she shifted him to the other breast. Life since his birth had been profoundly joyful. The supplies from Ulrich had enabled her to focus on caring for Kristian, who'd grown into an adventurous toddler fascinated by sticks, bugs, and the ships that plowed past. Deep down, she'd known that the pretense of their happy little family couldn't last, so she'd been squirreling rations. She and Kristian would need that food to survive through the winter and spring until the first harvest from the garden she intended to grow.

Apparently satiated, Kristian wriggled out of her arms. Normally he'd be drowsy by now, but the prospect of the journey, as well as her nervous energy, must have excited him.

"Stay." She wagged her finger at him as she began dragging the raft.

He followed her onto the pier.

Sighing, she stopped her effort and picked him up before he could fall in. "Can you help Mommy move the boxes?"

He nodded, even though he couldn't have fully understood her, and she set him in the grass. While he tried to catch a frog, she fastened the cartons to the wood with knotted bedsheet strips.

The sky was fading, and with it, their window of opportunity. She pulled an adult-size life preserver over Kristian's head and used the last of the ties to secure it to him. Then she secured her son to her via a makeshift, braided cord.

"You ready?" she asked with forced enthusiasm.

"Ja. Boot. Im Wasser." He ran onto the dock, swinging his arms.

Praying it wouldn't be their last, she bent down for a hug, and he lunged away.

She commanded him to stay put, shoved the raft off the pier, and placed him in the empty triangular space at the center of the boxes. "Your special nest," she said, thankful the phrase was similar in both languages. Since she couldn't tie him in place, given the risk of capsizing, she would have to talk him into staying put. "Tweet, like a little birdie." She flapped her arms.

"Tweet." He mimicked the motion.

She made the sign of the cross, said a quick prayer, and eased onto the wood. Cold water rushed over her bare feet, and she adjusted her position to balance the platform. With a board that would serve as her paddle, she pushed them away from shore.

A current tugged the raft. Furiously, she paddled to redirect their course. The dark form of the smaller of the Brethren Islands was just visible across the channel. Babbling with delight, Kristian nudged between two of the boxes, and she barked at him to stay put. Miraculously, he listened to her.

Waves rocked the raft, and she struggled to keep it from tipping. The gusting wind sprayed her with saltwater, leaving a taste on her tongue that forced her mind back to 1907. The thought of those sharks momentarily paralyzed her. While it had been romantic to think they'd saved her, they instead might have been fixed on devouring her. She paddled harder.

Her muscles burned from the exertion, and her forehead felt equally hot. A chill coursed through her, and she knew the fever had begun. A burning itch told her that pustules were emerging across her skin. She glanced back and decided they were almost halfway.

Repeatedly, she dug the board into the tidal strait, slowing her rhythm only to check on Kristian, who was soaked, shivering, and sobbing. To soothe him, she sang, "Row, row, row your boat," each word coming out hoarser than the last. Her throat felt like it had filled with silt, blocking the air from reaching her lungs. A coughing fit seized her, and she had to stop paddling until it subsided.

Kristian's howling rose above the roars of the wind and the river.

"What have I done?" she wailed. Nausea and fatigue were spreading through her like a plague, and she fought the urge to give in to them. Even if their vessel reached the islet, and she could stave off death for three days, she wouldn't have the strength for the return.

Regret and doubt wouldn't save her son. Only she could. *First, reach the shore. Then worry about the rest*, she scolded herself.

Gritting her teeth, she jabbed the board into the water and pulled herself toward it, again and again.

Behind her, Kristian shrieked for her.

"Almost there." She twisted to give him a reassuring smile and yelped in surprise. He was climbing over the cartons to reach her.

"*Bleib in deinem Nest!*" she yelled, harsher than she'd intended, for him to stay in his nest and he shrank back into a corner.

A current whipped them away from South Brother.

She paddled urgently, but it wasn't enough.

Soon they would be swept into the worst chop of Hell Gate. *Please, God.*

The raft jerked, and she bobbled and almost fell overboard. Regaining her balance, she checked on Kristian, who was hugging his knees.

Something had hit them. The heavily trafficked river was thick with flotsam; it could have been anything.

A second impact from below sent her to her knees, and the river ripped away her makeshift paddle. She grabbed Kristian's arm and clung to one of the tethered crates.

The platform pierced a whitecap, and the horizon tipped. She held on for both of their dear lives.

Frigid spray slapped her cheeks, momentarily cooling her fever.

The raft slid into a trough and abruptly slowed.

The chop dissipated, and her sense of balance returned. They'd escaped the current that had been pulling them toward the main channel.

Cora wiped the water from her eyes, gave Kristian a reassuring kiss, and looked for South Brother in the gaining light. Whatever had struck the raft had knocked them back on course. She scanned the surface for a pylon or other large piece of debris but saw nothing.

The wet skin on the back of her neck tingled, and she studied the water again, this time looking in vain for a shark fin.

Cora returned her attention to the tiny islet. Either through the assistance of luck or another force, they'd almost reached the beach.

The waves diminished, and the raft stabilized. The pebbly bottom, sloping upward to the rocky sand, appeared below them, and she whooped with relief.

Kristian continued to whimper.

"Mama's got you. We're almost there." Pushing aside the memory of children sinking around her, she exhaled to dispel the tightness in her chest. An inch at a time, she slid into the water.

She could hear their desperate shrieking all around her.

No, it's in my head. "I can't help you," she declared to quiet them, and Kristian's lips wavered, his mouth open in a soundless cry.

"It's okay. Mama's got you." She waded to the side closer to him, and he leaped into her arms. She set him on the sand, and with what little remaining energy she could muster, pulled the raft ashore.

With Kristian clinging to her, she dragged the boxes and finally the platform past the rim of the forest.

Collapsing from exhaustion, she pulled Kristian into a hug. "You are my everything," she hoarsely whispered into his ear.

Darkness closed in on her, and she resisted it just long enough to tighten the knots on the cord that connected her to her son.

Two Days After Reaching South Brother Island

Cora squinted against the light. Instead of a tree canopy, ceiling tiles blocked her view of the sky. She blinked, but they didn't go away. The still air carried a faint scent of antiseptic, and the cut of the worn cotton against her skin felt alarmingly familiar.

Propping herself up on her elbows, she rose to a seated position and met Ulrich's eyes, their anger barely obscured by the reflection off his wartime gas mask. He was seated a few feet beyond the side of the bed, with Kristian asleep in his lap.

Only his rage kept her from reaching for her son. The aching in her engorged breasts told her they'd been apart for too long.

Neither she nor Ulrich spoke. Averting her gaze, she recognized the vast room as one of the dormitories within the tuberculosis pavilion.

Kristian squawked in his sleep and hugged his security blanket tighter. The fact that he'd been reunited with it consoled her only momentarily. Her baby once again in the hands of her tormentor . . . she had failed.

Unable to bear seeing him sleep so peacefully on Ulrich's lap, she rolled to her side to climb out of bed and felt resistance. Amid a fresh spattering of smallpox scars, a needle extended from her right arm.

Her veins were carrying whatever toxin was dripping from that bag to every cell in her body. Once the side effects began, it would become even harder to stop him from stealing her son. She reached to yank the needle from her flesh, and Ulrich barked "Halt."

She froze, but her mind continued to reel. The skin around the site looked freshly washed, and her hair smelled of lavender. "What are you doing to me?"

"It's only a saline solution to treat your dehydration."

"You expect me to believe that?" she asked, tugging at a corner of the tape.

"I've no reason to lie."

Exhausted, she let her arms sink to the mattress. He'd always disclosed the rationale and risks for each of his trials, like he was providing the necessary details to obtain her permission. But in the end, her consent was always coerced. Unlike the inmates and orphan babies that had been experimented on throughout much of the twentieth century, to the outrage of a few good reporters, she had no human rights.

But Kristian did. Ulrich had filed a birth certificate with the New York City Health Department, listing Rollie and his new wife, Petra, as the parents.

"It's a good thing I found him when I did," he said, stroking the fine, blond curls at the nape of Kristian's neck.

She waited for him to continue, suspecting that once he'd recounted the details, she would agree.

"He was playing in the shallows of South Brother. He could have drowned. Undoubtedly he would have if I hadn't spotted him from the lighthouse roof."

Nausea surged, and she swallowed hard. "He was tied to me," she managed to croak out, as much for her benefit as his.

"We—I—almost lost my son," Ulrich said with a sob.

The heaving of his chest told Cora that he was crying. Only once before had she seen him do so—the day his mother and sister died.

Before now, she'd thought his cruelty had withered his tear ducts. *He does love our boy*, she thought and pictured him frantically searching the island for them. A sharp pang of guilt sliced through her. "I'm so sorry," she spluttered. "I shouldn't have—"

His chin jerked upward and he fixed her with a cold stare. "You're *sorry*?" From a nearby bed frame, he picked up the dirty, crusted remains of the cord, now ripped in two. "Your recklessness almost killed my son." He tossed the pieces onto the floor.

The noise startled Kristian, and he woke with a cry.

"It's okay, mein kleiner Bär," she said out of habit to soothe her "little bear."

He wailed for her and tried to slide off Ulrich's lap.

Ulrich repositioned him. "*Mutti muss schlafen.* Mommy needs to sleep. *Ich habe dich.* I've got you."

Why's he teaching him English? She sucked in her breath at the likely answer: just as she'd feared, he would take her son, and she would remain here alone. For eternity.

"This is your own doing," Ulrich stated as he struggled to control the flailing boy.

"You were planning to steal him from me," she said, loudly enough for Ulrich to hear over Kristian's escalating cries.

Ulrich managed to retrieve a chocolate bar from his black kit and broke off a block for Kristian. "You should have spoken to me about my plans *before* you endangered our child. Kristian's cognitive development requires socialization. However, he also still needs a mother's affection. I'd been intending to split his time between the city and here with you."

She pressed the back of her head into the pillow. It had to be a lie, but what if he were speaking truthfully? Over an eighteen-year span, with only a two-year interruption while Riverside had been temporarily closed, she'd observed Ulrich's commitment to providing Rollie and then also Greta with an idyllic childhood. He might have concluded that Kristian should remain close to his mother.

"That *was* my plan." He cleared his throat, and the knot in her stomach tightened.

"But because of your folly, you'll never see him again."

The pronouncement slammed into her and stole her breath. If she hadn't fled with Kristian, would Ulrich have let him live here part-time? She would never know. "Please. I'm sorry. I'll never do anything like it again."

"Correct. You won't."

Cold sweat clung to her sides, and her heart pounded in protest.

Kristian, who'd finished the treat, whined for another. His tears ran into the chocolate smeared around his mouth, and she felt an overwhelming urge to clean his face and kiss those little lips.

She swung her legs off the bed and reached for him.

"Mutti." He dove toward her, and Ulrich yanked him back and raised his other hand to strike her.

Cora flinched but didn't retreat.

"Please, he wants me." Her entire body trembled with exhaustion and fear.

Writhing to free himself, Kristian clawed at the protective suit, which forced Ulrich to thrust the boy at her.

She grabbed him, and Kristian quieted instantaneously.

Buckling under the extra weight, she staggered backward and collapsed onto the bed.

Her son burrowed under the gown to find her breast, and she inhaled his scent. Ulrich must have bathed him, and his diaper beneath the fresh pair of trousers felt dry. The long shadows on the floor told her it was late afternoon, but she could only guess how long she'd been unconscious.

As he suckled, his fingers flitted across her belly, and he hummed with contentment.

"He needs his mother." She stared into the round lenses of Ulrich's alienesque mask.

"He's old enough for cow's milk."

"That's not what I meant."

"I know. I'm anticipating a difficult adjustment period, but that will be only temporary."

"Ulrich, you know what it's like to grow up without a mom," Cora pleaded, desperate enough to broach a topic that had always been taboo. "Don't do this to your son. Give him what you didn't have."

"This is very different."

"No, it's not. I love him. He needs his mother's love."

Ulrich shook his head. "Soon, he'll come to think of Petra as his mother. And I'll be there to make sure she fully replaces you."

"No," she said, weeping, and Kristian looked up at her questioningly. He raised his hand to her face, and she grabbed his wrist for a kiss to keep him from touching her tears. She didn't want him to know this pain. But in the weeks to follow, he would. Although she was relieved to hear that Rollie—not Ulrich—would raise her son, the thought of Kristian crying out for her cut deeper than any scalpel ever had.

Kristian resumed nursing, and she caressed his chubby cheek.

Eventually, wrapped in the love of his false parents and deranged "grandfather," he would forget her. Oblivious to her existence, he would grow up in the city she'd fantasized about experiencing with him.

Meanwhile she would remain trapped in this hell, aching for him with every beat of her heart. Now death called to her, louder than ever before. "Your next visit, kill me, please."

"Ha. You're far too valuable to exterminate."

"Then I'll kill myself."

He laughed. "Go ahead. Then, someday, I'll tell Kristian his birth mother didn't love him enough to stay alive."

She stiffened. Kristian pulled away from her breast, so she shifted him to the other side. "Give me another chance."

"You don't deserve one."

Without disrupting Kristian, she sat up. "For six decades, I've been subjected to every form of torture, in the name of medicine, and I've never asked for anything."

A sly smile stretched to his eyes. "Perhaps I will bring him back sometime."

He was lying; she was sure of it. Ulrich would use the promise of a reunion to force her compliance and to torment her. She pressed her baby to her chest, and his warmth radiated through her. Before she would let Ulrich break this bond, she would destroy him. Just as she'd sworn to do the day the last ferry had departed from Riverside.

To conceal her hatred, she ducked her head and gazed at her baby. A sense of awe pushed aside her loathing.

Her scalpels might still be in his physician's bag, resting on the cart just out of her reach. Could she sever the vein that bulged from his neck? It should be as easy as slicing an apple. Not only could she do this, Cora reasoned, but she *had* to do this *today*. Once he'd removed Kristian from the island, Ulrich would be her only tie to her son.

"Your time is up. Give him to me."

"Please, one more hour." To fool him into thinking she was too feeble to resist, she raised an arm and let it fall.

He huffed through his respirator. "Fine, thirty minutes." He took out a magazine and settled into his chair.

If she failed, these moments with her son would turn out to be her last. Determined not to let Ulrich's presence ruin them, she laid Kristian on his back between her legs and played "This Little Piggy" with his toes. His cascade of giggles formed the most beautiful song she'd ever heard. Committing the sound to memory, she blinked back tears and kept up a smile for his sake.

"I love that sound," Ulrich murmured from his chair.

As much as Cora wanted this time to belong only to Kristian and her, she needed to lull him into thinking they were once again a happy family. Only then would he put down his guard, enabling her to grab his medical kit. Even if her scalpels weren't inside, the bag had to contain something else sharp.

"And this little piggy went wee, wee, wee, all the way home."

Kristian cackled as her fingers traveled up his leg and tickled his belly.

"He is quite remarkable," Ulrich said as sincerely as any father might say to his wife.

"Because of you. And me." She massaged Kristian's chunky thighs.

Despite his cruelty, she knew his principles had never wavered when it came to his family. Maybe he really would bring Kristian back to visit.

But not if she tried to slaughter Ulrich now. Given her weakened state, he could easily wrest a blade from her, and then there would be no question that she was unfit to mother their child. No, she couldn't risk it.

Instead, she would cherish these final moments with her baby, and hopefully, in the process, convince Ulrich that they were a family.

She lifted Kristian's other foot, and he pointed at her. "Mutti toes?"

Already he'd picked up the English word. "But your toes are much cuter."

He repeated his request, so she made a Bronx cheer on his stomach.

His laughter subsided, and he touched her wet cheek, triggering new tears. He crawled up her lap and examined her face with his hands. "Mutti boo-boo?"

"No, Mommy's not hurt. Mommy's sad."

"Ssssad," he said, trying out the new word.

She looked at Ulrich, who was no longer pretending to read the magazine.

"Mommy's sad because you're going on a trip. A boat! But you'll come back soon, and we'll hunt for spiders."

He nodded, though he couldn't possibly have understood, and wrapped his arms around her neck.

"And Vati, too," she said for Ulrich's benefit. "We'll play hide-and-seek with Vati."

Ulrich discarded the magazine. "Time's up." From his bag, he removed a syringe.

White spots bombarded her vision. "What's that?"

He tapped the tube. "A concentrated dose of . . . we'll call it *Veh Zeh*."

Cora knew he was referring to the letters *V* and *Z* in German. "What's it for?"

"The good of society. If you ever try to come after Kristian, you'll be dead before you reach the Williamsburg Bridge. It's a weaponized strain of a highly lethal disease."

She grabbed Kristian and scrambled off the far side of the bed. Another breed of microscopic monster, this one even deadlier. She couldn't allow it into her veins. "I've learned my lesson, I swear, and the germs already inside me, they'd stop me anyway. On South Brother they would have succeeded if you hadn't—"

"Roll up your sleeve," he commanded, and Kristian began crying.

She bounced her son to calm him, but the jerky motion only worsened his distress.

Ulrich came around the bed, yanked up her sleeve, and jabbed the needle into her flesh. She shrieked, and Kristian's wail sharpened.

Ulrich tore him from her.

"Mommy's okay," he said, bobbing the boy. "The shot will keep her safe, and everyone else. Do you want to ride in a boat? A *real* boat?" He sneered at her.

Kristian squealed and clapped his hands, and Ulrich wiped the tears from the toddler's reddened cheeks with his rubber glove.

"Say bye-bye to Mommy."

Kristian waved. To avoid upsetting him, she forced a smile.

Ulrich shifted their son to his hip, grabbed his kit, and strode from the room.

His footsteps echoed down the corridor.

He hadn't even let her kiss her baby good-bye.

Her howls to bring him back drowned out his footfalls.

She staggered to the window for one last glimpse of her son. Minutes passed, and the porch outside the central entrance remained empty. *Maybe he changed his mind*, she thought. Holding her breath, she listened for the sound of their return.

Below, the front door banged open, and Cora bit her knuckle so hard she tasted blood.

She pressed her forehead to the glass to bring them into view.

Ulrich hurried down the front steps and onto the lawn. The fair skin of Kristian's face, nestled in the crook of Ulrich's shoulder and hood, stood out against the black hazmat suit.

Cora threw open the window and screamed for her boy, for her *everything*. Without him, she would have nothing. Be nothing.

Ulrich didn't turn or break stride; he'd already disregarded her.

But Kristian hadn't. He spotted her at the fourth-story window and beamed.

She blew him a kiss and he mirrored the gesture.

Devastated, her cries primal, she caught his love in her palm and swore that she would never loosen her hold on it. Even while driving a scalpel through Ulrich's heart.

February 1967

The bitter cold seeped through her friendship quilt, down comforter, and parka, yet Cora wouldn't relinquish her post on the morgue roof; she'd been watching for Ulrich every morning since he'd taken Kristian four months earlier. Not once had he come to deliver provisions, resume the experimentation, or even discuss their son. Rather than seek her advice, presumably he'd been allowing Petra and Rollie to make mistakes as they learned. Undoubtedly Angela wouldn't have been sharing her expertise.

The transition must have been tough on Kristian. She pictured him, confined to a crib with wooden rails, wailing in the night for Mutti. Would they have figured out that he wanted his back rubbed? She hoped so. At least he had his blankie. She shivered and conjured the warmth of his body, snuggled against her, twitching as he dreamed important baby dreams. Did he still remember her at all? By his birthday, in less than a month and a half, she knew he wouldn't.

She would miss the marking of his second year, and every one after that.

Tears blurred the skyscrapers across the strait, and she was amazed by her body's endless supply. If only her food caches could likewise never run out. The ache in her hollow stomach had become an almost constant companion.

Although unlikely, Ulrich could be planning to return with Kristian once the weather improved. In the current conditions, the passage through Hell Gate would be dangerous for a toddler who liked to climb. The tension in her shoulders eased with the prospect. Maybe Ulrich would bring him on his birthday. Just in case, she would have a present ready, as well as an iced cake. From what Mary had taught her, and the two chocolate bars she'd been saving, she would manage something.

Such fantasies are dangerous, she reminded herself. An untouched torte on March 30 would only make the distance between them feel wider. Still, she knew that as the day drew near, she would prepare, just in case.

She raised her head above the wall to gaze across the river. The buildings looked as densely packed as the *Salmonella typhi* Ulrich had once let her view through the microscope. Which one held her boy? When Ulrich returned, she would beseech him to point it out to her, even though she knew he'd coldly refuse.

Now that she wasn't busy caring for her child, each day, empty of meaning, stretched on until dark arrived. Hourly, she berated herself for disobeying Ulrich. Now regret was constant and more punishing than any pain she'd ever known.

She shifted her attention back to the river and inhaled sharply. In the early light, she could just make out an approaching boat. Its shape matched the fishing trawler that Ulrich chartered for his trips. She dove to the ground, though it mattered little if he'd seen her, and peered through the spy hole.

The boat stopped alongside the dock, and Ulrich leaned out to buffer them from the pylons. Still, no sign of Kristian, although Ulrich might have made him stay in the cabin. Suddenly sweltering within her parka, she prayed that he would emerge.

Ulrich's usual henchman tossed him a line. It fell into the channel as Ulrich jumped onto the pier and bellowed her name.

His anguish hit Cora in the gut, and she knew something must have happened to their boy. She threw the blankets aside and raced down the stairwell and through the morgue. "Where is he?" she yelled as she neared the dock.

"Halt!" he ordered, raising his arm.

He wasn't wearing protective gear; he had no intention of stepping onto the island. Instead, Ulrich must have come to deliver bad news, and by the tone of his voice, he believed she was to blame. *Please God, let my baby be okay.* "Where is he?"

He glanced at the sailor, whose exaggerated efforts to arrange the bumpers made it clear he wanted Ulrich to believe he wasn't listening.

The wind tugged at Ulrich's coat, and he let it rip the hood from his head. "He's ill."

Her vision blurred, and she swayed. "How's that possible?" she asked, blinking rapidly to clear her head. All of Kristian's blood samples had been free of her pathogens, but they could've been hiding somewhere else within him, she speculated.

"He's got influenza."

Only the flu. Her headache dulled, and her breathing slowed.

"How is he?"

"Improving."

Then why was Ulrich here, and so angry? The answer struck her with the force of a bullet: they'd been wrong about his immune system. Apparently, he was just a normal boy. Except, possibly, when he was on North Brother. Her heart beat faster as her hope flew skyward.

"Maybe he's like me, and his immunities only work here."

If Ulrich had come to the same conclusion, Kristian might yet be napping in the cabin.

"I'm sorry," Ulrich said in a softer tone.

No, it couldn't end this way. "But you said . . . that your Aryan genes . . . our baby might turn out like Pettenkofer. There's no way I didn't pass my germs to Kristian. His body must have fought them off. That would mean his immunities are even stronger than mine. But like mine, they must only work while he's here, right?"

Ulrich sighed, and a gust amplified his frustration. "You think I haven't considered that?"

"Bring him to me." She bit her lip to stop herself from begging.

"You know that's not possible," he said in a gruff tone.

"Why?"

"Because he would miss his mother."

Her knees buckled, and she hit the pavement. A tingling sensation overran her face and hands, and she realized she was panting. She must have had the wind knocked out of her. Or her body couldn't bear the notion of Kristian wiggling out of her arms, crying for his new mommy.

Of all the things Ulrich had ever said to her, that comment had been the cruelest. She detested him, and someday she would end him.

But first she had to get her son back. Then her blades.

As much as she didn't want to grovel, she couldn't muster the strength to stand, so she pushed against the ground to raise her torso. "I may be a mutt, but I'm a mutt who knows her master better than anyone else. Compared to immortality for your genes, Kristian's bond with Petra is of little consequence to you."

"I've no proof that his longevity will match yours."

"And you never will if you don't bring him back."

Ulrich hesitated, and she knew he still believed in the possibility that Kristian would stop aging once he reached adulthood.

With the vigor of an eighteen-year-old, she scrambled to her feet and pulled away her hood to reveal her taut skin. "A month ago, I turned eighty-three. North Brother is my holy grail, and there's a good chance it's your son's as well."

"That may be true, but testing the theory is not worth the risk. If his immune system isn't stimulated by the unknown force here, your love will kill him." He cocked his head. "Although in a different way than I'd anticipated, Kristian is exceptional. In every area of cognitive development, he's years ahead of the milestones for his age. And—I have to admit—I can't stomach the thought of losing him. It's selfish, I know, and it goes against my scientific principles, but he brings me so much joy."

"But if he just visited me, and still lived near you?"

He exhaled with a groan.

"Please," she begged.

"I can't, Cora. My number one priority in life is my three children. Being a father means more to me than being a scientist. I can tell our friends think I'm far too involved in my children's—and grandson's—lives, and look down on me for doing a woman's work. But I refuse to feel ashamed for it. I love Kristian, and I will not risk any harm coming to him by bringing him back here."

There would be no visits, Cora knew. "What about my love for Kristian?"

"I'm sorry. But your love could kill him." He motioned to the thug, who unloaded a single medium-size carton.

"The next time I come," he continued, his expression hardening, "we'll continue where we left off years ago."

Her mind barely registered his promise. All she could think about was her son and the hole in her heart that would widen with each day that passed without him.

"What about trying again? Maybe another baby will have my immunities." Shocked by what she'd suggested, her mouth hung open. More appalling than the prospect of being repeatedly violated again was the notion that her love for Kristian could be transferred to another child.

He interlaced his gloved fingers. "I've further genealogical research to do before completing a second trial."

From the bitterness in his tone, she could guess what had happened: Angela had threatened to leave him if he ever impregnated Cora again.

The sailor finished unmooring the trawler, and Ulrich signaled that he needed a minute.

Folding his arms across his chest, Ulrich appraised her. "Do not ration these supplies. You'll need strength for my next visit."

He turned to board, and she raised a hand to keep his attention. Swallowing her dread and rage, she begged, "Please, at least bring me a picture of him."

"Maybe, but it'll cost you." He pivoted toward the boat, then twisted back to face her. "I almost forgot." From his coat pocket, he removed a package and carefully unwrapped it.

Cora recognized the thin silver and ivory handle—the first scalpel she'd stolen from Otto. To remind herself that God would forgive her planned sins, she'd etched a crucifix into its handle.

"Until your betrayal, you were doing an excellent job raising my son. That didn't go unnoticed, and I'm a man of my word." He dropped the knife, and it skittered across the wooden pier and stopped near the edge.

What good would it do her now? As long as he had Kristian, she couldn't use it on him.

She glared at Ulrich. The compliment had carried a taunt, the particular scalpel chosen for its symbolism: he—not God—ruled this island.

Ulrich stepped into the bow.

The motor roared, and the boat backed away.

Cora sank to the concrete, as cold as a block of ice. Hoping it would numb her, she pressed her cheek to the hard surface.

Soon, the crew of a passing ship might spot her, but she couldn't pick herself up. How she would ever take another step, she couldn't fathom.

March 2008

Eleven days before the new heron nesting season

March 10

Finn pushed Sylvia's wheelchair to yet another display of luxury watches. The constant hum of all that ticking, along with the smells of glass cleaner and leather, filled the showroom. It seemed to Finn like the only thing without enough time was his mom.

As she scrutinized the selection, the reflection off the glass and makeup that her aide had applied that morning animated her green eyes, infused with russet like his.

Kristian would be turning forty-three in three weeks. A decade ago, Sylvia had bought him the second in what had become an impressive watch collection—the first had been Ulrich's Eberhard. As her health had declined, she'd refused to give up the tradition.

"Any you'd like to see?" he asked gently.

Despite his reluctance to attend Kristian's upcoming birthday dinner, Finn was in no hurry for this excursion to end. His mother's joints had to be aching and her ears ringing. By the joyful look on the side of her face not paralyzed, she'd managed to block all that out.

"How about this one?" he asked, pointing at a watch he wouldn't be caught dead wearing. For his birthdays, his parents gave him money to help with the rent.

"I know you've been to North Brother," she slurred.

Startled, he turned to face her.

A saleswoman approached, and he curtly waved her off. "Dad told you?"

"After thirty-three years. In this family," she said in her slow, labored speech, "I know, the distant look on a Gettler's face. After a visit to that island. And her."

Finn dropped his gaze to his boots. "You—we—saw it far too often when I was a kid."

"And Cora," she said, attempting to shift forward in her seat, "is the cause of your rift with Kristian. I was surprised you came today."

"I'm here for you, Mom. Not him."

She nodded almost imperceptibly. "You've learned about their real research, and you don't like it."

"That's putting it mildly."

"I failed," Sylvia said, her thin voice cracking.

Finn put his hand on her shoulder, padded by a bouclé suit jacket that hid her frailness, and crouched beside her. "You've never failed at anything."

"All my life, I stood up for others. I was so," she said, lingering on the word, "strong. At least I thought I was. But the most important battle: I didn't have courage to fight."

"That's not true; you did everything you could."

Sylvia shook her head. "I should have made Rollie. Give up. I was afraid. If I made him pick. Between studying her and being with us, he would choose her. And I should have insisted he keep Kristian out. Kristian doesn't have. Right mind-set. But I told myself he'd be the one to cure her. So smart. Creative."

Finn leaned in. "Do you really think he can solve her?"

"Yes, I do. They've continued. Behind my back." She clutched his hand, still on her shoulder, and he could feel its tremors. "I know it's for me. It must end. Cost too high." Visibly exhausted from the effort, she lowered her arm. "Before . . . this . . ." She tapped the wheelchair. "I sometimes went. With them. I've seen the way Kristian treats—"

"It's like he's forgotten she's a human being, not some lab animal."

"Ulrich's influence." Her right hand tried to close into a fist. "They spent so much time together. I tried to teach Kristian to view her differently. Another failure."

Stepping behind her, Finn massaged her shoulders. "You didn't fail. It wasn't your job."

"It was my job to raise Kristian right, but I . . ." Her voice broke, and she began to whimper.

He knew she was trying not to cry. The clerks and other customers had retreated to the far side of the store.

"You did your best," he said, continuing to rub her shoulders.

If his mom believed Kristian could succeed, then maybe he could. But Finn knew that Sylvia would never willingly travel to North Brother Island to receive the experimental treatment if it had been developed at Cora's expense. "You can still put your foot down," he said firmly. "Tell Dad to stop for good. That you're on to him."

She grunted. "What happens when I die? You think Kristian will stay away then?"

"So, stay alive."

His mom clasped his hand. "You need to resolve. Because *you* will be the one still around."

Finn choked back a sob. He hated when his mother alluded to her own passing. "Lily thinks the best way to help Cora is for Kristian to find her antidote."

"That may be." Sylvia loosely gripped her armrests, as if preparing to stand. "Cora wants love, and family, more than anything. She deserves it."

"Lily thinks she should go back." Finn hooked his arms under his mother's and helped her up, positioning himself to catch her if she fell.

Leaning against the glass counter, Sylvia nodded. "Cora trusted me. Lily has a role to play, but this burden. Doesn't belong on her shoulders." Disjointedly, she turned to look at him.

Gently, Finn put his arm around her. "It's too dangerous for her anyway."

Over his mother's head, he surveyed the showroom. Everything looked new, polished, *civilized.* So different from Cora's world. "I found a note in Dad's journal from 2001. You said she suffered. What did you mean by that?"

"Rollie was kind to her. Cora assured me. But she has the right to say 'no more.' Her body belongs to her. You make sure that happens. That's why I left you that note."

"What?" Finn asked, arching his back.

"Last June, I watched you come out of shed. I could tell you'd found his expedition logs. You looked so determined. Just like him. I knew you'd decided to go. And that afterward, you'd return for a second look. So, I opened the shoebox, filled with all the ultimatums I'd written Rollie. But wasn't confident enough to give him. And took one out, knowing you would be strong for me."

Still doubting that she'd ever lacked the courage to put her foot down with Rollie, Finn studied her anew. He tried to picture her crossing the two-acre lawn in her wheelchair. "Did Mimi help?"

"It took us a long time!"

If she'd planted the message . . . "This'll sound weird, but do you know anything about a crate of horseshoe bats?"

Sylvia jerked her hand toward her chest. "That was us, too."

Staring at his mom, he saw past her feeble stature and recognized the fiery, capable woman he'd always admired. "How'd you pull that off?"

"Borrowed from zoo. Big donation."

Finn stared at his mother in wonder, though not in disbelief. She'd always gone beyond the seemingly impossible when something important to her was at stake. And she certainly had a talent for maximizing emotional impact.

"Why bats? And why the big setup instead of just pulling me aside?"

"Milo," she said, her arms settling onto the armrests. "When he was over, studying. I noticed drawings in the margins of his school notebook. He has a talent for it, like you."

An unsettling feeling congealed in Finn's stomach. "What did he draw?"

Closing her eyes, she whispered, "Coronavirus particles."

His eyes widened. "Are you sure?"

"I asked him. He said they were aliens. But I know microbes. Been in this family a long time."

"Kristian's bringing him into the fold," Finn reasoned out loud. "The fact that Milo's familiar with the SARS virus could simply mean they've discussed that pandemic. Or that Kristian does have live specimens in his lab."

Sylvia nodded. "I wanted you to see what's at stake. Not just hear it from your mom. With Milo involved . . ." Her words became indistinguishable.

He bent down to hear her better.

"It's time," she muttered to herself, seemingly forgetting Finn's presence.

He longed to plead with her for more details, but he could see the toll on her body from their conversation thus far.

Suddenly, she reached for him. "You need to go back. And give Cora a message from me."

"Of course." Finn cocked his head. "What is it?"

She beckoned to a clerk, and the woman rushed over to stand behind the case.

"That one." Sylvia pointed with conviction, and Finn remembered that although her body was failing, her mind remained needle sharp.

"What message?" Finn asked

"That it's time to tell him."

"Who's *him*?"

"She'll know," Sylvia said and set a folded square of paper on the glass counter. "I'd like this engraved on the back, please."

Baffled, Finn waited silently as the woman processed his mother's purchase and gave him the receipt.

"I'll pick it up for you when it's ready," he said, tucking the slip into his wallet.

"Good, because I want you to take it to Cora."

"Why?" Finn asked, taken aback. The watch had cost thousands of dollars, and it was far too big for Cora's wrist. "Then what will you give Kristian?"

"Something far more precious," she murmured.

The First Day of the New Heron Nesting Season

March 21

Finn scrutinized the duct tape on the underside of his rubber glove, this time covering a switchblade instead of her scalpel. Adhered to his other glove was pepper spray. If she noticed, he would remind her of the ticks and chloroform. Although she was a victim, he'd been foolish to view her as one. He wouldn't be making that mistake again.

So much has changed since the first time I came here, Finn thought as he took in the scent of the sandy loam. In the days after his talk with Sylvia, he'd revisited the times she'd encouraged him to stand up for the oppressed. *Someone has to be the hero.* It had hit him with an almost physical force that throughout all those years that Ulrich and Rollie had been grooming Kristian to inherit the project, Sylvia had been preparing Finn to take on the role of Cora's protector.

All those superhero comic cards and magazines she'd bought him ... God, he loved her. Finn silently vowed to show her that she hadn't failed. At least not at raising him. But he felt like he had a brick wall to punch through before he could make that claim.

To gauge how much longer he would have to wait beside his kayak, he studied the tree line beyond the field. Still, only Brooklyn's halo glowed above the canopy.

A low, trilling whistle replaced the calm, and Finn spun toward its source.

He could just make out the morgue, coal house, and smokestacks of the physical plant.

The noise could have belonged to a bird—Lily would know which type.

In January, she'd had another grand mal seizure, this one on the subway. Thank God a doctor had been in the next car. That night they'd agreed it was too risky for her to return here. She'd understood that meant Finn would go, but as far as she'd known, he hadn't finalized the date. To avoid causing her days of undue heightened stress, he'd planned to tell her the night before. Yesterday evening, however, she'd gone with her mother to see a Broadway show and spent the night at her mom's Chelsea apartment. Finn had left Lily a note on the kitchen table, next to a bouquet of daisies that would likely provoke more ire than romance, he now realized.

The birdcall sounded again, and Finn knew it had come from Cora, somewhere amid the cluster of buildings.

She must have been watching for him. Today marked the start of the heron nesting season; she'd accurately predicted he would return as soon as possible. Maybe he should have waited a week to prove her wrong. No, he would never add his name to the list of Gettler men who'd played mind games with her.

Although the noise didn't repeat, he knew she was expecting him to find her.

He shouldered his pack and lifted a duffel bag from his kayak. Since he couldn't use his flashlight while crossing the overgrown meadow, visible from the river, he would have to rely on the thickness of his rubber boots, and luck, to avoid ripping his hazmat suit.

As he carefully crossed the weeds, still beaten down from last winter's snowfalls, a hint of sunlight colored the horizon.

Reaching the cover of the buildings, he turned on his flashlight and swept the beam from one to the next. She could be lurking behind any one of their pitch-black doorways.

Irritated that she already had the upper hand, he considered dropping the supply-filled duffel and leaving. Taking a deep breath, he thought of his mother. "Now what?" he asked, turning off his light so he wouldn't be such an easy target.

Again, she whistled shrilly, and Finn spun to face the physical plant.

Silence filled the biting cold, an implied command for him to enter. At the threshold, he pointed his flashlight into the space. As he arced his light, eerie shadows danced like demons. Dark doorways led to other chambers, and a spoked valve wheel rested in the center of the room.

"Come in, out of the cold," said Cora from somewhere above.

He looked up at the rafters, crisscrossing an otherwise absent roof. In the fading night, he couldn't make out a single star, reminding him just how alone they were.

Finally, he spotted her perched on a joist.

"You do love heights," he said, keeping his light fixed on her. "Can you please come down?"

"If you stop blinding me with that thing," she said, her arm shielding her eyes.

"Sorry." He shifted the beam, and, like a spider, she worked her way down the maze of pipes bolted to the brick wall.

Her willingness to expose her backside made Finn feel slightly more confident that he would live through this day.

Appraising him, Cora smacked her gloves against each other, then straightened her "I [heart] NYC" sweatshirt.

Comforted by the ten-foot gap between them, Finn waited for her to speak.

She nodded at the bag. "That for me?"

"Depends," he said, jouncing it, "on whether you've realized that kindness isn't quid pro quo."

She cocked her head. "Did you bring the fourth *Twilight* book?"

Involuntarily, he chuckled. In the crate he'd dropped off in midwinter, he'd included the second and third novels. "So you like the series?"

"It's quite scandalous."

Finn took that as a 'yes.' "Unfortunately, the release date isn't until August second of this year." Hoping she'd request it, he'd checked.

Cora grunted in disappointment.

"I know. It does suck that you can't kill me today and still find out how the story ends."

"That drawing of the Astor Hotel, it was stunning. Because of it, I'd already decided to spare your life, this time," she added as she fingered the keloid encircling her neck, which, he realized, hadn't been one of the scars she'd explained on the morgue roof.

Nonchalantly, he set the duffel bag halfway between them, then retreated.

"You could have left this by the seawall, like last time," she said, eyeing it. "I haven't changed my mind about the Lyme or giving blood."

"I'm here on behalf of Sylvia."

Cora jerked her head. "Now, *that* I wasn't expecting. There's no way she'd ask me to be their guinea pig again."

"I have a message from her."

Cora's scowl vanished, and she blinked rapidly. "I'm listening."

"She says, 'It's time to tell him.'"

Her hand flew to her mouth. "You're sure? Those were her exact words?"

"I've a pretty good memory."

In the pale, early morning light, Finn could just make out the glisten of a tear on her cheek. He debated asking her to explain.

"I'm so glad Sylvia's come around to it." Cora looked past Finn, and he guessed she was once again speaking to the island. "And she kept her promise, that I could be the one. Rollie's okay with this?"

She was staring at him, and Finn surmised that the question had been addressed to him. "I've no idea what you're talking about, but Sylvia hasn't even told Rollie that she knows he's continued his research. I highly doubt she consulted him about this."

"They never told you." She clicked her tongue. "You'll find out soon enough, though you'll wish you hadn't."

"Am I the 'him'?"

"No," she said with a scowl.

"Is Kristian?" he asked, but she'd already turned away. From the shaking of her shoulders, he could tell she was crying.

Fidgeting, he felt uncomfortable witnessing this vulnerability from a woman who'd tried so hard to appear unbreakable.

This was a private moment; he knew he should leave. Debating whether he should slip away or say good-bye, Finn remembered the watch.

"My mom wanted me to give you something," he said softly, shrugging off his pack.

Plainly embarrassed, she ducked her chin and turned only partially to face him.

"Cora," he said gently, "you're human. It's okay to cry."

"No, I'm not. But don't worry: I came to terms with that long ago." Rummaging in her messenger bag, she pulled out an antiseptic towelette to wipe her cheeks.

He retrieved the small shopping bag and threaded his way through the debris to place it close to her. Keeping his light fixed on the package for her benefit, he backed away.

Clearly puzzled, Cora removed from the bag a patent leather box. Carefully, as if she thought it might be a trick, she opened the case and inspected the watch. After flipping it over, she read the inscription, then uttered a single cry.

Finn longed to know why she'd reacted so strongly to the simple German phrase.

Suddenly she glanced up and darted into the darkness of the adjacent chamber.

Faintly, he could hear her crying. Then she stopped.

The room was too quiet. He inhaled slowly, the air thick with the smell of rust and rot.

The brightening sky, visible through the missing roof, only increased the creepiness of the broken machinery around him. It was far too quiet.

He tore off the tape to access his switchblade.

The scraping of a metal bar against the ground behind him fractured the calm.

Whirling around as he fumbled for his weapon, Finn glimpsed a dark object flying toward him. As he yelled in surprise, the pipe crashed into his temple.

A single spike of torturous pain pierced his head.

The room blurred away.

1991

Nature has nearly reclaimed North Brother

July 4

A trace of blue entered the sky as Cora wove her way through the forest canopy, which had been progressively darkening the Riverside campus for the past twenty-eight years. Behind her, the calls of awakening black-crowned night herons filled the woods. Since the single, warning squawk that had roused her, the heron colony at the southern end hadn't made a sound. The only force capable of wholly quieting those birds was death, and she planned to silence whoever had served it to them.

Fingering the flap on the raccoon skin case she'd made to sheath her sole weapon, she stopped in a mulberry tree at the fringe of the nesting site. A breeze shook the leaves, and Cora recoiled at a familiar scent, like cut hay. Chloroform had always been a trademark Gettler tool, but Ulrich had grown too feeble to manage the crossing, and she couldn't envisage Rollie needlessly exterminating the flock.

Bright light hit her eyes, momentarily blinding her. Shielding her face with her arm, she flattened her body against the far side of the tree.

"She's over there!" shouted a wraithlike figure.

Cora studied the shifting shadow and decided it had to be a man in a black hazmat suit. His voice, warped by a gas mask, had sounded too young to be Rollie's.

Kristian, she thought, and her hand flew to her chest, just as one of her feet slipped from its toehold.

She dropped and her abdomen and the underside of her arms scraped down the bark as she attempted to bear-hug the tree. A branch slowed her fall, and she wrapped one leg around the trunk and flailed the other until her boot found new purchase.

From below came laughter.

She shrank against the trunk and tried to ignore the stinging from the raw skin on her abdomen.

"I thought you said she was agile," a man in a hazmat suit said to the foliage behind him.

Cora pressed her cheek to the bark, both hoping and fearing that the voice belonged to her son.

"She is, but you succeeded in surprising her. Congrats." Rollie stepped into the small clearing. "Don't worry," he called out, "your herons aren't dead. They're just sleeping in."

Even if the pair had killed off the entire population, at this point she wouldn't care. The twisting of her heart meant Rollie's companion could be Kristian. A few inches shorter than Rollie, the man's stature seemed plausible for her son, given she wasn't particularly tall. And his voice had sounded about the right age.

This past March, Kristian had turned twenty-six. Like every year before, using the goods she'd bartered for with Rollie, she'd readied a cake and present, only to throw them into the strait the day after. Despite begging Ulrich during each of his visits, Cora hadn't convinced him to reevaluate Kristian's immune system. Six years ago, when Ulrich had begrudgingly passed leadership of the project to Rollie, she'd begun asking Rollie to let her see her son. All his replies had been vague.

If Rollie had acquiesced, why wouldn't he have simply brought Kristian with him on one of his routine visits? Gassing the birds seemed far too shifty for a reunion. Although she'd warned him against entering the island's interior, he should have known she'd make an exception for her son.

The morning after Ulrich's first heart attack, in 1985, Rollie had promised to end the brutal experimentation and mind games. And he had.

Because Rollie had claimed he was within millimeters of a breakthrough—and he was her only tie to Kristian—she'd agreed to remain involved on a limited basis. Once a month, he delivered supplies she no longer relied on. Concurrently, he retrieved the blood bags she left for him in a shallow hole.

The predictability of their routine had given her a sense of control that still seemed as foreign as Gotham had become to her.

Yet this uncertainty now reminded her of the Ulrich years. She couldn't let Rollie see that he'd shaken her.

"You'd better hope they wake soon," she said in an arctic tone, patting her sheath. "Those herons aren't just protected by state and federal law. In my rules, trespassing is a capital offense." Even to her own ears, the threat sounded empty, given the stranger might be her son.

"Come down," Rollie said, "so we can do this the right way."

It must be Kristian! She covered her mouth to prevent a shriek of joy, and tears blurred her vision.

Even though she'd been preparing for this moment for twenty-four years, she clung to the tree as tightly as the kudzu vines around her. He'd aged at the normal rate, so they would almost look like peers. She wondered how they would convince him of the seemingly impossible.

According to Ulrich, they'd kept the truth from Kristian "for his own good," even after Petra died. Following Rollie's second marriage, Ulrich had reveled in telling Cora that Kristian had begun calling yet another woman "Mom."

Now she could set the record straight. But ever since the forest had grown tall enough, she'd kept to the canopy whenever a Gettler came ashore. Her intuition told her not to descend now, yet motherly instinct argued that she should.

Even though Kristian was a Gettler, he was her son. Staring into her open hand, she thought of that kiss he'd blown her. Despite the passage of so many seasons, her love for him hadn't lessened. Surely, somewhere deep within, he felt the same way.

She wiped her eyes and lowered herself to the next branch.

"Wow, she listens to you."

"Absolutely," Rollie said, pivoting toward Kristian and revealing a gas canister on his back. Cora reflexively held her breath. "We have a mutual respect."

Still too high to safely drop to the ground, Cora couldn't bring herself to descend to a lower branch. What if Ulrich had passed his Fascist ideals to their son, who in turn had now influenced Rollie? She decided to stay within her treetop network so she could flee at the first whiff of fresh chloroform.

Instead of that sickening smell, the memory of Kristian's baby scent, infused with the aroma of dirt from their time outside, filled her nostrils. And the sensation of tiny fingers, flitting across her stomach while he nursed, felt as real as it had the last day she'd held him.

Back then, she'd been more than a lab rat—she'd been a mother. *His* mother. And now that her child was here, she had to go to him, regardless of the risk.

Slowly, Cora lowered herself to the last branch and dropped to the ground.

Bright light hit her eyes.

"Incredible. A complete lack of cellular senescence. I'd been wanting to see this for myself for so long. Thank you, Dad."

Squinting against the glare, she could just make out the dark outline of Kristian's eyes through the mask. She knew his lashes were as thick as hers. Each night, while lulling him to sleep, she'd strained to see whether his eyelids were still parted.

Now it made her nervous that she couldn't see those windows to his soul. She clutched her satchel, where she kept the knit cap he'd been wearing the first time she'd held him.

"Coraline McSorley," Rollie gestured from her to Kristian, "I'd like you to meet Kristian Gettler, my son."

Rollie's firm tone had contained a warning, so she bit her tongue. "It's always a pleasure to meet another Gettler."

"Likewise," he said, nodding his head in a greeting. "It will be a pleasure to . . . accelerate my family's progress."

Unsure how to interpret that comment, she backed toward the tree she'd just descended.

Stepping toward her, he addressed Rollie over his shoulder: "With two of us, it'll be easier to force her compliance."

Cora reeled back, and her boot snagged on an exposed tree root. As she hit the loam, a rock gouged the flesh between her shoulder blades, and she rolled to her side. Sickened by how much her little boy had changed, she curled inward.

"That's not how I do things here," Rollie said, "and your grandfather has been very specific that you are to listen to me."

"Grandpa's senile, and you've made it clear you're unwilling to do what's right for the family—and science."

Their voices sounded distant, and the forest seemed to be darkening.

"If you forget your place again, you will lose it," Rollie stated, his voice rising above the chirping of the insects in the underbrush around her. "We've got less than fourteen hours to complete today's objective."

A prickling sensation, accompanied by a sickly-sweet smell, invaded her nose and throat, and the sound of her wheezing rattled in her ears.

The sky exploded in crimson and a *boom* shook the grating over the windows of the isolation chamber. Three amethyst rings supplanted the fading red, followed by a triple *bang* and a single, misplaced *crack*. Leaning against the fence, Cora listened for other incongruent noises.

Her hand drifted to her hip, where her scabbard should have been. Ever since she'd retrieved the scalpel from the pier, she'd kept it on her. Also missing was her satchel. Her fists balled, she pictured her golden guinea, bird stone, Susie's bunny barrettes, Emmett's locked crucifix box, Mary's tortoiseshell comb, and the baby cap, all now in the Gettlers' possession.

And, if the pair had scoured the island for her caches, they might have taken much more.

She smacked her palm against the grille, already vibrating from the rumble of the fireworks.

By her estimation, she'd been unconscious for twelve hours. Despite a lingering haziness, the memory of Kristian's reaction to her was razor sharp. And it cut just as deeply.

Fortunately, Rollie's authority over him appeared well established. So why had they gassed and caged her?

Because they were somehow altering Riverside, she decided. The misplaced rumbles meant that somewhere on this island, the two were setting off explosives. She'd been watching for flashes of local light, but the flickering of the rockets launched from the nearest platform in the East River toyed with her vision.

The sky brightened, and a series of crackles signaled that the grand finale had begun.

Rollie and Kristian had timed their clandestine operation perfectly. It was the kind of Machiavellian move Ulrich would have made, so she guessed that it had been Kristian's idea. Cora wondered at what age he'd been introduced to their vile work. The single photograph that Ulrich had given her—what she'd endured to get it had almost shattered her—had been of Kristian at age twelve. She kept it locked in a windowless room, away from the fading effect of the sun and the physical impact of her love.

The sky darkened, and the grating over the window stilled. She slid to a seated position and continued to listen, but the mistimed *booms* had ended with the show. With nothing left to do but worry, she lay down.

Only subconsciousness would give her a respite from the shock and disappointment that had accompanied meeting her grown son. Yet her mind refused to succumb to sleep.

The door creaked open, and she scrambled to her feet.

A man in a containment suit filled the doorway.

Based on his height, she knew it was Rollie.

"Give me my things," Cora demanded.

He tossed her the satchel, which she caught. "My knife?"

Rollie whipped an object across the floor to her.

She grabbed the sheath, clipped it to the loop of her jeans, and began inventorying the contents of her bag.

"It's all there." He pointed his flashlight to aid her effort.

Although she sensed he was telling the truth, she finished checking. "What were you doing with explosives?"

"I'm sorry for the way Kristian treated you. I've been trying to counter Ulrich's teachings. They spent so much time together, without me. He's a brilliant kid, with a lot of good in him. He's in medical school now."

"Another Dr. Gettler?" she said with a huff. "That's supposed to make me feel better?"

"I suppose not. But here's something that should: Cora, he's not just book-smart; his curiosity and creativity are astounding. I believe, wholeheartedly, that he'll be the one to cure you."

"Is that before or after he tortures me in the name of science? Just like his mentor."

"I won't let that happen, I promise," he said, shaking his head. "But I need him involved, as a lab assistant. Already he's made a brilliant observation. In comparing the older data with my recent work, he noticed some anomalies in the CBCs. The composition of your blood changes when it leaves the island. We need to be extracting the antibodies from the blood samples while they're still local."

"This was about building a secret lab? What a waste. I would have let you set something up. So much for that 'mutual respect' you mentioned to your 'son.'"

She tucked her fingers beneath the flap of the raccoon-skin case, and he backed into the hall.

Even though she couldn't see his face, Cora could sense his unease, and it thrilled her. She pulled out the scalpel, flipped it upward, and caught it by the handle. "How stupid of you to return this."

She flicked her wrist, and Rollie ducked behind the corridor wall just as the blade landed in the door frame.

"I know how much it means to you," he said from out of sight.

"Where are the rest?" She darted forward to grab the handle and returned to the fence.

"I've told you; I don't know what Ulrich did with them," he said, edging down the corridor. "If it's not enough for bird-hunting, I'll find something better. You shouldn't be reliant on us ever again."

"Hunting. That's right," she said, raising her arm. "I'll give you a thirty-second head start."

He snorted. "You can't hurt me. I'm the only one who can control your son."

Her hand fell to her side. "Why's that?" she asked despite her premonition.

He stepped into the doorway. "Ulrich may have screwed up Kristian in a lot of ways, but he did instill in my—your—son obedience and respect. As long as he believes I'm his father, he'll listen to me."

Her intuition had been right. The scalpel fell to the floor with a clatter.

Rollie sighed. "Ulrich gave Kristian his diaries, one for each year, beginning in 1926. Kristian studies them like they're medical textbooks. He now has so many astounding theories, any one of which might work. I need him focused on this puzzle."

"Surely Kristian read about his birth."

"There's no mention of it. Ulrich must have been afraid that Angela would find them. After he admitted what he'd done, their marriage was never the same. Even after she began dragging him to church. Whatever the reason, he gave up on that heinous master race delusion."

"Thank God for her." Cora tried to swallow a lump in her throat. "What if Kristian decides to resume the experiments that Ulrich detailed in those journals?"

Rollie raised his hand. "I won't let him touch you."

You won't be around forever, she thought. "Why can't you tell him I'm his mother? He would never harm me then."

"Because"—he stepped into the corridor and flashed the beam in each direction—"I also don't want him rethinking his relationship with Sylvia, whom he practically worships." Rollie winced. "That was insensitive. I'm sorry. Anyway, for years, he's heard Ulrich refer to you only as 'the subject' or 'mutt.' In those journals, it's no better. Sylvia's the most effective countervoice to that cold, clinical mentality."

Her insides roiling, Cora simultaneously hated and felt overwhelmingly grateful to that woman.

Rollie consulted a watch, looped around his utility belt, and an eerie green glow reflected off his mask. "Did you know that breast milk contains antibodies? Certainly not," he muttered. "It was only recently discovered."

Breast milk? He wants to talk about breast milk? This day can't get any worse, she decided. "You'd better go," she said, edging toward the door frame so he couldn't lock her in again. "Your 'son' is probably worried about you."

Rollie waved his hand, still holding the flashlight. "My point is, Kristian may have your same immunities."

She squinted to shield her eyes from the shifting beam. "What are you talking about?"

"It's only a theory, but hear me out."

Cora nodded for him to continue.

"The entire time Kristian was living on the island, he was nursing, and thus receiving your antibodies. Those antibodies must have been killing the microbes you were passing to him before they had a chance to take up residence. Back then, scientists hadn't yet discovered the benefits of breast milk. So it never occurred to Ulrich to remove that variable when assessing Kristian's immune system while he was still living here. Cora, Kristian's physiology may work the same way as yours."

A warmth spread across Cora's chest. *Maybe I can have my son back*, she thought. "Why didn't Ulrich test the theory after he learned about the milk antibodies?"

"Because Ulrich loves Kristian too much to risk losing him if our theory is wrong."

"What about infecting Kristian with something benign, like the common cold, while he's here?"

He shook his head. "That won't give us the data we'd need. Only the strongest of pathogens have ever been able to coexist with your immune system."

Desperately searching for an alternative, she squeezed her temples.

"I know this is hard to hear, since I'm sure you still love him, but you need to believe me when I say you don't want him staying at Riverside with you."

It wasn't Rollie's decision to make. Before she could tell him that, the sound of gas escaping the canister on his back filled the cell, followed by the reek of chloroform.

"I wish I didn't have to do this again, but I can't have you following me."

Her entire body began to tingle, except her heart. That felt like lead.

March 2008

March 21

Rot. Finn smelled it before his eyes had finished sorting the light from the dark. He squinted against the blinding white that had breached the dank room through its only window. Where the hell was he? A wintry draft passed across his bare chest, not nearly as cold as the metal beneath him. Cursing, he moved to rub the spot but was stopped by a pair of plastic ties, each encircling a wrist and a rusted metal bar. He jerked his legs; they were restrained at the ankles.

Ignoring a spasm, he twisted his neck to inspect his surroundings. The decaying walls and floor were free of the pipes and machinery that had characterized the physical plant—the last place he'd been before . . . that blow to the head.

He listened for noises that would cue him into his location. Through the paneless window came the sounds of lapping water and shrieking herons. The room smelled of mildew and death. He must still be on North Brother, he decided, in one of the buildings along the river's edge. Likely the morgue.

Finn recalled the rusty examining table he'd seen during his spine-chilling walk to the roof and feared that he was strapped to it. He tried to thrash free, but the cords held, stinging his wrists and ankles. Tucking his chin despite the misery in his neck, he tried to inspect his body but couldn't see beyond his chest.

Already, deadly microbes might be coursing through his bloodstream. Panic, along with acid, rose in his throat.

He raised his head to sniff for the lingering presence of insect repellent on his skin. The pungent odor confirmed he still had some protection, but it couldn't be much.

The drone of a boat's engine intensified, then waned. No one in a motorized watercraft would hear a scream through these walls.

Where is Cora? Gritting his teeth through a pulsating headache, he flashed back to her crying in the other room, then silence. And the rush of air from a metal pipe.

Had she done this to him? Undeniably she was capable. And sufficiently angry. Her weepy reaction to Sylvia's message could have been a ploy. Or a trigger.

Frantically, Finn inspected the cord binding his right wrist. It looked like something used in a psychiatric hospital, which Kristian easily could have procured. His brother could have also returned here on the first day feasible.

Alternatively, Cora could have stolen the ties from Kristian's bag at some point over the years, adding them to her hoard of "resources."

Aside from the rickety table beneath him and the rubble and dormant vines on the floor, the chamber contained only a metal cart against the far wall.

Squinting, Finn tried to discern the objects on its top shelf, which appeared sideways in his vision. The glinting of silver suggested medical instruments. Beside them rested a newspaper—quite possibly the *New York Times* that he'd just given her.

"Shit."

With a disturbing premonition of what else she'd left there, he scrutinized the cart again. Beside the newspaper rested a test tube with a strip of orange near its stopper.

The ticks!

"Shit."

Visualizing a dozen tiny arachnids crawling on him, sinking their mouth hooks into his flesh, he twisted his neck to inspect what he could see of his body—only his chest and shoulders, none of the warm, dark places ticks prefer.

Infecting him with the antibiotic-resistant strain of *Borrelia burgdorferi* would be fitting retribution for the sins of his family.

Pinned down, he was helpless and exposed—exactly the way she must have felt each time a member of his family had given her one of those scars.

Ten Minutes Later

Desperate to escape, Finn yelled.

To combat the pounding in his injured temple he regained his composure by slowing his breathing. He listened for his aggressor.

A *thwack* sounded in the hallway and ricocheted. Finn snapped his attention to the interior door, his muscles tensing.

Cora wouldn't have been so careless. Unless she didn't care if he'd heard her.

The rusted, flaking door opened with an ear-splitting squeal, and a figure in a black biosafety suit rushed toward him.

Finn recognized his brother through the visor.

"Are you okay?" Kristian asked.

"How'd you know?" Finn responded, relieved that his brother hadn't been the one who'd tied him down.

"I heard your scream." With a gloved hand, Kristian pulled back Finn's hair and peered closer. "That's a nasty contusion on your parietal bone. You may be concussed."

"Have you seen Cora? I think she's planning to release those ticks on me." Finn nodded his chin toward the cart. "If she hasn't already," he said and tried to look down at his body.

"I wouldn't put it past her." Kristian inspected Finn's wrists, then his ankles. "Those lacerations will need to be treated."

With one of her scalpels readied for an overhand throw, she could be aiming for his brother's spine this very moment. Strapping Finn to this table might have been a stratagem to lure Kristian here for an easy kill. He craned his neck to see the doorway beyond Kristian's bulky figure.

The space was empty, but she could be waiting on the far side of the wall.

"We need to get you to Dad's clinic," Kristian said.

"Where's your kayak?"

"It's with Lily's in the mulberry grove."

"She's here, too?" Finn asked, his stomach hardening.

Kristian folded his arms. "I'm sure she'll have the same reaction to you being here."

"She swore to me that she'd given up the idea."

"You know her better than that."

"Why would you help her?" Finn asked, suddenly aware of the goose bumps that had spread across his frigid, bare skin.

"She presented a very compelling case." He shrugged. "I knew from the get-go that I would stay close to her."

"Where's she now?" Finn couldn't let her see him like this.

"Safe in the tunnel."

Finn winced. Rollie had refused to show it to him, yet Kristian had allowed his girlfriend access.

"It's not what you think," Kristian said, raising a hand. "Her suit ripped during our landing. She's hunkered down, holding the gap closed, and probably freaking out that I'm not back yet with new gear."

"Let's get going then," Finn said, rattling the cords for emphasis.

"Not quite yet." Kristian ducked his head apologetically. "I'll complete my work as quickly as possible; I don't like her stuck down there any more than you do."

Work? It was as if Finn had been sucker-punched. *Kristian did this. Cora must be in danger,* he thought. *Lily, too.*

"You tore her suit, didn't you?"

Kristian drew in his breath. "I love her like a sister, even if she'll never become one."

Finn glared at him. "Get these cords off me."

"She's fine. There are no mosquitoes down there, and we used bug spray."

"What if she has a seizure?"

"The quicker I'm done with Cora, the less chance of that."

Cora's sudden silence, moments before the metal had met Finn's head, likely meant that Kristian had tranquilized her, Finn reasoned through the throbbing in his temple. "Where is she?"

"Nearby, and prepped."

Alarmed, Finn eyed the medical cart. "What's under that newspaper?"

"You think I'm hiding something from you?" Kristian asked in an injured tone. "Why would I do that? I simply took her paper because the mutt doesn't need to know what's going on in the world. It'll only increase her feelings of isolation, and the temptation to break her quarantine."

"When did you become such an asshole?" Finn asked as he noticed the flask with red tape, signifying chloroform, beyond the one containing the ticks. Cora must have had the vials with her.

Kristian looked up, pretending to be lost in thought. "The day I read that it took three months for the Chinese government to disclose SARS to the public." He clasped his gloved hands. "Or maybe it was the day we concluded that the IV antibiotics weren't working for Mom."

"So, you're planning to infect me with Lyme," Finn stated. A million imagined pinpricks of pain, like those his mother experienced daily, overwhelmed his nervous system, and he thrashed to shake them off. "Because you think that'll make Cora cooperate."

Moving the tube out of view, Kristian cleared his throat. "They're not meant for you. A slow infusion through the natural feeding process of the ticks should reduce the probability that her lymphocytes will wipe out the *Borrelia burgdorferi* the way they did with Ulrich's original strain." He sniffed. "A secondary delivery method in case this," he said as he held up a syringe, "doesn't work."

"Then why did you remove my hazmat suit?"

"You'll see in a minute." Kristian fiddled with the instruments on the cart, then abruptly left the room.

Over the pounding in his head, Finn strained to hear his brother's movements.

A moment later, the sound of wheels crushing debris came from the corridor, and a gurney appeared in the entrance. Protruding from it were Cora's worn work boots.

Finn recoiled in horror. "Kristian!" he thundered.

Heaving, Kristian pushed the stretcher into the room and swung it around, bringing her feet even with Finn's head.

Cora's lithe form lay motionless, her wrists and ankles strapped to the four joists. Although her khaki pants shielded her lower half, from the waist up she was bare, her history of past torture fully exposed.

"Untie her!" he said, seething. "Now!"

"Soon. How often do I get a chance to work on her like this? Thanks to whatever you said that upset her, I was able to catch her off-guard. So now

I have a rare opportunity to accomplish several objectives. In addition to introducing *Borrelia burgdorferi* into her microbiome and collecting several liters of plasma, I can further my research on coronaviruses. That, by the way, has been limited to specimen cultures, *not* host animals," he said, rolling his eyes. "I've decided that before infecting her with SARS-CoV, I should study the initial interaction of the virus with her cells in an isolated environment."

"You're crazy," Finn said with a growl.

"Don't worry," Kristian replied as he retrieved an antiseptic towelette from a carton on the bottom shelf of the stand. "This won't cause her any trauma. She'll be asleep during the procedure."

"What procedure?" Finn asked in a demanding tone.

"A lung biopsy. I'll be using an aspiration needle, so the entry point will be small. See, I do care about her. And, of course, you."

"Me?" Finn asked, jerking his arms, restrained at the wrists.

Kristian sighed with impatience. "I need a control group of typical lung cells."

Finn's mouth gaped open. "Why are you doing this?"

"Isn't it obvious? The SARS virus damages the air sacs of the lungs. These samples will enable me to observe how Cora's lung cells respond to an attack from the virus, compared to the response in typical lung cells."

"This is wrong."

"Let's save the discussion on moralities until after the next novel virus emerges, and our family has stepped forward with a scalable technology that can quickly produce millions of vaccine doses," he said, wiping clean a patch of Cora's chest. "I've got a lot to do before she wakes, including dressing your lacerations and getting you back into your suit. Then we'll collect Lily."

His anger surpassed the point of containment, and Finn yanked on the cords in an attempt to rip free the rails of the examining table.

"Stop that. You'll worsen the abrasions. Those are your own fault, though I am sorry for the head injury." Kristian discarded the towelette in a bio-hazard waste container beside the cart. "I only had enough chloroform in my bag for Cora, and I feared the window of opportunity might close while retrieving more."

With Cora's limp form only four feet away, Finn wasn't worried about himself. "Does Dad know? There's no way he'd allow this."

"I don't need his permission."

"Mom will be livid."

"At this point I'd rather have her alive and angry than dead."

Finn couldn't let this happen. But how could he prevent it? The slightest tug on his cords ignited the already raw skin.

His rage surged through his veins, and he released a primal, animal-like yell.

"That's very distracting," Kristian chided. "It's imperative that I'm able to concentrate," he said, picking up a gleaming needle.

Moments Later

Ignoring the fiery sensation of plastic digging into raw flesh, Finn battled the restraints as he screamed at Kristian.

"Shhh," Kristian said, prodding Cora's chest to determine his entry point between two ribs. "Ideally I'd be doing this with the aid of a CT scan."

Finn clenched his jaw. So far, his rage had been futile. Although silence would make him feel complicit, it would be better for Kristian to quickly, cleanly complete this violation of her basic human rights.

Kristian leaned forward, and with his usual surgical precision, inserted the needle.

Finn longed to shut his eyes, but he felt a responsibility to bear witness. Such a small puncture likely wouldn't even scab over, leaving no physical proof.

Deftly, Kristian withdrew the needle, just as the exterior door groaned and light swarmed the room.

"Stop!" Rollie bellowed from the doorway.

Kristian lurched backward.

A cold draft blasted Finn. "Thank God you're here."

"Thank Lily, too," he replied, glaring at Kristian. "She was worried about you, so she came to the surface, where her phone has reception."

"But the mosquitos," Finn exclaimed.

"I instructed her to go back down and wait for us." Rollie bent over Finn. "What happened to your head?" He peered into Finn's eyes. "Follow my finger."

"Kristian hit me with a pipe," Finn replied, tracking the motion.

"What is wrong with you?" Rollie asked Kristian as he examined the contusion on Finn's temple.

"He's fine. At the most, a mild concussion." Kristian responded. His hands remained tucked behind his thighs, and Finn realized he was hiding the aspiration needle, now filled with Cora's lung cells.

"The same cannot be said for her." Finn jerked his chin toward Cora.

Rollie shook his head in clear disgust as he rifled through his bag and pulled out a can of insect repellent. "You know her strain of RVF is lethal," he said to Kristian as he sprayed Finn. "It's sheer luck that none of the vandals who've come here during the summer have caused an outbreak."

"The first thing I did was spray him."

Coughing from the chemical mist, Finn glowered at his brother. He didn't attempt to speak; the next statement he planned to make would be in the form of a fist to Kristian's face.

Shaking his head, Rollie moved to inspect Cora. After checking for breathing, he visually examined her bare chest, narrowing in on the patch of skin still slick from the surgical wipe. "I'm appalled. After we thoroughly discussed this, you still . . ." He grunted—an obvious effort to keep his irritation in check.

Finn stared at his dad. Evidently, Rollie had been aware of Kristian's desire to collect the tissue sample from her, which meant he must know more about Kristian's side project than he'd admitted. Yet he apparently hadn't insisted on overseeing the effort, so that he could ensure ethical boundaries were maintained.

Because, Finn realized, their father had a weakness: his wife. To avoid alienating Kristian, and losing him as a lab partner, he'd allowed Kristian to work independently.

From his bag, Rollie removed a space blanket. Gingerly, he covered Cora's torso.

Their dad had picked the wrong son to bring into the fold, Finn thought, grinding his teeth.

"Where do you think you're going?" Rollie asked Kristian, who'd backed toward the interior doorway, the aspiration needle still presumably palmed in his hand.

"You need to stay and face the consequences of your actions." Rollie retrieved a buck knife from his bag. "How could you do this behind my back?"

"Because I knew you wouldn't—"

"Exactly. We do *not* operate on her. It's counterproductive, and a distraction from our priorities."

Defiantly, Kristian stood ramrod straight, his hazmat suit adding three inches to his stature and fifty pounds to his heft.

"Your involvement in this project has always been conditional on your adherence to those parameters." Rollie turned to saw through the plastic cords restraining Cora.

"I wouldn't do that yet," Kristian said in a low tone.

Rollie lowered the knife, and Finn knew they were anticipating a violent reaction from Cora when she did wake.

"Pack this stuff up." Rollie pivoted toward Finn's bound ankles.

"Hang on. There's a syringe with *Borrelia burgdorferi*," Kristian said, pointing at the cart. "We've been waiting for this opportunity for six years, and we likely won't get another chance before losing Mom."

Slowly, Rollie lowered the knife.

"You cannot be seriously considering it." Finn kicked against the cords.

"What makes you think she'll ever give us blood samples now?" Rollie asked Kristian.

"I've accounted for that as well. My theory will work."

"You can't do this!" Finn shouted.

"If I don't, your mom will die." Rollie stepped toward the cart.

Through Rollie's face shield, Finn could see the same resolute expression he'd witnessed from behind his cracked-open bedroom door as a child, when Sylvia would beg Rollie not to spend the day at North Brother Island.

A long-forgotten memory broke through Finn's subconscious: *She's human, too.* His mother's plea.

Rollie's response, as his features softened: *I know, sweetie. Don't ever let me forget it.* Taking her chin in his hand, he'd kissed her, and Finn had slipped back into bed.

Rollie has forgotten, Finn thought now as he recalled Cora's comment to Lily about the research poisoning their souls. His dad had feared that outcome. So he'd relied on Sylvia, who'd ironically become the catalyst for Rollie's departure from the values he'd espoused throughout Finn's childhood.

Finn pictured his father, poring over his patient files at the kitchen table, explaining to Finn why he jotted down the name of the person each patient loved most. *Your great-grandfather shouldn't have stopped the habit. Make sure I don't.*

Then, when Finn had surprised his parents with the news that he'd changed his college major to biology, Rollie had grimaced. *You've got a more important role to fill. Switch it back.*

And, just three weeks ago, Sylvia's hand on his shoulder: *You need to resolve. Because you'll be the one still around.*

Finn's heart pounded. All those years, while he'd been struggling to understand why nothing he did was ever good enough, his parents had been grooming him to stop Rollie if he ever did stray from his principles. *Once Rollie lost sight of Cora's humanity, after Sylvia's diagnosis, he didn't want the "fail-safe" he'd designed anywhere near this island*, Finn thought bitterly.

Regardless of whether keeping Rollie in check had been his "purpose" all along, today he would succeed in doing just that.

He rattled the ties. "Get these off me."

"Just a minute," Rollie said, uncasing the syringe.

"We don't expect you to understand, Finny," Kristian said smugly as he stored the aspiration needle within an insulated bag.

Racking his brain for an argument that would dissuade Rollie, Finn squeezed shut his eyes. And saw that array of patient files, a name scrawled at the top of each.

"Finnegan Gettler," he announced.

Kristian chortled. "Congratulations. You know your name."

Finn craned his neck to see Rollie, who now stood beside Cora.

"That's what you should write in the upper corner of her chart."

Rollie stiffened.

"I'm sure there've been others, but she's lost them all. Now all she has is me. And she loves me, Dad. I know it," Finn said with forced conviction. Rollie hadn't witnessed his interactions with Cora; he couldn't know the animosity that had prevailed each time she'd begun to soften toward Finn. "She *is* human, and she's in love with your son."

From the interior came a high-pitched hiccup.

In the hallway stood Lily, one hand gripping the tear in her suit, the other covering her mouth.

"Lils," he stammered.

She shook her head vehemently and stepped out of sight.

Finn longed to explain that he'd grossly exaggerated Cora's interest in him, but he couldn't, not yet.

Rollie wavered. The syringe in his hand trembled. "What am I doing?" he asked himself. "I promised her that I'd never cross this line; that I'd never stop *seeing* her as a patient, not a test subject," he stated, returning the syringe to the cart.

"Let her go," Finn said softly.

Nodding, Rollie retrieved his buck knife from the tray and cut loose Cora's bindings.

"Kristian, what have you done?" Lily asked from the doorway.

"I was trying to help you, and Sylvia."

She looked to Finn's nearly naked form, then to Cora. "Not like this," she said, crumpling to the ground.

"Lily!" Finn shouted as Kristian rushed to help her up.

"Get off me!" she said to Kristian, pushing him away.

Rollie moved to Finn's side. "I'm so sorry I let it come to this. Thank you for being the son I truly needed," he said as he inspected the lacerations on Finn's wrists and ankles.

"We're finished here," he said, addressing Kristian. "For good."

"I'm not abandoning our research," Kristian declared, stepping toward Cora. "Before you showed up, I had things completely under control."

With measured strokes that told Finn his father was trying to keep his anger in check, Rollie cut Finn's cords. "As long as I'm still alive, everything on North Brother is under *my* control."

"Except Cora. She's become a feral, savage dog."

"Kristian!" Lily said sharply.

"As wild as this island," he continued without looking her way. "But I can change that."

Rollie broke the last tie.

Finn bolted upright. Hit by a wave of dizziness, he nearly fell off the rickety table.

Light and dark blurred together, and he swayed.

"Take it slow." Rollie held him steady while reaching into his bag for a water bottle.

As Finn guzzled the room came back into focus. He lunged toward his brother.

A loud crack sounded, followed by a shriek from Lily, and Finn spun toward the noise.

The table had landed behind him on its side. Plaster dust filled his nostrils. Coughing, he waved at the cloud to disperse it and resumed his advance on Kristian.

"Finn," his father said firmly, "we need to get Lily home." He looked to Kristian. "Get them suits. Then start dismantling the onsite lab."

Cora groaned, and all three men spun to face her.

Her eyes flew open and Finn registered fear in their blue depths. Blinking rapidly, she sat up, and the foil blanket fell away.

Grasping for words that could quickly pacify her, Finn concluded there were none and braced for her fury.

Cora looked down at her naked upper torso, clearly searching for a freshly sutured incision. Her fingertips met the reddened injection site, and she raised her chin and fixed her stare on Rollie. "You promised," she said in a glacial tone.

Instinctively, Rollie raised his hands to shield himself, then dropped them. "I'm sorry. I didn't know that Kristian was planning this. He's never gotten over Ulrich's death. I'd underestimated how unforgiving and resentful he'd remain. That was my fault."

"Ulrich's death wasn't my fault," she hissed.

"Let's not go there now." Rollie shuffled backward. Beyond her, Kristian had slinked toward the corridor, where Lily had backed up against the far wall.

"I tried to stop him," Finn said, embarrassed by how empty the claim had sounded.

Her focus didn't stray from Rollie. "I suppose I'm now a carrier of Lyme," she said far too calmly for the circumstances. "And God knows what else."

"He didn't inject anything," Rollie said.

"But he did 'take,'" she replied, rubbing the spot. Her emotionless tone, boiling with anguish beneath its surface, agitated Finn. He wanted her to know that he hadn't been involved, but what good would that do now?

Shaking her head in apparent disgust, her hand drifted to her hip and her eyes narrowed. "You'd better give it all back."

"Of course," Rollie said, glancing at Kristian.

Cora didn't follow his gaze. "Then get the hell off my island."

"Kristian, go get the suits," Rollie said without taking his eyes off her.

"I'm not—"

"Now!"

"Fine," Kristian said curtly and left the room.

Wrapping the foil around her chest, Cora addressed Rollie: "We should have told him years ago."

"It was the right call. I still believe that."

"Sylvia doesn't think so. According to Finn, she wants me to tell him now."

Rollie turned to him, a questioning look on his face.

Finn shrugged. "Mom knows you never gave up your work."

"How?"

Finn raised his hands. "I didn't say anything."

From the hallway, Lily scoffed. "She knew the same way any woman would: intuition."

Rollie released a long, tired sigh. "I guess I shouldn't be surprised. Despite her illness, she's still incredibly perceptive. Cora, I swear to you: we are done. This," he said, waving his hand at the stretcher beneath her, then the medical cart, "has shown me it's impossible to ensure we stay within the boundaries you and I established."

"It took *this* for you to realize that?" she asked, raising one eyebrow.

"No," he said softly. "It took Finn for me to realize it."

Finn's chest tightened, and he glanced at Lily, hoping she understood why he'd played up Cora's feelings toward him.

Her attention fixed on the ground, she didn't acknowledge him.

"I'm mothballing the project," Rollie continued, "which is more reason not to tell him. If Kristian knows, it'll be harder for him to give this up."

"What are you talking about?" Finn asked, the sting from his abrasions flaring.

Shaking her head, Cora bypassed the overturned examining table and moved outside. Standing among the dormant weeds, she held the space blanket tightly around her.

Something bumped into Finn's back, and he spun around and accepted a gear pouch from Kristian.

"Sorry for the rough treatment earlier."

"Drop dead." Finn hurriedly put on the suit as Lily, still in the corridor, did the same.

Kristian surveyed the room and located Cora outside. "I want things to be better between us," he said in a surprisingly gentle tone.

"Give me my sweatshirt."

He grabbed a plastic bag from the corridor and tossed it to her.

"And my satchel and scalpels." She stepped out of sight, regaining a modicum of privacy while she put her top back on.

Kristian gesticulated to Rollie that they shouldn't return her blades.

Finn had to agree that doing so right now could be deadly for them all.
"She'll need them to survive on her own, as is her wish," Rollie said loudly, clearly for Cora's benefit.
She stepped into view. "My things."
Crossing his arms over his chest, Rollie mouthed the word "go" to Kristian.
Kristian stalked into the hallway, almost knocking into Lily.
"Not a word," he said to her.
She huffed. "You're a hypocritical, chauvinistic pig."
Finn stifled a smile. No doubt she had a few choice words lined up for him, too.
Returning moments later, Kristian handed the items to Cora, and quickly retreated.
"I'm sick of fighting," he said from the interior wall.
"That's only because you've lost. If you didn't worship the memory of a man who tortured me, and thousands of others, I'd still be giving you monthly blood specimens."
Kristian raised his index finger. "Ulrich's experiments at the work camp were meant to ultimately save lives. He took far too many liberties in the name of the 'Greater Good,' but that doesn't change the fact that people will keep dying because of your selfishness. All those tiny, burned bodies you saw lined up on the lawn after the *Slocum*, that's nothing compared to those that will stack up outside morgues and in freezer trucks if a pandemic hits New York City."
Her face had twisted in anguish.
"I know those memories haunt you. My family still hurts, too, from our loss." Kristian put his hand to his heart. "I read in the library archives about the hero diplomas. The empress of Germany presented them to fifty-one nurses, but not you. If you'd received one, I'm sure it would be in that bag of yours. You wish you could have saved even more people that day. This is your chance."
Momentarily, Finn thought she might acquiesce. Then her expression hardened.
"This latest theory of yours," she said, her voice rising, "will lead you to the same place as all the others—a dead end."
Kristian shook his head. "Not this time. All we need is thirty units of your blood, and your permission to let us conduct a trial on the island, aboveground." He stepped toward her. "Sylvia's the same passionate

woman you once knew, even when a sliver of light or a whisper is enough to make her wish she were dead. You'd enjoy seeing her again, and watching her heal through your generosity. And then we'll use that same technology to help the world prepare for the next viral threat."

Shaking off the vision of a brighter future, Finn marveled at Kristian's skill in manipulation.

"I do care about Sylvia," Cora said, rubbing her pocked cheek. "And mankind. Just because I'm stranded here doesn't mean I've forgotten the value of their lives." She gestured toward Manhattan. "Unfortunately, though, I've realized that the power that would come with harnessing my immunities, in your hands, could do more harm than good."

"You conniving bitch," Kristian said, his sneer visible through the protective face shield.

"Kristian!" Rollie barked.

"You think I should take that from her?" He turned to Cora. "My motives have always been pure—not that you'd understand morality. As Ulrich liked to say, you're just a lowly mutt, no different from any other lab animal."

"What would you do with a vaccine?" she asked, clearly choosing not to dignify his insult with a reaction. "Who would get the first doses?"

"Americans," Kristian stated. "Every single one of them, regardless of race, color, or gender."

"What about the people in the Mideast? And China? Would you help them next?"

"You're too ignorant and simpleminded to understand geopolitics."

"Boys, let's go home," Rollie said, stepping between Kristian and Cora.

"Am I the only one here who cares about Mom?" Kristian asked.

"Cut the family loyalty crap," Finn spat. "Two hours ago, you hit me on the head with a pipe and tied me to a table! You're pathetic."

"Boys!" barked Rollie, but Kristian's arm was already in motion. His fist connected with Finn's mask, and the pain from the whiplash momentarily stunned Finn.

His ears rung, and he realized it was Lily's screaming.

He charged at Kristian and pinned him to the wall.

Kristian's arm snaked around Finn's neck in a chokehold. Gasping, Finn writhed to free himself.

"He can't breathe," Finn heard Lily say.

Kristian loosened his hold just enough to free Finn's air passage.

"I'll kill you if you ever touch her again."

"You *do* have feelings for the mutt." Kristian made a *tsking* sound, and his visor knocked against Finn's. "Poor Lily. Such a sweet girl, whereas you can never touch that petri dish."

Finn kneed him in the balls. Kristian groaned and doubled over.

When he stood back up, he was holding the Lyme syringe, which he must have grabbed from the ground.

Rollie, Cora, and Lily screamed for him to stop.

"You're insane!" Finn yelled.

"What genius isn't?" He thrust the needle at Finn, who jumped out of its range.

The edges of the room and the others faded away. All Finn could see was the hypodermic pointed at him. His hands outstretched, he darted around his brother and grabbed an instrument from the tray.

Kristian sprang toward him, and Finn waved the surgical knife in a defensive arc.

The blade met resistance, and Kristian grunted as a ripping sound signaled that his suit had been punctured.

The knife fell from Finn's grip and clanged against the ground. A moment later, Kristian's syringe landed near it with a *ping*.

Cora's wail splintered the fading echoes.

Clutching his abdomen, Kristian fell against the cart, bringing it down with him.

A sharp crack filled the room like a rifle fired from close range.

Medical equipment clattered as it hit the ground.

Finn gaped at his brother and then his empty hand.

"Oh my God," Lily said with a gasp and rushed to him as Cora shrieked, "What have you done?!" and leaped over the toppled examining table.

The women almost collided above Kristian.

"Your pathogens, get back!" Rollie yelled to Cora and rushed to Kristian's side.

She gasped and sprinted back to her spot beyond the outer doorframe.

"You, in the hall!" he barked at Lily, then said to Finn, "Help me get this off him!" and began cutting the Teflon away from Kristian's abdomen. Crimson red spilled onto the floor.

"He's losing blood fast."

Finn yanked on the material. "I'm sorry. I'm so—"

"There's no time for that."

"Should I call nine-one-one?" Lily asked, fumbling in her bag.

"They won't get here in time," Rollie said, "There's an emergency kit in our lab. Can you find your way back to the tunnel entrance?"

Lily scrunched her face in concentration. "I'm not sure. I was running. There were so many trees."

Rollie locked his eyes on hers. "You can do this. Head toward the single-story maintenance building, that way," he said, pointing. "Once there, you'll recognize the way. Be careful not to rip your suit again. Now go."

She nodded and ran down the corridor.

Finn returned his attention to the horror before him. His dad had resumed cutting away the suit, the gap now revealing a deep gash above Kristian's navel.

Rollie surveyed the medical instruments scattered across the rubbish. "Cora, get the suture kit from my duffel."

Now wearing an N-95 mask and gloves that must have come from her messenger bag, she retrieved the kit, handed it to Rollie, and returned to her post outside. "Please don't let him die," she said, sobbing. "Please."

"He needs a transfusion. We've got to get him to a hospital before . . ." His father's voice trailed off.

Finn could tell his brother wouldn't make it that far.

Seconds Later

Blood covered Finn's hands. No matter how much pressure he applied, it continued to slip past his fingers, pooling around Kristian's large intestine. "Hurry! I can't stop it!"

"Let him concentrate," Cora said from the doorway, her hands raking its concrete frame.

Seemingly oblivious to both, Rollie continued suturing a severed artery in Kristian's abdominal cavity.

Fighting off a wave of nausea at the sight of his brother's innards and the warm, wet sensation of so much blood, Finn gritted his teeth, willing his father to work faster.

"Almost ready." Rollie tied off the stitch and rethreaded the needle. "I need to get where you are. Switch to one hand, and apply more pressure."

While pressing firmly, Finn shifted to give his dad more space. He leaned over to make eye contact with his brother, and a tear landed on the inside of his face shield, directly above Kristian's cheek.

"Stay with me. Milo needs you; Hannah needs you; Mom needs you." Only minutes earlier, he'd threatened to kill Kristian. Now Finn wished he could take it back. "I need you."

Kristian's pupils seemed to lock onto Finn, then his eyes rolled back into his head.

A memory pushed through Finn's panic, at the movies, sharing popcorn with Kristian while watching *Terminator* 2. He'd been too young for the R-rated film, so Kristian had sneaked him in. So many times, Kristian had been the big brother that every younger brother wished he had. Finn blinked back hot tears.

He cuffed the side of Kristian's hood. "You can't die now, not before paying me back for that kick to the balls. You hear me?"

The sound of Kristian's labored breathing through the respirator dimmed to a barely audible gasping.

"No!" Finn shouted. "Don't you dare give up!"

"Is he breathing?" Cora asked, her usually gritty voice now laced with shrapnel.

Finn put his ear to the side of Kristian's face shield. "Barely."

"He's lost too much blood," Rollie said without looking up. "He's not going to make it."

Cora wailed, and the desperate sound ended in a series of racking coughs, barely muffled by her surgical mask. With one hand clutching the door frame and the other pressed to her chest, she began hyperventilating.

Her entire body swayed.

Finn feared that she might collapse, but neither he nor his father could leave Kristian.

"Wait." Finn sat up. "What's my blood type? Is it the same?"

"No." Rollie grabbed another suture thread. "If it were, you'd already have a needle in your arm."

"Cora," Kristian stammered so feebly, Finn thought he might have imagined it. He brought his head closer to his brother's visor but Kristian's lips didn't move again.

Why had Kristian mentioned her? Finn glanced at Cora, whose wheezing had become interlaced with appeals to God, and back to his brother. And why was she so emotional, so desperate for him to survive?

Kristian's eyes had closed, his head slumped to one side. *No!* "He's unconscious."

Rollie checked his pulse. "He needs CPR," he said, rising on his knees. "Move."

Finn scrambled out of the way, and Rollie removed his hood and then Kristian's.

"CPR means he's not breathing?" Cora asked quietly from the doorway. "My God!" her voice rose to a wail. "He's dead!"

"Not yet. Keep praying." Rollie began chest compressions.

"He asked for her. For Cora," Finn said in disbelief. "Why would he?"

"He did?" Cora asked in a shrill tone. "He needs me. Let me go to him."

"No," Rollie said without breaking his rhythm. "He was referring to your blood." He gave Kristian two breaths and resumed the compressions. "You're O positive. A universal donor, just like him."

"We're a match," she whispered, gazing into her cupped palm, then fisted her hand. "It's the only way," she said, looking straight at Rollie as she crossed the threshold. He returned her stare while continuing to count.

Finn's heart raced. "No way. Cora cannot be his donor. She'll kill him!"

Cora pushed the N-95 mask against her face. "Finn's right. It's too dangerous."

"He'll die for certain if we don't," Rollie said, winded from his effort.

She fidgeted with the tips of her latex gloves. "What if—"

"We'll figure it out later. If he makes it." Rollie dropped his head to expel air into Kristian's mouth.

"Are you crazy?" Finn jumped to his feet. "This is murder. Her pathogens. He'll never . . ." Even as he said it, he knew there was no alternative.

"Finn's right. Rollie, I can't do this." Cora tugged at her crucifix pendant. "If it doesn't work, I'll have killed my—"

"I need tubing and IV needles. Where's Lily? We can't wait for her. There might be some in this mess. Start looking." Rollie listened for Kristian's breathing. "I've stabilized him, for now. Hurry."

Cora's eyes flashed with hope. "He might make it?"

"Only with your blood." Rollie rifled through the fragments within reach.

She dropped to the ground behind the toppled examining table to search for the needed supplies.

Still shocked by the plan and Cora's willingness, Finn tried to focus on the immediate task. He spotted a handful of white packets beside the overturned cart and crawled over to them, his slick gloves leaving behind red streaks. In the dim light, he strained to read one of their labels: gauze. Continuing his search, he turned toward Cora and the upended table.

"I found tubing," she called out and tossed the package to Rollie.

Finn shuffled closer to her. "Why are you doing this?"

"Because," she said, furrowing her brow, "I have to."

"This is your chance to be rid of him." Just voicing the notion sickened him, yet he needed to understand. "If he makes it, he'll never leave you alone."

"The pain will be worse if he dies."

"This was my fault," Finn said, choking on the words. "You don't need to do this to clear your conscience."

She shook her head. "That's not it."

"Then why?" he asked, squinting to distinguish her face from the sunlight behind her.

Her sky-blue eyes looked heartbreakingly soulful. Finn felt the urge to embrace her, despite all the reasons he knew he shouldn't. He looked down at the river of brittle vines that ran past him. Soon they would be supple again. The seasons would repeat. If Kristian lived, he would find a way to torment her despite their father's edict. Cora would pass the next years the same way she had the last hundred.

He pictured the scars that traversed her body and remembered what she'd said about her interior being even uglier. Although incomparably prettier than Frankenstein's monster, she, too, had been transformed by scientists who'd believed they could play God. It made perfect sense that she'd revolted against the family that had viewed her as their creation—and property. So why was she helping them now?

He leaned forward and lifted her chin, so she had no choice but to look at him. "You owe me an answer."

Her eyelids fluttered, their long lashes shining with tears.

Rollie called for them to hurry, but Finn didn't stir.

Neither did Cora.

At last, she met his gaze. "I love him."

He must have misheard, yet her words had been crystal clear. "How could you possibly?"

Already turning away from him, she plucked a package from among a scattering of antiseptic wipes. "Needles!"

"Bring them here!" Rollie commanded.

"Where do you want me?" she asked, rushing to his side.

"On the gurney." Rollie connected a needle to each end of the tubing. "So the blood can flow down to Kristian. Finn, help her."

Stunned, she stood stock still, staring at the surface she'd been bound to minutes earlier.

Finn's stomach lurched. They couldn't ask her to lie back down on that, so he scrambled to his feet and righted the examining table. After testing its sturdiness, he extended his hand to her.

"Hurry, we're losing him!" his father yelled, breaking Cora's trance.

She looked at Finn, and he could see her fear.

"I won't let anything happen to you; I promise." He squeezed her hand.

Exhaling slowly, she sat down on the rusted metal which creaked and wobbled beneath her trembling frame. He lifted her legs onto the footrest and grabbed the needle now connected to the tubing.

She shrank away from it. "I don't know if I can."

"Do you want me to?" Finn asked, though he doubted he could properly insert it into her vein.

"I'll do it!" Rollie shouted.

"That's not what I meant," she said, her teeth chattering.

"Would you rather be asleep?" Rollie stood up. "As God is my witness, I swear no harm will come to you. Though you may need a breathing tube."

Slowly, she sat up. "Okay, but first, I need to say good-bye, in case . . ."

Rollie backed away and signaled Finn to do the same.

Cora bent over Kristian's still form, whispered into his ear, and kissed his forehead.

Suddenly comprehending that the two had a history together, he wondered what had happened between them that made her so forgiving now.

With renewed poise, Cora climbed back onto the table. "Don't worry: I've got something."

Rollie nodded and took the needle from Finn.

From her pocket, she removed the vial of chloroform, which she must have recovered while searching for the needles and tubing.

With an uncharacteristically peaceful expression, she gazed into the palm of her other hand. Finn strained to see the object, but her fingers had closed around it.

She looked from Kristian to Finn, then laid down. After a whispered prayer, she removed the plug from the chamber, closed her eyes, and held it to her nose.

Silently, Finn reminded her of his promise.

Moments later, her hand slipped from its resting spot atop her abdomen, and her fingers uncurled, revealing an empty palm.

Rollie inserted the needle, connecting Cora and Kristian.

Though unconscious, she seemed to be smiling.

Six days later

March 27

A black sedan careened through the stale yellow light.

Finn grabbed Lily's coat sleeve and yanked her back into the pool of lamplight on the corner of the sidewalk.

"Ouch!" she said, surprised.

The surge of adrenaline had reminded him of the times he'd almost lost her, and he shivered in the misty rain. He longed to pull her to him. Instead, he didn't even offer the now obvious explanation.

Throughout their commute from the Bronx hotel where they'd spent the past six days in quarantine, she'd been seemingly oblivious to the bustle of evening rush hour. And quiet, worrisomely so. During their second stint in isolation, the few times Lily had answered his calls she'd only been willing to discuss Kristian's health.

According to Rollie, who'd run their diagnostics while caring for Kristian in the Tuberculosis Pavilion, Kristian had tested positive for Ebola, Rift Valley fever, and Spanish influenza—all three of Cora's diseases without vaccines. To prevent the physical side effects of stress from hindering Kristian's healing, Rollie had been keeping him in a medically induced coma while watching for symptoms to emerge.

Although Lily's aloofness since leaving North Brother was justified, it had exacerbated Finn's own agitation. He'd taken for granted how open she'd always been with him. In comparison to his family's secrets and evasiveness, Lily's honesty and chatter had provided a welcome contrast. It was just one of the many reasons he loved—and needed—her.

Now he'd likely lose her, right as his family was falling apart.

Finn followed Lily across Madison Avenue, the mist glistening in the headlights of the waiting cars.

In a few minutes, they would enter his parents' warm, bright, deadly quiet apartment. Finn couldn't do that with this wall between them.

"Come here a sec," he said, abruptly moving under an awning to escape the biting wind.

Glancing in the direction of his parents' apartment, Lily frowned, and Finn surmised that she was debating between two equally unpleasant alternatives: continuing there without him or having the conversation she'd been avoiding.

"Can we please talk?"

From her rigid jaw and posture, he knew her standoffishness would be hard to crack.

During the past six nights, his hotel bed had felt achingly empty—a preview of life without her.

More than anything, he wanted Lily to be happy and healthy. Remaining entwined with his family would threaten her chances at both. She needed to move on. If he dictated that decision, however, their split would be even harder on her. And, he knew, she would assume that he'd developed feelings for Cora.

"I love you," he said unintentionally. *Too much to keep you.*

Her shoulders slumped, and she released a single, strangled whimper. "I love you too."

Ignoring reason, he wrapped his arms around her and kissed her deeply.

She responded with an intensity that shocked—and guilted—him.

"I don't know if I can handle this stress," she said, burying her head against the front of his jacket.

Finn pressed his cheek against the damp hair atop her head. "You shouldn't have to."

"It was so horrible, seeing her tied up like that. And you."

He hugged her tighter. *His own brother*, who soon might die because of Finn's reckless retribution. "I'm sorry."

"It's not your fault," she said, leaning away.

"If I hadn't lost my shit after he punched me, Kristian would be fine right now."

"He was only there in the first place because of me." She shook her head in frustration. "Do you know the worst part?"

He tensed, waiting for her to continue. There had been so many worst parts.

"When Rollie announced that the project was over, I was disappointed. It's so wrong, but throughout all this, I couldn't help but think that maybe, eventually, they'd find a way to cure cancer with her immune system. I was even fantasizing about us starting a family."

Wishing he could fill the hollowness he knew she felt because of her infertility, Finn slid his hand between her coat and sweater to rub her lower back.

"In that moment," she said, sobbing, her face hidden against his jacket, "I was as bad as Kristian."

Finn stepped back to look into her russet, reddened eyes. "Don't ever think that. You've been through so much. It's natural that you didn't want to lose a reason to hope."

She returned her head to his chest, and he rubbed her back again.

"I have to tell you something," she said, her voice muffled, and Finn's hand froze.

"I've always felt uncomfortable around your dad, even before last summer."

Cocking his head in surprise, Finn waited for her to continue.

"When you're not around he asks me really probing questions, about my childhood, our relationship, stuff like that. I'm sure he assumed that I thought he was just making small talk, since he didn't know you'd told me about the project. But given what I did know, it always felt too intense." She bit her lip, coated in a cinnamon-smelling gloss. "While I've got my own legit reasons for not wanting to get married, the vibes I get from your dad haven't helped."

"Why didn't you tell me? I thought you liked him."

Lily sighed. "It's complicated. Most of the time, the way he treats me is what I always wanted from a dad. And you were so happy that we got along. I didn't want to disappoint you."

"That's ridiculous."

"I know," she said, brushing back her windblown hair. "I'm sorry. Right now, though, I'm not just worried about your family's screwed up values. I'm also worried about myself. I still find myself wondering what it would be like if your brother and dad succeeded. We could have a family then. Two kids? Or three? Is that sick?"

"No, not at all," Finn choked out. "We should be parents."

She wiped her eye, smearing her makeup. To Finn she looked no less stunning.

He held her chin in his hand. "Let's do it."

Immediately he regretted the comment. A child would fix nothing. Not to mention: he should be helping her realize that she should move on, not giving her more reasons to stay. He shifted gears: "You are nothing like them. You're a good, kind, beautiful person."

"But not as beautiful as Cora," she blurted out, then cringed. "That came out wrong."

Finn gripped her shoulder. "I told my dad that Cora loves me so that he'd remember she's human, too. I was desperate to get him to stop. It's not even true."

"I gathered that's why you said it. But it's got to be true! She's just as much a woman as me, and all the reasons I'm attracted to you, she must see, too. And she's so lonely. How could she not love you?"

"Because I'm a Gettler," he said, thinking of his brother, now at her mercy. Although he was furious at Kristian, he couldn't simply dissolve the bond they'd developed over Finn's lifetime. The thought of Kristian stuck on that island, separated from his family while pathogens festered within him, made Finn feel queasy.

"He might be okay," Lily said, evidently sensing his distress.

"I hope so." Finn wiped the light rain from his forehead. Rollie had told them that Kristian's body might be compatible with her immunities, given their matching blood type. Right now, Finn didn't want to think about the alternative.

"It doesn't matter if Cora loves me or not. I love you." The words had escaped before he'd remembered that he shouldn't be convincing her to stay with him.

Fully aware of all the reasons he shouldn't, he leaned down to kiss her, and tasted cinnamon.

She responded passionately, then abruptly pulled away. "I know you love me, not her. The fact that she's so contagious means she's not a threat, which makes me feel guilty. Again."

"Lils, you're the only one for me," he said automatically, wrapping his arms more tightly around her. *But she'll be better off without me,* he reminded himself and loosened his hold. "I want you to be—"

"If Kristian survives," Lily said, cutting him off, "you won't be able to walk away from Cora. She'll need you on her side."

Finn felt the onset of a headache. Lily was right: now that he understood his true role within his family, he couldn't shirk the responsibility.

"Your relationship with her won't—can't—stay platonic," she said, staring past him.

"Why would you say that?"

"One of two things will happen: either you'll fall in love with her, or this project will poison your soul, like she warned me. It's happened to all the other men in your family."

"That's ridiculous!"

"Is it? From what I've seen of your family's obsession, the only thing that'll keep you from losing sight of her humanity is love." She stepped out from the doorway, and a sharp wind whipped her hair across her face.

He wanted to dismiss her claim, but what valid counterargument was there? His dad had been a genuinely good man, and yet he'd caved to the temptation of a cure at any cost. Sylvia had been able to keep Rollie in check for only so long, and Finn wouldn't have that support even initially if Lily broke up with him, which she should do.

"Let's go," Lily said. "Your parents are waiting."

Finn wanted to draw her to him for a final kiss but stopped himself.

She must have sensed his hesitation; she turned on her heel and left the shelter of the awning, her figure briefly illuminated by the lights on the next storefront.

Rollie opened the apartment door.

He looks ten years older. Suddenly overwhelmed by their situation, Finn didn't greet him.

"C'mon in," Rollie said, his voice equally aged.

Finn moved so Lily could enter first and shrugged off his jacket.

The spacious living room looked immaculate, only possible through Rollie's recent absence.

"Where's Mom?"

"Asleep in the bedroom."

"How's she handling it?" Finn asked, nervous that Sylvia blamed him, despite Rollie's reassurances to the contrary.

"Not well." Rollie studied his age-spotted hands. "Hannah should be here soon. Milo's at swim practice, thankfully."

"Shoot," Lily said, smacking her forehead. "We forgot soda. I'll grab a liter from the deli."

That morning she'd offered to engineer a way for Finn to talk to his father alone. In response, he'd invited her to be part of their conversation. "Finn," she'd replied, "I don't want to." His throat constricting, he'd nodded, relieved yet saddened that she was distancing herself.

Closing the door behind her, Finn turned to his dad, who'd moved to the windows facing the East River.

"How's Kristian?"

"The same. No symptoms yet."

Finn released his breath. "When they do start, you'll call the CDC, right?"

"If it becomes clear that Cora's antibodies aren't helping him, then yes, I will." Rollie rubbed his chest. "Maybe I should've involved them long ago. I'm so ashamed of myself. You've shown me this mantle is too much for one family to shoulder."

The knot in Finn's stomach loosened. If his brother did recover under the CDC's care, and they assumed authority over Cora's case, maybe his family could find some form of normalcy. And he and Lily could stay together.

Alternatively, if Kristian died, how would any of them ever move forward?

"Finn, there's something I need to tell you," Rollie said, running his hand down his pants leg.

Weary of any more bad news, Finn clutched his arms to his chest. "What?"

Rollie lowered himself to the couch and indicated that Finn should sit in the recliner across from him.

"There's a reason I'm hopeful that Kristian will remain symptom-free, even though that didn't occur with Ulrich's test subjects who received her blood."

Finn felt his own blood chilling. "Go on."

"There's no easy way to say this," Rollie said, fidgeting with a coaster on the end table. "Kristian is Cora's son."

"How could you?!" Finn roared and stood up.

"No, no, no." Rollie put his hand up. "He's not *my* son."

"Then whose?"

"Ulrich's," Rollie said in a bitter tone.

Speechless, Finn dropped back to the recliner.

Numb from the shock, he listened to Rollie explain Ulrich's theory, ensuing experiment, and its incomplete conclusions.

"So, he might be like her, and we never knew it," Rollie said. "Or he might begin showing symptoms any time now."

"That's why you allowed the transfusion," Finn murmured. "Does Kristian know?"

"Not yet."

Finn recalled the message that he'd passed from his mother to Cora, as well as the inscription she'd picked for the watch. Now they made sense. As did Cora's reaction.

The room felt crushingly small. The urge to run gripped his muscles.

A shocking realization hit Finn, forcing his spine ramrod straight. "He's not my biological brother."

Rollie's hand drifted to the scar on his jaw. "He's your uncle. You are my only son."

Finn's throat constricted. He looked at his dad anew. "But you always favored him."

"Not true. I had to keep a closer eye on him, given how much time Ulrich spent with him. They did so much together, like baseball games and Cub Scout camping trips, that I always marveled at the fact that neither he nor anyone outside our family figured it out."

"Why'd you keep it from him?"

"We were certain that if he found out, he'd test his limits. Now, this week, I find myself worrying about that once again."

"Why didn't you tell me? All this time."

Finn knew the answer. No child could be expected not to divulge such a destructive truth during an argument with a cocky, older brother.

"I'm sorry. I love you so much," Rollie said. "I'm sorry I haven't been a good enough father to you."

Although he had been fully attentive and supportive when home, the man had so often been absent. And while Rollie's sky-high expectations for Finn had been flattering, each time Finn had fallen short, it had hurt that much more. An apology now couldn't undo the past. Finn thought of Lily and her relationship with her dad. He wished she were beside him now. So effortlessly, she'd coolly rebuffed Leonard's request for forgiveness.

Conversely, looking at his frail, defeated father, Finn felt sympathy. And because Finn believed himself to be a good Christian, an obligation to forgive him. Yet he did also feel anger.

"Given Kristian's predicament, we obviously can't mothball this project. It's embarrassing to have to ask this, but I need you to keep me from crossing that line again," Rollie said, looking toward the bedroom.

Finn twisted to see his mother on her scooter in the doorway. Her cheeks were wet with tears.

"See, sweetie, you didn't fail," Rollie said to her. "Look at him."

"Not with him," she slurred. "With Kristian." She looked at her hands, folded in her lap. "And with Cora, when she begged me to give her son back."

"That was not your fault," Rollie said. "We did a thorough medical risk assessment."

"I should have been stronger. Should have insisted you tell Kristian the truth." She motored into the room. "Out of everything that's been done to her, I hurt her the most. Because she believed in me."

Rollie grunted in frustration. "I failed Cora; not you."

"Mom," Finn interjected, "you did come through for her, with what you left for me in the shed."

She waved her hand, clearly dismissing his point. "Hannah will be here soon." She tapped her good hand on the arm of her wheelchair. "What do you plan to tell her?"

Rollie pressed the knuckles of his right hand to his lips and began to pace.

Finn settled into the recliner. He knew Rollie had already confessed to Kristian's wife that they'd secretly resumed their research following Sylvia's diagnosis, which hadn't surprised her. Then Rollie had informed her that Kristian had been exposed to Cora's pathogens.

Finn guessed that his dad had been hoping to delay the tougher conversations until he had proof that Kristian could fend off the three viruses he'd contracted. But Hannah had insisted on coming over tonight to speak with Sylvia.

"What do you think we should tell her?" Rollie asked, revealing just how severely his confidence had been shaken.

Irritated that Rollie was expecting Sylvia and Finn to sort out this mess, Finn averted his gaze from his father, and noticed an old family photo on the end table. The photographer had captured Finn looking up at his brother.

Throughout Finn's entire life, he'd been trying to prove that he should be involved in his family's secret initiative. Now that he was so desperately needed, why would he even consider backing away? Finn asked himself.

"What do *you* think?" Sylvia replied, and Finn smiled. His mother was not about to let Rollie off the hook.

"I suppose we should tell Hannah about Kristian's parentage, so she knows he's got a shot at pulling through this."

Sylvia raised her arm in support.

"Doesn't she have the right to know what Kristian did to Cora?" Finn asked.

No one spoke. Hannah should be told. But what would that do to Milo?

"The lying and secrets have to stop," Finn stated.

Rollie shifted his weight from one foot to the other. "This truth will destroy their family."

Kristian had been raised with a false sense of identity, and both brothers had been lied to. Repeatedly. With the sting of Rollie's revelation still fresh, Finn abhorred the thought of that same deception being repeated with the next generation.

Rollie looked to Sylvia, so Finn did the same.

The functional side of her face had tightened in anger. "Men in this family use family to get their way. I'm sick of it. Milo's well-being is the priority here, and the truth will crush Hannah. Milo needs her, and his dad." She turned her scooter toward her bedroom. "But I won't be part of another lie."

A knock on the door effectively ended the debate.

Finn looked for confirmation from Rollie, who, white-faced, agreed. Then he went to answer it.

Moments Later

The door opened, and Lily's stomach dropped at the sight of Finn's ashen face. Her right shoulder began to twitch, and she willed it to stop.

He beckoned her inside, and she complied while forcing herself to remain calm.

Whatever had just happened between the two could not—should not—deter her from what she had to do later this night, before she lost the courage.

While counting out the exact change at the deli, she'd decided that she had to break up with him. Her doctors, her mother, Finn, and his family: they'd all been telling her that too much anxiety could lead to more health problems. She needed to reduce the stress in her life.

Finn hung up her jacket. By his troubled expression, she surmised the conversation with Rollie hadn't gone well.

"Hannah will be here any minute." Finn set the soda in the kitchen.

Lily moved into the living room.

His back to her, Rollie was staring out the window. Never before had he not greeted her. *He's ashamed. Rightly so.* Yet a pang of sympathy shot through her. She now understood that his actions—however misguided—had been well intended. And she had to give him credit for his foresight and humility in fostering in Finn the strength to dissent.

Reciprocating his lack of greeting, she asked, "What's the plan?"

"It's premature to tell her certain details." Rollie turned to face her. "Kristian might be dead within two weeks," he said, his voice cracking.

A knock on the door sounded, and a sour taste filled Lily's mouth. She pitied Hannah for what she was about to learn, and not learn.

Lily didn't want to become her; she had to leave Finn. Tonight.

Finn helped Hannah with her coat, her long blond hair catching in the zipper. When Lily had first met her, she'd envied Hannah's big blue eyes, ample curves, and runway-model height. Now, wearing no makeup and likely having slept little in days, Hannah looked strung out.

Rollie gestured for the two women to sit on the couch.

Lily cleared her throat; she didn't want to be associated with this conversation. "I'll order the pizza," she said, stepping into the kitchen, from where she could still hear Hannah quietly inquire about Kristian.

"His wound is healing well," Rollie said. "So far there've been no symptoms, but we're not in the clear yet. Hannah," he said more loudly, and Lily stopped her search for the delivery menu and shuffled to where she could see into the living room, "there's something I need to tell you."

Lily braced herself.

Rollie dropped to an ottoman across from Hannah. "Kristian's not my son, or Petra's."

"What?" Hannah asked fiercely as Lily's hand flew to her mouth.

"His biological parents are Cora and Ulrich."

Gripping the counter to steady herself, Lily shifted to see Finn. From the chagrined yet composed look on his face, she could tell that Rollie had dropped this bombshell on him while she'd been at the corner store.

Her hands out, as if to ward off any further disturbing revelations, Hannah had sunk into the couch seat, the implications of this development working through her features. "He'll be okay? If he's like her?"

"*If* he's like her, then yes." Rollie smiled thinly.

"Why didn't you tell me sooner?" she asked, her chin trembling. "He's been keeping this from me?"

"Kristian doesn't know yet. I've sedated him until he's strong enough to process it," Rollie said, scratched his balding scalp. "Then Cora will tell him herself."

"I'm . . . at a loss."

"He was only seventeen months old when Ulrich brought him to us. He couldn't understand then. And, as the years passed, it grew harder. Ulrich insisted we keep up the pretense, so that Kristian wouldn't be tempted to experiment on himself." Rollie rubbed the dark circles under his eyes. "And we were a family. He was—is—my son. I didn't want to lose that."

"Well, now we might have all lost him," she snapped. "I'm disgusted that you allowed Ulrich to kidnap—steal—him from his mother. You're complicit in that crime."

Rollie stared at his hands, gripping the knees of his pants so tightly that his knuckles had turned white. "It was wrong," he mumbled.

Hannah's eyes widened. "Shit. If Cora is Kristian's mother, then Milo has a quarter of her genes."

Rollie nodded.

Lily's empty stomach twisted.

Visibly stunned, Hannah tipped her head back and pressed her hand to her abdomen.

"If Kristian is like her, will he have to stay on the island?" she asked, wiping a tear from her cheek. "I won't be able to see him."

Rollie's shoulders curled inward. "In a biosafety suit, you could."

"What?" She jumped to her feet. "The only way to be with my husband again is in a suit?"

Lily bit down on her thumb. That desperate scenario had wrenched her heart, despite her anger toward Kristian. Hannah didn't deserve that.

"We don't know yet how his body will react," Rollie said flatly.

"Milo," she said, swaying, "he's so close to his father. They've been spending so much time together in Kristian's lab. If he's like them, he could see his dad, right? But then he'd become an asymptomatic carrier? I won't be able to touch him, either?"

"All of this will take time to sort out." Rollie stepped toward her, offering his arm to steady herself.

She waved him off. "How exactly did this happen?" she asked, looking at Finn expectantly, as if he were more likely to tell the truth.

Finn clasped and unclasped his hands, and Lily could almost see the weight of his guilt in his slouched posture. The temptation for him to lie must be strong, she knew, and that neither she nor Rollie would counter his story if he decided to bend the truth.

"We got in a fight," Finn said, shifting to the edge of the recliner. "It started with fists, but Kristian picked up a syringe, so I grabbed a scalpel to defend myself, and—"

"You cut him?" Hannah asked, her mouth hanging open. "You did this to him?" She lurched toward him, her fists balled.

"I'm sorry," Finn said, his long, folded legs visibly shaking.

"'Sorry' doesn't cut it. What were you fighting over?"

He glanced at a framed picture of Kristian and his family at the beach, then at Rollie, who subtly shook his head no. Earlier, Finn had stressed to Lily that Hannah should be told the full truth. Yet now Lily guessed that he was thinking of Milo, currently in a swimming pool and blissfully ignorant of the worst parts of this debacle.

Lily thought of her own childhood, and all the nights she'd lain awake, crying into her pillow, wishing she had a father who loved her. *They have no right to take that from Milo.*

Lily stepped into the room. "I was there."

"You?" Hannah stared at her incredulously.

"He was upset with Finn for getting involved with Cora." *What does this lie matter,* Lily thought, *given that I'm breaking up with him tonight?*

"Kristian was worried about Finn being exposed to her germs," she continued, "and him then passing them to me."

Finn looked like he'd just been sliced open, yet he said nothing to dispute her story.

"He always has been so selfless, to a fault," Hannah said in a sluggish tone, her burst of energy undoubtedly depleted. "What happens next?"

"We wait and see how Kristian's immune system responds," Rollie said. "If he has her same traits, and now cannot leave North Brother, we work like hell to eradicate the germs so he can return to you and your son."

"And daughter."

"What?" Lily exclaimed at the same time as Finn and Rollie.

Hannah placed her hand back on her stomach. "I'm pregnant. Twenty weeks." Despite herself, she smiled.

A twinge of envy shot through Lily. "Congratulations," she managed to say.

Then it hit her: This second child also wouldn't be able to have direct contact with her father, if Kristian even survived. Unless the baby had inherited Cora's unique immune system. In that scenario, if the girl contracted any of his viruses, then she would have to remain with him, away from her mother.

"That's wonderful news," Rollie said, his voice hoarse.

Hannah burst into fresh tears. "I need to get out of here." She grabbed her jacket from the hall closet. "Please don't tell Sylvia. That's why I came tonight," she said with a sob. "I still want to be the one, even though our baby won't technically be her grandchild."

Before anyone could respond, she exited, shutting the door behind her so hard its frame rattled.

Instead of Sylvia, Lily realized, Cora would be the grandmother. She pictured Cora, completely content, cradling the infant. For years Lily had been trying to stifle the longing for a baby. Cora must have experienced that same emotion—likely with a greater intensity given that Ulrich had ripped her existing child from her. That year and a half of raising Kristian must have been sheer bliss for Cora. Having access to her granddaughter—essentially a second chance to nurture and adore a child—would bring utter happiness to a woman who'd experienced an unconscionable share of suffering.

But this would only happen if the baby were brought to the island, which depended on Kristian's status. They wouldn't risk exposing a newborn to such lethal pathogens. *Do they make PPE that small?* Lily wondered.

She turned to Finn, seated in the armchair, and could almost see the remorse pressing down on him. Evidently consumed by the destruction his fight with Kristian had wrought on his brother's family, he presumably hadn't turned his thoughts to how Cora would receive Hannah's announcement.

Lily's heart constricted and she recognized the sensation for what it was: love. For an innocent baby girl, who in less than five months would be born into whatever devastating circumstances had emerged by then. An urge to protect her coursed through Lily, and she knew that she couldn't break up with Finn this night. Perhaps her longing to care for a child of her own needed this redirection. Whatever the cause, she felt compelled to be there for this one and do everything she could to give Cora this opportunity to love and be loved.

THREE DAYS LATER

MARCH 30

The smell of antiseptic wafted through the blackness. Kristian snapped open his eyes, expecting to see the hospital that had been his second home for the past fifteen years. Blinking rapidly, he tried to bring into focus the familiar ceiling tiles, but their perfect right angles wouldn't emerge. Instead, an irregular swath of flaking ivory paint materialized. From the two-toned ceiling hung a series of rusted metal frames, their lightbulb sockets bare. Old surgical lamps. A chill raced down his spinal cord.

Kristian knew this location: an operating theater within the tuberculosis pavilion. Cora's territory.

Jolted, he sat up, a spasm of pain igniting his abdomen, followed by a crushing wooziness. He gripped a pair of side rails and recognized the bed as the gurney where he'd bound her.

Just as his dad had burst into the room . . . Finn thrashing with a surgical knife . . . the acute sting . . . Cora's wailing and Lily's shrieking. The last thing Kristian remembered seeing was Milo's face—obviously a sign that he'd been in hemorrhagic shock.

He raised his hospital gown, the same style they kept in the onsite lab, and inspected his professionally treated wound. It had to be his father's work, as was the IV needle in his arm connected to a bag of saline and another of morphine, hanging from a pole. Rollie must have been here, but where was he now?

"Hi. You're awake."

Kristian whipped his head toward the sound of Cora's scratchy voice and recoiled at the sight of her only three feet away.

He hadn't heard her arrive. *Has she been here this whole time?* he wondered, his skin tingling. "You're too close; back off!"

As if she hadn't heard, she simply stood there, smugly beaming at him, her eyes practically sparkling. How could she be gazing at him like that after all he'd done to her?

He hated that smile.

She must be envisioning her revenge. Instinctively, he checked his wrists and ankles: they weren't bound. Her scalpel pouch was missing from her hip, which only heightened his mistrust.

Not constrained by her usual braid, her reddish-brown hair looked untamed—so emblematic of the wild beast she'd become—and her face and folded hands were free of the protective gear he'd rarely seen her without.

After twenty years of adhering to proper contagion procedures, he felt a compulsion to rebuke her, but he held his tongue. The absence of her PPE must be intentional, part of her plan to be rid of him. "Where are the others?" Hopefully his dad and Finn had taken Lily home. He shouldn't have brought her with him. Because of his obsession—and overconfidence—he'd endangered that sweet girl, he realized, now angry at himself.

The room spun, but lying back down would reveal his weakness.

Cora's arm snaked across his back, supporting him. "You need to rest."

Her foul breath warmed his neck, and he pictured highly lethal virions landing on his skin. "Get away from me."

Wincing, she jumped back. "I'm sorry," she stuttered, wringing her hands. Her cheeks flushed, she turned her head toward an open, dark supply closet. "Rollie said to take it slow," she whispered. "I should have listened. I'm just so—"

The hairs on Kristian's arms rose. "Who the hell are you talking to? Why am I here?"

Cora fixed her attention back on him, her soft countenance and relaxed posture highly disturbing. This could not be the same woman whose behavior and anatomy he'd obsessively studied for two decades, whose actions he could usually predict with nearly 100 percent accuracy.

"Spit it out."

"Your idea worked," she said gently, "for me to give you blood."

Appalled, Kristian looked down at his chalk-blue hospital gown and the IV in his arm. With an urge to scream welling in his throat, he longed to rip the needle from his flesh, but that would accomplish nothing. By now, Ebola, Rift Valley fever, and 1918 H1N1 microbes had to be teeming within his cells.

"I don't believe you," he said through gritted teeth despite a murky memory of pointing out that Cora had his same blood type. "I was delirious. Rollie would never have allowed it."

"I'm so glad he did," Cora said, her obnoxious grin returning.

Kristian's hand quivered with the urge to push her away. Three concurrent systemic infections. He wouldn't survive the onslaught of symptoms. "Where's Rollie?"

"I asked him for this time alone with you."

His heart palpitated, and he was suddenly aware of cool perspiration trickling down his sides. "He would never allow that."

"Well, he did. I've got something for you," she said coyly.

"You've already given me plenty." He narrowed his eyes. "The symptoms will start any day now."

"Actually," she said, enunciating each syllable, "Rollie kept you sedated to give your body time to recover before . . ." Her voice trailed off as she made the sign of the cross, then she kissed that trite pendant of hers. Several times throughout the years following his grandfather's death, when he'd impulsively thought to call Ulrich to share his latest successful patient surgery or achievement of Milo's, he'd fantasized about choking Cora with that necklace.

"Kristian."

"What?" he grunted.

"It's already been nine days."

Stunned, he shook his head, then blinked as he finished processing her words. Feverishly working through the implications, he felt his forehead. Still cool. Early signs, such as a headache, abdominal cramps, or muscle aches, would be masked by the morphine drip. Also, the incubation period for Ebola could be as long as twenty-one days. But the Spanish flu and RVF took only two to seven days to incubate.

"Rollie ran the tests, I assume."

"Yes." Cora's voice had sounded like they were underwater. "Rollie, Lily, and Finn are all fine—physically, I mean. Finn and Lily are helping with Hannah and Milo, who're both in shock."

Finn must have told Hannah and Sylvia everything. *His* version of it. Imagining their reactions, Kristian felt an urge to vomit. Even if he weren't currently in isolation, Hannah would refuse to see—or forgive—him. Likely, Sylvia was equally angry, and disappointed in him. *This is Finn's fault*, he thought. The plan would have worked if it hadn't been for his brash, halfwit half brother. Regardless, he would have to be the one to make things right, even if it meant accepting full blame. Because it was his family's well-being at stake. "I need to get home."

"Kristian, you're . . . positive for the three without vaccines."

"What?" He inhaled deeply but only felt more light-headed. The morphine, messing with his mind, must be blocking the initial symptoms, he concluded. Or, alternatively, along with her pathogens, she'd transmitted her active, unique antibodies. Overcome by that possibility, Kristian rose onto his elbows. "Holy shit." *But that approach failed with Otto's mice and Ulrich's human test subjects*, he reminded himself.

His chest heaving, Kristian projected the outcome for each scenario: either he'd be dead within a week or his survival would signify a major breakthrough.

"It's going to be okay," she said, patting his shoulder.

Repulsed by her touch and needing space to think, he knocked her away.

Stumbling, she regained her balance, then clutched her necklace. "Oh, right. You don't know."

"Know what?" he asked, glaring at the dried blood stains spotting the ratty sweatshirt he'd thrown to her after Rollie had sawed through the plastic cords. His blood, all over her. Her blood, coursing through him. *How has she not cleaned herself up yet?* he wondered. He wanted off this rock, now.

"Kristian, the fact that you're symptom-free shows that, as I always hoped and prayed, you're just like me."

"I'm nothing like you," he said vehemently. "Go to hell." He wished there was an afterlife, with a special barbed-wire cage there just for her, far more miserable and cramped than this island. And beside it, an operating table.

"It's a lot to take in, I know," she said in a soothing, condescending tone.

"What are you talking about?"

Her attention shifted to a pair of metal carts against the yellow-tiled wall. One contained medical instruments. The other held a case of water, a small package wrapped in newsprint, and what appeared to be a misshapen chocolate cake.

"There's something more you need to know," she said, wheeling the cart with the amateurish cake closer to him.

"I'm done with this conversation. Whatever it is, Rollie can tell me."

"No. This has to come from me," she said, examining the palm of her right hand. "There's no easy way to say it, so I just will." She looked him straight in the eyes, the same way she had seconds before she'd killed his grandfather—the man who'd so patiently supported him through everything from overcoming his early childhood speech impediment to studying for his board exams. He yearned to lunge from the bed, grab an instrument from the tray, and stab her.

Curiosity, however, held him back; he returned her stare.

"Ulrich, his research spanned far more than"—her voice quivered—"virology. One of his goals was to create immortality for the Gettler lineage," she said, watching for his reaction.

He kept a straight face to deny her the pleasure of knowing she had his attention.

"You're, um, the result of that experiment, using him and me," she concluded, her lips closing in a smile.

"What?!" Kristian roared.

Blinking hard, he tried to make sense of his surroundings and what she'd just said: Ulrich, not Rollie, was his father. And *she* was his mother.

"Shit!" Why hadn't Rollie—his *half brother*—told him?

"You were born in this very room."

Serenely smiling, Cora gazed at an empty spot near his gurney, and a tear ran down her scarred cheek.

It couldn't be true. It simply couldn't.

They both, however, did have the O-positive blood type. He pictured the Punnett square that proved the inheritance feasible. But they also shared this trait with 38 percent of the world's population. Why would he have suspected it was anything more than coincidental? "If I have your immunities, which only work here, how have I been able to live in Manhattan my entire life? Surely you infected me with your germs during the birth."

"The antibodies in my breast milk. While you lived here with me, I was nursing you," she said, her eyes closed. "You loved hunting for spiders, digging in the dirt, watching the ships from my spy holes on the morgue roof."

Groaning, Kristian tried to block out her words, yet he couldn't ignore a nagging sensation that they were factual. Once, he'd asked why there were no baby pictures of him, much less an album. Rollie had shrugged off the question with a vague line about Petra not having been good at that sort of thing. Yet in Finn's baby book, some of the entries had been penned in Rollie's neat, tight script.

"You are *not* my mother," he said, "and you never will be, you vile piece of filth."

As if he'd just punched her, Cora staggered backward.

"I'm done here." He swung his legs off the gurney and reached for the IV needle.

"You can't go yet," she said, rushing to block his path. "You're still recovering, and I need to teach you how to move within the tree canopy so you don't leave germs at ground level. If an outsider were to catch something, the CDC would swoop in. They'd build a base right here to study us. Put us in glass cages."

"Us? There is no *us*," he said with a growl.

Hannah and Milo. And the baby. If what Cora was saying were true, it wouldn't matter if Hannah forgave him; he could never be with them again. He wouldn't be at her side in the delivery room, or even ever hold the baby. "No!" he wailed. "My family!"

As if she too felt his pain, Cora covered her mouth with her hand.

"Milo can't grow up without a dad," Kristian said, horrified by the possibility. "He needs me, just like Ulrich needed Otto. I swore to Ulrich that I would always put family first, that I would never neglect my children. And I've only just begun Milo's training."

"This isn't at all like what happened with Ulrich," she said, her voice cracking. "Milo will be surrounded by love, and he'll be able to visit you in a containment suit."

"That's not good enough," he snapped. "And the . . ." He stopped himself from revealing Hannah's pregnancy.

"You're right; it's not. I know how you feel. It was hard for me to accept this life at first, too."

"You can't possibly understand. You were nothing before you came here. You had nothing."

"That's not true. I lost my family as well. But now I have you back. Please," she said, rubbing her palm, "give me a chance. It's your birthday. Every year, since Ulrich took you from me, I . . ." She glanced at the cart.

Kristian eyed the lump of chocolate. Of all the days to wake up to this nightmare.

Hannah was a wonderful baker. He should be at home right now, celebrating with her and Milo. *Milo.* A quarter of his genes had come from Cora. Same with the baby in vitro. Conceivably both—or one—could possess the superimmunity trait as well. But it could take years for Kristian to design a safe, effective method for evaluating them. Meanwhile, Milo would come of age without his father's daily guidance, and the baby would experience all her firsts without him. While he was stuck here, with *her.*

Vaguely, he recalled the lung tissue extraction that had led to this disaster. If all that Cora had claimed were true, he would no longer need her specimens to continue his research. The means of preventing another coronavirus outbreak—or a pandemic caused by a different novel pathogen—now resided within him. But what did that matter if he couldn't be with his family? Any time spent on attempting to harvest and replicate his antibodies would be time not devoted to finding a way to eliminate the three viruses now colonizing within him because of *her.*

He glared at her. "You call that a cake?"

"I worked very hard on it," she said, seemingly unaware of his disdain. She set the wrapped box beside him.

"I want nothing to do with you."

"During my labor," she said, as if she hadn't heard him, "Ulrich and I were so scared we'd lost you. He had to do an emergency C-section. But your first cries; they were so sweet. You were so sweet. You loved cuddling against me." Putting her hand to her heart, she breathed in deeply. "There's a lullaby your dad and I used to sing to you. Ulrich learned it from his mother. It goes like this," she said and began singing, her voice hoarse and off-key, "Weißt du wieviel Sternlein stehen an dem blauen Himmelszelt?"

He had many fond memories of his grandfather—his *father*—singing that lullaby to him in his crystal-clear baritone. Kristian, in turn, had sung it to Milo, whom he now couldn't see without PPE between them. Kristian blinked back the sting of tears.

Cora nodded toward the package. "Open it. Please?"

He lifted the box to hurl it against the wall but found himself sliding his index finger beneath the edge of the newsprint. He'd never been one to stifle his curiosity; why start now?

As the paper fell away, he recognized the embossed symbol of his favorite watch brand. The rich scent of the patent leather box cut through the mustiness of the operating room. *This can't have come from her,* he thought with a sideways glance.

Cora had stepped back, seemingly afraid he might strike her. Despite the gloom that had engulfed her, he could still make out *hope* in the upturned corners of her lips and the darting of her eyes.

He could crush her spirit now, so easily. With a simple flick of his wrist, the case would fly.

But he had to know how she'd gotten this. Slowly, he opened the lid, and a gift receipt fluttered to his chest.

He snatched it and inhaled sharply upon seeing the store's name. "Where'd you get this?"

Shyly, Cora smiled. "Sylvia. She wanted me to be the one to give it to you."

The room seesawed and Kristian fought to restore his sense of equilibrium.

Instantly, he'd understood the message that had accompanied his mother's gesture. Everything Sylvia did was with intention and from the heart. She'd anticipated his rejection of Cora, rightly so, and planned accordingly.

Since Sylvia's Lyme diagnosis, every stroke of his pen, every pipette filled and dispersed, every microscope slide he'd prepared had been in her honor. How could he accept Cora, his father's assassin, as his mother? He didn't know if he were capable of that, even for Sylvia.

"Do you want help putting it on?" Cora asked, her raspy tone scratching his nerves.

No, he did not want help.

"Get out of my sight, you . . ." Kristian bit his tongue to hold back that habitual, final word: *mutt*. Given that 50 percent of his genes had apparently come from her, what did that make him? And his children?

Her grandchildren.

Picturing Sylvia in her wheelchair at their window, staring across the East River toward North Brother Island, he slowly raised his arm so that Cora could affix the watch.

As she removed it from the box, Kristian noticed an inscription on its chrome back. He grabbed the watch from her to read it. *Du bist mein Ein und Alles.*

You are my everything. A tingling sensation prickled his eyes. While he had no distinct memories associated with that phrase, it felt strangely familiar.

"I used to tell you that every day, when you lived here."

He brushed his cheek to erase a tear. Intuitively, he knew she wasn't lying. "Where did Sylvia learn that?"

"I told her, when I was begging her to help me get you back."

Kristian thought of Milo, whom he already missed. And the baby who'd be born without him there. He couldn't fathom this heartache worsening with more time away from his children, and Hannah.

For over thirty years, Cora had been enduring this same intense longing for her child. For *him.*

He looked at her anew. She was biting her lip, visibly nervous. Her eyelids were fluttering; Kristian realized he'd inherited his long lashes from her.

For Sylvia, just like everything else he did on this island, maybe he should try to accept Cora.

But, he thought, squeezing the watch in his grasp, *she killed my father. Right before my eyes.*

He would discover a way to eradicate the pathogens from his system, Kristian vowed. Until then, he would do everything within his power to ensure that Cora understand one simple, new rule: North Brother Island now belonged to him.

Don't miss the unforgettable
sequel to *The Vines.*

Coming soon!

Author's Note

Like far too many COVID-19 patients, I've spent dozens of nights hospitalized. While in the ICU on oxygen therapy, repeatedly, I feared that my lungs would fail me before daybreak. I know the terror of struggling for air. But not because of the virus; in my case, it was an acute form of leukemia that caused pooling of blood in my lungs. My feelings heightened by my past trauma, I have deep empathy for those who've experienced severe and/or chronic complications from COVID-19 and for those who've lost loved ones.

I hope and pray that through the tireless efforts of the health care heroes and essential workers, as well as the breathtaking medical innovations being achieved, we will soon emerge from this crisis. Then, we can collectively begin the healing process, which won't be easy for many. Despite the passage of nearly a decade since my diagnosis, I still grapple with fear and anxiety.

The first symptom of my cancer was the death of our baby at twenty weeks gestation. For the over forty days I was inpatient, I lay awake each night, weeping over our loss and for our eighteen-month-old, whom I was forbidden to see because her germs could kill me. Frequently, I needed IV pain medication, which barely dented the emotional anguish. Daily, I received blood transfusions. Throughout, I experienced 105-degree fevers, dangerously high blood pressure, hemorrhaging of the eye, a full-body hive outbreak, migraines, vomiting, and severe bone pain. During this period, I spent a total of two hours with my toddler. Before I returned home, she'd stopped asking for me.

For the three years of treatment that followed my diagnosis, my writing focused on my cancer blog, highlighting the themes of disease, fear of death, isolation, loss of a child, infertility. But also survival, courage, healing, and hope. Through that therapeutic writing process, Cora—and her foil, Lily—were born. Before these two strong female characters, however, came the setting:

In 2014, during a descent to LaGuardia Airport, my husband elbowed me in the side and directed my attention to a spit of land in the East River. "You should write a book about that island." Returning the elbow jab as I leaned across him, I gasped at the decaying buildings, visible in winter with the trees barren. Once we landed, I immediately consulted Google and was hooked.

So often people make that comment: "You should write a book about [x]." Typically, writers just smile and nod in response. But a novel set on such a fascinating, abandoned, forbidden place within plain sight of millions of New Yorkers was too tantalizing a concept to dismiss simply because I hadn't thought of it myself.

Diving into research, I learned that North Brother's past is rife with misery. The haunting online images of Riverside Hospital provided gut-wrenching context to the grisly historical essays.

I decided that a novel set there should incorporate Riverside's 125+ year evolution, its actual inhabitants, and the details captured by online photographs and Christopher Payne's stunning coffee table book, *North Brother Island: The Last Unknown Place in New York City,* for which I attended a standing-room-only book signing. After meticulously cataloguing every map, image, and historical detail available, including the report from research led by University of Pennsylvania preservationist Randall Mason, I took a deep breath and began structuring an epic tale that I believed I'd earned the right to tell.

To incorporate the island's full modern history, I knew I'd have to get creative. At the time, I was still very raw and traumatized by my cancer ordeal and terrified that I was going to die. The notion of a character blessed with immortality and superior immunities appealed to me. Through telling Cora's story, I could also tell North Brother's.

While plotting the novel, I studied the photographs available online and in Payne's book. Many details from these photos appear in *The Vines,* as a nod to all the North Brother enthusiasts out there. For example, Payne's book includes an image of the exposed bathroom on the first floor of the staff house where Cora showers in the opening scene. Similarly, if you do a quick Internet Image search of the island, you'll see the rusted examining table in the morgue.

Regarding the characters, Cora, the Gettlers, and Lily are all fictional. However, many of the secondary characters were real people who lived on the island. The most famous was Mary Mallon, whose permanent quarantine on North Brother Island hits too close to home for us all during this pandemic. To accurately incorporate Typhoid Mary's history and personality, I extensively researched her, and in the process fell in love with *Fever,* by Mary Beth Keaton. Because of Keaton's book, I was able to add Mary Mallon's beau, Alfred Briehof.

Richard O'Toole, John Canne, head nurse Kate Holden, and nurse Puetz all lived on the island. From an essay about Riverside Hospital by Jacob Riis, I learned that the staff actually believed that nothing could kill an O'Toole. Riis' writings were tremendously helpful in my understanding of conditions for the poor immigrant class at the turn of the nineteenth century. Additionally, the survivors named during the *Slocum* scene were real people. Adella Wotherspoon, who passed in 2004 at the age of 100, was the last living survivor of the tragedy. *Ship Ablaze* by Edward T. O'Donnell, a gripping, poignant, detailed account of the most lethal disaster in New York City's history prior to 9/11, served as an invaluable resource for me while reconstructing the catastrophe.

In creating the fictional Ulrich Gettler (and the subplot involving Lyme disease), I drew inspiration from *Lab 257* by Michael Christopher Carroll. Yes, that's right: Lab 257 is an actual secret germ laboratory, run by the US government. This extensive and chilling piece of investigative reporting will shock you.

Much of my understanding of the Gettlers' appropriate level of medical sophistication throughout the decades came from Paul de Kruif's *Microbe Hunters*. This classic history of microbiology is a must-read for anyone who enjoyed my references to the field's pioneers and advancements in immunology.

The sinking of the *HMS Hussar,* rumored to have been carrying eighty shackled Revolutionary soldiers and a golden guinea payload for the British army (potentially now worth hundreds of millions of dollars), is also factual. The *Hussar* will play an important role in the sequel. Because who doesn't find fascinating the fact that there's a treasure-laden ship still sitting at the bottom of New York City's East River?

Unfortunately, the diseases and past pandemics mentioned in *The Vines* are fact as well. As I was finalizing the manuscript in spring 2020, I incorporated a few references, such as SARS, that set up the series to tie in COVID-19. The island's original use as a quarantine facility drove my decision to center the plot on pathogens, vaccine development, and medical research (and its corresponding ethics). The fact that *The Vines* is now so topical is tragically coincidental.

The COVID-19 pandemic took far too much—far too many—from us. But it has given us renewed confidence in the resiliency of the human spirit, awe-inspiring innovations, and proof that we are stronger together even when we must be physically apart. The real-world immunological advancements made since Dr. Otto Gettler first began studying Cora's blood in 1902 are breathtaking. And the acceleration in the vaccine process that occurred in 2020, in my opinion, is as great a feat as putting a human on the moon. We, as a global society, achieved this feat by working together. My hope for *The Vines* is that its historical context highlights just how remarkable these medical advancements are. Thank you to everyone who, through grit and global collaboration, is bringing us out of this crisis. Because of you, the future of health care innovation is even brighter.

To see a historical timeline and collection of resources on North Brother Island, as well as to sign up for notification of the sequel's release, please visit my website, www.shelleynolden.com.

ACKNOWLEDGEMENTS

First and foremost, thank *you*, the reader.

Throughout the several years of writing before sunrise and on commuter trains required to finish *The Vines*, what kept me going was the vision of Cora's story in your hands. It means so much to me that you chose to spend your time immersed in North Brother Island. More so than I could ever express here.

Thank you to all the health care heroes and essential workers who've selflessly served throughout the COVID-19 pandemic, including those involved in developing the vaccines at breakneck speed. These scientists accomplished what the Gettlers couldn't, even with Cora's supercharged antibodies at their disposal. On that theme of medical advancements... I owe my life to all those who've contributed to cancer drug research and development, countless blood donors, and the oncology staff who kept me alive during some very dicey times.

From kernel of an idea to polished manuscript, my editor, Benee Knauer, guided me every step of the way. Benee, thank you for all those seven a.m. conversations, plotting advice, superb edits, and most importantly, your friendship and support. Thank you to Bill Drennan and NY Book Editors for the copyediting assistance. And a big thank you to the team at Freiling Publishing for shepherding this novel into the world. Tom Freiling and Christen Jeschke, thank you for believing in me and making my vision a reality.

I feel so fortunate to have had such a strong team working with me to bring this novel to readers. Thank you to my publicist Rachel Gul, whose enthusiasm for *The Vines* combined with her talent made the marketing process so enjoyable. Thank you to: Deborah Lewis at Freiling Publishing for the gorgeous book cover; Matthew Prodger for a stellar author website; mapmaker extraordinaire Travis Hasenour for the beautiful rendering of

North Brother Island; and actress/narrator Jessica Nahikian for a riveting performance in the audiobook. To all four artists: your professionalism, kindness, passion for this project, and talent blew me away.

Thank you to all the reviewers, bloggers, and Bookstagrammers for your kind words, gorgeous pictures, and enthusiasm. I admire and adore your passion for reading and the creative ways you share it with the world. Also, thank you to my local postal workers, who processed all those Advanced Reader Copy packages that I repeatedly stacked on your counter. Every day through this pandemic, you served us all despite the personal risk.

Thank you to the talented authors who generously gave their time to support this debut novelist: Sarah Pekkanen, Greer Macallister, and May Cobb.

To my GRYT Health family, thank you for staying by my side throughout the ups and downs of cancer survivorship, as well as for your support during my publishing journey. Dave Fuehrer and Ellis Emerson deserve a special note of gratitude for their moral support.

Thank you to all my New Jersey friends, who supported me both during my illness and the writing process. A special thanks to Ken Silber for his writing support and Brooke Silber for her fabulous inspirational illustrations and first rendition of the North Brother Island map. Thank you to my Wisconsin swimmer friends, especially Jen May and Julie Van Cleave for their roles in the draft review process.

Thank you to Jen Miller, Gina Miller, Matt Miller, and DiAnne Nolden, who whole-heartedly embraced their role as both early readers and listeners. I'm so grateful to the rest of my family as well for believing in me and my dream. I love you all.

A special thank you to my mother. All those English papers in high school that you helped me edit, sitting side by side at our desktop computer striving for perfection, long after I knew the paper was an A, gave me the foundation for writing this book. And thank you for reading several versions of this manuscript, with a keen eye to detail, and for lending your science expertise to help me get the medical details right.

And finally, thank you to my husband, Rob, and our two amazing daughters. Rob, ever since that elbow jab on the airplane after you spotted North Brother, you've been unwavering in your support. Not only have you always believed in the potential of this book, but I know that you also value the happiness that writing brings me. And so you've always helped me carve out time for it. That means the world to me. To our fiercely creative, brilliant, loving girls, thank you for believing in me. With passion and determination, you can and will achieve whatever you set your minds to. I love you.